"Typical of abuse victims, Maranatha pushes everyone away, suspects all men, and fears emotional and physical intimacy. As Maranatha slowly learns to trust, the reader experiences the grace of God working in her life and slowly healing her heart. *Wishing on Dandelions* is by far the best inspirational fiction I have read on this subject of recovery and healing."

— MICHELLE HUTCHINSON, caseworker and former CPS supervisor working with adult and child victims of sexual abuse for eighteen years

"Mary had me from the first page of *Wishing on Dandelions*. I loved her fallible characters, lyrical prose, and memorable imagery. And the world needs to hear this book's theme: finding Christ's healing (and falling into His arms of love) after suffering traumatic events. I can't wait for Mary's next novel!"

— DENA DYER, author of *Grace for the Race: Meditations for Busy Moms*; coauthor of THE GROOVY CHICKS' ROAD TRIP series

"Maranatha pleads, 'Jesus, show me your love.' Her longing to be reassured of God's love in the face of her past will resonate with readers as they share her journey. Step into words so beautiful they hurt, pages of rich symbol, and emotions so genuine you can't look away. Experience a powerful, lyrical voice in contemporary fiction."

— SHARON HINCK, author of *The Secret Life of Becky Miller* and *Renovating Becky Miller*

"Mary DeMuth offers up a great story that's a feast for the senses. Her characters' struggles and triumphs resonate with readers long after the last page has been turned."

— SANDRA GLAHN, ThM, coauthor of *Lethal Harvest* and *False Positive*

"*Wishing on Dandelions* is a journey into the heart and mind of a young woman caught ⬚⬚⬚⬚⬚ painful childhood. Natha is both ⬚⬚⬚⬚⬚ s life's injustices, overcoming the ⬚⬚⬚⬚⬚ ish at a time."

— T. SUZANNE ELLER, s⬚⬚⬚ *...e Mom I Want to Be: Rising Above Yo...ut to Give Your Kids a Great Future*

WISHING ON DANDELIONS

A Maranatha Novel

MARY E. DeMUTH

NAVPRESS®

BRINGING TRUTH TO LIFE

OUR GUARANTEE TO YOU

We believe so strongly in the message of our books that we are making this quality guarantee to you. If for any reason you are disappointed with the content of this book, return the title page to us with your name and address and we will refund to you the list price of the book. To help us serve you better, please briefly describe why you were disappointed. Mail your refund request to: NavPress, P.O. Box 35002, Colorado Springs, CO 80935.

NavPress
P.O. Box 35001
Colorado Springs, Colorado 80935

ISBN 1-57683-953-2

Cover design by Kirk DouPonce, DogEaredDesign.com
Cover photo by Steve Gardner, ShootPW.com
Author photo by Rogier Bos
Creative Team: Terry Behimer, Lissa Halls Johnson, Kathy Mosier, Arvid Wallen, Kathy Guist

This novel is a work of fiction. Names, characters, places, and incidents are either the product of the author's imagination or are used fictitiously. Any resemblance to actual events, locales, organizations, or persons, living or dead, is entirely coincidental and beyond the intent of either the author or publisher.

Unless otherwise identified, all Scripture quotations in this publication are taken from the *King James Version* (KJV). Other version used: the *New American Standard Bible* (NASB), © The Lockman Foundation 1960, 1962, 1963, 1968, 1971, 1972, 1973, 1975, 1977, 1995.

Published in association with the literary agency of Alive Communications, Inc., 7680 Goddard Street, Suite 200, Colorado Springs, CO 80920 (www.alivecommunications.com).

DeMuth, Mary E., 1967-
  Wishing on dandelions : a novel / Mary E. Demuth.
    p. cm.
  ISBN 1-57683-953-2
  1. Girls—Fiction. 2. Rape victims—Fiction. I. Title.
  PS3604.E48W57 2006
  813'.6—dc22
                    2006013610

Printed in the United States of America

2 3 4 5 6 7 8 9 10 / 10 09 08 07 06

FOR A FREE CATALOG OF
NAVPRESS BOOKS & BIBLE STUDIES,
CALL 1-800-366-7788 (USA)
OR 1-800-839-4769 (CANADA)

To those who wish for healing

Acknowledgments

PATRICK, IT BLESSES ME THAT YOU read *my* novels — even though you don't read novels — and tell me how they move your heart. I love you.

I couldn't have written this book without the insight of my critique group, Life Sentence. Leslie and D'Ann, thank you for plowing through the first draft with me and offering valuable words of encouragement and clarity. I love our Wednesday phone calls. I only wish I could import you to France!

Thank you, prayer team, for faithfully praying me through this book: Kevin and Renee Bailey, Valerie Bertrand, Gahlen and Lee Ann Crawford, Suzanne Deshchidn, Colleen Eslinger, Sandi Glahn, Jack and Helen Graves, Kim Griffith, Ed and Sue Harrell, Justus and Samantha Heyman, Debbie Hutchison, Hud and Nancy McWilliams, Michael and Renee Mills, Kim Moore, Marilyn Neel, Caroline O'Neill, Kathy O'Neill, Don Pape, Catalin and Shannon Popa, Brandy Prince, Katy Raymond, Tom and Holly Schmidt, Carla Smith, Kelli Standish, Erin Teske, Jim and Stacey Tomisser, Janet Turner, Todd and Kari Urbanowicz, JR and Ginger Vassar, Rod and Mary Vestal, Rita Warren, Jodie Westfall, Denise Wilhite, Betsy Williams, Jan Winebrenner, and Liz Wolf. If this book touches souls, the glory rests on the shoulders of Jesus, on the wings of your prayers.

Beth Jusino, you've helped make my dream come true. I'm a novelist! Thank you doesn't seem a big enough sentiment.

Sophie, Aidan, and Julia, thanks for understanding when

I cranked out words upon words. Thanks for "woo-hoo-ing" when I finished. Thanks for being such amazing children.

Jesus, thank You for giving me words to write. You've rewritten my story in so many ways and answered so many wishes. It's all for You.

Introduction

I STILL CAN'T TELL MY STORY up close, like it was me in it, breathing the tangled wisteria on the fence posts of Burl, Texas. There are times I still can't bear to say it was me. The book of my life continues to open, painful word by painful word, page after page. I get real close to typing the whole story with the word *I* in it, but I hit delete every time, replacing *me* with *she*.

Zady tells me I'm ready to write my story honest, but I'm not so sure. She says she's there to help me remember my healing, even as she puts an arm around my shoulder when a tear slips through. "It hurts," she says. "Real bad. Lord, I wish it didn't rip at you so."

She tells me I survived that story — that I should be proud — yet her presence brings back its horrid validity written on the backdrop of her tender love. Reminds me in a kind, wild way that this is *my* story even if I can't seem to admit it on the page.

Summer 1983
Burl, Texas

Uncle Zane appeared disheveled when Maranatha pestered him. His silvery hair, normally combed and parted in the exact same place, was instead bunched and unkempt, his part like a winding Burl road.

"Camilla and me, well, we want to go to the fair. Can you drive us? Please?" Maranatha practically danced, shifting her weight from one foot to the other.

"No," he shouted, an odd outburst for such a quiet man.

Gangly and with a sinewy will of her own, she pled, "C'mon, Uncle Zane. Everyone will be there. Besides, Camilla promised we'd shoot the fair — ride every single ride from the merry-go-round to the Zipper. This year I promised her I'd do it without getting sick."

"I said no."

Three plain words. Maranatha almost turned away in a thirteen-year-old huff, but she lingered long enough to see him sit down in a parlor chair, then bend forward, pressing palms to temple.

"We'll ride our bikes," she told him. The room echoed her words. "I'll be back later." Her words stung even as she said them, particularly because Uncle Zane, usually a man without reaction, looked up at her with a strange sort of look in his blue eyes. A look that pleaded, *Please stay.*

She left him there. And didn't look back.

Camilla and Maranatha raced down the road toward the embrace of the fair, miles away. "You're going to barf on me, I know it," Camilla teased.

"I will not. My stomach's better."

"Oh, right. Now that you're a teenager, you're not nauseous? If I were you, I'd be cautious. I don't trust your stomach. Neither should you."

They raced, tire to tire, until Camilla saw a wrought-iron gate and, behind it, a burnt skeleton of a house. "I smell mystery," she said. She stopped her bike. Maranatha nearly crashed into her.

In lieu of a ride on the Tilt-a-Whirl, and despite Uncle Zane's pained blue eyes, Maranatha and Camilla climbed over the gate. They searched the scorched scene, pretending to be arson investigators. They concluded a cat had set fire to the house, taking feline revenge on an evil master. "All scary houses have names. This one's Black, sure as night," Camilla said.

As the day's shadows lengthened, after they'd explored the woods behind the house whose once-grand pillars stood charred against the Texas sky, Camilla said, "I want to come back here another day." She put her hands on her hips and tilted her head back. "Let's go back to Black." She wailed and screamed the words like AC/DC. Maranatha laughed so hard, she nearly wet her pants.

Maranatha and Camilla never made it to the fair.

Tired from their investigating, they pedaled lazily back to town. "I'll see you soon, baboon." Camilla waved a good-bye to Maranatha.

Something niggled at Maranatha as she walked the stairs of the big white house. Everything looked the same, but nothing felt that way.

"I'm home, Uncle Zane." Her voice echoed, bouncing off tall ceilings. She called Zady's name, though she knew it was unlikely the housekeeper would be there on a weekend. She shivered. Loneliness pierced her.

She walked past the parlor to look out the kitchen window at Uncle Zane's parking spot, figuring he'd probably left to look for her — again. He had swung on a wild pendulum from disinterest to overprotection the day her name changed from Mara to Maranatha three years ago, but his protection kicked into high gear when she turned thirteen. On her birthday, he gave her a bike that sported a crudely shaped bow. He handed her a hockey helmet. "Be careful," he said. And he meant it.

She stopped in front of the window. Uncle Zane's white Cadillac sat silent in the driveway, the same place it'd been when she'd ridden away earlier.

Panic ripped through her.

Maranatha ran to the parlor. On the floor, Uncle Zane lay prostrate, face kissing the oriental rug, arms and legs outstretched like he was making a prone snow angel.

"Wake up," she wailed.

But he didn't.

An ambulance came and whisked him away, while the word *stroke* hung in the hot Burl evening.

Zady'd tried to soothe Maranatha during his long rehabilitation. "It's not your fault, Natha," she said. "I should've checked on him. He seemed altered, and I should've known."

Though Zady wore guilt in the lengthening lines around her eyes, she pestered Maranatha with all sorts of don't-blame-yourself words, meaningless blather that never made it past Maranatha's terrible heart. The best way Maranatha could explain it to Camilla was that she and Zady stood before a giant chalkboard, with the words *should have* and *could have* scrawled over and over again like naughty kids' sentences. While Zady tried to erase Maranatha's *coulds* and *shoulds*, Maranatha rewrote them line by line.

One

Summer 1987
Burl, Texas

EVERY YEAR ON THE ANNIVERSARY OF his stroke, and
many times in between, Maranatha retraced the route she and
Camilla had ridden that day. In front of her bike tire beckoned a
serpentine of gray pavement radiating heat. The more her shirt
clung to her body in a sticky embrace, the better she liked it.

Penance.

She'd learned the word from Bishop Renny. He said something about trying to make things right by abusing yourself.
Said Jesus took the need for all that away. But she knew Jesus
would say something different to her, considering how she'd
nearly killed Uncle Zane because of her selfishness.

The hot Burl breeze tangled Maranatha's hair so that it
whipped and wrangled about her face. She didn't mind, didn't
even brush a casual hand to her face to clear the hair from her
eyes. At seventeen, she welcomed the wildness, wearing her
tangles like a needed mask. A gust of sideways wind whipped
the mask from her face.

Maranatha passed the costume shop where, behind a

cracked front window, one headless mannequin sported a faded Santa suit and another, a sequined Twenties dress. She pedaled past the farm implement shop whose yard was dotted with ancient rusty plows. This strip of road held most of Burl's broken dreams — a turn-of-the-century white farmhouse, now converted into a bed and breakfast that no one visited, a hand-painted For Sale sign declaring the dream dead. A mobile home stood way back on a fine piece of property, the structure tilted oddly to the left where the cement blocks had deteriorated. A goat preened on its roof, claiming it for himself. Four years ago, children had played out front. She and Camilla had even waved to them. So carefree for such a day.

Wiping the sweat off her forehead with the back of her hand, she glanced down at the too-small bike, despising it, as if it had once held her hostage, carrying her away from Uncle Zane's need four years ago when she and Camilla had been drawn toward the lure of cotton candy and caramel apples.

Maranatha veered onto the familiar gravel driveway flanked by crepe myrtles. She stopped, straddling her bike, catching her breath. She listened for cars but heard only the labored noise of a tractor, far away, until the engine sputtered and died.

The silence roared at her.

It should have blessed her with peace; instead, she remembered Uncle Zane's hair askew and wondered why God let a selfish girl like her take up space in this world.

She looked behind her. Her thoughts shifted as a deeper worry played at her, taunting her. Though she never voiced it, she lived with a constant fear that someone would burst from the silence and grab her. She hated that she always looked behind, like she was expecting some crouching phantom to nab her. She'd been running from monsters bent on destroying her ever since General first drawled, "Hey, Beautiful" in her ear.

Even though she was sheltered in Uncle Zane's white house and safety was no longer elusive, she always felt the presence of evil five steps behind her. Ready to suffocate her.

She glanced at her wrist to soothe her fears. Circling it was her name, MARANATHA, each sterling letter separated by a bead. Zady'd given it to her a year after she found out that her real name wasn't Mara but Maranatha. Part of her quest in discovering her identity was a need for a name that meant more than "bitter." When she learned that her real name meant "Come, Lord Jesus," a part of her heart enlivened, as if it knew she was named that all along. She touched each letter, thanking God that He added Natha to the end of her name, that He changed her from bitter to a heart where Jesus could live. If He wanted to, that is.

She got off her bike. The same wrought-iron gate stood erect before her, chalkboard black and foreboding, with an out-of-place silhouette of a squirrel at its arched top. It always reminded her of Willy Wonka's gate, the gate that prohibited children from seeing the mysteries within the glorious Chocolate Factory. She laid her bike in its familiar dusty place behind the crepe myrtles and approached the gate. Locked.

As usual.

Heart thumping, she tried the handle, a ritual she performed every time she ventured to this place, the scene of her selfishness. Why she thought it would magically open today, she didn't know. When she tugged at it, the gate creaked a warning, but it didn't budge. Looking back toward the road, she listened again. Nothing. Only the sound of a dove calling to its lover and the crackle of too-dry grass rubbing against itself like a fiddle against its bow. She breathed in the hot air and touched the angry wrought iron. She returned to the bike, unzipped the pouch behind her seat, and stretched on her bike gloves.

Attacking the gate again, she pulled herself up, up, up until she could swing her leg over the gate's pointed top. She scampered down, preferring to jump the last three feet.

Maranatha smiled. Before her was an open field whose hair was littered with dandelions past their prime. Bits of dandelion white floated in front of her like an idle snowfall, only these flurries drifted toward the sun, away from the ground, in lazy worship. Beyond the field stood the remains of the charred mansion.

Now shaded by the house's pillars, she remembered Uncle Zane's eyes the day of his stroke. The smile left her face.

She ran to the middle of the field, trying to shake the memory — her laughing, laughing, laughing while Uncle Zane pled for her. She stopped. Maranatha picked one dandelion, held it to her mouth, and blew a warm breeze over its head, scattering wishes toward the has-been mansion. *Jesus, You know my name. I want to live up to it. I want my heart to be a place where You want to come. But I'm afraid it's too dark there. What I've done. What's been done to me.... I'm sorry I'm so needy, but I have to know, have to know it in my gut. Please show me You love me anyway. Whatever it takes.*

It had been her wish since she met Jesus under the pecan tree at her home, back in the days when Uncle Zane had a quiet will and Zady, his housekeeper and her friend, kept house without the intrusions of Georgeanne, who had invaded their peaceful home with her schemes. Zady dished out helpings and helpings of His love every day at Uncle Zane's table, but Maranatha never seemed to be able to digest even a scrap. She experienced Jesus at church, surrounded by Mama Frankie and faces darker than her own. When dark-skinned Denim spoke or his pale-faced stepdaughter Camilla rhymed truth, Maranatha thanked God for making unique folks, for giving her friends. Still, Jesus' love seemed far away, and she, undeserving.

A portion of her little girl's heart had been abducted by General, the boy-turned-man who violated her so many years ago. His pocked face visited her in nightmares where she had no voice, no safety, no escape. He seemed to lurk behind every stray noise. He didn't haunt Burl anymore, but he lived firmly in her mind, igniting dread. She feared he'd stolen the only part of her that could have understood God's love. She feared he held the middle piece to the puzzle of her life.

Am I wishing for something I'll never have?

Maranatha shielded her eyes from the pursuing sun and walked toward the burnt house. Four once-white pillars stood tall, blackened by angry flames. She remembered when she'd first seen Uncle Zane's home nearly a decade ago, how it loomed large on its street, how she'd longed to be the owner there someday. But reality was more complicated than that. Sure, she lived there now. Little by little, she was renovating it to splendor, but lately the joy of transforming it had waned thin, like a pilled swimsuit at summer's end. Fixing things was hard. She'd painted and painted until her fingernails were permanently speckled. Then the pier and beam foundation settled further, cracking her handiwork.

As she gazed upward at the four pillars that reached for the sky, where the abandoned house's roof once lived, she wondered if she'd ever have a home of her own, children about her legs, a husband to love her. The thought of marriage both repulsed her and pulsed through her. Hatred and longing — all in one girl.

She walked through the rubbish, darkening her red-dirted shoes, looking for a sign from heaven. She played this game sometimes, asking God for signs, for sacred objects that showed her that He saw her, that He knew she existed. That He cared.

Something glinted off and on as the sun played hide-and-seek through the trees. She bent low to the ashes, her body blocking the sun. The glinting stopped, so she stood and let the sun have its way again. There, spotlighted beneath the gaze of the pillars, was a simple, thick-banded gold ring. She retrieved it, dusted the ashes from the gold, and examined it, turning it over and over in her hand.

Inside the ring was a faint engraving. *Forever my love.*

"Thank You," she whispered, but her words melted in a hot wind. Dark clouds obscured the sun. The sky purpled. She'd seen a sky like that before. She slipped the ring into her shirt pocket and ran toward her bike, climbed the hot gate like a criminal pursued, and dropped on the other side.

She mounted her bike. From behind she heard a bustled scurrying, like the furious bending of too-dry alfalfa.

Then darkness.

Someone's hands suffocated her eyes, obscuring the day, stealing her screaming breath. She kicked her leg over the ten-speed, struggling to free herself from the firm grip, and tried to holler. Like in her nightmares, she was mute from terror. Though she knew General's presence was illogical—he'd been shipped off to some sort of juvenile-offender boot camp—she could almost smell his breath as she gasped for her own. She heard a laugh but couldn't place it. It sounded familiar, like family.

She kicked and elbowed like a kindergarten boy proving his manhood against a playground bully, but the hands stayed enlaced around her eyes.

More laughter. Even more familiar.

She took a deep breath and screamed. Real loud.

Thunder answered back.

Two

"COOL IT, NATHA. IT'S ME!"

Maranatha spun around to see Charlie, Zady's son. She slapped him on the side of his brown face. "Don't you *ever* do that again."

Charlie rubbed his cheek and smiled. "Great left hook you have there. Is that how you greet all your boyfriends?"

"Only the ones who sneak up on me and scare me half to death." She let out her breath — finally — and smiled.

He stepped closer. Errant raindrops fell between them like a beaded curtain. "It's good to see you smile."

Something in her stomach roiled, mimicking the clouds rumbling above her. She longed to bridge the gap between them, to permeate the rain curtain with the joy of new love, but she couldn't. Someone watching from the outside might think she hesitated because Charlie wore a different color on his skin, but she'd learned a long time ago that a house's exterior paint meant nothing; it was the foundation that was important. She knew Charlie's construction was good, but she wondered if he hid behind pretend goodness, if something darker lurked there behind the nice-looking wallpaper. She stepped back.

"When will you let me kiss you, Natha?" She could see that

Charlie wore an expression of grief and hope while Maranatha played this painful tug-of-war with his heart.

"When I'm good and ready," she said. Part of her wanted to fling her pale arms around his neck and touch her lips to his; the other part wanted to sprint as far as she could in the other direction.

"There's not much daylight left in summer." As he said it, thunder rumbled the earth and heat lightning illuminated the crepe myrtle behind him.

"There's not much daylight left in today," she said. The rain bucketed from the clouds now, hissing, then drenching the pavement a few yards away. "Best get going," she shouted through the rain.

"I got my pickup. Want a ride?"

"Why should I ride with a creep who lurks and grabs me?" She smiled as she said it, but she could detect a slight wavering to his smile — a tinge of hurt.

"Suit yourself." He turned toward the road, head down.

Maranatha reached through the rain and grabbed his elbow. "No, I'm sorry. Of course I'll ride with you."

As she said it, wind blew through her, making her feel as though it might lift her off her feet. In a moment the rain ceased, revealing a sky no longer purple but sickly green. A siren moaned in the distance. After the wind's violent gust, stillness settled where earth met sky, a stillness that felt like punishment delayed.

"Too late." Charlie grabbed her arm. "Over the gate. Hurry."

"Why can't we take the truck?"

"Not enough time. It's having trouble starting." He pulled her toward the gate.

They climbed over the wrought iron, both dropping on the

other side. The dandelions stood perfectly still, their translucent heads reflecting the sky's angry green.

"Is there shelter here?" Charlie ran toward the house as he said it. "Real shelter?"

"A cellar in the woods," she gasped. Her legs sprinted through the dandelions, their fuzz clinging to her legs. "Beyond the house."

The earth and sky roared anger. Maranatha stopped and looked up. The green sky snarled, churning clouds around and around, like they were headed down a toilet bowl. Only there was no bowl for the sky to flush. No hole deep enough to contain its fury. She could see the funnel now, landing right near the trailer home she'd passed. Fascination and terror rooted her to the ground. Love and tornados had the same hold on her — of utter panic and irresistible lure. Charlie seemed far away now, almost to the pillars of the house. He didn't see her. Lightning zigzagged the sky above her in rickracked abandon. It struck a pine tree in the distance with a furious flash. She smelled the distant odor of campfire, but she stood still.

Perhaps this is what penance looks like — a tornado headed for the likes of me.

Charlie's voice was indistinct, like a radio station untuned. The tornado spied her, changed directions, and raced toward her. There was solace in knowing that it was coming for her. At least she knew it was there. At least it didn't sneak up on her and throw its windy hands around her eyes. This enemy she could see.

"Natha!" Charlie shouted in her ear, his breath coming in heaves. "What're you doing? Come on!" He seized her hand and pulled her away from the place she had stood, the place marked X, where the tornado was seeking its treasure. She ran until her lungs hurt from heaving air in and out.

"Where is it?" Charlie was looking wild-eyed at the ground, searching.

"Where is what?"

"The shelter! Where is it?"

"Near the birdhouse. Back there." She pointed toward the woods. In front of the stand of pines stood an unscorched yellow birdhouse, high on a pole. She led Charlie toward it as the sky chased them, rolling, rumbling, yelling at their heels. The house behind them exploded. Charred debris flew in wild trajectories. A burnt two-by-four catapulted past Maranatha's head. "Here!" she yelled above the relentless wail of the funnel cloud. She pointed to a door hinged on a cement platform anchored to the earth.

Charlie pulled the rusted handle. It broke in his hands. He crouched lower, bloodying his fingers around the outline of the door while the wind blew in horizontal terror. Maranatha wedged her thinner fingers into the jam and pried, heaving the door one inch above the ground. Her body lightened. She wondered what it felt like to fly. Charlie pushed his hands beneath the door and flung it heavenward. The hole beneath the ground was as dark as the sky. The house's ash swirled around them and stung their eyes. Maranatha still had one hand on the door's frame as her body lifted. Charlie snatched her free arm, pulling her down toward laddered stairs. "You first," he yelled.

As he pulled the door almost shut, something hit him, toppling him over Maranatha. He thudded to the cellar's earth below.

She scrambled down the ladder as the door was ripped from its rusty hinges.

"Charlie, are you all right?" She yelled the words, but even she couldn't hear them. Bits and pieces of burnt house fell through the cellar opening where Charlie lay motionless. She squeezed her eyes shut, forcing them to adjust more quickly to the darkness of the earthen hole. When she opened them, she saw the size of the room. Grasping him under his arms, she pulled Charlie away from the gaping mouth above to a more sheltered corner. "Wake up!"

He didn't stir.

"Help," she said, but the tornado devoured her words.

Wet warmed her hands where she'd touched Charlie's head. The heat congealed his blood, made her fingers sticky. Her weak stomach lurched, threatening to erupt, burning her esophagus.

The open doorway rained dust and wood and foliage just as the clouds had spat rain minutes before. Dust sprinkled down as light filtered the particles. The emerging sunshine illuminated her bloody hands.

"Help." This time she could hear herself speak, but her voice sounded swallowed. "Charlie!" She shook him lightly at the shoulders. Nothing. She bent close to his lips, the lips she longed to graze but was afraid to kiss, and felt his breath against her cheek. Alive.

"You stay right there. I'll be back." She touched his cheek with her sticky hand before climbing the ladder. Popping her head above the surface of the ground like a curious prairie dog, she planted her red hands on the red earth. The pillars that had stood tall, had defied the attack of fire, were gone, leveled instead by wind. The cement slab looked as if it were ready for carpenters to start framing, as if God had taken a push broom and swept it near clean. The dandelion field beyond had lost its white hair and all of its wishes. Green slender bodies without heads swayed in the cooler breeze. The always-locked gate stood cockeyed on one hinge, and the squirrel that once looked toward the sky gazed earthward, as if he were praying.

Maranatha ran toward the broken gate. The storm's grit

tasted like charred sand in her open mouth. Her hair twirled around her head, but this time she didn't welcome its wildness. She shook her face free of it as she loped through the gate's skewed threshold. At the road, she prayed. Asked God for help. Asked God for someone to please drive by.

Unfortunately He answered in the form of Georgeanne Peach. Maranatha waved down the red Thunderbird, only to watch her drive beyond, stop, and circle back around.

Georgeanne parked in front of the gate, pulled her rearview mirror to herself, checked her reflection, and then got out. "What's all this about, Maranatha?"

She puzzled at Georgeanne's nonchalance. "The tornado — it passed right over us."

"Us? You and Zane? Where's Zane?"

"Isn't that *your* job? Knowing where he is? Why aren't you at the house?"

"Dead? Is he dead?" Her perfectly mascaraed eyes registered panic.

"No, Uncle Zane's not here. Charlie is. Hurry. He's hurt. We need to get him to the hospital." Maranatha started toward the slab, shoving her blood-caked hands in her pockets. Georgeanne certainly would not approve.

The fiftyish woman followed, but very slowly, her heeled feet picking their way through the dandelions. Maranatha turned back and pled with her eyes.

Georgeanne planted her hands on her hips. "Charlie? Isn't he that black boy? Why, what in the world were you two *doing*, Maranatha?"

"Running from a tornado. Now hurry!" Surely she'd let her racial prejudice go just this once, letting her home-health-aid ways be of service to Charlie.

Georgeanne stopped. "Tell you what. I'll go get you some

help. I'll call you an ambulance, okay? Why don't you come with?" Her voice was slow, painfully slow, drawn out like Ed McMahon's "Here's Johnny," only there was no Johnny to her slowness, no real ending to her sentences. She was the kind of talker who left you wondering if she was ever through. She always ended her voice high and drawn out, like there was something else to say.

"And leave Charlie?"

"Of course. He'll be fine. He's a strong boy, isn't he? Not like your uncle." She examined her nails and picked at a hangnail.

Maranatha stared at the blondish woman. "I'm staying here. With Charlie. Get an ambulance *now*."

"Sure thing," the perfect red lips said. "But I can't say I didn't warn you."

"Warn me about what?"

"Other folks won't like it, darling. Not one bit." She shook her head, her hair staying in one place like an over-hair-sprayed wig. "Finding you with a colored boy out in the middle of nowhere." She shook her head, nose in the air. "You know how my friends will talk and talk. It'll make a terrible muddle for your Uncle Zane too. Chocolate and vanilla, they never mix, baby." Her perfectly spoken words had the cadence of molasses, painfully slow and forever stained.

With that, she meandered to her car and left, leaving Maranatha alone with her hot anger in the decapitated dandelion field.

Though the sun followed Maranatha, she shivered as she jogged back to the cellar.

Three

FROM THE CELLAR, MARANATHA HEARD THE faint siren of Charlie's rescuers. When the noise crescendoed, Charlie's eyes opened. "You okay?" were his first two words.

"'Course I'm okay. It's *you* I'm worried about."

Charlie rolled to one side like he was ready to prop himself up.

"Stop it!" Maranatha put a hand on his shoulder. "Might be a concussion. Best stay down. I need to flag down the ambulance. Stay right here."

"Yes, ma'am!" Charlie saluted her.

"Very funny."

The tornado sky had departed like a rent-avoiding tenant, leaving hyacinth blue where green had been. Not one cloud traced across the sky. Maranatha ran toward the ambulance parked beyond the gate. Its lights twirled, but there was no sound. The last time she'd needed an ambulance was when Uncle Zane . . .

Two firemen started toward her. They met her in the dust between field and gate. "The tornado get you? I heard it didn't touch down," said one, his gear too large for his skinny frame.

"You heard wrong. And no, it didn't get me. Do I look like

Dorothy? Anyway, I'm not the one — "

"Let's get you inside." The other fireman, his volunteer helmet skewed atop a head of curly red hair, put his hand on her arm.

She jerked her arm away. "Charlie's the one who's hurt. Banged his head." She turned toward the cellar, then looked back when the men didn't follow. "Um, you're probably gonna need a stretcher."

The hodgepodge crew of two obeyed, scuffing up dust as they plodded behind.

A shrill voice pierced the journey. "Maranatha! Maranatha!"

Without stopping, Maranatha looked back to see Georgeanne run-skipping toward her — fast.

Maranatha kept walking.

"Your Uncle Zane's back at the ambulance."

Maranatha turned, looked at the nearly sweating woman.

"I picked him up and brought him here. He wants to see you. T'make sure you're fine."

She wanted to run and hug him, to will him back to himself, but she couldn't, not with Charlie the way he was. "Tell him not to worry. And can you please contact Zady?" Maranatha increased her stride to a jog, leaving Georgeanne in the red dust.

Maranatha followed behind Charlie's stretcher until she saw a herd of flowery-dressed ladies surrounding Georgeanne near the ambulance. She stopped.

Beyond the crowd, alone, stood Uncle Zane, hat in hands. Maranatha skirted the ladies and ran to him, but stopped short of throwing her arms around his thin body. His emotions, the little he had before the stroke, had left altogether the day the ambulance came for him. She couldn't bear needing him, felt guilty for wanting a hug returned, so they stood there, staring at each other.

"Where's Zady?"

"Coming." His eyes didn't meet hers. He looked at his hands. "You safe?"

"Yeah. But Charlie —"

Uncle Zane coughed and walked away. The ladies behind Maranatha murmured and hushed.

Bert and Ernie, Maranatha's unspoken nicknames for the volunteer firefighters, steadied Charlie into the ambulance's open back. Maranatha once again flanked the whispering flowered ladies and stood at the tailgate. "Your mom's on her way, Charlie," she said. Inside she could see him raise his pink palm, as if he was trying to silence her. Ernie pulled a white gauze strip around Charlie's head, reminding her of the World War II movies she and Zady loved.

"Best tell her he's on his way to Mama Frances," said Bert.

"It ain't Mama Frances. It's *Mother* Frances," Ernie corrected.

"She knows what I mean," Bert snapped. He looked at Maranatha. "Probably needs stitches."

In tandem, Bert and Ernie slammed the back doors, got in the ambulance, and sputtered gravel on the flowered ladies. The vehicle turned left toward downtown Burl, where Mother Frances Hospital sat on a bluebonnet hill. The sirens ripped through Maranatha, sucking resolve clear out of her, reminding her. When she faced the ladies, what scrap of energy she had dried up.

"So what were you doing out here, child?" Georgeanne's voice snaked its way into Maranatha's heart. She waited for the venom to take effect.

"Where's my uncle?"

"He's waiting in the car." She looked beyond Maranatha. "He's waiting for me to take him home. Away from here."

"I know." She looked at the dirt, kicked it a bit. Every time Georgeanne talked, Maranatha could hear blame. She worried that if by some chance she could erase the *coulds* and *shoulds* from her chalkboard, Georgeanne would find a way to rewrite them, this time in indelible paint.

The posse of ladies, whose cars littered the shoulder of the road, smiled simultaneous white grins.

Georgeanne met the grins with her own and sighed. "You're fixin' to break your uncle's heart, fraternizing with that colored boy."

Maranatha had to get out of here, needed to flee from Georgeanne and her snooty friends. It was a circle she never felt privy to, having grown up as a foster child primarily in the "bad" section of town, the illegitimate offspring of a crooked judge and a sickly woman who were caught in the crossfire of Burl politics. "I'll see you later, Georgeanne." She backed away, seeking solace from the stares. She looked behind the crepe myrtle bush where her bike had been, but the tornado had apparently snatched it clear away. Lord knew where it had ended up. Probably in a tree somewhere, wheels spinning.

A car roared to a stop. Zady stepped out of Maranatha's blessed getaway car, a Dodge Aspen station wagon. "Where's my boy?" she asked, ignoring the now-dispersing crowd of flower ladies.

"On the way to Mother Frances. He needs stitches, they think." Maranatha closed the small distance between them.

"What in tarnation was he doing out here? What were *you* doing out here?"

"I'll explain in the car. Let's go."

Maranatha couldn't understand Zady's tight-lipped silence. Driving faster than her Aspen-doting husband would have let her, she kept shaking her head and saying, "Mm-mm-mm."

Maranatha watched as the ribbon of road she had ridden hours earlier raced by. She missed her bike, her one prospect of freedom, and wondered if she'd get it back. She remembered the truck then.

"Charlie's truck—"

"We'll get it later." Zady stared straight ahead. She slowed the car at Burl's Loop and turned right.

Only four words. Maranatha and Zady had shared hundreds and thousands of words in car rides before—about dreams, Jesus, the proper day for harvesting purple-hulled peas, the beauty of garage sales, friendships. But on this ride where so many words could be said, those four snapped like rattraps at her heart.

Zady turned right, up the road splitting the now-grassy hill of Mother Frances. Every spring the hill hosted millions of bluebonnets. Families sat on its girth, snapping next year's Christmas photos. Bees flitted above the white-tipped flowers, too busy visiting blossoms to sting. But now, under the gaze of the summer sun, the hill was reduced to mere grass—browning, at that.

In front of the hospital, a bride preened. Little girls ran around in miniature versions of wedding dresses while a boy in a too-small tux sat on a red rock and smirked. One of Burl's sad facts was its lack of outdoor wedding spots, so folks got married in front of the hospital where a rose garden and fountain provided Burl's only wedding vista. A photographer leaned on his tripod and swatted at mosquitoes. Zady exited the car. Maranatha followed.

People in varying degrees of pain filled the emergency room. One woman screamed, clutching her abdomen as her five children watched with wide eyes. A man held a Coke can in his bloodied hand and spit in it. Zady pressed past them and interrupted the ER receptionist who was talking on the phone, smacking her gum. "I'm looking for my son. Charlie Wilson."

The stringy-haired girl, eyes rimmed with caked-on blue eyeliner, barely looked up. "One minute," she said to the receiver. "Down around the corner, ma'am." She gestured to the left.

They followed the girl's directions. Rounding the corner, Zady nearly collided with a man in scrubs. "If you'll please wait, ma'am, I'll let you see him in a minute." The ER doctor pointed to three mustard yellow chairs in a hallway. Maranatha and Zady sat. Unspoken words stood in the air between them. Maranatha glanced at her sticky hands and decided to wash them, leaving the worrisome silence behind.

In the bathroom, she saw her reflection above the sink — tangled hair, dusty face, a deep, old look of pain in her eyes. Had it not been for the sad eyes, she'd have said she looked like the Tasmanian Devil from Saturday morning cartoons. She turned on the water to full hot and scalded her reddened hands beneath the faucet, shampooing them with antiseptic soap. Grit and blood washed down the drain, as did a bit of her hope.

When she returned to the mustard chairs, they were empty. She poked her head into one room. An elderly man moaned under white covers. She looked into a second room to see a puffy-eyed mom with a screaming baby. In the third, she saw Charlie. Part of her heart leapt to her throat; the other part bottomed out on the heels of her feet. Dear Charlie. His forehead was bandaged white against brown skin, making him look patchworked. He smiled. "Hey there, Natha."

"Hey." She walked to the foot of his bed.

"They'll let me out in a few. Only seven stitches and I'm as good as new. I figure I'll look a bit like Frankenstein."

"Where's your mom?"

"Calling Daddy. No doubt telling him a near-death story.

Should have seen the look on her face. Priceless."

Maranatha hoped Zady's zipped lips were a result of motherly worry and not something else. But deep down, she knew. Zady was mad. Zady's silence felt exactly like Georgeanne's narrowed stare. Uneasiness crept in, all fast and furious, like a gecko pursued by a hungry cat. She could bear, even argue back, Georgeanne's prejudice, but she didn't know what to do with Zady's disapproval. It knocked her end over teakettle, as Zady often said.

"Cat got your tongue?" Charlie sat up and winced.

Maranatha shook her head. "I'm worried about you."

"A little fall, that's it. That cellar ground was awful hard. Hit my spine. I'll be fine tomorrow."

"What about work?"

"What about it? I'll be there tomorrow."

"You can't work in the warehouse if your back is sore. Can't you call in sick?"

"Yeah, if I want to lose my job. No such thing as sick leave, Natha. Not at the warehouse. You know that."

"But if you're injured . . . surely they don't expect — "

"Stop your preaching, girl. I'm paying my dues. Without college, I don't have a chance at much. You know that. But at the warehouse, I can move up. I'll be manager someday."

He said *manager* as though the job were president of the United States. He sat straight up now, hands by his sides. His face held a hint of pain.

"You don't have to be strong, Charlie."

"It's not a matter of *have* to be. It's a *need* to be."

Zady filled the doorjamb. "Need to be what, Tornado Boy?"

"Calm yourself, Mama."

Immediately, Zady stood by Charlie's side, holding and stroking his reluctant hand.

The Sesame Street song about one thing not being like the others mocked Maranatha. *I'm one of these things that doesn't belong. Anywhere.*

Zady turned to her. "Best be getting home, Maranatha. Your uncle wants to see you."

Maranatha nodded, first to Charlie, who nodded back, and then to Zady, whose face showed no emotion at all.

"See you." She left the foot of the bed and walked her skinny body through the wide doorjamb, past the lobby with the still-hollering lady, and out into the boiling heat. The sweaty bride and groom posed in front of fading roses. They turned toward each other and held hands, their rings reflecting the late afternoon sun.

Maranatha remembered the golden gift hidden in her pocket from what seemed to be seasons ago. She shoved her hand into her shirt pocket as she walked toward home, searching for the wedding band from Jesus.

Not there.

She fished again.

Nothing.

The burden of the day suffocated her as rebel tears dared to wash her cheeks. *So this is what happens when I ask You to show me Your love. It figures. A tornado hurts Charlie, takes my bike, steals my ring.* The day's fickle joy flickered in front of her like a decaying black-and-white film — fuzzy dandelion heads waving in the breeze, the familiarity of the charred pillars, the butterflies in her stomach at the first sight of Charlie. The film broke and flung itself around and around its reel. A full color movie played in its place — a movie where her wishes blew hither and yon on an angry breeze.

Penance.

Four

SHE MEANT TO WALK STRAIGHT THROUGH town, cross the Loop, and climb the crooked stairs of the big white house where an emotionless Uncle Zane awaited her. But her feet turned, meandering toward Camilla's blossom-filled yard. With Camilla gone most of the year at college, Maranatha tried to absorb as much of her friend as she could over the summer.

Camilla's mom, Rose, was tangled among a stand of climbers. She peered at Maranatha through the brambly hedge, nodded, and kept at work under an Australian gardener hat, shielded from the sun and the gazes of passersby. Still somewhat of a recluse.

Maranatha climbed Camilla's steps, noting their sheen. The porch and steps had been Camilla's project for summer weekends, between her weeks of counseling at Shady Pine Girl Scout Camp. It maddened Camilla, Burl's self-proclaimed poet laureate, that not much rhymed with porch, other than fire words like scorch and torch. "I'd soon as torch this porch," she'd said at summer's beginning, but the rhyme didn't really work, and she laughed when she said it. That's when Maranatha started encouraging her to write unrhymed poetry.

"Rhyming limits you," Maranatha said.

"Limit, schlimit. Rhyming's an art."

Still, Maranatha's comments seemed to put Camilla in a foul mood that summer. The porch had been the better for her wrath—bearing the fury of rhyming Camilla and sandpaper unleashed.

Before Maranatha could knock, the door flung open. "Well, look at you! What's with your hair?" Camilla kissed both of Maranatha's cheeks, French-style. Camilla, clad in a red and yellow bikini, held a pitcher of tea.

"Tornado," Maranatha said.

"Today? Ain't no twister, sister."

Maranatha rolled her eyes. "I was out visiting Black, and one came up all of a sudden-like."

"You okay?" Camilla stepped aside, welcoming Maranatha inside.

Maranatha stepped around the tea-wielding girl and plopped herself onto their ragtag sofa. Its cushions absorbed her. Made her sweat.

Camilla set the pitcher down and gave Maranatha a curious look. She sat next to Maranatha and put her arm around her. She didn't say a word, didn't have to. In a simple embrace of friendship, Camilla stroked Maranatha's hair. Told her everything would be fine.

A tear escaped her eye. Camilla noticed and wiped it away. "Sorry," she said.

Maranatha simply nodded.

Camilla stood. "Tea?"

"Sure."

She disappeared into the kitchen, reappearing with a McDonald's collectible glass with the state of Alaska emblazoned around its circumference. "Tea's colder in this glass," she said.

"Thanks." Maranatha took a long, cool drink, letting the sweet liquid cool her throat. She felt better instantly.

"So, a tornado. Do tell." Camilla now sat opposite her in a reupholstered easy chair, rescued from the roadside. She propped her chin on her hands.

Maranatha recounted a portion of the tale, omitting Charlie. "The wind blew the dandelions clear away. Took my bike too."

"Oh, no. Your bike."

"I know."

"How'll you get around now?"

"I don't know. I guess I could ask Uncle Zane."

Camilla gave her a hard look. "I don't think you should. He scares me. I don't think he's all there."

"He's fine," Maranatha said too quickly. She looked away. She hated hearing the truth, like if it were said out loud like that, Camilla-style, it would make it even more true. She remembered Uncle Zane's limp hand, the way his body gave no resistance when she rolled it over, the way his unblinking eyes stared past her to the ceiling fan above. All because she allowed Camilla to convince her to go to the fair.

Camilla cleared her throat, snapping Maranatha back to the parlor.

"Were you hurt?" Camilla sat back, hands behind her head, revealing unshaven armpits.

"Well, not really." Maranatha remembered Charlie, lying still on the cellar floor. She kept nothing from Camilla, not a thing, but this detail about Charlie's being with her she couldn't tell. It wasn't that she was ashamed or anything, just that she wanted a secret all her own. Away from the inevitable flow of Camilla's questions. "I did break a nail." Maranatha smiled. She was never one for manicures.

"C'est dommage."

"What?"

"French, silly. Why else do we kiss-kiss when we meet? I'm trying to get some culture into you." Camilla crossed her legs and bent forward. "French is my minor, I decided. *C'est dommage* means, 'That's too bad.'"

"Oh. What's your major, then? Still religion?"

"Yeah. I guess I'm stuck with it. Changed my major so many times, the school nearly kicked me out. But I have mostly religion credits." A crooked grin crossed her face. "At least I like my minor. I like French. Like the way the words roll off my tongue. French is very chic, you know. Very with it."

"You've been home all summer and you've never told me this." *So I'm not the only one with secrets.*

"You never asked."

Maranatha took another drink, draining Alaska of its icy lake of tea. Camilla poured more into her glass. They existed in a strange sort of tandem, knowing each other's thoughts and needs before they were expressed, even after Camilla left her friendless three years ago when she packed her bags for the University of Illinois. "Well, how would I know to ask that? What else should I ask you that you're not telling me?"

"Like what I eat now."

"What do you mean?"

"I'm a vegetarian. No more meat for me."

"Is that why you aren't shaving?"

"Nah, that's laziness, I suppose, or maybe I'll keep it. I'm into nature now."

"Since when?"

"Since I met folks like myself. Take William, for instance."

"Who's William?"

"Just a guy. His family owns a cattle ranch somewhere around Nebraska or Kansas."

"Why would a ranching boy—"

"He's no boy, Maranatha. He's a man."

"Fine. Why would a ranching *man* be against meat? Makes no sense."

Camilla sighed. She had a way of sighing when Maranatha didn't *get* her words. "It makes perfect sense."

The day's events settled into her. Her body looked seventeen, her heart felt forty-three, and her mind was far too tired to figure out Camilla's words. She wanted the old couch to envelop her, to welcome her for a three-hour nap. She shut her eyes. For a moment.

"I'm sorry. I forgot you've had a rough day."

Maranatha opened her gritted eyes. "Yeah." She waited for Camilla's easy words—words of reassurance that always came when Maranatha was at the end of her lasso.

"I'll make it easy on you. William, he raised Black Angus cows. Grew 'em, killed 'em, ate 'em. And pretty soon, he got tired. Tired of the cycle. Tired of the big, brown eyes. Tired of the blood. And he convinced me of the murder and mayhem. I decided I couldn't do it anymore. I can't eat dead animals. Can't wear 'em either. Leather is *dead.*"

Maranatha stood. Hardly the conversation she was looking for. "I need to get home. I need a shower." She walked past unshaven Camilla and over the home's threshold, letting the screen door slam behind her. As she tramped down the perfectly painted steps, she could hear Camilla squeak the screen door.

"Wait."

"I'm tired." Maranatha turned. She expected a repentant Camilla. She found a red-faced one instead.

"I thought you of all people would be interested in my life. I haven't shared that stuff with anyone. And you walk out the door?"

Maranatha started to say, "I'm sorry," but then thought the better of it. Camilla had a rat snake way of slithering an apology from anyone, even when there was no offense. "It's been a hard day. I need to go," she said as she measured her steps. She half expected Camilla to run after her, to beg her to stay, to say she was sorry for not shouldering the burden of Maranatha's day. Instead, the screen door slammed shut, vibrating the doorjamb.

Maranatha walked through the picketed gate, turned right, turned right again, and walked the dirt-streaked sidewalks of Burl to her home like she should have done in the first place.

Five

MARANATHA STOOD AT THE FRONT DOOR for a bit. She sang "The Star-Spangled Banner" in her head once, turned the knob, and walked in. Uncle Zane sat in the parlor, newspaper unfolded like an oversized book. She wondered if he was really reading or just trying to appear to be.

"Hi, Uncle Zane," she said.

"Yes?"

"You left with Georgeanne. And you seemed angry."

"No, not angry."

"Then what?" She picked at a hangnail.

"I was worried, that's all." He ruffled the paper, then folded it like a map. "With you running around while a tornado chased you."

"I'm fine."

"Just be careful."

"Uncle Zane?"

He held his hands on his lap, didn't answer.

"It's just that — well, my bike. It disappeared."

"I'm sorry," he said. And nothing more. Chin lowered to chest, he fell asleep.

She heard footsteps and turned. Zady stood in the dining

room, an apron around her waist. "Best let him sleep. You gave him a scare."

Maranatha wanted to run to Zady but stood near the parlor alone. She hugged herself. "I know."

"Scared me half to death too."

For a moment, she wondered if Zady's silence at the hospital masked fear for her. She released the breath she'd held in.

"If something had happened to my Charlie—"

Maranatha sucked in another breath. Held it. Of course. Zady'd be afraid for her own flesh and blood. Not for Maranatha. She was to blame for Charlie's pain today. For Uncle Zane's afternoon nap.

Maranatha turned and mounted the stairs to her room. She thought she heard Zady's voice leak a little tenderness as she walked higher and higher, but she convinced herself it was silly imaginings.

Summer never really ended in Burl. Like a grandmother in love with administering guilt trips, the sun could never let go of the red East Texas earth, could never let it rest for even a minute or two. It kept at it, beating Burl's residents with rays and rays of heat. The heat settled into Maranatha's bones, sapping her energy. The days following her date with the tornado blew on and on in lazy circles.

Camilla sent a conciliatory note via the U.S. Postal Service. Never good at face-to-face apologies, she'd mastered the art of cleverly written ones.

Maranatha Girl,

About that sassiness, I've enclosed a tangled poem of repentance. It's not my best work, particularly pulling Barbados out of my literary hat, but there aren't a lot of words that rhyme with tornados.

Cheeks, Camilla

Maranatha smiled. Used to be they hugged when they saw each other, that is, until Camilla apparently became Frenchified, greeting her like Napoleon or Brigitte Bardot, with a kiss on each cheek. Maranatha looked inside the envelope again. A small boat-folded note crouched in the envelope's corner. She examined Camilla's origami handiwork, complete with artistically rendered portholes with cartoon drawings of Camilla and Maranatha smiling from within. Camilla always drew herself like a pirate — one-eyed with a purple patch and several blacked-out teeth. In the belly of the boat, Camilla's truth-poem read:

A terrible thing, those tornados
Tossing friends like they're potatoes
Around and around
Flying up and then down
Flinging folks clear to Barbados.

She refolded the boat. Maranatha winked at the pirate girl, smiling half-toothed from the paper boat. "I forgive you," she said.

Charlie defied his stitches and went right back to his warehouse work. Camilla returned to singing, "Make new friends but keep the old. One is silver and the other gold" with green-outfitted Girl Scouts bent on learning how to tie a fisherman's knot. Uncle Zane maintained his daily schedule of eggs, newspaper, and naps. Zady kept to herself and the housecleaning, only now she didn't sing.

Or whistle.

Or hum.

Georgeanne Peach, who'd wheedled her way into their lives after Uncle Zane's stroke, made it a point every night to fuss with Zady in the kitchen. Though her duties ended before dinner when she gave Uncle Zane pill number twelve, she took to staying. Meddling, really.

In quiet wrath, Zady and Georgeanne crafted dinner together, each bumping into the other, each claiming the kitchen as her domain. It had taken Zady one full year to convince Uncle Zane to abandon night after night of Red Heifer's rib dinners — an amazing victory — but it would take longer to convince him to rid the kitchen of Georgeanne, if he could find a bit of the will he once had.

On the surface, it was all okra and purple-hulled peas between Zady and Georgeanne, but Maranatha knew there were more than vegetables underneath, like angry scorpions concealed beneath a proper piecrust.

Dinner that night was a sweaty occasion. The window air-conditioning unit had busted earlier in the day, coughing black ash all over the oriental carpet, putting Zady in a contemptuous mood. So they ate fried chicken while a fan's breeze ruffled the napkins on their laps. Uncle Zane kept his seat at the head of the large table. To his right, in Maranatha's place, Georgeanne preened. Over the past year, she'd elongated her home-health-aid duties to include helping Uncle Zane eat every meal, including dinner. Maranatha sat next to her in the crooked chair. Zady muttered to them all as she clanked china to table.

"Nice weather." Georgeanne placed a pointer finger inside her napkin and dabbed the corner of her down-turned lips. No sweat glistened through her powdered face. She could have been dining in an air-conditioned oasis.

Uncle Zane *humphed* and lifted an eyebrow her way. Why he kept Georgeanne, even after he improved, Maranatha didn't know. He certainly wasn't looking for someone to talk to. Maybe that was it. Maybe he grew tired of his own silence and liked the familiarity of Georgeanne's voice to drone and prattle the days away.

"Tell me, Maranatha," she chirped, "have you heard anything from Zady's boy?"

A dish clinked. Maranatha could see Zady's back, a room away, her shoulders hunched over the sink, her head shaking no.

"No, ma'am. I guess he's back at work." She tried to make her words smack of nonchalance, as if the mention of Charlie meant nothing more to her than the day's weather or local politics. The fan's breath passed by her wet face.

"Work, does he? I didn't take those boys much for workers. That's downright commendable, don't you think, Mr. Winningham?"

Humph.

A dish clacked against another.

Maranatha stabbed her chicken, remembering Camilla's sudden hatred for all things meaty — all for the sake of a boy. Defending Charlie suddenly seemed futile. She looked directly at Georgeanne, who had taken to separating the sinews of Uncle Zane's chicken pieces and lining them up neatly on his plate like a row of happy soldiers. She pushed the plate back to him.

"All folks need to make a way in this world, don't you think?" Maranatha ate a bite of chicken and swallowed.

"I suppose, but it's so *commendable* of him — to break out of his circumstance to become a laborer. Where did you say he worked?" She scooped a small bit of chicken onto her fork and placed it carefully in her mouth so as to avoid smearing her perfectly applied lipstick.

"I didn't."

Zady entered with a pitcher of ice water. She poured Uncle Zane's where it sat, passed by Georgeanne's glass, and poured Maranatha's — an inefficient use of time. She then doubled back, grabbed Georgeanne's glass, placed it near the table's edge, and poured from high up. Water splashed Georgeanne's face, but she sat stock still, staring straight ahead. Zady kept pouring. Maranatha almost reached out to steady the near-full glass, but stopped. Burl lacked suspense these days. May as well relish this one small bit.

Zady poured until the water spilled over the top of the glass and tipped over onto Georgeanne's neatly folded lap napkin.

Georgeanne sat there.

"What was I thinking?" Zady mocked. "Here, let me get you cleaned up."

"Mr. Winningham," Georgeanne said in an even tone, "it will be lovely when outside help is unnecessary, won't it?" She took her wet napkin off her lap, still looking forward. She folded it neatly, placed it back on her lap, and turned toward Maranatha. "I suppose now would be as good a time as ever, right, Mr. Winningham?"

Humph.

"You see, Maranatha," she said, "your uncle and I have decided to get married. In two weeks."

Maranatha watched Zady walk to the kitchen, watched her look out the window, her big shoulders slumping a bit. The window opposite framed her like art. She needed this job, Maranatha knew. Needed it to feed the family. Why she thought first of Zady, she didn't know. Her mind didn't have the clarity in the heat to let the significance of a marriage seep into her.

"Did you hear me, Maranatha?"

"Yes, ma'am." She stood, crumpled her napkin, and went to the kitchen.

She put a tentative hand on Zady's shoulder. Together they watched the sun play peekaboo with a peach tree while the two people behind them clattered fork to plate in premarital bliss.

Georgeanne enunciated her way through hoards of sentences — all about appropriate flowers for summer weddings ("Ones that don't wilt in the heat"), why Margie *had* to play "Ode to Joy" on the accordion during the reception, which plastic forks were acceptable ("Not those white flimsy things. They must be those clear bluish ones from Jasper's Rentals"), what role Maranatha should play ("Not an important role, mind you, but a small one. Maybe tending the cake or helping folks with the guest book, that sort of thing. And by all means, make the child wear a proper dress"), and precisely which lighting made her look best.

All the while, Uncle Zane said

not

one

thing.

Not even *humph.*

$\mathcal{S}ix$

IN LESS THAN TWO WEEKS, ON August's "premier day," as Georgeanne called it, Uncle Zane would veer from his *humph*-uttering ways and actually repeat words after Preacher Byers. Maranatha got a queasy sensation in her stomach every time she thought of it, like how you feel when someone else's wound gets infected or you smell a nursing home for the first time. That kind of thing.

Maranatha tried to busy her mind with other things. Would she survive Calculus under Mr. Morrison this year? Where could she apply for affordable but good colleges far away from Burl's borders? There was always Southeast Texas Community College, but every person she knew who haunted its yellowing walls ended up frying french fries at Fat Cow's Burgers, civilizing prisoners at the correctional facility ten miles down the road, or spending day upon day stocking pale red tomatoes at Value Villa, bragging a ten percent discount around the holidays.

That was it. STCC birthed Burlites, who then took it upon themselves to marry other Burlites, thus producing future Burlites. Entirely too predictable.

Two Mondays before the August 1 wedding, and Maranatha was stuck. Stuck at home wondering where her poor bike had flown to. Stuck listening to the ill-suited silence of Zady, who seemed to be holding all her current problems against Maranatha. Stuck hearing the slow, exasperating voice of Georgeanne, who made it everyone's business to know each detail of the wedding. Stuck watching Georgeanne rearrange the innards of the big white house to suit her own tastes.

"Burgundy," she'd blurted. Maranatha watched in amazed silence. Georgeanne faced the floor-to-ceiling bay windows. Every blonde hair in place, she perched on high heels, flipping through paint chips.

Like Tolkien's Gollum, she argued with herself. "No, maybe not burgundy. *Southern Living* says the new color is hunter green. Yes, hunter green."

A pause, then, "No, hunter green is too dark for this room. This is a gathering room, a music room. Peach. Yes, peach. That will do. Bright and happy and so modern."

Another pause. "No, not peach. Peach washes me out. What was I thinking? Certainly not peach. Mauve. Oh, yes. Mauve. Here's one. Dusky purple dawn. Yes, that will do. Dusky purple dawn."

Maranatha tried to sneak by the room, but the floor wouldn't allow it. Beneath her shoes, ancient planks squawked.

Georgeanne turned around, her paint swatches arrayed like an oriental fan. "Oh, it's you. How nice of you to interrupt me."

"Aren't you supposed to be helping Uncle Zane?"

"He's sleeping," she said.

"I was just leaving."

"Leaving where? You don't have anywhere to go, do you? No car. No life. Seriously, Maranatha, what *do* you do all day? Hmm? You sleep in until ten o'clock, mope around the house, and read silly books. Really. Don't you think it's time you pulled your weight around here? Like painting, for example." Instead of examining her fan, she turned her paint samples over, fanning her fingers instead. She looked at each nail and smiled.

Never one to say something quippy in the moment, Maranatha remained as mute as Uncle Zane. Suddenly she understood him more. Why talk if someone else can field all the words? Why even try? Georgeanne had already pegged her anyway — considered her a nuisance. What could she say? Still, the silence begged for words, so she blurted, "I'm actually quite busy, ma'am. Busy fixing up this house. Busy getting ready for school. Busy — "

"Really, now. How nice. How *industrious*. Maybe you can put that skill to work in the future, building houses for homeless black people or becoming a plumber. Plumbers make a lot of money, you know. Nothing to sneeze at. You'll never get anywhere in this world if you're lazy, if you sulk around expecting to inherit your uncle's wealth. Best make your way in the world, I always say."

Maranatha examined her own cuticles, anything to escape Georgeanne's eyes. Those eyes bled something she couldn't figure out — not hate, exactly, but something like that. All masked with the spit-polish of Southern hospitality, like a chocolate-covered June bug. "I need to go," she said.

"Of course you do, dear. Of course you do. Gotta go roam the neighborhood, I suppose. Looking for your beau."

"Good-bye, Georgeanne," was all she could say.

"Yes, well, yes. Good-bye then."

As she walked down the hallway, Georgeanne's words echoed behind her, bouncing off the high ceilings like funeral music in an old church. "When I'm married, you'll be sure to help me paint, right? If you really care about your uncle, that is."

Though the outside smacked her with heat when she pushed

through the back screen door, she felt relief. Anything to get out of that house. Away from that woman. She'd worried for three days about Zady and her well-being, but now the heaviness of what the wedding meant sweltered her like a down hunting jacket in August. Maranatha decided to do something, anything, to alleviate the suffocation. Though she'd been ignoring the Almighty lately for being such a terrible Answerer of Prayers, she thanked Him today that *she* remembered to put her money in her pocket.

She walked down the tree-root-buckled sidewalk seven blocks — three east toward Camilla's home, four south to the heart of Burl. Mackenzie's Odd Lots stood tall amid the rapid decay of the downtown corridor. Most businesses had moved outside Burl's Loop, creating almost a ghost town in its dying center. But Mackenzie's had stayed, in part because Bret Mackenzie hated change more than innovation. Rumor had it that he inherited a mint when Pop Mackenzie died, which left him enough money to stay in this same place, selling the same tired merchandise to no one in particular.

Maranatha pushed open the door and was greeted by the same stifling air as outside, only this air moved. Mr. Mackenzie had purchased the largest fan Maranatha had ever seen. Larger than an airplane prop engine, it blew from the back of the store to the front door so folks were greeted with a gust when they opened the door. Her hair danced around her head, calming down slightly when she stepped to one side, out of the wind's howl.

"Good afternoon, m'lady." Mr. Mackenzie stood behind the counter of an antique soda fountain, his long fingers splayed out on its top, as if ready to launch himself over its girth.

"Hi, Mr. Mackenzie." She noticed his silver hair first — bowl cut meets mullet — and decided he probably tried to cut it himself but couldn't reach all the way around with his scissors.

"Maranatha Winningham. You know by now not to call me that. M'name's Old Mack. Y'know that, don't you, dear?"

"Yes, sir. I do. Sorry. It seems so disrespectful."

"You couldn't be disrespectful if you tried, little lady." When he shook his head, the mullet swayed back and forth. His eyes, blue as the Texas summer sky, squinted into a smile.

Maranatha smiled back. Old Mack was the only Burlite of late who actually liked her. Who seemed happy with her. Who liked being in the same room with her.

"What can I do you for?" He smiled, this time with his mouth, revealing four front teeth, perfectly straight, surrounded by gums. Had it not been for the two extra and the fact that he lacked padding, she'd swear he'd be a perfect Narnian beaver.

"A bike. You have any bikes?"

"Hmm, let me see. Got me a BMX, but that wasn't what you had in mind now, was it?"

She shook her head.

"But you have a bike, right? You lookin' to upgrade?"

"No, mine got blown away in that little tornado."

He scratched his head, then pulled on his braided gray beard. "Hmm. I heard about that. Heard some couple was stuck out there, and one got 'im some stitches."

Had it really made it to Old Mack? That we were a couple? "Oh." Maranatha turned away. Looked out the window, hoping a passerby would warrant her distraction. No one walked the streets of Burl in this heat. A crow hopped down the street, cawing. Even his caw seemed tired. Maybe it was time to go.

"I do have another bike. Want to take a look?" He stepped around the counter and walked toward the fan. The gray mullet now strewn behind him, he fought against his braided beard that kept smacking him in the face.

She followed behind, letting his thin body draft hers so her hair wouldn't fly so much. No matter, it whipped her face like an overzealous jockey. He maneuvered around the five-foot-tall fan and walked through an open doorway. Old Mack reached over his head and pulled a long white string, illuminating a storeroom full of bedsprings and empty bottles on a long line of shelving. "Keep my good stuff back here. Away from prying eyes. Promise you won't tell?"

"Sure thing."

Old Mack squeezed around the shelving. "I'll be right back," he said.

He returned moments later with a salmon-colored bike, brand-new. "This," he said, "is a good bike, Maranatha Winningham. A bike-shop bike. It'll outrun that Huffy you used to ride."

Under the single lightbulb, she could see he was right. Though its tires were knobbier and its handlebars straight, it was a Raleigh — the brand she'd wanted for three years. She'd seen one at a bike shop in Marshall and coveted it ever since.

"Called a Seneca. You can take it on any county road you want, and even beyond that, on them dirt roads out by your church. Yep. A real nice bike."

She bent low to its frame and ran her left hand along the top. She fingered the gearshifts and inspected the chain. It had never touched a road, she could tell. No red dust clung to its tires. Brand-spanking-new. "How much you want for it?" She remembered the money in her pocket and fretted.

"Not a red cent, girl. It's yours."

"No, Old Mack. I'll buy it from you. I can make a down payment and pay you back each month."

"Looky here, Maranatha Winningham. You listen up. The good Lord brought this bike here. Told me, 'Old Mack? I want you to give this here bike to the first gal who asks to look at a bike, you hear?' I told Him yes, of course. No use fooling with God, you know?"

"It's just that — well, it's perfect, and I don't understand."

"Plain as day, darling. Plain as day." He wheeled the bike out of the storeroom toward the front counter, this time his mullet blowing around his face. "Jesus wanted to give you a pretty pink present, that's all. Must've known you needed it. He went to all the trouble to drop it here in my lap. I've been burning in antici- pation ever since."

He took a hankie out of his denim shirt pocket and dusted the bike as he went on. "Who would it be? I had wondered each time a new shopper showed up. Ellen Shreeves? Nah, she wanted a gas lamp, of all things, in case her power went out in the summer. MaryBeth Hawkins? Nope. Needed her an ironing board that adjusted to short, being as how she's a hair under five foot. Wilma Walker? Not her. Wanted a dead animal, preferably an elk, to mount on her wall. Wanted it smiling down on her as she quilted."

"I don't know what to say."

He bent low to the bike, dusting under the aluminum frame. "That's a precious gift, Maranatha Winningham, not know- ing what to say. Sometimes it's the best thing t'be silent. Like today. You could've talked about Charlie and you and how you weren't a couple and that it was all a misunderstanding from the chicken spaghetti-toting church crowd and such. No. You let me say my words. Let them hang out there. I like that about you, Maranatha Winningham. Like it very much."

Maranatha winced. So he did know. So the gossip really had made its Burl rounds. She felt heat rise to her already warm cheeks, but Old Mack didn't seem to notice. Instead, he stood back from the bike and filled the silence with kind words.

"It's yours. Please take care of it. A present from the Almighty should be cherished." He winked a blue eye her way. "I have an inkling that this bike will save you. Will help you through this next year."

"Thank you, Old Mack." The giant fan blew hair into her eyes as she wheeled the bike away. It *tick-tick-ticked* beneath her.

"Maranatha Winningham?"

She turned, still holding the Raleigh's handlebars. "Yes?"

"Be careful."

She knew his words went beyond the bike. Like chiggers, the advice itched her whole life. "I will, Old Mack. I will."

Seven

MARANATHA RODE THE BIKE RAGGED THAT week, more out of frustration than a need to exercise. Georgeanne insisted Maranatha help arrange peach and mauve silk flowers for the wedding. "But, Georgeanne," Maranatha had said, trying not to sound snotty, "peach for your bridal flowers? I thought you said peach washed you out."

"Only as wall paint," Georgeanne said, with pure conviction. "As flowers it's okay."

Maranatha would rather trap rat snakes with her bare hands than twist roses and oversized daisies around each other. Rather eat fire ants.

But tonight, as she pedaled away from the big white house, her stomach flip-flopped. She was headed to Zady's, which also meant Charlie's. She hadn't seen him since the tornado, though they'd talked several times on the phone. Charlie's voice had a needy twang lately, like he was longing to be near her. As she pedaled toward his house, a movie played in her mind. She could see herself ride up. Charlie standing in his yard, the sun highlighting his head like God was pointing a friendly finger at him. For her. She embraced him, threw her arms around him while the halo of sunlight smiled down. She smiled too in this movie, a smile that held hope. But, as usual, her feet disobeyed her heart. Maranatha watched as the "dream Maranatha" broke free from the shelter of Charlie's arm and ran away, her bike left in a heap. As she ran, her heart twisted, whispering words like *rape* and *General* and *betrayal*. Maranatha shook her head to break free from the movie and focused again on her bike beneath her, the bike heading toward Charlie's house.

Maranatha gazed at the quilt of yards flanking her as she rode. One yard sported appliances, rusted and tilted, and no grass to be seen. Fire ant mounds erupted in a circle around a doorless dishwasher as if the ants were plotting to storm its open gate. Overgrown flowers crawled through a chain-link fence of another yard, red and orange and yellow, daring to crowd out the Bermuda grass by sheer determination. Another yard shouted grass victory. No shrubs, no flowers, no fire ants — simply a perfect buzz-cut lawn. A low-pressured sprinkler danced lazily on the green surface.

They suited Burl, she thought. Burl was a hodgepodge, a real cross-section of humanity, where uppity ups shared sandy ground with those of lesser luck.

But it was the mixed yard that brought back memories. Half flowered, part grassed. General's house. When she pedaled past, she felt her heart hollow. He wasn't there anymore; she knew that. That he could no longer see her did nothing to calm her. After the authorities sent General away, his family disappeared, leaving the house vacant for years. She'd gained tentative peace in its emptiness. As long as it stood vacant, as long as unpruned wisteria vines entangled themselves around the porch, as long as the windows emitted no light from within, she was safe.

But two months ago, the eyes of the house brightened. A mom puttered in the yard, planting sunflowers. A dad trimmed the lawn on Saturdays. A toddler giggled in a soggy diaper under the sprinkler. It was something that should've made her feel safer, she knew. But instead, she felt mocked. As if they could move on when she couldn't. No matter how many flowers they planted, how much grass they cut, how many times the sprinkler spat upon the pale shoulders of the half-naked child, they couldn't erase General from that spot of Burl earth. Couldn't make the memories go away.

Maranatha quickened her pace. Once she turned away from town, she'd have less than a mile until she'd have to face Zady and maneuver around Charlie's pleading eyes. Though she was hot, she didn't sweat this time. The sun started to disappear behind the sycamores lining the street, but that didn't mean a thing in Burl. The heat always stayed with the sun's departure. And yet her body seemed to notice its absence.

She pulled up to the house and set her new bike inside the gate and stood there, stalling. Zady's father, Daddy Dale, had built the rock home from the bounty of the ground. He'd work all day in the cornfields in summer, in the rendering plant in winter; but by night, he'd build. Every rock imbedded in the house's walls he retrieved from a riverbed a mile down the road. The way Zady told the story, the good Lord provided seven rocks a day, always in the same place. Daddy Dale called it a miracle. In two years, he'd erected its walls. He scavenged bits and pieces for the house the following year until it resembled a home. Windows of different sizes gleamed at Maranatha.

Maranatha wished she could've met Daddy Dale. She could shake his hand, Zady joked, if she wandered down to the river where the rocks appeared. Folks said his spirit inhabited the place.

Before she could muster up the courage to mount the red stone steps, the front door opened. Zady stood there with a look that could only be described as a frown-smile — a thin-lipped line that said neither *Good to see you* nor *Good riddance.* "What you need, Natha?"

"I stopped by for a visit. Is Charlie here?"

"Not yet. Still at work. Why don't you wait with me on the porch? The house is too stuffy." She motioned to the porch swing.

Maranatha sat, thankful they could talk hip to hip, not eye to eye. They sat facing forward, letting the trailing sun highlight the last stand of sycamores.

Zady started the swing rocking, gentle-like. "I don't know what I'm going to do, Natha-girl."

Maranatha didn't know what she meant, which subject she referred to, so she kept quiet.

"Mama Frankie always told me about beauty, child. I wish to God her mind wasn't going, because I could use her words right now. Could use her perspective."

"What do you mean?"

"I'm prejudiced, child. M'heart's dark."

Maranatha let the words settle into her, but she could make no sense of them. *Prejudice* was a word white folks wore proudly in Burl, but it was not a badge for a black person.

"You and Charlie, child. I went to talk to Bishop Renny about it all. He cleared my head a bit, but the nagging stuff kept coming back. I know they's been talking, been chattering about this in certain circles. It bothers me more than I can say."

Maranatha shifted on the swing as the sun left the horizon. "Why? I thought you didn't care what Burl ladies thought."

"I don't much, but this here's my boy, Natha. I have a fierce sort of mother-need to protect him. From you."

"Zady, we're not going out. We're not a couple. There's nothing to fret about."

"Don't matter. Other folks think so. And I see my Charlie's eyes, child. He's taken by you."

Maranatha put a hand over her stomach. It felt like it did after one too many rides on the Zipper. "I still don't understand. You're not prejudiced."

"Yes, I am. Against you. Against your skin. Mama Frankie used to tell me this rhyme: 'Beauty is skin deep, but ugly is to the bone. Beauty will fade, but ugly will hold its own.' I believe that, Natha. Problem is, my ugly is to the bone. I care more about what Georgeanne Peach thinks than about the heart of my son. And if I dare get to admitting it, I'm worried what *my* friends will think."

"But you always told me that skin color doesn't matter."

"It's a truth worth repeating, shouting even, 'specially in Burl. It don't matter, to be sure. But this past week, I realized it does matter. At least to me."

Maranatha crossed her other arm over her stomach. She could barely handle Charlie's interest, but that paled to Zady's admission. "So, what does that mean?"

"It means I'll be a-praying, Natha-girl. I'll be wearing out my knees until my stubborn heart listens. It means I'll stop pouting, stop blaming you for my own muck. I'm sorry, Natha. Will you forgive a foolish old woman?"

Maranatha smiled. The tension Georgeanne created in the big white house was thick, but it hadn't compared to the pain of Zady's withdrawal. In one instant she felt the sticky humidity in her heart lift, replaced by clear, spring air. "Of course I forgive you. Of course."

Zady patted Maranatha's leg and then clasped her broad black hands together on her lap. The swing swayed as a gentle breeze fanned them both.

"Can't we stop this wedding?"

"Doubtful," Zady said, shaking her head.

"I mean, she's just weaseling in. Why would he ask her to

marry him?"

"I don't know. Maybe security? Or maybe she convinced him."

"He's not easily convinced, Zady."

"That was the old Uncle Zane, child. Not the new one. He's different."

Maranatha watched as a bee buzzed around Zady's lap. Zady sat still, never minding the stinging insect. Maranatha tried to swat it.

"Don't be doing that, Natha. You'll make her sting. Leave her be. You never know what'll happen when you swat a bee."

Maranatha fiddled with her hands. "What are you going to do? Once Georgeanne moves in?"

"Don't know, child. Raymond says the Lord sees us all. Says He'll take care of us here in the stone house. I wish I had that faith. I've been working for Mr. Winningham your whole life and then some. Eighteen years, child. And we need that money."

"What about Raymond's woodworking?"

"Brings in a pittance. He's the best cabinetmaker Burl has, but no one appreciates it. Folks, 'specially rich ones, lowball him every time."

"Can't you find another job?"

"Been looking. Nothing's coming up, though. Charlie joked that he could get me a job hoisting boxes at the warehouse. He got mad when I took him seriously."

"You can't do that. Your back —"

"I knows it. But we gots to eat. Gots to pay the electricity."

"I'll miss you, Zady."

The words hung in the thick air, hovering like tired mosquitoes over a cow trough. She hadn't meant to say the words. She measured her emotions in very small doses, teaspoon by teaspoon. Any more than that, and a heap of crying would pour out by cupfuls. But these words were a cup. Zady had been her mother, had been her life. Not seeing her every day, well, it was too much. Besides, who would bear the guilt with her? If Zady weren't there to erase her *shoulds* and *coulds*, the chalkboard would fall under the weight of all those words. A tear snaked down her cheek, but she didn't wipe it. Didn't want to admit it.

After a long silence, Zady choked, "I knows it, Natha. I'll miss you too."

They sat on the swing, staring forward as dusk put the day to bed. Street shadows gave way to a dimmer world, where night bugs came out to frolic under cover of grayness. Charlie's truck, white and in need of a muffler, broke through the dusk like a snorting white horse. He turned into the driveway, pulled up the emergency brake, and stepped outside. It wasn't until his foot hit the first rock step that he saw his mother. And then Maranatha.

"Hey, what're you doing here, Natha?"

"Came by for a talk." She looked at her hands, didn't meet his gaze. "With your mama," she added.

"How was work?" Zady asked.

"Tiring, so quit bothering about it, Mama. You ain't gonna work there. If you try to, it'll be over my dead body." Charlie smiled at Maranatha. "I shouldn't have even joked about that job. She's been bothering me about it ever since. Made me talk to my boss about it." He looked at Zady. "I'm telling you, Mama, you're going to get me fired, all this messing around with the management."

"We need the money, Charlie Boy. Simple as that."

Charlie dropped his lunch box on the porch and faced them both, leaning against the railing. "I knows that, Mama. That's why I am working."

"I wanted that money to go toward college." Zady picked

her teeth with her left hand.

Maranatha twisted her hair and examined her split ends. *Charlie should go to college, should see the world beyond Burl's tight grip. There has to be more to life for him than hoisting boxes.*

"I've told you a thousand times — I am not going to college. Got me a good job here, with a chance for advancement. No need to go any further. No need for more book learning. Besides, I *want* to help provide. You've worked long enough."

Zady sighed. When she exhaled, it seemed like too much air, like she'd been holding her breath for a year. "I gotta make supper. Best get washed up. You smell like the warehouse."

"Mind if I walk Natha home, Mama? I'll be back real soon."

"Suit yourself, Charlie Boy, but mind that you come back soon. I'm fixing burgers and onion rings."

Maranatha's salmon bike stood out like a color picture on a black-and-white background. "Hey, nice bike, Natha."

"Thanks," she said.

"Where'd you get it? Your uncle?"

"No. I got it at Old Mack's store."

"I didn't know Old Mack had bikes like this."

"He doesn't normally." She was too proud to tell him it was a gift, that she didn't buy it herself, so she let silence take over.

"Here, let me." He held the handlebars and pushed her bike toward Maranatha's house.

"You okay, Natha?"

"Yeah, why?"

"Nothin'. You seem awful quiet."

"Got a lot on my mind, that's all."

Crickets fiddled happy songs while she walked on one side of the salmon bike, he on the other. "Why don't you want to go to college?"

"Gotta grow up sometime. Make my way. I already make more than my old man."

She noticed how his strong hands gripped the bike handles, as if he were glued to them.

"I'm going to college. Probably far away."

A dog barked in the distance. A motorcycle roared to life. A child shouted. But Charlie walked in silence as the bike rolled beside him.

Side by side, with a bike between them as a chaperone, they walked — neither speaking, neither risking a noise that might sound like a conversation starter. When they reached Maranatha's home, Charlie stopped. The arms of the giant pecan tree reached down, nearly touching the top of Charlie's neatly shaven head. Maranatha wished the tree would swoop her up and away, anything to get away from a tense home and a silent Charlie.

He handed the bike to her, not in a shove, but gently, yet without emotion. "Here."

"Thanks." Maranatha held the handlebar grips, still warmed from Charlie's fingers.

"Charlie?"

"Yeah."

"I'm sorry."

"For what?"

"Just I'm sorry. Can't that be enough?"

"It's enough for today, Natha."

Eight

"GLORY! GLORY! GLORY!" MT. MORIAH'S multigenerational church choir rumbled and rhythmed to the cadence of Bishop Renny's hand clapping. His hands, larger than the Bible he usually held, caused his clap to resonate against the walls, rallying his parishioners. Maranatha sat in her usual place, next to Zady's family, right in front of Mama Frankie, who shouted, "Amen!" at odd moments.

"We've got problems, church." Bishop Renny clapped.

"Amen!" said Mama Frankie, her usual hankie lightly dusting Maranatha's ear.

"Big ol' problems." Another clap.

"Amen!" Mama Frankie tickled Maranatha's ear again.

"But Jesus!" The bishop shot both hands heavenward, eyes looking beyond the ceiling.

Mama Frankie fell silent.

"But Jesus!"

Maranatha heard more "amens." The choir swayed in sync with Bishop Renny, who danced a Holy Spirit–choreographed jig.

"Glory," he shouted.

"Glory! Glory! Glory!" The choir belted and swayed.

On and on the *glorying* went until Maranatha nearly shouted, "Amen!" Almost.

Zady fanned herself something fierce, an act that cooled Maranatha's face. Every few minutes, Raymond would mutter a "Yes, sir," while Zady shouted, "Preach it" in a fiery cadence rivaled only by the kindly bishop. For another hour, Bishop Renny preached "Jesus" while the choir chanted "glory." When it was all over, Maranatha felt as though the choir had bathed her, that their voices had washed over her weariness. For a moment, she tasted glory and forgot about Georgeanne Peach's eyes, Uncle Zane's silence, and Charlie's neediness.

But it all came back soon enough.

Mama Frankie poked Maranatha on the shoulder with her closed fan. "It's going to be a green 'mater year, baby."

"Hello, Mama Frankie," Maranatha said. "You look beautiful today." She'd learned from Zady to keep the conversation to weather and clothes and grits; otherwise, she'd end up on a strange rabbit trail with the old woman — a thing that usually ended in Mama Frankie's yelling at the top of her lungs.

"Shut up about beautiful, will you?" She pointed a bony finger at Maranatha's face. "I'm older than Ronald Reagan. And let me tell you, he ain't pretty. Least not in my opinion."

"Some people think he's handsome, Mama Frankie." Maranatha waited for the yelling. She stepped back one step.

"What do you know, anyway? You're too young to know the difference 'tween ugly and beautiful anyway. Takes years to learn that. Takes years to see into people's hearts. Takes years to see beyond the layers of fluff on the outside."

"You're probably right." Maranatha stepped forward to let Zady and Charlie pass behind her.

"Darn sure I'm right. As I am about the green 'maters." The old woman coughed then. Coughed from the deepest part of her soul, hacking, sputtering, wheezing. She supported herself on her metal walker, sucking in breath.

Maranatha looked around for someone to help. She didn't know if she should pat Mama Frankie on her hunched-over back or give her some space.

But as quick as the coughing came, it stopped. Mama Frankie looked up, leveled a gaze at Maranatha, and winked. "I'm telling you, Sweet Potato Pie, it's a green 'mater year for you. And not the fried ones neither. I like the fried ones, like 'em as they smack against my lips. Likes me the cornmeal, the grit. No, ma'am. This'll be your green 'mater year." She winced, looked like she'd swallowed a lemon. "Sour. Stinging. Someone's gonna attempt to pluck you before you're ripe, before you get a chance to sing. I sees it, I do." With that, she grabbed Maranatha's wrist with freakish strength, indenting the MARANATHA bracelet into her arm.

"Okay, Mama Frankie. Okay. You can let go now."

"I can't and I won't."

"Please, you're hurting me." Her hand tingled.

"Not until you give me a promise." Her hazy eyes seemed to termite a hole through Maranatha.

"What promise?"

"That you'll run the other way. Run far away when the plucking comes."

Maranatha laid her hand across Mama Frankie's. "I promise."

The old hand relaxed its grip on her forearm, but her pale skin still registered the woman's grip. The letters MARA reddened her wrist. Maranatha could almost see Mama Frankie's fingerprints on the surface of her skin.

"There, I warned her, Jesus." She reassigned her hand to the walker and stared at the ceiling. "Told her about the 'maters.

Told her to run. Told her to be careful. You going to let me die now?" The woman's voice crescendoed. "I'M AWFUL TIRED. SICK OF THIS OLD, WORN-OUT BODY. I'M A-READY TO DO SOME DANCIN', JESUS. READY TO FLYYYYYYY!"

Zady popped her head back in the sanctuary and gave a scolding look to Maranatha. "I told you," she yelled. "Weather. Clothes. Grits. Nothing more. You've started a ruckus!"

Mama Frankie raised her right hand and waved it back and forth like she was greeting a friend who happened to be flying through the sanctuary. "I'M RIGHT HERE, JESUS. COME AND GET ME. I'M READY FOR GLORY! GLORY! GLORY!" Her knees buckled all at once. She slumped in the pew, her head strangely angled.

Maranatha shouted, "Someone please help me!" She climbed over the pew and lifted Mama Frankie's head. Her eyes were open, her mouth painted into a teeth-bared grin. "Mama Frankie, wake up! This is *not* funny." She shook her at the shoulders, but Mama Frankie kept smiling. A gurgle of spit drained out the left corner of her mouth.

In that small moment, Bishop Renny landed near Maranatha and plunged his finger into Mama Frankie's neck. "Lay her down! Raymond? Someone get Raymond!"

Maranatha didn't know what to do, where to be. She backed away as Raymond came through the back doors, wide-eyed. "Call 911!" he said to Maranatha. She ran toward the phone. Raymond pinched Mama Frankie's nose and blew puffs of air into her lungs. Bishop Renny did chest compressions.

She grabbed the phone and stared at the receiver as Zady put an arm around her. "I'll call, child. Sit yourself down."

So she sat. And watched as Mama Frankie breathed with Raymond's breath, lived by Bishop Renny's push. Over and over the two men tried to bring Mama Frankie back to Mt. Moriah, the church she'd mothered, but she would have none of it.

Sirens blared.

Medics arrived.

Folks gathered around in circles, praying.

Moaning and cries punctuated the rhythm of CPR.

But Mama Frankie refused to wake up.

They carried her out on a stretcher under a stark white sheet. Maranatha followed behind, remembering the day Aunt Elma wore a similar sheet, feeling the same rock in her stomach. Bearing the same guilt. As they wheeled her out the double doors, a crow flew in. Charlie later told her how it went crazy-like, how it thrust its black body against the window on Mama Frankie's side of the church until it broke free through the window and flew heavenward.

Maranatha shielded her eyes from the angry sun. The moment it stared at her, she started sweating through her cotton dress. Mama Frankie didn't sweat, though. The medics, whom Maranatha recognized as Bert and Ernie from tornado day, paused briefly at the back tailgate. Maranatha moved to stand at Mama Frankie's side, wondering if perhaps God would pull a Lazarus. She willed Mama Frankie's chest to rise, for her to yelp in a big breath of Burl air and shout, "Amen!" She touched Mama Frankie's hand that had slipped from beneath the sheet, her fingers pointing lazily to the ground, then lifted the limp hand and placed it once again beneath the protection of the sheet and stepped away. Bert and Ernie lifted the gurney and jarred Mama Frankie into the ambulance and shut the doors. The two got in and drove away without turning on the sirens, like a hearse.

Someone put a lazy arm around her shoulders. Charlie. She shrugged him off and looked down, where she could still see the imprint of Mama Frankie's live grip on her forearm. MARA. She wondered how long the impression would last. Wondered if from now on, she'd be bitter. Wondered if Jesus had flown away with Mama Frankie, never to return to her heart. "Come, Lord Jesus," she whispered to the air, swirled with particles of red dust. "Please come."

As the ambulance broke over the hill in a slow dirge, a tear flecked her cheek. She wiped it with the back of her hand. *When someone wants to pluck, I'll run, Mama Frankie. Maybe I'll ride my bike.*

Nine

"THE FUNERAL'S TOMORROW?" GEORGEANNE PEACH cornered Maranatha in the kitchen the day after Mama Frankie's death. "It's scandalous! Don't they know I'm getting married four days later? Well, I've never heard of such a thing. Funerals and weddings don't mix that close together." Georgeanne turned back to the cupboard next to the sink and pulled down more glasses. Needed more room for her crystal, she'd said. She placed each glass upside down, lining them up perfectly straight like pawn pieces on a chessboard. "Don't know why your uncle wants to go."

Though she wore a skirt, she hoisted herself onto the countertop and started bleaching the emptied cabinet.

"Will *you* be there?" Maranatha stayed rooted near the doorway, providing herself a quick escape. Already the straight bleach stung her eyes.

Georgeanne scrubbed the cabinet floors in vigorous circles, occasionally looking at her sponge and frowning. "Not sure. I'm not that comfortable in mixed crowds. I guess I'll let Zane go by himself."

"It's probably for the best that you stay behind. He seems to be doing better." Maranatha breathed an internal sigh of relief.

A chorus of *hallelujahs* echoed in her head. The last person she needed at Mama Frankie's funeral was this hired woman who'd sunk her claws into Uncle Zane in four short years.

Georgeanne turned, sponge in hand. "And what's that supposed to mean?" She smiled an incredulous grin.

"Uh, nothing. With all the wedding preparations, I figured you can't spare a moment away." The *hallelujahs* faded, replaced by a screechy electric guitar solo.

"Are you saying I'm insensitive?" As Georgeanne jumped from the counter, her skirt lifted, revealing nylons with runs above the knee line stopped by dots of maroon fingernail polish, making her look scabbed. "That I'm too busy for a funeral?" She smoothed her skirt, pretending it hadn't flown up, and smiled again. Her teeth were perfectly straight, perfectly white, but the words hissed through them when she spoke.

"Not at all. I thought you wanted everything to be perfect — for the wedding."

"Of course I want everything perfect. It'd be a bad omen if it wasn't. My first wedding to Jimmy, God rest his soul, was perfect. If this one isn't, it'll be jinxed."

"I'm sure everyone will understand if you aren't there." Maranatha implored with her eyes, hating herself as she did it.

"I suppose you're right."

Hallelujahs broke through again. Maranatha let out a breath.

Georgeanne turned and faced the household glasses arranged in military rows and gently placed each one in a liquor box that waited open-mouthed at her feet.

Maranatha stiffened. "What're you doing with our glasses?"

"They don't match each other. Can't have mismatched glasses, child. Trust me. You'll like my new glasses. They're crystal. Inherited them from my grandmother. And now they've finally found a proper home."

"The old ones are fine."

"They're fine for someone who is aesthetically challenged, I'm sure, but they don't complement my upcoming decorating scheme. You'll understand one day when you have your *own* house."

"This *is* my house." There, she'd said it. Not with a shout, but with a twinge of shake in her voice.

Georgeanne lifted one plucked eyebrow. "Things will change, Maranatha. Starting Saturday. You haven't had proper rearing, what with Zane's quiet ways. And who knows what that Zady woman has taught you. The good Lord put me in your life. At the right time. For your refinement."

And what exactly could Uncle Zane's nurse have to say about refinement? She wanted to say what she thought, but, unlike Camilla, Maranatha lacked gumption.

Georgeanne dropped the last glass into the vodka case and shut the lid.

Maranatha took the box. "I'll take those," she said to Georgeanne, not meeting her eyes. "They're mine." She wanted to add, *just like this house,* but, again, couldn't voice her words.

She turned her back on Georgeanne, bleach still blitzing her nose. She toted the box out of the kitchen.

Her kitchen.

On the way up the stairs, she snagged a brightly colored envelope sticking through the mail slot like a toddler's teasing tongue. *Camilla.* In the quiet of her room, she placed the heavy box in the middle of the floor. She sat on her unmade bed, then ripped open the envelope.

Inside were puzzle pieces painted white. She walked over to her desk and emptied the pieces onto its top. Thankfully, words written in blue ballpoint helped her configure the pieces. She read the short poem:

> Mama Frankie's flown
> Behind, nested, we wither
> Without her flutters

Beneath it, Camilla wrote:

Dear Mara,

I'm writing Mara for a reason this time because I know you must be awfully bitter and sad with Mama Frankie dying. I wrote my first haiku for you (pardon the rhyme, I can't help myself). I figured a nonrhyming haiku would capture the remorse better. (See, sometimes I do take your advice.) I'm really sorry. I know she was your friend, in her funny old-lady way. Hope my truth-poem eases your tears.

Beaucoup de cheeks, Camilla

Maranatha held a hand to her mouth, like she'd prevent tears from escaping there. She padded back to her bed while tears watered her face. She pulled the covers to her chin so that they embraced her body. She shivered despite the seepage of heat through the space between her single-paned window and the nearly broken air-conditioning unit.

The puzzle haiku made Mama Frankie's death real. Another loss. She looked at the box in the room's center. It screamed orphan to her — solid proof that she had no parents. No home. No one to really care that she took up space in Burl.

She pulled a framed photograph from the shelf behind her bed. Her mother. She'd ripped her up in a fit of anger one day, but Zady had taken to repairing the confetti she had become. Tiny white lines wormed through the picture, but that made it all the more dear to her — evidence of her mother's face and Zady's hands of love all woven together.

She used to imagine her mother materializing from nowhere to give a thought about literature, a hint of motherly advice, or a shake of the head when Maranatha wore mismatched clothing. She used to have one-sided conversations with Mama at her graveside as she weeded honeysuckle tendrils from around the marker.

She wished her mother sat on the bed with her now. Today she wanted to ask Mama questions. Wanted to hear her voice just once during her teen years. She could barely remember the hint of Mama's voice; it had been so long since her death. She died before Maranatha had a chance to memorize her face, appreciate the touch of her hand, or purr under her embrace. Mama died, left her orphaned.

"Mama?" she asked the picture. "Why is life so hard? Why can't it be easy? Do you see me here?"

But Mama stared back at her with a plain white smile, eyes fixed, flowered dress severed in white-lined rips. No voice. No melody.

Maranatha placed the picture on her bed and stared at the box in the middle of her room. The air-conditioning cycled on. She pulled the covers to her chin again. She needed Camilla to rhyme for her, reminding her that life would turn out fine, despite her anxious whine.

Though Zady would be in the house a few more days, she could already sense her absence. Georgeanne had relegated Zady to muck patrol, cleaning behind wardrobes and dusting under beds, so that she barely had time to bump into Maranatha, let alone share her soul with her. One thing was for sure. Georgeanne predicted life would change.

And it already had.

Ten

MARANATHA EXPECTED BLACK. WANTED BLACK, even. But when she stepped into Mt. Moriah Church wearing a straight black skirt and a black and mauve blouse, color bloomed everywhere. Flowers rioted the altar. Women wore white dresses with still more flowers, complete with hats covered in white netting. The place hummed excitement. She looped her arm through Uncle Zane's and intended to walk him to the front of the church, left side. Used to be he'd drag his right foot, but he fought back to where no one would detect a limp.

"In the back, please," Uncle Zane said.

Though she felt a need to sit in the same place as always, part of her was relieved. The last time she sat there, Mama Frankie screamed and died. She half expected Mama Frankie's place to be roped off, in reverence for her long-used pew. But, as happens in life, another family sat there as if Mama Frankie'd never been there at all. It made Maranatha want to cry and yell at the same time until she realized the interlopers were Denim and Camilla. An ache caught in her throat. She decided to go say hey once she found a seat for Uncle Zane.

Uncle Zane slid down the pew on the right side of the church, three rows from the back pew. Not many white folks attended the funeral; she counted only seven, including Camilla, Zane, and herself. She thanked the Lord that Georgeanne wasn't one of them. She'd been as surprised as anything to hear her uncle say he'd come to Mama Frankie's funeral. They'd talked a few times but hardly had anything called friendship. "For Zady's sake," he'd mumbled hours earlier.

Maranatha looked at the view from her unfamiliar seat. In a way, it was good to be in such a different place. She had the advantage of seeing everyone else all dressed up. Like a spectator at a Friday night football game, she could observe but not play in the game. Maybe the grief she felt rising at the back of her throat would stay put, would not erupt, if she stayed on the outside looking in.

"I'll be right back, Uncle Zane. I'm going to say hey to Camilla."

Uncle Zane nodded as he removed his hat.

"Hey, Natha." Charlie met her at the pew's end in a white suit and rose-colored tie. "Why aren't you sitting with us?"

"Too crowded," she lied. Even though Uncle Zane was a man of few words, they had an unspoken understanding between them — a familial bond that covered for the other. She wouldn't dare say, *Well, Uncle Zane is shy ever since . . . you know.*

Uncle Zane nodded at Charlie. Charlie cocked his head in response, like he knew the right way to "talk" to Uncle Zane. He walked to his pew, but Maranatha didn't follow. Camilla could wait. She sat down again.

"I like that boy," Uncle Zane said. "He's a respectful one."

"Zady and Raymond know how to raise children," she said. "I'm going to miss Zady." She didn't mean to let the words tumble from her mouth, but they did nonetheless, like they had a toddler-sized will.

"Yes, me too," he said. "You know, we could — "

The church erupted in music, interrupting Uncle Zane's words. He folded his hands on his lap, smiled at Maranatha, and then looked straight ahead.

She wanted to yell over the din of "Every Day with Jesus," *We could what, Uncle Zane? Keep her on?*

But the moment for the conversation had passed. She knew that much. Maybe during the car ride home they could finish what he started.

It was then she noticed the casket, right in front of Bishop Renny's podium. The simple light wood box sat closed, like a book after it'd been savored. The life Mama Frankie lived culminated in the pine rectangle before her. But more than that, it was the people overflowing the pews that revealed the old woman's real life. Maranatha traced the lifeline of her left hand, wondering how long she'd live, how many lives she would touch.

"Today's a day of glory," Bishop Renny said, a genuine smile parting his lips. "A day for celebratin'."

Shouted "amens" chorused from around the sanctuary. She could hear Zady's voice above the rest. But she could not smile.

"Here lies Mama Frankie." He pointed to the casket below him. "But she ain't here."

"Uh-huhs" resonated around the room. The organ played a jig.

"'Cuz she's dancin', folks!" Bishop Renny jumped to the side of the podium and kicked up his legs, nearly toppling himself.

As if on command, the congregation stood, jumped, and laughed.

"I want you to tell your neighbor, 'She ain't here!'"

"She ain't heres" shouted around the room. Uncle Zane looked at Maranatha with a pained expression. He used to be one who didn't like to obey such commands, especially from a stranger, but ever since the stroke, he'd become more obedient.

"She is not here," he muttered.

"She isn't here," Maranatha said back.

"Yeah, that's it, folks. That's the gospel right there. Mama Frankie is dead, but she lives today. Lives forever in heaven!"

"Hallelujahs" echoed off the church walls. Denim waved his hand in the air. Camilla stayed seated.

Bishop Renny went on as he usually did, each phrase getting louder as his face sweated like a cold tea glass in summer. Seeing perspiration fly from his face made her fan herself a little harder and worry a little more about Uncle Zane's reaction.

"The woman who mama-ed this church is GONE! NOT HERE! FLOWN THE COOP! SOLD HER LAST FRIED PIE!"

A chorus of "Swing Low, Sweet Chariot" mingled through the congregation, first quietly, then louder. Maranatha half expected a chariot to carry Mama Frankie out of the church right then.

When the song died down, Bishop Renny wiped his brow with a white hankie. "I'm gonna miss that woman," he said above a whisper. "Gonna miss her prayers. The moment she left us, I felt it in my soul. Felt all the prayers fly away. Felt like my holy armor sported a hole. Felt like a piece of my heart became vulnerable. I'm gonna miss her."

The sanctuary quieted, except for the swishing sound of funeral fans.

Bishop Renny was giving a gift right then. He was giving folks the words of grief. Showing them how deeply pained they felt but couldn't say out loud. Maranatha wiped a tear that angled down her face.

"She may be jitterbugging with Jesus," he said, "but she left her dancin' shoes behind. And none of us can fill her shoes. Not a one."

Grief lived a sheltered life in Maranatha's heart. She was

never one to let her grief come out and greet the world. Keeping it carefully locked behind a steel door, she fed it, but didn't give it light. Bishop Renny's words opened the door wide, letting in a flood of light, beckoning the grief to come out.

Like a too-full creek after a gully-washing rain, Maranatha's grief overflowed the banks of her soul and came out her eyes.

In a flood.

She covered her face, ashamed. She peeked out the left side of her opened fingers to see Uncle Zane's reaction. He stared ahead, not noticing. Eyes blurred with grief, she wept while the music came and went with the rise and fall of Bishop Renny's words. She gulped in huge buckets of air and exhaled in gasps. Her pain shamed her. If Mama Frankie had been there, she'd have scolded her for such a display.

The truth was, she grieved for much more than Mama Frankie. Maranatha grieved her own life. She couldn't put it that way in spoken words, but she knew more than anything that life was not as it should be, that pain was present all around, and that she'd have to muddle through more.

Someone shuffled beside, then in front of her. She moved her knees aside as rose-scented perfume wafted by.

Georgeanne!

"It's nice to see you." She sat between Maranatha and Uncle Zane, smelling like flowers but bringing the scent of death.

Maranatha turned away, wiping her tears, hoping Georgeanne hadn't noticed. The grief she felt now was more pronounced. It had been a sweet release, now soured by the perfumed woman beside her.

"Don't carry on so, Maranatha." Georgeanne arched a manicured eyebrow as she offered Maranatha a delicately embroidered hankie. "You'll see her in heaven, right?"

Uncle Zane remained mute. Maranatha wanted to climb

over Georgeanne and throttle her uncle, screaming, *How can you marry this woman? Can't you make her stop? Say something!* But decorum and fear anchored her to the pew, kept her from screaming a scene.

Bishop Renny prayed now, a weepy sort of prayer that threatened to steal more tears from her eyes. Head bowed, she stared at the floor, afraid if she closed them, her eyelids would spill. She examined her bracelet and prayed, "Come, Lord Jesus" over and over like a nursery rhyme, erasing the bishop's tear-inciting words.

"Mama Frankie wanted no fuss," Bishop Renny said. "She's probably scolding us right now for all these flowers." Laughter echoed through the church. "But she did request one thing — that we sing her favorite song on the day of her service. Turn with me to hymn number 357, 'His Eye Is on the Sparrow.'"

Everyone rose, even Georgeanne, who shared a hymnal with Uncle Zane. Maranatha opened her own, although she knew the words by heart. In hushed voices, the congregation moaned the words:

> *Why should I feel discouraged, why should the shadows come,*
> *Why should my heart be lonely, and long for heaven and home,*
> *When Jesus is my portion? My constant friend is He:*
> *His eye is on the sparrow, And I know He watches me.*

Maranatha wiped a tear with Georgeanne's hankie. The perfume stung her eyes. *I hope You're watching me, Jesus.* Bishop Renny pointed to the duct-taped window, reminding them all of the bird that broke through the day Mama Frankie died. A wail rose up to the heavens, on the wings of Zady's voice that sung above the others.

I sing because I'm happy,
I sing because I'm free,
For His eye is on the sparrow,
And I know He watches me.

Maranatha closed her eyes, trying to picture Mama Frankie singing, happy and free. For a moment she smiled. One moment.

"These spiritual songs are downright inspiring," George-anne said. "I'm so glad I came."

Dark thoughts circled Maranatha's heart. In a strange fit of jealousy, she wished she were in heaven singing bird songs while Mama Frankie was here, dealing properly with Georgeanne — using heavy doses of truth. She wondered how she would bear living with this woman, until Jesus answered her heart in the next verse.

"Let not your heart be troubled," His tender word I hear,
And resting on His goodness, I lose my doubts and fears;
Though by the path He leadeth, but one step I may see;
His eye is on the sparrow, and I know He watches me.

She'd heard many times from Bishop Renny's lips that this congregation was the body of Jesus, but today she was convinced it was His holy mouth, singing life and hope into Maranatha's breaking heart.

Whenever I am tempted, whenever clouds arise,
When songs give place to sighing, when hope within me dies,
I draw the closer to Him, from care He sets me free;
His eye is on the sparrow, and I know He watches me.

A quavering voice, loud and off tune, seemed to amplify itself in her ears, singing the last stanza like a prayer over her. Mama Frankie! She turned around to see who sang so much like the old woman. A little girl with her father stood there in their Sunday best. No one else. Only the wall beyond them.

Thank You, Jesus. She turned her bracelet around and around, remembering the cadence of her name. *Mara-natha. Mara-natha. Thank You for not leaving me as Mara, for adding to me, for coming toward me.*

Bishop Renny prayed a winded, meandering prayer. At "amen," as if on cue, folks walked to the front of the church. A little boy kissed the coffin. Zady placed a daisy on top. Raymond ran his hand along its top. Maranatha meant to go up there, to say her good-bye, but she lost her will.

Folks milled around in groups, buzzed in conversation.

Georgeanne was speaking, but her words filtered around Maranatha as if they were far away, like a fly trying in vain to make its escape out a closed window. "Maranatha! I'm talking to you. Listen to me."

"Yes, ma'am?"

"We drove separate, you see. And I don't want to drive to the cemetery alone, so your uncle and I are riding together. We'll pick up the Cadillac on the way back. It's one of our only alone times before the wedding, so do you mind catching a ride with one of your *friends*?"

"I can't think of anything else I'd rather do," she said. She handed Georgeanne her hankie, slightly dampened. "Thanks."

With that, she left the cushion of space that reeked of too-strong rose perfume and hunted for Camilla.

Outside the church, groups stood together. Still before noon, the sun hadn't decided whether it would shine or hide, but its presence was very much felt, drenching the armpits of several dresses and suits. Trees off to the side of the building created a smatter of shade relief.

"Must be near 103," a voice said behind Maranatha.

She turned to see Camilla all decked out in a violet-covered dress and wondered how she knew what to wear. "I meant to say hey before things began, but the music started and — "

"And you were afraid of me, right?"

"No, like I said, the music — "

"It's all right. I understand you way down deep. You cried like a baby, didn't you?"

Maranatha wanted to deck her right then, and almost did. She thought of the belly laugh Mama Frankie would have in heaven over such a show — two white girls pulling hair at her funeral.

Camilla moved in next to her, cradling Maranatha's shoulders with a skinny right arm. "Hey, I'm sorry. I've been a bit, what shall we say, *self-absorbed*. Can you forgive me?"

"Of course." A smile sang from her lips to her heart. Maranatha couldn't stand it if folks held stuff against her. She hated living under a pile of hidden anger, particularly toward those she loved. Camilla's words were the perfect fit to the grief-shaped hole in her heart. The flood that Georgeanne had stopped with a word roared out again, and Maranatha wept in the open under the canopy of trees, the arms of her best friend in the world wrapped around her like a love-worn quilt.

$\mathcal{E}leven$

JULY 31. WEDDING EVE, GEORGEANNE CALLED it. It made Maranatha wish Uncle Zane had let her get a summer job. She'd have something to do to whittle away the hours—frying fries, blending milkshakes, stocking shelves. Anything would be better than putting precisely one tablespoon of rice in a round piece of netting, tying it with a bow, and gluing a mauve rose to its center.

"Not like that." Georgeanne ripped a rice bundle from Maranatha's hand, spewing rice everywhere. "Now look what you've done." The snippy bride-to-be dropped to her knees and carefully gathered the rice, as if it were fine chocolate or gold flecks. "*This* is how you do it." Georgeanne dumped the rice back into the bag and scooped out one tablespoon, leveling it with a knife. She placed the heap in a perfect circle, then scrunched the netting around it before tying a symmetrical bow. She smiled like the Grinch, a wide, thin smile that pushed her cheeks upward in a heap. "Then you put the flower on. Right here. Now, do you think you can do that on your own without making any more mistakes? There are less than one hundred to go, and I have to tend to more important matters."

Maranatha nodded as Georgeanne left the room. She viewed the piles of ribbon, flowers, and rice as punishment, something she had to endure. By tomorrow it would all be over and she could get on to other things — like school and planning for college. Soon, she'd be out of Georgeanne's perfect hair, her greatly inflated personality.

A knock sounded at the door. She set down her pile of netting and descended the creaky stairs to the front door. She opened the door to find Camilla wearing a smirk, hair tied back in a fetching red bandana. "Thought you might be needing some help," she said, brandishing a pair of scissors.

Maranatha wanted to hug her.

"I figured Georgie Porgie would be slavin' you, this being the day before the wedding, so here I am. How's it going?"

"Slow."

"Put me to work," Camilla said with a wink.

"Follow me to the room of peach clouds and purple flowers." Maranatha and Camilla creaked their way upstairs.

"Lord, have mercy!" Camilla grabbed a handful of netting and threw the pieces in the air. Like misshapen, oversized snowflakes, they floated to the ground, kissing the hardwood floor.

"I know. I have near one hundred of these puppies to do. Perfectly, mind you."

"So the Peach has graced you with a job, huh? I'm all yours. Show me what to do."

They worked for over an hour until rice littered the floor. Every time they stepped, it sounded like the crunch of dried spaghetti under tap shoes.

"You know, you're not *supposed* to do rice anymore," Camilla said, breaking the silent reverie of rice-ball production.

"What do you mean?"

"I heard it's bad for the birds."

"What birds? Last I heard two *people* were getting married. Not birds."

"Hah. Very funny. Folks are supposed to untie this bee-ewe-tee-full peach thing and throw rice at your uncle and Georgie Porgie, right?"

"Yeah." Maranatha tied another crooked bow.

"Well, outside the church, the ground will look like this floor, won't it?"

"And—" She glued a flower to the ball, askew.

"And birds will come by and eat the rice, sure enough."

"So the problem is?" Maranatha threw the completed mess into a heap.

"Birds will explode!" Camilla gestured wildly with her arms and clapped her hands together.

"What?"

"Explode, sure as pie."

"Pie doesn't explode."

"Very funny," Camilla said. "No, consider this. One of our avian friends flies overhead and sees Uncle Zane walking out with Georgie Porgie all dressed in white. He whistles to his other bird friends, knowing that there will be a treat coming. A flock of birds alights on the ground where rice is aplenty. So used to scavenging from dumpsters behind Value Villa, they see this as a feast and gorge themselves on rice."

Maranatha still couldn't see the point. "And?"

"You know how rice is, right? It absorbs water as it cooks."

"It does?"

"For crying out loud, Maranatha Winningham. For such a smart girl, you sure do lack cooking smarts. Didn't you take home ec?"

"No time. Took honors classes instead." Maranatha spilled rice onto the floor, adding to the chaos below.

"Okay, Miss-Smarty-Pants-who-lacks-common-sense, here's the thing. The rice expands in the poor bird's stomach and — *kablam*! It explodes!"

"You're making that up." Maranatha grabbed the last peach circle.

"No, I'm not. I'm thinking of writing a truth-poem about it."

"Interesting. Where'd you hear the exploding bird theory, by the way?"

"In college."

"I'll be sure not to go to your college. I thought you were learning Shakespeare." She finished the last one and threw it on the pretty peach pile.

"Very funny. No, in my environmental group, silly. People for Perpetuating Plants and Protecting Populations. We call ourselves the Five Ps."

"Okay." Maranatha gathered the peach bird killers and placed them in a gigantic basket tied in wide rose raffia.

"That's where William and I learned more about the carnage of killing and eating animals."

"What are you talking about? Is William your boyfriend?"

Camilla helped her gather the last stragglers. "No. He's just a good friend."

"Really?"

"Yeah, so snip it. William, you remember, is my friend who convinced me to become a vegetarian."

"Too bad for Red Heifer. Folks like you will put the poor man out of business." Maranatha walked down the stairs. Camilla followed. She placed the basket of rice-throwing-thingies on the dining room table.

"You ever looked at Red? Certainly *not* the picture of starvation. My bet is he's eating forty head of cattle all by himself. The carnage!"

All Maranatha could do at that moment was picture a

porterhouse steak so large it lopped over the plate. She could almost taste it.

"You want to walk me back to my house?" Camilla stood by the front door, hands on hips. Accustomed to being a formerly stick-straight girl, she seemed to pride herself that she had a place to set her hands now that her body had morphed from straight lines to curves. Maranatha wondered if she'd ever develop beyond knobby knees and a too-flat chest.

"Yeah, that'd be fine. I have to get back, though. George-anne's wanting me to 'attend to last minute details,' as she says."

They walked under the canopies of tired trees, leaves droop-ing from days upon days of heat and sunshine. With every step, a bit of life drained from Maranatha. The heat had its way with her, and she lost.

"You okay?" Camilla asked.

"Yeah, it's so hot."

"And how long have you lived here? Face it, this is Texas. Can't get much hotter than Texas. By the way, did you see Faith Assembly's sign?"

"What sign?"

"Their billboard thing next to the church. They're always putting Jesus slogans there. Stuff like, 'Seven days without prayer makes one weak,' only they spell week with an *a*. Get it? We're weak if we don't pray."

"Yes, I get it. So what did their billboard say?"

Camilla laughed. "Well, it's not the most inviting sign. I spied it as ladies in dresses were bringing Jell-O salads to a potluck. Seemed kind of funny. The sign read, 'You think this heat is bad? Wait until you live in hell!'"

"Really? It said that?"

"Sure as pie. I wouldn't lie!"

Shared laughter felt good. They giggled at the quirkiness

of the town they both loved and hated. As red dust rose from under their feet, they padded in silence in that comfortable place called friendship where words were unnecessary.

"You ever been in love?"

Maranatha kept walking.

Camilla elbowed her.

"Ouch! Why'd you have to do that?"

"To get your attention. You didn't answer my question. You ever been in love?"

"I heard you." They turned left onto Camilla's road. Only one block to go and Maranatha would be free from this line of questioning. "You're almost home."

"Mama wanted to say hey to you. Won't you come in for some tea?"

"Only for a minute. I have to get back to Georgeanne, you know."

Camilla stood in front of their picket gate and seemed to measure Maranatha with her piercing eyes. "I can see it all over your face. You're in love. Swear on a cat it's not true, and I'll believe you."

"I don't know what you're talking about."

"Lying does not become you, friend." Camilla swung open the gate with a flourish and looked back at Maranatha, a glint of all-knowing dancing on her face — the kind that comes from someone intent on pulling out the truth like a dentist yanks a stubborn tooth that refuses to let go of its gums.

They sat inside the parlor. In the exact places they were during the last argument. Maranatha got a funny rumbling in her stomach, the same one she got when bad history repeated itself. "Where's Rose?"

"How should I know? Am I my mother's keeper?"

"But you said she wanted to talk to me."

"Did I say that? I don't remember. Let me get you some tea. You look downright flushed."

She left Maranatha alone in the high-ceilinged room. Camilla had painted it cream earlier in the summer. There was still tape on the ceiling. No pictures adorned the naked walls.

"Here you go. Some sweet tea for you." Camilla set two sweating glasses between them, sat back in her chair, and folded her arms. "Now, where were we? Oh, yes. Your love life."

Maranatha grabbed her stomach. She remembered the first time she'd told Camilla a secret, when their friendship was one hour old and she whispered parts of General's abuse to her without thinking. Though she knew having feelings for Charlie was not the same sort of secret, it felt that way, like a forbidden topic, not to be entrusted even to Camilla. "I liked a boy. Once."

"Kevin Arthur?" Camilla rolled her eyes. "Don't get me started on Kevin. You didn't love him. He worshipped you. And you kept him at arm's length. He was the best catch in Burl, and you hooked and released him." Her eyes said, *Shame on you.*

"Kevin was nice," Maranatha said. "But not my type."

"Wonderful is not your type? A gentleman is not your type? Heavens, Natha, who *is* your type?"

"I don't know. Not Kevin." She took a long drink of tea, hoping it would settle her stomach. Instead, her stomach wrestled itself.

Camilla emptied her glass. "I know you're in love."

"I told you. Kevin and I didn't work out."

"I'm not talking about Kevin."

An uncomfortable silence embraced the room. The air-conditioning hummed.

"I'm tired," Maranatha said. "And I need to get back."

"Tired but in loooooove," Camilla mocked.

"What do you care? Why does it matter?"

"Then there *is* an 'it' to talk about!"

"It's Charlie." Just like she regretted whispering General's antics to Camilla years and years ago, she regretted spilling Charlie out in the silence of the room. It almost felt like Charlie stood between them, head bowed, naked. Talking about him seemed humiliating.

"Charlie Barley, buck and rye." Camilla winked, then continued, "What's the way the Frenchmen fly? Some fly east, some fly west, and some fly over the cuckoo's nest." Camilla smiled. "How'd you end up choosing a guy from a nursery rhyme? Or a freaky movie?"

"Very funny. He's not a nursery rhyme. Or a freaky movie. You know me better than that."

"Well, then, it's got to be Charlie Bucket. I loved that kid too. Loved how he inherited Willy Wonka's factory." Camilla looked irritated. "Come on. Just admit you made that name up."

Maranatha breathed an internal sigh of relief. "You got me, Camilla. You know how I loved Charlie Bucket. The actor's name is Peter Ostrum, you know. Was born in Dallas."

"C'mon, Maranatha. Don't change the subject. I'm not talking about schoolgirl crushes on child stars. I was kidding you. I don't know many Charlies here, other than a buttoned-up violin player — not your type, I might add — and Zady's Charlie, and we both know he couldn't be *the* Charlie."

"Why not?"

Camilla laughed. "Because you two are like brother and sister. You can't be in love with your brother. Sheesh. We're not in Arkansas, you know."

Maranatha smiled. *Well, that made perfect sense.*

"You know what I think?" Camilla asked, her plucked eyebrows raised just so.

"What?"

"I think you said a name to put me on a possum trail." She tapped the fingers of her left hand on her knee. "This fictitious Charlie. He live in Gumbo? Or Hastings?"

Maranatha stood. "I have to go. Thanks for the tea."

Camilla stood and smiled. Her face looked catlike then, like she had a secret behind her smirk. "Tea for two and two for tea, I always say."

"See you at the wedding," Maranatha breezed, hoping that the Charlie subject would be happily buried, but knowing he'd be dragged out of her sooner or later. While she looked past Camilla, she could see a hint of knowing in her eyes, like Camilla already knew the truth but wanted to torture Maranatha until she spilled the beans.

"I wouldn't miss it. You know that. Wouldn't miss watching Old Miss Peach marching down the aisle to 'The Yellow Rose of Texas.' I hope she trips." She handed Maranatha a piece of paper folded like a collared shirt. "Here."

"What's this?"

"A sonnet, to commemorate Zane and Georgeanne's nuptials."

"I can hardly wait to read it."

"Good, because it's my best truth-poem yet. Billy Shakespeare, eat your Macbethian heart out."

Maranatha smiled. She'd somehow been able to outmaneuver Camilla, turning her from overt questioning to poetry giving. "If you don't mind, Miss Poet, I'd like to read it right now. Out loud."

"I don't do poetry readings." Camilla bit a fingernail clear off, examined it, and threw it on the floor.

"It's not a poetry reading—it's a listening. I'll read. You listen."

Camilla plopped on the couch and worked on another fingernail.

"Nice folding, by the way," Maranatha said.

"Thanks." She spit out another nail. "I have a new paper-folding book. I can fold all sorts of clothes out of paper now: dresses, underwear, pants. Rose said she wishes I'd get as much out of folding laundry."

"Why do you call her Rose and not Mama?"

"Because it's her name, that's why."

Maranatha unfolded the shirt. She read:

Georgeanne, she went and caught herself a
     man,
A quiet man who drives a big white car.
She chased him more, but all the while he ran.
A little slow, he didn't get too far.

She hooked him with her womanly good charm,
And hair-sprayed hair that grabbed him in
     embrace.
His heart, it did not come to any harm,
While hair surrounded him about his face.

That Zane, he likely stood right there,
     bewitched.
Medusa, she continued curling 'round,
Until their hearts were with a needle stitched,
And Zane compelled to give a ring profound.

They'll say their vows about a love so rare.
If truth be told, it's all about the hair.

Maranatha laughed. "A more tragic love poem there never was," she said, trying to refold the sonnet into a shirt.

"Here, let me do it." Camilla, smiling, grabbed the paper. In seconds, she transformed it from a romance poem to sensible clothing. "I guess they won't be reading this poem at the altar."

"No, I suppose not."

"I can't wait to see how her hair looks tomorrow," Camilla said.

Maranatha headed toward the door. "Might want to bring a few small coffins with you."

"What?" It wasn't often that Camilla looked puzzled.

Maranatha smiled. "For the exploding birds."

Twelve

WALKING DOWN THE STREET. THAT'S ALL. Not inviting anything. Anyone. Simply walking as the Burl heat melted the skip in her gait. But footsteps pounded hard behind her. Before Maranatha could turn to see where the pounding came from, a hand grabbed her mouth and jerked her neck to the left, stifling her breath. Another hand covered her nose. The hands were connected by arms that engulfed her. She was suffocating, she knew. She could struggle only so much until her breath was silenced forever, so she stopped and went limp in the strong arms. She could smell a workman's body. She wanted to scream. Wanted to will a scream, but couldn't. Clamped beneath dirty palms, she could say nothing. Do nothing. Behind her closed eyelids, she saw Jesus standing by, arms crossed, looking impatient and bothered. *Help me, Jesus.* But He couldn't seem to read her thoughts, or He merely chose to watch with a disinterested look as she fell to the pavement in a heap.

As her body thudded on the rough cement, her eyes opened to the stillness of her bedroom.

Another nightmare.

The nightmare had a way of weaseling into her mood all day long. She already wanted to run the other way on this

W-Day, the day Uncle Zane wedded the likes of Georgeanne Peach. Her hidden pleasure came when she remembered something Camilla said. "She'll be a rhyming bride. Georgeanne Winningham. Poetic, ain't it?"

Maranatha ran downstairs, expecting a bustle of activity. Instead, a note was taped to the fridge.

Maranatha, I dropped by this morning but you weren't awake, so I left without you. Be at church by 10:00 sharp. Please bring your dress, but don't wear it. There's work to be done.

Georgeanne signed it with a flourishing *G*, curlicues circling like praise around it. She looked at her watch. 9:54.

The church was seven blocks away, and, for whatever reason, Uncle Zane's Cadillac was gone. She ran upstairs, pulled on some work clothes, grabbed her hideous peach and mauve dress, and ran out the door. She jumped on the salmon-colored bike and pedaled, holding the handlebars in one hand and the dress made for fairies in the other. Above her, gray clouds thundered, and she wondered if she'd get caught in a storm. She pedaled harder as lightning highlighted the tree-lined street. The bike jostled her as it hit the buckled pavement. She almost let go of the dress to steady herself but regained control as more lightning split the sky above First Baptist. Almost there.

Without warning, Maranatha found herself hurtling headlong toward the First Baptist parking lot, her bike wheeling over her. She stopped herself hands first. Red grit embedded itself into her palms as one finger bent nearly backward. Her body followed after. She hit her shoulder, then rolled over and over until she was on her back, staring up at the happy purple of a crepe myrtle. Fat drops of rain dotted her face, rain she didn't wipe away. In a stunned stupor, she rolled back over to her knees and stood. The world spun off-kilter, like a home movie taken by an eager child — jerking, circling, focusing in and out. She placed her hands on her forehead and pushed hard on her two temples.

Ten feet in front of her was her dear bike, crumpled upon itself, the dress entangled in it.

"You okay?" a male voice came from behind her.

She turned to see Old Mack standing there, shaking his head.

"I don't know, Mr. Mackenzie."

"M'name's Old Mack, child. How many times do I have to holler it at you?" He smiled the scolding.

"I guess I fell." Raindrops splattered lazily between them.

"You guessed right. I saw you riding up the street on my way to church. Loved seeing you enjoy your bike, that is, until you flew head over foot." He walked toward the bike as the sky continued its spitting. "Here's your problem." He showed her the dress, caught in the derailleur system. "Got yer dress mixed in with the wrong crowd. Chains and dresses, last I checked, don't mix."

Dresses of that color didn't mix with her sensibilities either. She watched as Old Mack carefully untangled the dress from the oily chain. "I'm trying not to rip it, dear, but I don't know if I can."

"It's okay. It's not like I'm *in* the wedding. I'm only serving cake."

"I'm playing the organ."

"Really?"

"Yeah, Georgeanne asked me, and I said all right. Her being my cousin and all."

"You're Georgeanne's cousin?"

"Yep." He freed the dress. A ragged black scar divided the dress in half. "She's my Uncle Clarence's only child. A bit too spoiled for my taste, but hey, blood is blood."

The sky darkened and the rain came down in sheets. "Georgeanne's gonna be cross with the Almighty on this one. You can be sure she ordered sunshine on her day. Expect a sour mood." He was yelling above the rain now. "Best get you inside. I'll carry your bike." He handed her the soiled dress. They ran to the tall white doors of First Baptist, which were locked. A note was taped there to use the side entrance. "You stay here and I'll let you in." Old Mack disappeared through the rain, lifting the salmon bike.

"Just look at you. *Look* at you." Georgeanne *tsked* her head back and forth. "What'd you do? Choose today to mud wrestle? Get in the bathroom and clean up. I need your help. It's raining, you know."

Maranatha let rain drip from her hair. The bathroom mirror revealed a red dirt streak across her forehead, a soggy head, and muddied hands. She washed with Ivory soap and tried to rake her fingers through her tangled hair. What she really needed was a hair dryer, but that was back at the house, and the rain would make it all worthless anyway.

She walked into the sanctuary. It was five times larger than Mt. Moriah's and full of stained glass windows showing a white Jesus. It startled her to see Him so pale. She'd mostly known Him as near-ebony. How could He be two colors at once? The song "Ebony and Ivory" tickled the back of her memory. She knew that, in Burl at least, white folks and black folks were separate, living tandem lives, but not in harmony. She felt sad seeing this ivory Jesus with His plastic smile. She wanted to introduce Him to ebony Jesus. She was sure at least *they* would get along.

The carpet was a perfectly groomed dark burgundy. The room held an air of hush about it, like you had to tiptoe under the stained glass to be approved for membership. It gave Maranatha the creeps. She missed the liveliness of Mt. Moriah, missed the noise she heard the moment she entered the simple brown doors.

"All right," Georgeanne said from behind. "Bows. You need to do the bows." She handed Maranatha a large box. She wore soup-can-sized rollers in her whitish blonde hair. Above her lip was a bleach mustache.

"But I can't tie bows. I'm terrible at it."

"They're already tied. Don't you think I knew to take care of that? Now, alls you need to do is gently hook them over each pew with this florist's wire and then drape a ribbon to the next one. Like this." She hooked a mauve bow on the very last pew and draped a ribbon to the next one, where she hooked a peach bow. "It's simple, see?"

"Yes, I see."

Georgeanne left.

Maranatha looked down the aisle. To her it seemed as long as a city block. Slowly, painfully, she hooked ribbons, trying to make sure the in-between ribbons dipped at precisely the same places. She felt alone in the empty church. The only light shone through the white of stained glass Jesus' face, but that wasn't much considering the storm outside.

A single organ note blew its breath and sang a clear note. Maranatha looked up to see Old Mack with braided beard and mullet sitting at the organ in his OshKosh overalls. "I thought you might like some music to work by," he yelled. His voice echoed off the sterile walls like laughter.

"That would be great." Maranatha smiled. Camilla could write an epic poem about Old Mack, she knew.

From Old Mack's fingers came bits and pieces of geniuses. Bach for five minutes. Then a sample of Beethoven. Mozart showed up for a few. All the greats Maranatha listened to with headphones in her room. She'd found the albums at a thrift store a few years ago and fallen in love with all things classical. No one knew this, of course. The albums were hidden under her bed. But Old Mack seemed to know. Knew parts of her heart she couldn't share with a soul.

Music filled the sanctuary. Suddenly the white Jesus didn't seem so menacing. In the light of sixteenth notes dancing on the air, He seemed to be smiling down on her as she performed her Georgeanne chore. Old Mack played and played, his fingers racing each other on several keyboards, running over and under in a near tangle. At times the music moved through her, giving words to her sadness. Other times, a joy hidden in her heart wanted to arouse itself and crescendo with the music. Old Mack was playing the song of her life in minor and major keys. She wanted to laugh and cry all at the same time.

When she finished the last bow, Old Mack ended his sampling of the masters with a slam-bang Liberace ending.

When he met her at the aisle's end, all she could say was, "Thank you."

"No, thank you."

"I don't understand." She placed the remaining scraps of ribbon back in the box.

"I can't usually play that stuff. Not without the proper audience. I needed you. Thank you."

She didn't know what to say. Didn't know how to convince him of her own thankfulness. Just as Georgeanne had the ability to heap pain upon her, Old Mack piled blessings, gifts.

His old face smiled. "He gives and takes away, child."

She sat in the last pew. He sat next to her. "What do you mean?"

"You think I give to you, but I think you give to me. That's how life should be with friends. Lots of giving. But sometimes it's not that way with Jesus." He pointed to the smiling Jesus, where children scrambled upon His lap. "He knows us deeper than the ocean, knows that we need discipline now and again. So sometimes He takes. Sometimes He gives. But it's always in love. Remember that, okay?"

"I don't like it when He takes away," she said, barely above a whisper.

"Not many do. The way you'll know you're a-growing is if you learn to shake hands with the taking-away stuff, welcoming it as a way to be more like Jesus."

"That's hard."

"Don't I a-knows it, Maranatha Winningham. This is one of those pruning years for you. I can see it. Stuff's going to be cut out. But underneath, what Jesus leaves of you, is the best part. He cuts away the bad stuff so the good stuff can grow."

Georgeanne burst through the back doors. "*There* you are. I need you, Maranatha. Need you right now."

Maranatha stood. So did Old Mack.

"Hello, cousin," he said.

"Yes, thanks for coming so early. You have the song list?"

"Yeah, I do."

"Well, I don't hear it being practiced, now do I? Bunch of old-fashioned music for dead people is what I heard. You're not going to play that junk at the wedding, are you?"

"Of course not," he said. He turned and winked at Maranatha.

"And your hair. Something must be done. Slick it back and tuck your beard under your bow tie. It's embarrassing."

"Whatever you wish. When do you want me to start playing the prelude music?"

"At 2:30. Precisely."

"But the wedding isn't until 4:00."

Georgeanne huffed. "I know *that*. But you never can tell who'll be getting here early. I can't have guests sitting in silence. It ain't proper and you know it."

"Very well," he said, caressing his braided beard.

"So, 2:30 then?"

"Yes, you can be sure of it."

She turned toward Maranatha. "The reception hall is a mess. Ironically enough, it's a good thing you're a mess too — I need you to be cleaning."

Maranatha followed her through the back doors. She turned to see Old Mack smiling.

"He gives and He takes away," he mouthed.

When the doors closed behind her, she knew what he meant.

Thirteen

"I'LL BE CHANGING YOUR ROOM INTO a guest room," Georgeanne said as she handed Maranatha a mop and bucket. "I hope you don't mind."

Before she could say anything, Georgeanne added, "It has the best light. I'm painting it peach. You'll have to move down the hall to your mother's old room. I figured you'd like that."

Maranatha looked around to see if anyone else heard the woman's words. Not a soul to witness them. "Let's not be hasty, Georgeanne. Let me talk to Uncle Zane first." She remembered the first time she'd been in that room, before she knew it was Mama's. So long ago. Her nine-year-old hands had caressed the wardrobe in the stark, empty room, wondering what it held. When she opened it, beautiful dresses scented with rose beckoned her. Her Mama's scent.

Georgeanne planted her hands on her hips. "Already talked to him, child. He's fine with changing rooms." Her large curlers now hung loosely about her head. Maranatha wondered if she'd look like Medusa when all was said and done and the curlers were freed from the layers of Aqua Net. She was wearing a flowered skirt and a crisp white blouse, as if she were heading to a picnic at the club, but large rounds of sweat wet her underarms — a chink in the beauty armor if there ever was one.

There was no arguing with the woman, not today. Maranatha sighed. "What should I do about my dress? It's stained now."

"Finish mopping first and then run yourself back to the house and find another dress. Be sure it matches."

"But it's raining. And all I have is my bike."

Georgeanne rolled her eyes. "Go find your uncle then. He'll take you back. But mind you, don't let him see me. It's bad luck, you know." With that, she turned and clicked away in impossibly high heels.

When they ran to the car, Uncle Zane still had his everyday clothes on, still looked the same. Part of Maranatha wanted to grab him and say, *It's not too late! Stay home and let Georgeanne have her wedding without you*, but the sight of his fidgety hands kept her mouth shut. He turned on the radio to Denim's show, only to twirl the dial to oldies. Then he turned it off. But the silence seemed to fidget him more, so he turned it on again, this time to country music. Someone sang a song about leaving his heart in Texas. Maranatha wondered if Georgeanne was stealing Uncle Zane's heart, in a crash and dash way, not in a syrupy love way.

"Uncle Zane?" she asked.

"Yes," he said. The rain had slowed to a drizzle, but he didn't turn on the wipers. It drove Maranatha crazy seeing life all blurry like that.

"Do I really have to move rooms?"

"'Fraid so. Says she needs it for a guest room. Has the best light, she says." His hat, firmly pressed into his angular head, made him seem smaller. His voice sounded thin.

"But it's my room. It's been my room ever since I got there. Why can't she find a different room?"

"She's the woman of the house now. Best respect her."

She wanted to echo the advice Denim gave her last year when she was struggling with an unfair teacher who demanded her respect. "Respect is earned, not granted," he had said. Instead, she watched the rain slink down the window in tiny lines. A minute later, Uncle Zane parked in the rear of the house.

"I'll wait here," he said.

Maranatha ran upstairs to her room. *Her* room. A crush of sadness pressed in upon her. The walls seemed to be closing in on her, Star Wars fashion. In a few days her happy yellow walls would blush peach. Antique furniture would replace her twin bed. Smiling posters would frown as they were ripped from their home. And Maranatha would be displaced—to the room she seldom ventured, to the room where her mother's scent lingered.

For a year after knowing who her mother was, Maranatha had spent a little time each day pressing her nose into the folds of her mother's dresses, trying to picture her mother holding tea and chatting on patios. But after that year of drinking in the scent of the woman whose face had faded, she stopped outright. The pain associated with Mama's smell riveted her heart, poking hole upon hole in it in ways she couldn't talk about.

So she had kept that door shut. For years. Sometimes Zady would dust in there and accidentally leave the door ajar. Every time Maranatha would shut it and walk on by.

Maranatha remembered Uncle Zane in his hat, waiting in the car. She rummaged through her closet. None of her dresses would match. Panic rose within her. She touched the fabric of each dress, most of them being too small, and remembered again the touch of her mother's gowns. Without letting herself think, she left her room, moved down the hall, and opened her mother's room in one single motion, as if it were something she'd done for years.

She opened the wardrobe. The scent of her mother spilled out like huddles of rosebushes along a path. Every dress was lined up in perfect order, from white to black with every color in between. She pulled out a peach dress. Too dated. One lavender dress screamed the 1960s. She almost shut the door, until she remembered. White went with anything, right? She pulled out the white dress that kissed the left wall of the dark brown furniture. Sleek lines, simple neck, silken texture. Perfect. She threw everything off and gently pulled the dress over her head. It fit. Like a glove. She shut the door and stared at herself in its mirror, wondering if she had her mother's eyes, her mother's hair, her mother's hands. She noticed another red dirt streak across her face from the bicycle incident and decided to wash up.

Face clean, she pulled her hair back in two clips, pulled white nylons over her tanned legs, and shoved too-small pumps onto her feet, wicked stepsister style.

Maranatha squeaked open the back screen door. Every drop of water became a diamond in the sun-sparkled yard, reflecting the green of the trees, the blue of the sky. She picked her way around the mud and slid into the car. Not one to turn his head much, Uncle Zane defied himself and looked straight through her with probing blue eyes. "That dress," he said.

"My mama's," she said.

"I know." A look of pain creased his face, like he'd been slugged in the stomach. "I bought it for her."

He turned forward, adjusted his hat, and started the car.

"You loved her," she said, smoothing the dress skirt.

"I did. Still do."

"I know."

They sat staring forward as the car seemed to drive itself. Between them lived a Burl hillside of grief, a shared pain they'd never discussed, a love lost, never to be returned. She wanted to soothe the ache in his face, to touch his hand maybe, but she didn't want to risk having him retract. She'd never really lost a man, a lover. Only a mother she'd barely met—a mother who sang sweet songs to her, whose melodies wafted in and out of her soul like a wild, meandering rose.

They pulled into the parking lot. Maranatha expected Uncle Zane to kill the engine and walk away in one move. Like always. But the engine died and he sat. He held the steering wheel, staring off into a past neither of them could bear, perhaps watching the vitality of Maranatha's mother fade away to empty photographs. He released the wheel and rubbed hands on pants. With his right hand, he took off his hat and set it between them. He turned to her then. Blue eyes wet with tears. He reached over the hat and held her left hand for a moment. Squeezed it, then released. "I'm sorry," he said.

He opened the door, took up his hat, and left.

Fourteen

THE SANCTUARY LOOKED LOPSIDED, LIKE A seesaw with a round kid on one end and a skinny toddler on the other. Hundreds of guests murmured on Georgeanne's side of the church. A few of her people spilled over into the right back rows, according to the bride's directions yelled from an adjacent room to unsuspecting ushers. The right side held five full rows in front — indications of Uncle Zane's hermit life — bank folks from his old life before the stroke, a few merchants, and some family and friends. Maranatha saw pieces of her life assembled in those five rows. No one sat in the front row. Someone she couldn't make out — an old woman, she thought — sat in row two. Zady's family sat in row three. A few cousins and aunts-twice-removed chattered in row four, while the business people murmured in row five.

She'd spent the last two hours with Georgeanne's hair, a painstaking procedure. First, she carefully removed the woman's triple-hairpinned rollers. Then, the bride brushed out all the curls until her hair resembled combed wool ready to be twisted to yarn. "I put the curlers in first," she told Maranatha, whose face must've shown bewilderment, "to give it body. Then I brush it out so that I can recurl it. I should patent my procedure."

After brushing out the first curls, she emptied one tall can of super-grip hair spray on her hair. Then, she pulled one-inch strips of hair and curled them around a hair spray–stained curling iron. "I only use a beautician's curling iron," she told a peachy mauve bridesmaid. "The other ones aren't hot enough." She sprayed each curl while it was still circling the curling iron and then carefully removed it. Finally, she sprayed the curl again until it crisped. In an hour, she looked like a cross between Shirley Temple and Farrah Fawcett, neither of whom was anywhere close to being fashionable.

In between curling and spraying, she barked orders to a bridesmaid to tell Old Mack to please stop playing that old-fashioned music and play something fashionable like Engelbert Humperdinck for God's sake. She told the ushers where to place each guest. "Fay Rains can't be seated farther back than row seven. She'll be insulted. But don't put her near Ellen Brack. They hate each other." Eventually, she turned on the brides-maids, scolding each one for poor hair design or improper makeup. And in between it all, she chastised Maranatha.

"White? What's with white? Trying to compete with me, I see."

"It's the only one I could find. White matches everything—"

"I have a right mind to send you back again, but there's no time. Be sure you're only serving cake, child. I don't want you standing next to me in that *dress.*" The way she said *dress* sounded like a kid saying a swear word for the first time. Like she knew it was a dirty thing to say but loved to say it anyway, for the sheer thrill of being naughty.

An alert bridesmaid noticed an uncurled piece of George-anne's hair. A flurry of activity buzzed around the bride while Maranatha slipped away and watched the five rows of her life.

She didn't want to walk down the aisle, and she was sure it wasn't in Georgeanne's plan, but an usher grabbed her arm while Old Mack, beard tucked into tux, played a prelude. Georgeanne's friends and relations now took up most of the church, leaving only one pew between Uncle Zane's people and the rest of the guests. Though usually not self-conscious, she knew the eyes of every person were on her; she swore she heard whispering. Her white dress swished as she walked. She wondered if anyone recognized it as her mother's.

The usher walked her by pews four and three. Charlie's eyes stayed upon her, seeming to soak her in. She tried not to catch his gaze, but couldn't help herself. There was something about him, something that had happened in her heart toward him, that she couldn't explain. He'd been her friend for nearly a decade, someone to hang around with, shoot baskets with, talk about books with. In the past year, he'd become something more.

She sat down in front of Charlie, right next to the old woman she now recognized as cousin Mabel — a senile woman with a glass eye, a larger-than-dime-sized mole below that eye, and a whiskered chin. She was known to frighten trick-or-treaters by showing the eye with one hand (while her socket remained hollow and wrinkled) and offering a Hershey bar with the other. "Who's that next to me?" Her voice had the caliber of Mama Frankie's, albeit with a little more muffled Southern twang, like she was chewing a handful of peanuts.

"It's me, Maranatha," she whispered back.

"Speak up, Methuselah. I'm hard of hearing, don't you know." Her voice echoed above Old Mack's prelude.

Proper folks from the left side of the church turned toward row two in tandem. Maranatha sensed the attention. Heat crept up her neck and into her face. "Turn this way," she whispered louder.

When Mabel turned, her one good eye brightened. "Well, why didn't you come out and tell me who you were, Josephine? I would've given you a proper hug. How's that child of yours, anyway?"

Old Mack played louder now, like he understood Maranatha's embarrassment. Slowly, the volume rose over the old woman's voice. His transition between prelude and processional was a quick hiccup, no pauses.

"I'm not Josephine," Maranatha said. "I am her *daughter*." As she said it, a hatless Uncle Zane walked in through the baptistery door, followed by two of his cousins. Sweaty Preacher Byers emerged from another door, his too-tight suit squeezing still more droplets from him. On cue, four peach and mauve bridesmaids walked down the aisle and took their place. For a blessed moment, Mabel kept her good eye on the processional, entertained by the comings and standings of the flowery bridesmaids.

Maranatha checked her watch.

Camilla, bless her, slipped in next to Mabel, on her good side. Denim and Rose took the pew behind, next to Zady's family.

Mabel poked Maranatha. Hard. "You're the spitting image of Sephie, you are. How's yer mama?"

Old Mack stopped playing the processional right before "How's yer mama?" The entire church heard Mabel's question. "How's yer mama?" took on a life of its own, bouncing off the stained glass of pale Jesus, looping through mauve and peach ribbons, igniting a hush of murmurs behind Maranatha and to her left.

She wanted to die.

Camilla looked around the half-blind woman and winked, trying her best, it seemed, to lighten Maranatha's sudden death wish.

A warm hand embraced her shoulder from behind as Old Mack rescued the silence with the wedding march. She turned slightly. Zady's cleaning-worn brown hands lay atop her white sleeves. The church stood, thankfully, passing the moment. But Mabel kept poking Maranatha with her left index finger to the exact rhythm of the march. The march continued for minutes upon minutes while the crowd stared at the two closed doors.

Old Mack played the processional again, louder this time, but the door didn't move.

Camilla leaned forward and whispered around Aunt Mabel, "It's the hair, I'm telling you what."

Maranatha crammed a giggle back down her throat.

Zady bent close to Maranatha's ear. "She was always one for dramatic entrances."

Maranatha smiled, despite the constant poking from glass-eyed Mabel. She turned to see Uncle Zane. He looked smallish up there, particularly without his hat. Hardly the intimidating man she thought him to be when they first met years ago, when a hellish existence was exchanged for a protected, but lonely, one.

He fingered the button on his coat, but not in a way that anyone would notice. His were actions of varying degrees of slightness. But Maranatha knew. His robotic movements suddenly changed to erratic, twitchy ones. He looked nervous. Or maybe it was regret that put a tremor into his hands. With the wedding march pounding in her ears, Mabel poking her to the beat, and the haunting of Uncle Zane's "I'm sorry," she wished she could for once climb into that man's head and know what in the world he thought. Especially now as Old Mack played the wedding march a third time and the crowd started wagging heads.

"Whose wedding is this, anyway?" Mabel shouted. "And

where is that crazy bride?"

Maranatha laughed now. At least Mabel got one thing right.

At round four of the wedding march, the doors opened, ever so slowly, revealing Georgeanne Peach in a Princess Di puffed-sleeve dress. No one accompanied her. Her father had died the previous year. No one else would do, she had said. She carried a parasol in one hand, while peach and mauve roses dangled over the cradle of her free arm. It looked awkward to Maranatha, like she was trying to carry too many groceries. Her smile reminded Maranatha of Malibu Barbie, painted on and fixed in a sappy pink-lipped grin. Her unadorned hair — a veil would ruin her curls, she said — was pinned tight from her forehead to her ears until a mass of curls erupted from behind like a colander of too much spaghetti. But not one spaghetti strand moved. It didn't dare.

Georgeanne walked as though "Mother May I" told her she could take 458 baby steps. "Does she have arthritis or something?" Mabel had stopped her poking now and thankfully modulated her voice.

Camilla laughed, a hand clasped to her mouth.

Maranatha didn't answer back, hoping to educate Mabel on proper wedding etiquette by example. And for a time, she succeeded. Mabel kept quiet.

Thankfully, so did Camilla.

By the time Georgeanne reached the threshold, Old Mack had played the march two more times. Preacher Byers raised his hands and lowered them, leveling the congregation to their seats like a magician. From the back, Georgeanne looked like a princess. For a brief moment Maranatha imagined herself in a wedding dress one day. She wondered if Burl was a big enough town for a wedding like hers, where the couple who stood upon the top of the wedding cake would be black and white, ebony and ivory.

Maranatha's stomach ached. She couldn't wear white. Shouldn't wear white. Scorching anger seared through her. There were times she never thought of General, never thought of what he stole under Burl's tree limbs. But then there were times like now when she knew he had taken everything away. Even her wedding dress.

She looked down at her lap at the white silken gown that graced her knees. She half expected it to sprout hideous spots right there so that everyone would see how unclean she was. Even Charlie. Zady'd assured her that no one except Raymond really knew her secret (well, and Denim and Camilla and Uncle Zane). Anyone else was either incarcerated or dead or had moved on to another Texas town. But even that was little reassurance. She felt it. From the inside out. Like the stain on her heart would never be removed, like eventually the cancer within would spread to her skin so that everyone could see. Like Hester Prynne from American Lit class, she was marked. She knew it.

Preacher Byers wiped his head with a dullish white hankie while he took Uncle Zane and Georgeanne through the wedding ceremony.

While he spoke about dearly beloveds and holy matrimonies, Maranatha couldn't help but blame herself for the whole wedding. If she'd only been there that day Uncle Zane fell prostrate, he would've been okay, wouldn't have lost his resolve, would've sent Georgeanne packing. Logic swirled further in her mind. If Uncle Zane had been spared the stroke, there'd have been no need to hire a home-health aid, which would have meant no Georgeanne in the first place.

But here they were, a puffed-sleeve bride and her prey,

listening to the preacher, whose eyes clung to the black leather book in front of him. Everyone knew Preacher Byers wasn't carrying his King James Bible, but a small book called *Preach a Wedding Three Easy Ways*. It had been the petty joke of Burl that if you were to be married at First Baptist, the script was right there in that book. No surprises.

"Do you take this woman to be your lawfully wedded wife?" he monotoned from the book, never moving his eyes away from the script.

Uncle Zane whispered, "I do."

Georgeanne sniffed.

When Georgeanne said, "I do," she said it with such resolve that the congregation snickered. The Peach blushed. Then she whispered something to the preacher, whose eyes got wide while his sweat dripped heavier.

"It appears," he said with a nervous twitter in his voice, "that the bride wants to say her own vows."

Maranatha could see Uncle Zane tense. He probably was horrified being in front of so many people and had been ticking off each part of the ceremony in his head, anything to bring its end and get on with his predictable life in the big white house.

"I do," Georgeanne said again in a quavering voice. "Zane," she paused and held his hands, "I choose to caress you in the way you want to be caressed."

A collective gasp shot through the crowd.

Uncle Zane's eyes darted left to Maranatha. For a moment their eyes connected, and she could see humiliation there.

"Knowing the undulating journey we thus trod today, I choose to be your undying companion." She swiped at her cheek. "Until the world around us collapses or one of us breathes our last."

Mabel leaned over to Maranatha. She could smell the Juicy

Fruit gum the old woman smacked. "What's this lady doing? This ain't a show."

"And on this, our wedding day," Georgeanne continued, "I will ride off in the sunset as your saddle companion, ever mindful of snakes and coyotes and dead of night. Always watching your back and tending to your campfire."

"She doesn't make no sense," Mabel whispered. "Sounds like she crossed a girlie magazine with a Bible and a cowboy movie."

Maranatha stifled a giggle. Georgeanne had toyed with writing her own vows but said she didn't know where to begin. She'd traveled to Dallas to make photocopies of vows from various wedding books. What Mabel said actually rang true.

"Forever, my love. Forever. That is our love. It shouts enduring joy like the grains of sand on the sea, like the playfulness of a frolicking puppy, like the intricate web of the spider." Georgeanne's hands shook now, making Uncle Zane's shimmy with hers. There was a long silence as she stared into his eyes.

Preacher Byers cleared his throat. "You done, ma'am?" he asked.

Georgeanne nodded.

Uncle Zane's shoulders relaxed.

The preacher opened his black book, seeming relieved. "By the authority vested in me by the Lord Jesus Christ and by the honorable state of Texas, I now pronounce you man and wife. You may kiss the bride."

"I can't," Uncle Zane said. Plain as day.

"Why not?" the preacher and Georgeanne said in unison.

He pointed to his left ring finger. Empty.

Preacher Byers scolded himself with a shake of the head. He flipped backward through the black book and read through the ring portion of the ceremony. Though he'd already said it, he repeated, "By the authority vested in me by the Lord Jesus Christ and by the honorable state of Texas, I now pronounce you man and wife. You may kiss the bride."

Which a red-faced Uncle Zane did. Just a peck.

"I now present to you Mr. and Mrs. Zane Winningham!"

Old Mack responded with an organ symphony, and the happy couple walked in strange tandem down the aisle, Uncle Zane trying to hasten Georgeanne's pace. She won the battle, though. It took three recessionals to get them down the aisle.

Charlie offered Maranatha his arm, but at that moment, Mabel tugged at her other arm and pulled Maranatha to her. "Should've been you up there, Josephine. That Zane, he sure did love you. Loved you right down to your toes."

Maranatha turned to Charlie, trying to communicate with him to stay, but a curtain of hurt covered his eyes. He walked down the aisle without her.

Camilla stood behind Mabel. She was wearing the same dress she had worn to Mama Frankie's funeral — a happy, flowery gig. "Hey, Miss Mabel, I didn't get a chance to say how lovely you looked."

Mabel grunted, then sat down, rummaging through her ample purse. Maranatha wondered if she had several different glass eyes rolling around in there, perhaps a different color for every occasion.

Camilla inched around Mabel and sat next to Maranatha.

Maranatha bent closer to Camilla. "Nice dress."

"Thanks. I'm of the mind that if one has a new dress, one must wear it to any and every occasion. And of course, this counts as an occasion, don't you think?"

"Certainly. Thanks for coming."

"No problem. I wouldn't miss the marriage of Georgia Peach to Mr. Quiet. It *was* quite a show, wasn't it? You see your uncle's face when she spouted off those vows? By the looks of him, I'd say this was a dreading wedding for him."

Maranatha smiled. "It *was* unusual."

"No doubt the reception'll be the same. I'm only sorry I'll be missing it."

"Why?"

"You know how Rose is. Besides, I'm not the wedding reception type. All that ceremonial stuff. Garters. Cake. Toasts. Not my glass of tea."

"When do you leave for college? I forgot."

Mabel dumped the entire contents of her purse on the pew. Something rolled off and bounced on the floor. Maranatha shuddered.

"Two weeks. Right after Burl's schools start. Don't worry; I'll have a party. Maybe then you could invite this Charlie and the Chocolate Factory character, who, by the way, I know is real."

She should've known Camilla would see right through her, would know that Charlie was real. She wondered if Camilla had noticed her pained exchange with Charlie. Her stomach lurched. Part of her ached from knowing Camilla would needle her to death until she spewed out every secret. But a bigger part was sad Camilla was leaving again. Their friendship had survived the last several years, but every nine months away made for more challenges, less shared stories, more unknowns. Before she could respond to Camilla's revelation, Mabel poked her. Hard.

"Lost my other eye," she said. "Could you help me find it?"

"That's my cue to be on my way," Camilla laughed. "I'll call you."

Maranatha bent low to the pew and saw the errant greenish eye three feet away, staring at her. She'd hoped she'd see its backside; seeing it like that gave her the willies. She stood, walked around the pew, grabbed a silk rose from the pew's end, and scooped the eye up with the petals, never touching it.

"Many thanks, Josephine. You always were such a dear. So kind. Too bad you were bent on breaking that man's heart."

"But—"

"I blame you, that's what," Mabel said, wagging her finger in Maranatha's face. "Zane never was the same after you left him, after you took his heart."

Maranatha wanted to explain it all but thought the better of it. She decided to heed Zady's advice about Mama Frankie—to keep the conversation to weather, clothes, and grits. "Nice day it turned out to be," she said.

"Purt'n near 105, I reckon," she said.

"I like your dress," Maranatha said.

"Value Villa. $7.75. A bargain, I always say."

"Someday you'll have to give me your grits recipe. I hear it's legendary."

"Yep, it is. Won me a prize at the fair one year. Got a blue ribbon and five dollars to boot. Don't tell anyone, but I bought me some chewing tobacco with it."

"I won't. I'll see you at the reception."

"Not likely," she said. "Gotta go tend to my hogs. They git hungry this time of day, 'specially in the heat. Good-bye, Josephine."

"Good-bye."

Maranatha tried to imagine a Josephine-shaped love coming from the likes of silent Uncle Zane. He must've been the kind of guy who only loved once, whose passion spilled over a weakened dam, never to be rebuilt.

As her dress swished down the aisle, she knew she'd never spill out like that. Knowing how it haunted Uncle Zane, she wouldn't dare take the risk.

Fifteen

"I'M WRITING MY OBITUARY." OLD MACK sipped sweet tea in the corner of the reception hall while Maranatha nursed a small plastic cup of Hawaiian Punch.

"Really? Why?"

"It helps me rethink my life."

"Are you sick?" She scanned the crowd for Zady's family but couldn't see them anywhere. She knew they'd be easy to spot, being the only black family there. Perhaps they felt the heaviness of that and left.

"Well, I know I'm going to die, if that's what you mean." He pulled his beard out of his tux. He handed her his tea. "Can you hold this a second?" Unbraiding his silver beard, he hummed Handel. "This too?" He handed her a small rubber band. With the deftness of a French-braiding champion, he plaited his whiskers in no time, taking back the rubber band and then the tea, all the while humming.

"I'm sorry to hear that," she said. "What have the doctors said?"

"Not a thing, Maranatha Winningham. I don't believe in docs."

"So how do you know you're dying?"

"We all are dying. All are one day closer to the pearly gates."

Maranatha nodded as though she understood what he meant. She seldom thought about death, at least not during daylight hours. Only when she sat in bed at night, fighting to sleep, did death haunt her. With both parents dead, night often threatened to strangle her. It whispered words like *You'll be next* and *You'll die young, just like they did.* On the nights death worried her, she'd have nightmares — of faceless men grabbing her, of running away from killers, of specters hiding in closets or under beds, of hoarse whispers of *help* never heard.

"You ever thought of writing your obituary?"

"You mean what goes on my gravestone?"

"No, what the newspaper says about you."

She scolded herself for forgetting something so elementary. "I knew that. I must've left my brain somewhere."

"Don't be so hard on yourself. We all leave our brains from time to time. But seriously, someday you ought to try to write your obituary. It'll change your life. Give you some perspective. Sometimes life gets so thick and dark that the only way you can crawl out of the hole is to think about how you want to influence the here and now. And besides, thinking about heaven will change everything — well, maybe not your circumstances, but certainly your perspective. It's worth a try."

They walked together to the food line, grabbed clear plastic plates and peach napkins, and piled their plates with pigs in a blanket, sausage rolls, bacon-wrapped dove breasts, and jalapeño poppers. "This here's good eating, don't you think?" He motioned for them to sit in a small grouping of chairs. Old Mack flung his braided beard over his shoulder and attacked the food on his plate. Maranatha picked at hers, still scanning the crowd for Charlie.

"Your bike's in the storage room to the right of the entrance," he said between pigs in a blanket. "I gave it a look-see. It's fine. Needs a bit of a cleaning up, maybe some touch-up paint, but it's good to go."

She thanked him for his kindness and ate in silence, nibbling here and there but tasting nothing.

When the time came for cake serving, Maranatha stood dutifully behind the four-tiered production with gallons of Crisco-based frosting swirled in every nook and cranny. The plastic couple atop the cake looked young, a nuptial Barbie and Ken. The pang in Maranatha's heart groaned. Would she ever have her own multitiered wedding cake?

Carla, First Baptist's catering coordinator, approached. "You ever cut a cake?"

"No, ma'am."

"I'll be right here t'help you." Carla stood probably five feet tall and was as skinny as a stray dog in winter. She'd pulled her brown hair striped with gray into a haphazard twist and secured it with a clip.

"Thanks."

Carla held a cup of red punch in one hand, a long, sharp knife in the other. "First, we take off the top layer and give it to the couple. That's the one they use for the official cake-cutting ceremony. Then we take off the rest of the layers and cut around in circles until we've fed everyone."

They set the little cake in front of Uncle Zane and Georgeanne on a small card table. Georgeanne tapped a nearby microphone over and over until people stopped milling and looked up. "It's time for the cake-cuttin' ceremony. Gather 'round, everyone." With the skill of a surgeon, Georgeanne cut two pieces of perfectly square cake, a strange feat since the cake was round, and placed them on clear dessert plates. She handed one to Uncle Zane, who searched the crowd, eventually finding Maranatha. His eyes seemed to ask, *What in the world do I do now?*

Georgeanne picked up her piece of cake with her French-manicured fingers and held it to Uncle Zane's closed mouth. Maranatha mouthed, *Pick up the other piece.* In silence, he obeyed.

"One. Two. Three," Georgeanne said, cramming the piece into Uncle Zane's face, his mouth closed.

Do the same thing, Maranatha mouthed.

But he didn't. He set his cake down, grabbed a peach napkin, and wiped his expressionless face.

Georgeanne laughed a nervous giggle and snatched the microphone. "I always knew I'd marry a proper Southern gentleman," she quipped. "We want to thank y'all for coming to our wedding. Being temperance folks, there won't be a toast, but we'd sure love for you to stay and eat some more, mingle a bit, and greet us." Her voice trailed off. Others filled the uncomfortable air with conversation.

From her vantage point, Maranatha watched Georgeanne scold Uncle Zane, could see the top of his head bent forward as if he were a four-year-old caught with his hands in the cookie jar. Only she was scolding him for not putting his hands in there, for not playing the wedding game properly. Maranatha wanted to give Uncle Zane his backbone back, the will he had before the stroke, but he slumped forward all the same — a sign that her life at home would never be as it was. Once ruled by Uncle Zane's silence, it would now be governed by a peach-loving woman with an unstoppable mouth.

As she served cake alongside Carla, Zady and Raymond approached.

"I need to attend to the kitchen," Carla said, and then left.

"Where've you been?" Maranatha handed them each a large slice of cake.

"Milling about the church," Raymond said, "waiting till everyone else was served."

The way he said it slapped Maranatha. Though she knew she'd had nothing to do with making Zady's family uncomfortable, she knew the guilt of it, like she had to bear it simply because she was white. But she was glad they stood near her now and they could have a chance to talk.

"You'll be coming around the house, right?" Maranatha glanced at Zady's hands, the hands that had cleaned and loved her home for so many years. She loved those hands, so much so that *I love your hands* almost burst from her mouth.

"On Monday, to gather my cleaning supplies. Raymond'll come with me to load up the Aspen."

"Just like that?" Maranatha hadn't intended to allow her emotion to escape, but a deep cry caught against her tonsils.

"Just like that, Natha. I'm so sorry. Wish I could change things for you."

Raymond put his arm around Zady.

The three stood silent, a cake table between them. How could Zady apologize when *she* was losing her job? How could she care more for Maranatha than her own family's survival?

Standing there, cake server in hand, Maranatha decided she wanted to be like Zady when she grew up — a woman full of character, strength, and undying beauty that only enhanced with age, perseverance, and grace. She asked Jesus to please make her more like Zady. She added a PS: *And though I'm unworthy, please show me that You love me — in a way I can see. I need to know.*

"I'm going to miss you," Maranatha said, her voice choked.

Zady reached across the white table and grasped both of

Maranatha's hands. "Me too, beautiful girl."

"I'm worried about you."

"Don't you be worried, Natha. The Lord sees us; He does. He'll take care."

I hope you're right. She couldn't bear to picture Zady and Raymond's family hungry.

Carla returned from the kitchen and set her pale hands on her skinny hips. She leveled a look at the two grasped hands, as if they were involved in criminal activity. Maranatha let go first, scolding herself for letting the likes of Carla, a stranger, ruin a moment between friends.

"Best be going, Natha. We'll see you Monday," Raymond said.

She wanted to ask where Charlie was, wanted to see if Zady'd found a job, wanted to know how they were feeling, but she didn't. She let Carla's heavy glare rule her silence.

"Time to clean up this mess," Carla said in a thin voice.

Maranatha wanted to protest, wanted to get on her bike and leave, but where would she go? Home would never be the same. The longer she stayed to clean up, the longer it'd be until she had to go back there. Caught between a home she once knew like the back of her hand and the home she'd now have, she stood behind the demolished cake, knowing it conveyed home perfectly. Tumbled down. Consumed. Picked through.

She shadowed Carla the caterer, picking up napkins, discarded plates, plasticware underfoot. Carla did very little other than pick up one thing while whispering more tasks through Hawaiian Punch–stained teeth. Maranatha had to stay close to hear the next command. Peppered between the commands were sermonettes, words Maranatha grew increasingly tired of.

"Don't mind 'em," she said. "Don't mind 'em at all."

"Who?"

"Those folks you were talking to."

"Oh, you mean *black people*?"

"I'm all for equal rights," Carla said, wiping her hand along a banquet table. "As long as it doesn't mean togetherness, if you know what I'm saying." She pointed to a piece of cake on the floor.

"Not really." Maranatha picked it up and deposited it in the trash.

"The way I sees it, it's like that newfangled recycling stuff the Northerners are trying to make us do." She pointed to a pig in a blanket sitting lonely on a plate, but before Maranatha could grab the plate, she snatched the pig and put it in her mouth in one fluid motion.

That pig didn't see her coming. "I'm not sure I follow you."

Carla stopped at the punch table. She lifted the crystal punch bowl, poured some into her plastic cup, and drank it empty. Then she refilled it halfway, holding the cup in her right hand while her left hand pointed at trash. "They have those separate bins. One for paper. One for glass. One for plastic. Burl's like that. We have our separate bins. One for white folks. One for blacks. One for Mexicans. No need to mix 'em together. We're all happy in our little bins, fulfilling our purposes."

"Separate but equal," Maranatha said, remembering *Animal Farm's* haunting words, how pigs swiftly became more equal than the rest of the farmyard.

"Exactly! Everyone can get a job. Everyone can go to church. Everyone has their own circles." She turned toward Maranatha and motioned with her free hand. "All equal. But separated." Carla stepped backward, but her loafer heel slipped on a small puddle. As she tried to catch herself, Maranatha instinctively reached for Carla as Hawaiian Punch flew from her cup and splattered Maranatha's dress. Carla fell with a thud, then scrambled to her feet. "What do you think you're doing?" she asked, as if Maranatha had caused the whole mess.

But Maranatha said nothing as the red soaked through the white dress clear to her skin. Red saturated her mother's dress, like she'd been shot and the blood was spreading outward from a wound. Forever stained.

Carla spilled more words, but Maranatha walked away. She retrieved her bike from the storage closet, walked it behind the church under the canopy of a ripening pecan tree, and lifted her leg over the center bar, not caring if she looked ladylike or not.

"What's wrong?" Charlie emerged from behind the tree's trunk and stood next to her.

"Where've you been?" She didn't care if she sounded angry or mean or accusatory. She wanted to get home.

"Out here. Waiting for you under this tree."

"How nice."

"What happened to your dress?"

"Life."

"What?"

"Life happened to it, Charlie. It's what happens when you pray about something. God answers by throwing life at you."

"Natha, what's wrong?" He stepped closer, held her handlebars.

"This is, I mean *was*, my mama's dress." She let the words hang out there. The rain that had pelted the day had long since dried up, leaving the air hot and humid. The air between them muffled words that might've been spoken while the pecan tree's limbs swayed back and forth like a lazy hammock.

Charlie kicked a black, shiny shoe at the dirt.

Maranatha looked at her dress.

He placed a hand on her arm.

A tear raced down her cheek, followed by another. And another.

"I'm sorry," he said. And she knew he meant it.

They stood there, she on her bike, he at the handlebar, for what seemed a holy moment. Lazy mosquitoes circled between them. The breeze picked up, blowing her hair gently across her face, shaking the tree's leaves. She looked into his eyes, his deep, brown eyes, and stayed there, thankful for his touch, thankful for his understanding.

He moved a little closer.

She stayed where she was while her heart leapt to her neck.

Still closer.

She could smell his Tic Tac breath.

"Natha, I—"

A loud honk interrupted Charlie's sentence. He pulled away, tried to act casual, as Uncle Zane's car drove by on the street beyond the tree. Cans clanked behind. Shaving cream marred the prized car with "Just Married." Maranatha couldn't imagine Uncle Zane ever honking. As the car rounded the corner, she squinted and saw the reason for the honking: Georgeanne was driving.

And she wore a face of rage.

"Best be going," Maranatha said.

"Yeah." Charlie took a right and walked toward his home.

She took a left and rode in the direction of the big white house, wondering what life would await her there, thanking God that a Padre Island honeymoon would keep Georgeanne away for a good five days.

Maranatha mounted her bike, pulling the skirt up with one hand and steadying the bike with the other. She tried to pedal without looking down, for fear if she saw the red splatter, she'd cry some more. She remembered Charlie's sincere face and wondered what it would have been like to kiss him. Part of her wanted to throttle Georgeanne for interrupting, but another part silently thanked her. A kiss was a frightening thing, to be sure.

Safely home, she parked her bike near the back porch and entered the kitchen. She ran upstairs to her room and shut the door. She stripped off her mother's dress, revealing a stained pink stomach. She kicked off her shoes, pulled off her nylons not caring if they ran, and put on a pair of shorts and an old T-shirt.

The dress rested in a heap in the center of her floor.

She sat on her bed and grabbed her journal from under her pillow. Pen in hand, she wrote:

Maranatha Winningham, formerly Mara Weatherall, died from a broken heart. No one of circumstance survives her, her mother dying before Maranatha understood her smile. Nanny Lynn, the woman who really loved her, died when Maranatha needed her most. Aunt Elma, who wasn't really her aunt, died. Her father died too, rightfully so. Her best friend survives her, but she's almost always living up north now. Her housekeeper survives her but is too busy trying to make ends meet to notice. A boy named Charlie weeps somewhere, but no one hears his cries. Her uncle survives her, but he was abducted by an alien named Georgeanne shortly after Maranatha neglected him and he had a stroke. There's nothing really of note that Maranatha Winningham did in her life, other than survive one day to the next. She fixed an old house. She sang a few songs at Mt. Moriah Church. She got good grades in English. Other than that, not much.

She placed her pen beside the notebook, found a box in her closet, and started packing. This room was no longer hers. It belonged to Georgeanne now.

$\mathcal{S}$ ixteen

SCHOOL STOLE SUMMER FROM MARANATHA, EVEN whisking Camilla away, before she could have that promised party, to more adventures of what she called "liberation theology," where a gun-toting Jesus liberated the poor, particularly those in South America. Two weeks after the wedding, Maranatha found herself surrounded by friends named Calculus, American Lit, and Chemistry. She'd spent one blessed week alone, making her mama's old room a haven. At first she decided the wardrobe with Mama's things had to go, but the more she lived in the room (coupled with the fact that there was no one to help her move it), the more she wanted the piece to stay. To anchor the room. To anchor her heart.

So it sat along a blank wall, although the other three wore posters and prints. She couldn't adorn the wardrobe wall. Like a sacred object or a rare piece of art, it needed to stand alone. Apart. Every once in a while, she stole a whiff of her mother's lingering scent and pulled the dresses from their dry-cleaning bags, holding them to herself and wondering, *What did Mama look like in this one? In the blue one?* But the still-stained white dress always made her close the wardrobe's doors.

But homework needed her. Or maybe she needed

homework. It'd become her escape route from all things Georgeanne. She never had a moment's peace with that woman around, snooping through her things while she labored at school, barging in on her when she dressed in the morning, sighing and making exasperated noises while she snacked in the kitchen. Maranatha picked up a pencil, sat on her bed, and cracked open Calculus, thanking the good Lord for numbers that made sense, for black-and-white answers to complicated problems. If only life were that easy.

Downstairs, Georgeanne screamed.

Maranatha winced. *What tragedy is it now, Mrs. Drama Queen?*

Heeled shoes clipped up the stairs in a flurried rush.

Surrounded by logarithms, Maranatha looked up when Georgeanne burst through as though she were in crisis — a habit so common Maranatha wanted to call her "The Woman Who Cried Wolf."

"You're always in here," Georgeanne snapped.

Maranatha reread the equation before her. "I have homework."

"Don't know why you have to do that while there is mayhem all around."

Maranatha sat on the edge of her bed, caressing her Calculus book — something she envisioned her teacher Mr. Morrison would do, he was so in love with it. "Mayhem?"

Tea Rose perfume met Maranatha before Georgeanne sat next to her. She sat close, only the Calculus book between them. "Yes, mayhem. Turns out we have mice. An entire family of them skittering around the kitchen. While I was cooking. Scared the bejeebers out of me."

"I can only imagine." And she could. The mere imagination of it sent laughter through her thoughts. Mice and

Georgeanne—a comical combination, to be sure. The poor mice were probably crying, longing to make a nice, crispy nest in Georgeanne's perfectly spun hair.

"I want you to exterminate them. Now." She drew her hand through her hair, but her hand got stuck at the crown. Too much hair spray.

"And how should I do that?" Maranatha thumbed through the next pages of Calculus, hoping Georgeanne would get the hint.

"How should I know? Do what you did the last time."

"There *was* no last time," Maranatha said. "We've never had mice—until *you* moved in."

"Very funny. With this old creaky house, I know you're lying." Georgeanne stood, hands on hips. "I want those wicked creatures gone. In ten minutes. Or sooner."

"I could call Charlie. He's off work today."

"Zady's son? Yeah, I suppose he's killed his share of vermin, what with where he lives and all. You can call him, but no fraternizing, you understand? It doesn't look right you being near him—with your pale skin and his black face. It ain't right. Makes it wrong to be near."

Maranatha stood. She measured her words in her head before she unleashed them. "Georgeanne, do you mind if I ask you a question?"

"I guess not." She walked across the floor, her heels creating divots in the pine floor between them, and stood in the doorway.

"Why do you care?"

"Because I'm a good Christian lady, that's why. I care about what folks say about you, Maranatha. Care about your reputation, your standing in Burl. I care about your Uncle Zane. I care about whispers made about you and that colored boy—"

"His name is Charlie," she said, heat rising in her voice, "and he is much more than a mouse exterminator."

"Yes. Oh, yes. I forgot. He's a warehouse worker too. With your pretty face, I would have thought you'd be destined for someone greater."

Later she would think of all sorts of witty comebacks — things like *Yeah, well, I was hoping Uncle Zane would've been destined for someone greater too* or *How can you fit so many words into such a narrow mind?* or a Camilla-ism: *Ugly is as ugly does.* But none of these words sprouted from her lips. For a brief second, the two of them remained in their places in suspended animation, Georgeanne framed like a tacky Marilyn Monroe poster in the doorjamb and Maranatha standing next to her bed, Georgeanne's heavy perfume suffocating her. The silence bore into Maranatha's stomach like an ulcer, but she couldn't speak.

Georgeanne shifted her weight. "You gonna call him or not?"

A simple question, she thought. *At least I can answer that.* "Depends on how much you'll pay him."

"Pay him? Why'd I do that?"

"Because you would have to pay an exterminator anyway."

"Tell him I'll give him twenty bucks if he can rid the house of the mice." She left the room, her scent loitering, her words poking about in Maranatha's mind. She didn't care much for Georgeanne's opinions, but a little thought bothered her. What if Charlie wasn't good enough? Could she really see herself tethered to a laborer while she scrubbed toilets in Shady Grove nursing home? Would Charlie be enough? For her mind? For her hope to someday leave Burl's Loop, to venture beyond its stifling heat?

The scurrying continued, like the mice had somehow cut a NASCAR track behind the cabinets and were competing to see who could get to the fridge first. Back and forth they scampered while Charlie waited with the patience of a cat on the prowl.

"I would've done it for free." He sat cross-legged in front of the sink, the doors opened, his face resolute.

"I wanted Georgeanne to pay you. You need the money, right?"

He looked at her then, taking his eyes off the cabinet for a moment. "What's that supposed to mean?"

She bent her legs under herself and sat next to him, hoping to smooth his ruffled ego feathers. "Nothing. It's just, with your mama out of work, I figured you could use the money. For groceries."

"We are all eatin' fine, Natha. Thanks for your concern." He looked back at the cabinet. "Fine."

"I didn't mean any harm. None at all. Charlie?"

He turned to her again when a mouse raced past. "Ah, I missed him."

"Charlie?"

He grabbed a plastic Kroger bag and climbed into the cabinet, the plumbing above his head.

"Don't hit your head. Be careful."

"You fixin' to be my mama? Now quiet!"

Maranatha stood. She wasn't used to Charlie's anger, hadn't seen this side of being a man — of pride wounded, of honor and shame helplessly intermingled. She went to the fridge, opened the door with barely a noise, and pulled out a jug of sweet tea, Zady style; only her tea never tasted quite the same. She'd watched Zady brew it hundreds of times. Bring three cups of water to a boil. Add eight bags of Luzianne and a half-cup of white sugar, and boil to death. Drain teabags, squeezing them as tight as possible to suck all the caffeine and juice from within. Pour hot mixture into a half-gallon milk container. Fill with cold tap water and chill. She'd followed the steps exactly, but the tea hinted bitter. She missed Zady.

She grabbed two crystal Georgeanne glasses from the cabinet in stealthy quiet and set them on the kitchen table. She poured tea, being careful not to touch plastic to glass, and sat down.

The scurrying stopped, as though the mice knew their captor was lurking nearby. For several minutes Charlie stayed wedged into the sink's underbelly while Maranatha gulped tea. Waiting.

Little feet made noises to Charlie's left. They scurried — right into Charlie's open-mouthed Kroger bag. In one motion, he closed the bag around them and pulled his body from beneath the sink, holding the twitching bag.

"What are you going to do with them?" she asked.

"Set them free."

"Georgeanne wanted them exterminated."

"I'm not a killer, you know that."

"You're not a vegetarian, are you?" For a second, a happy Camilla chomping on raw soybeans flashed in Maranatha's mind.

"Not on your life, Natha, but I can't see the point in killing the mice. They're dislocated."

The bag squeaked, sending nausea through her. "You mean *displaced.*"

He stepped away from her. "Why're you correcting my words? Am I not good enough for you? Or are you too good for me? Is that it?"

"Of course not. I didn't mean — "

"I'll see you later. Tell Georgeanne she can keep her twenty." Charlie stopped in the doorway and turned. "Remember one thing."

"What's that?" She stood, offering a sweating glass of tea to Charlie's mouseless hand.

"That I am a very patient man, but there comes a time when you have to trap and run. Just you remember that." He left out the back door, mice in one hand, nothing in the other, as she offered the glass of tea to an empty space.

Later that evening in the quiet of her room, Charlie's words bounced through her head like a Ping-Pong match.

I am a very patient man.

She knew he was patient. How many times had he begged a kiss from her with his eyes and she'd darted her gaze away? How many times did she determine to brush lips against his but then retreat in utter terror? All that unfulfilled yearning stirred within her — like a tug-of-war between conflicting needs. She'd wanted a father, someone to stroke her hair and tell her everything was going to be fine, probably ever since she learned most families had fathers. In Charlie, she longed for that — for the comfort, for the protection, for the companionship, for the admiration. But that comfort, in the form of a teenage boy, had sexual strings attached, and that terrified her. Would one kiss be enough? Or would Charlie be hungry? Would he want Maranatha's soul? Would he rip it away as General had?

The word *man* worried her. Why did Charlie think of himself as a man? She'd called him Charlie Boy for as long as she could remember — until last year when he'd scolded her for calling him that; now only his mama could string *Charlie* and *boy* together. It never occurred to Maranatha that in all their Boardwalk-conquering Monopoly games, their lazy spring afternoons fishing at the lake, their races down Live Oak Street, the boy he had been would so soon become a man.

And if he called himself *man*, it meant that she'd have to call herself *woman*. She wasn't ready for the title yet. She'd yet to live a real childhood, yet to dance and play at make-believe. Though her outsides were young, she felt older than the East Texas hills. The sad fact was she simply didn't know how to play and enjoy each of life's moments.

She'd loved it when Bishop Renny spoke of Jesus, how He was the sort who put grown-ups off so He could welcome clamoring children on His lap. How she longed to shed her old self and run unencumbered to the Savior's lap — to feel His caress against her cheek, to hear that everything was going to be fine, to know His utter delight in her. But in her mind, she was one of the disciples, grumbling, standing aside, while the children chatted and laughed and were blessed. *Someday I want to sit on Your lap, Jesus.* Her eyes fell on her mama's once-ripped picture and wondered if Mama ever sat on Jesus' lap. Though Mama's eyes looked mischievous, they held that same sense of age that Maranatha knew. She wondered if it was a silly notion, this lap-sitting thing. Wondered if Jesus answered prayers like that. He certainly hadn't answered her *Show me You love me* prayer.

Somehow it was all intertwined — the terrible in-between of becoming a woman yet not ever really having been a child. Somehow Jesus' loving her had to do with recapturing bits and pieces of stolen childhood. She picked up her Bible and opened it blindly, hoping her eyes would fall upon life-giving words. Instead, her finger pointed to Leviticus 15:19: "When a woman has a discharge, if her discharge in her body is blood, she shall continue in her menstrual impurity for seven days; and whoever touches her shall be unclean until evening."

She laughed at the irony. Becoming a woman was inevitable. Like the cycle of menstruation, it would happen whether she welcomed the title of *woman* or not. Still, she didn't like Charlie's calling himself a man. Didn't like it one bit.

She undressed, slipped on an old T-shirt, and returned to her bed. She sat upright, the covers dusting her feet, and thought about Charlie and the mice.

There comes a time when you have to trap and run, he had said. She worried she'd pushed him away for too long. It ached her heart every time, something she couldn't help. Every wounded look he'd give thrust her stomach into turmoil. The last thing she wanted was to spoil her best friend's joy.

It was one year ago, under the wide canopy of trees flanking Mt. Moriah Church, where Maranatha noticed her loyalties change. Camilla'd been her best friend for forever and a year, but she'd gone away to college again and nothing filled the void, not even Zady's kindness. She'd sat across from Charlie then, eating watermelon and fried green tomatoes and drinking Diet Coke during a back-to-school church picnic. The tables — sawhorses with old plywood placed on top — were covered with red-checked oilcloth. Bees hummed in the background near the four hives Bishop Renny tended. There was nothing spectacular about the moment, no happy "We Are Family" songs blaring from the church's PA system. Mama Frankie sat next to Charlie, stealing his watermelon seeds, putting them in her mouth, and spitting them as far as the pecan tree.

That was it. But something happened there. Charlie said, "You want to go for a walk, Natha, while summer's still here?"

"Sure," she said.

They walked around the corner, down an old county road to a small lake. A rickety dock stuck out in the water like a tongue. Without talking, they walked to the end of the dock, took off flip-flops, and dunked their feet in the lukewarm water. She couldn't remember what they talked about, but she remembered how close he seemed, how his knee sometimes brushed hers. She remembered his smile.

"I think you're my best friend," she told him then.

"I know you're mine," he said.

And that was that.

She turned off the light next to her and let the bed hold her. The dock memory dawdled through her tired mind, mingling with dreams of what life should be. Her mama alive, happy, married to a kind-faced, healthy Uncle Zane. The big white house fixed up to its finery, the envy of every Burl citizen. Zady and Raymond visiting on Saturdays, bringing picnics, accompanied by Old Mack and a meat-eating Camilla. Raymond as a sought-after carpenter. And Charlie holding her hand. And she letting him. No one turning a nose in the air at the mixing of black and white. A beautiful dream . . .

The door opened.

Uncle Zane stood awkwardly. Georgeanne's head peeped around him.

"We're moving," she said. "T'the other side of town. I've convinced Zane to put the house up for sale, Maranatha. I thought you might want to know."

He shrunk away.

Georgeanne shut the door.

To her room.

To her home.

To her life.

She swore she could hear Georgeanne laughing down the hall.

Seventeen

MARANATHA WROTE SCADS OF LETTERS TO Camilla, the last one about the great mouse caper, being careful to mention Charlie as that brother-like friend who helped rid Georgeanne of vermin. She told Camilla about Georgeanne's propensity for stealing her house, for weaseling her will against a man who now seemed to say yes to everything.

School drudged. Life drudged without Camilla. Camilla had written scattered letters here and there about greenhouse gases and Sandinistas. Without her, there was really no one to talk to, other than Charlie, who was now working a shift and a half a day, endearing himself to Jimbo, his overweight manager, who chewed Big Red gum as much as he spit Big Red tobacco. As she walked the halls of Craigmont High School, she felt isolated, as if the kids parted around her like they were the Red Sea and she, Moses' staff.

The For Sale sign had dotted the yard a week now. She half thought of stealing it, stowing it in a dumpster behind Old Mack's store, but the inevitability of another, no doubt bigger, sign stopped her thieving hands. When she arrived home on her salmon bike, the sign had been kicked over, resting on its back, watching the clouds meander above it. She slowed her bike and stood over the sign, debating whether she'd be a good girl and right it or leave it be. A moment later, she walked her bike around it, climbed the porch stairs, and opened the front door. There, ready to leave, stood Uncle Zane. His hat was in his hands, his eyes examining his shoes.

"Hi," she said, balancing the front door against her hip.

He backed away.

"Hello," he said.

"Where are you going?"

"Into town," he said.

"Why are you going into town?"

"Georgeanne needs periwinkle."

"The flower?" Maranatha set her backpack on the wood floor at the foot of the stairs. The front door swung closed.

"No, the color. Wants our bathroom in the new house to be this purple blue color — periwinkle." He put his hat on his head and rustled keys in his pocket. He inched toward the back door.

"I see. I thought mauve was the color of the day. Or peach."

Uncle Zane shrugged. He did that a lot since the stroke. It was the first thing he actually communicated after weeks of staring at his bedroom wall. "Would you like some water?" Maranatha had asked to her vacant uncle for the hundredth time. He shrugged. She cried, welcoming the shrug. Now it maddened her.

"Why do you want a purple bathroom?" Maranatha walked around him and started up the stairs.

"Periwinkle," he said. A faint smile played on his thin lips.

"Sorry." She laughed. "I mean, do you really want a periwinkle bathroom?"

"It's not what I want that matters. I'm married now."

She sat on the lowest stair, setting her chin on her hands. "Uncle Zane?"

"Yes." He took out his keys and looked at them as if they held a secret.

"Do we really have to move?"

"I reckon so."

"But isn't the house mine too? I mean, don't I have a say in this at all?"

He placed the keys in his other hand and examined them afresh. "There is a way," he said. "But it's a legal way. You do have a choice. You don't have to lose the house."

"But what — "

The front door flew open. A blonde head of hair entered, followed by bags and bags. "I need your help, Zane. I got us some curtains and towels for the new house. Can you help?" Georgeanne noticed Maranatha then. "You too."

Maranatha wanted to kick Georgeanne. Truly. She'd never been a violent girl, always thought those girls who were women's-libbing their way to a spot on the bowling team or screaming like banshees during the annual powder-puff football game were weird. Violence didn't appeal to her, but for some reason, seeing Georgeanne flaunt new periwinkle towels brought out the barbarian in her.

She needed another rare moment alone with Uncle Zane so she could find out what kind of say she had in the house sale. So without saying a word to Georgeanne, she walked around her, following Uncle Zane to the red Thunderbird parked askew in front of the house.

"Uncle Zane?"

He pulled several bags from the trunk. "Yes?"

"You said there was something I could do — for the house."

"I did?"

"Yes, just now. You said there was a way legally."

"Right. Yes." He handed her a bag and looked beyond her.

She followed his gaze. The door to the big white house was ajar, but Georgeanne was not framed within it. They were safe. "A lawyer should be able to settle things," he said.

They walked slowly toward the house's open door. "A lawyer? But I don't know a lawyer."

"I hear there's a new one out at the courthouse. A lady. Might try her."

"But why don't you stop all this, Uncle Zane? You can, you know."

They neared the bottom of the steps, nearly in Georgeanne's earshot. "I fouled it up with Sephie." His voice cracked. "I'm not doing that again."

"Don't you think she'd love you no matter what?" She lowered her voice. "For who you are?"

He stopped and looked at her, confusion and pain painting his face. "Sephie, she always loved everybody. Even me."

"No, I mean Georgeanne. If she loves you, she'll listen to you, even if you don't agree, right?"

"I'm not taking that risk," he whispered. "But you can."

"But I don't have any papers—"

"Papers for what?" Georgeanne stood in the doorway again, her hair haloing her like cotton candy gone awry.

Uncle Zane gave Maranatha the *look*—a kind of panicked control that said, *Don't mess with what I have going here. You're on your own.*

"For school," she said, not looking up. "Financial aid forms for college. I need to get them soon. Fill them out."

"I should hope so. I've always thought it noble when kids paid their way through school. Your uncle simply can't afford your college tuition, you know. All those medical bills. It's good you're fixin' to find more funds."

Maranatha walked up the stairs of *her* home. The home she

determined to save at any cost.

She tossed her backpack on her bed, spewing its contents all over her quilt. Chemistry, in the form of the periodic table, beckoned her. She could see the paper peeking out from her notebook. Instead, she opened the wardrobe, pulled out a simple rose-colored dress, removed the dry-cleaning bag, and pressed it to herself. "This house was supposed to be ours, Mama," she told her reflection in the mirror. With the dress just so, and as her eyes bored into herself, she remembered something. Dress in hand, she grabbed the photo album Zady had put together of all the black-and-white Mama pictures she could find. She flipped a few pages until she saw it. Staring back at her was Sephie — in that very dress. It seemed to Maranatha that her mama was trying to say with her eyes that certain things were worth fighting for. Maranatha may not have been a violent girl, but today she sensed her mama's anger at injustice rise up in her heart, ready to attack. Ready to save something precious.

She slipped the dress onto its hanger and gently smoothed the plastic protector around it. Though the dresses were ordered by color from white, pink, red, orange, yellow, green, blue, purple, brown, and black, she hung the rose dress to the far left, next to the . . .

Wait. The white dress that kissed the wardrobe's left side was gone. A shell of plastic wrap hung without the dress, like its soul had been removed. She grabbed the ghost hanger and stared at it, wondering why it had allowed Georgeanne to take the stained dress without a fight.

Every day something was amiss when she opened the door to her room after school. A book skewed differently on her nightstand. A crooked lampshade. Her bed straitjacketed with hospital corners. Her curtains closed when she'd left them open. And now her mama's dress gone. Bile tickled her throat; revenge enticed her heart.

Georgeanne is going to pay.

She left her room in a fury. She needed fresh air to clear her head, needed to pump her lungs in and out until her breath labored. She ran downstairs, pushed open the front door, and jumped on her bike. She pedaled past the Loop where poor met rich, past the costume shop with Santa's suit still faded in the window, past the implement shop, past the for-sale bed and breakfast, past the crooked trailer house claimed by a goat, past field upon field of cows and farms and bowing brown cornstalks.

She pushed herself to ride the route faster than she ever had. When she was young, as an only child to Aunt Elma, she'd time how long it took her to jump rope one block or skip backward down an alleyway or hold her breath. And then she'd beat her time.

She smiled while the hills of Burl sped by. With furious pedal pumping, she was sure to beat her time by three minutes. That simple act of besting herself like she'd done as a child created hope that perhaps one day she'd understand what it would have been like to have a carefree childhood — maybe even experience it.

Maranatha came to a sudden stop in front of the crooked squirrel gate, panting. She checked her watch. Yep, three minutes faster. She parked her bike behind the faded blooms of the crepe myrtle and stood in front of the gate. She breathed in and out so much her lungs hurt, but it was a good kind of hurt, the kind that makes you know you're alive. A little of the bitterness toward Georgeanne had trailed off behind her on the road beneath her bike. Instead of vengeance, she revisited logic.

A No Trespassing sign was wired to the crooked gate, but she didn't pay it any heed. She walked around instead and stared at the blank spot where the burnt house used to stand.

Seeing how the tornado had leveled the burnt house reminded Maranatha of her nearly leveled life. Had she not gritted her way through her childhood circumstances, she'd have been flattened too. She'd soon learned that all she had to do was take care of herself and things would eventually work out. She'd been doing it so long, she knew instinctively how to preserve herself. She knew that if she needed to be taken care of or protected, it would be up to Maranatha Winningham and no one else. She walked through the vacant field where the dande-lions used to wave and stood on the burnt house's cement slab utterly alone. The smell of smoke was gone.

She stood there a long time, contemplating what plans could save her own house from a similar devastation. Having made up her mind, she walked back. A flash of white caught her eye. To her left stood one defiant dandelion, head full of fluff. She picked it without even praising its tenacity and blew a heavy breath over its top. Little white ballerina-fluff flew on a hot breeze in lazy circles, dancing and flying and frolicking.

"Show me You love me, Jesus — by saving my house." Though they were the first words from her mouth on the entire bike ride, she'd been breathing that prayer ever since Georgeanne said they'd be selling the house, so the words were familiar friends. It was good to say the prayer out loud; it gave her a strange sense of peace, that if it were spoken on the breeze of dancing dandelion fluff, God would hear more clearly. And then, He would answer.

A red truck slowed in front of the gate. She could hear the spinning of tires and the crackle of gravel. The truck backed up, blocking the entrance. A man got out and walked around the truck toward her. She didn't know if she should be alarmed because his face registered nothing — not anger, not confusion. Nothing. He walked with a slight limp. His black shock of hair nearly covered his eyes. She guessed him to be about forty years old, though not really knowing how to judge the age of adults, she could be wrong. He wore gardening gloves with red earth still clinging.

"This here's my property," he said, not lifting his head.

"I'm sorry. I used to come out here. To think."

"Well, it's mine now. I'd take it mighty kindly if you'd think on someone else's property." His voice didn't seem angry, but then it didn't register friendliness either. Just the facts.

"Okay," she heard her voice say, but something grumbled inside her—a vague inkling that something was not right. "I'll get my bike." She started toward the bike when he pushed up his hair and looked at her. Through her.

"No matter. I'll be driving back to town anyway. Could use the company. I'll get your bike."

She could hear Mama Frankie's voice whispering in her head, something about running away. Maranatha shook her head. *I'm sure he means no harm*, she reasoned. But Mama Frankie's voice got louder until she shushed it back down.

Before she could protest, he took her bike gently and lifted it into the bed of his truck. "Nice bike," he said.

She knew it was wrong to ride with a stranger, but she did it anyway. What was it about her that followed orders so easily without an ounce of gumption to say no? Maranatha found herself in the truck because this man told her to. Simple as that. She did the only thing she could do, one little act of defiance that revealed a shred of will—she sat as far away from him as she could, her right thigh warming the door handle, a wide path of vinyl seat between them. She glanced behind her to see her bike in the truck's bed, its rear wheel spinning in the wind.

He started the truck and turned right. Away from town.

"Excuse me, sir? I live in town. The other way."

One hand on the wheel, he took off one glove with his teeth. Then the other. "I figured that," he said.

"You'll need to turn around." Her pulse throbbed in her neck. She gripped the door handle until her right knuckles whitened. He went through the gears quickly, bringing them to cruising speed in a matter of seconds.

"I will when I'm good and ready," he said.

Jesus, get me out of here. She knew she couldn't jump — the road's broken white lines blurred as if they were connected. She scooted even farther away from the gearshift and prayed the *Get me out of here* prayer over and over like a skipping record.

He reached across the empty seat, placed a sweaty hand on her thigh, and smiled. "There you go, darling. No need to be afraid. Relax. We'll be there in a minute."

The heat from his hand seeped through her, and at once she knew she'd throw up. Her stomach started heaving.

"I'm glad we have a chance to talk now. Get to know each other a little better. I think you know what I mean." He squeezed her thigh tighter while he watched the road. Her eyes widened.

Jesus, get me out of here.

Jesus, get me out of here.

Jesus, get me out of here.

She bent forward and gagged. Today's school lunch burned her throat.

"Not in my truck, you hear? I can't stand the smell of barf." He removed his hand.

Jesus, get me out of here.

"I'm . . . I'm going to be sick."

"Nice try," he said, keeping his gaze forward, racing miles and miles away from home.

She looked in the truck's side mirror and saw her bike tire spinning happily in rhythm to the wind. She knew she'd miss that bike. She touched the truck's door handle and started pulling.

At the moment she heard the handle click, the man slammed on his brakes and swore. "Of all the days," he yelled.

Directly in front of him was a line of longhorn cattle, lowing as they crossed the road. A farmer halted traffic with a dirty palm. She saw this all in a split second, as she shoved the door open.

"No, you don't," the man said. He tried to grab her, but by that time she was out. In one swift motion, she nabbed the bike, yanking it over the truck's side, scratching the paint in the process. In a second motion, she was on the bike and pedaling. Toward home. Hemmed in by a semi behind and longhorns in front, the man was trapped.

Tears stung her eyes as she raced the miles of road home. Every few seconds she looked back, waiting for the man in the red truck to reach her, run her off the road, and steal what was left of her damaged heart. Before she got to the squirrel gate, she turned a sharp right onto CR 156 — a road that took much longer to get to town, but might prove to be her protection. It ended at Mt. Moriah Church and then T-ed, either cutting back to Burl down a winding, wild hog–visited road or leading to the little lake. If she could just make it to the T, where Mt. Moriah waited. Ahead of her was a long hill; beyond that hill was the church. She stood on her pedals and rode faster, actually gaining momentum up the hill.

She looked behind her. Nothing.

Yet.

At the crest of the hill, she saw the church, but she didn't see Bishop Renny's car.

She looked behind.

A red truck approached, engine revved.

Jesus, get me out of here.

She sped down the hill and into Mt. Moriah's gravel parking lot, nearly toppling over herself. She steadied her bike, rode it around the church, and threw it down. She ran to the side door.

Locked.

She could hear the engine roaring, seeking to devour her.

She banged on the door. A cry escaped her lips. Panic settled into her shaking hands. She put her hand to the knob, but before she tried it again, the door opened. Zady stood there with a mop in her hand.

Maranatha ran past her. "Shut the door. And lock it. Now!"

"What in the world?" Zady asked, but she shut and locked the door anyway.

"A man," she panted. "Tried to take me." She ran into the center of the sanctuary and turned around and around, eyes wide. "He's coming. He's right behind me."

Zady's look went from surprise to panic. She ran to the side window where the bird had shattered the stained glass the day Mama Frankie died. "Someone's here all right," she said as she peered through. "Someone in a red truck. A man with dark hair. He's pacing back and forth. Got kind of a limp. He the one?"

"Yes." Her stomach took charge. She knelt on the ground and heaved all over the red carpet.

"I'll call the police."

The side doorknob jiggled, followed by a banging. Then silence.

Maranatha could hear Zady's voice, her soothing voice talking to the police. "Yes'm," she said. "He's right here. Best hurry."

Maranatha leaned against a pew, not caring that she sat near her own vomit. Her head felt hot, her mind fuzzy. Zady walked toward her, white towel in hand. "It'll be fine, Natha. I'm here, you see?" She wrapped the rolled wet towel around Maranatha's head and held her shoulders.

"The throw-up," she said.

"Yes, I see it. I'll get to it. Don't you worry. I'll protect you." She sang hymns to Maranatha, strung together like there were no rests, rocking her in gentle rhythm with her tender, soothing voice. Songs of deliverance and hope and peace wafted around Maranatha's tired head. Into her terrorized heart.

Another bang reverberated the side door.

Maranatha hugged her knees to her chest.

"Don't worry. We're safe in God's house." Zady stood and went over to the cracked window. "Thank You, Jesus!" She opened the door. Bishop Renny stood there, looking confused.

"Why'd you lock the door, Zady?"

"You see a red truck around?" She pulled him in and locked the door again.

"Yeah, someone was leaving as I was pulling in. Spinning his tires." He looked beyond Zady and saw Maranatha. "What happened?"

"Natha said that man tried to nab her."

Bishop Renny closed the gap between the door and Maranatha in a few strides. "You all right?" He knelt so they were eye-level. He took an errant strand of hair and tucked it behind her ear like a father would.

"I don't know," she said.

He sat on one side of her while Zady sat on the other, sandwiching her, embracing her. Engulfed in such protection, Maranatha wept.

"Dear Lord in heaven," Zady prayed, "be so near right now. Touch this poor girl with Your amazing love. She feels alone and scared and unprotected. Help her to know Your eye is on her, that You see her. Thank You for delivering her today. Thank You for the gift she is to me."

When Zady said the word *gift* Maranatha cried all the harder, not because of the kind sentiment, but because she realized afresh that Zady wasn't around the house anymore, that Zady couldn't envelop her in the warmth of mamalike hugs.

"Jesus," Bishop Renny prayed, "You love us all, don't You? But sometimes it's hard to see. And sometimes this world is such a mess, full of people doing terrible things. Protect Natha right now. Protect her thoughts, her dreams, her heart. Thank You for bringing her to us."

She wiped her eyes and smelled vomit.

Zady must've been reminded too, because in that moment, she left. She returned with a bucket of sudsy water. On hands and knees, she scrubbed Maranatha's stain clean. If only she could scrub Maranatha's soul. Bishop Renny helped Maranatha to her feet and sat her down in a nearby pew — Mama Frankie's, actually — and told her he'd be right back. He returned with a tall glass of cold water from the water cooler. "Take a long drink. It'll help your stomach."

While sitting there, she remembered Mama Frankie's green tomato prophecy. She'd told Maranatha to run away when someone came to pluck her. And she had done just that. Well, rode away, actually. She could almost hear Mama Frankie's voice there sitting in her pew. She looked to her right toward the taped-up window and wondered if Mama Frankie's prophecy had been completely fulfilled today, that from now on no one would chase her, either in her dreams or on the streets of Burl. She hoped the green tomato year, though barely begun, had ended.

The police came and asked her more questions than she could answer.

No, she didn't get the license plate.

Yes, he said he owned that property.

No, she didn't catch his name.

Yes, he walked with a limp.

No, he didn't hit her.

Yes, he had dark hair.

Yes, the truck was red.

Yes, she got her bike back.

No, when he lifted her bike into the truck bed, he wore gardening gloves. No fingerprints. *But I can still feel his hand on my leg, does that count?*

The police officer offered to take her home, but she refused. She didn't know him, didn't trust him. She remembered riding with Officer Gus so many years ago, what he smelled like, what his character reeked of. No, she would only ride home with someone she knew. Of that, she was certain.

Bishop Renny took Zady and Maranatha home. Turned out Zady had been cleaning the church that day for extra money. Sometimes Raymond drove her there and picked her up. Sometimes she walked the seven miles to get there. But she went twice a week, scrubbing the church until it shone.

Maranatha let Bishop Renny and Zady talk. Her head ached. She didn't want to say any more words. She looked out the window, watching the brown grass sway beneath sycamore trees. She remembered when she'd been helpless under General, when he'd forced himself upon her. He'd taken something from her then, but he'd also given her something — a strange mark seen only by other men like him, like a fluorescent spot that shows up only in black light. What was it about her that seemed to attract men like the man in the red truck? It was like he knew she was an easy target, as though General had marked her indelibly for all the creeps of the world to see.

"Don't tell anyone," she said when they stopped in front of

the big white house. "I'll be fine."

Zady reached out and grabbed her hand. "I won't tell anyone, 'cept the Lord and your uncle."

"Please don't tell Uncle Zane."

"It'll be fine," Zady said. "He's not so far gone that he can't protect you still. He needs to know, being kin and all."

Maranatha nodded, still fretting. "Please, Zady, can you make him promise he won't tell Georgeanne?"

"I'll try, child, but that uncle of yours, he still has a stubborn streak. It's hard to convince him of anything."

"I'm not so sure."

Zady exhaled. "I'll do my best." She paused. "I'm praying, Natha."

Bishop Renny nodded his agreement. Maranatha could see tears in his eyes. She quickly looked away, knowing if she kept her gaze there, she'd explode into weeping.

He opened the trunk and lifted her bike from it. "You take care of yourself, you hear?"

"I will. I'm fine. Really," she said again, avoiding his wet eyes.

Under the shadow of the pecan tree, the place where she had met Jesus, she set her bike down. She ran upstairs to her room, only to find it painted peach. It took a moment to realize she'd entered her *old* room. She walked to her real room, shut the door, and took off all her clothes, throwing them in the corner like rubbish. She grabbed a blanket from a basket and wrapped it around herself like a cocoon.

She shivered though the sun angled through the windows.

Still in her cocoon, she sat on her bed. It was then she spied a pile of stacked papers on her pillow.

She leafed through them and discovered her name and lots of legal words: *deed, said property, undivided interest.* She silently thanked Uncle Zane. Tomorrow she'd call that lawyer, but tonight all she wanted to do was stop shivering and sleep.

And forget.

Eighteen

BUT SHE COULDN'T FORGET THE MAN in the red truck. Couldn't forget his face or the hot shape of his sweaty hand on her leg. The moment she fell asleep, he was there — tormenting her. He'd joined forces with General. Together they chased her through Burl's mean streets, the red-truck guy limping, General hollering *Beautiful* at her.

But she couldn't yell one bit. Not a whimper. No words flew over her vocal chords, only pale panting that disappeared on the hot air. At the end of her dream, she ran home, but home had changed. The big white house had turned periwinkle with peach trim. Odd, Seuss-like trees dotted the yard. And no matter how far or hard she ran, her home remained the same distance away, like she was moving on a treadmill, getting nowhere. All she wanted to do was reach the front gate, creak its hinges, and run up to her room — her old room. But the more she ran, the more the house seemed to back away from her.

When she finally vocalized the word *help*, the house moved closer, except that Georgeanne stood on its periwinkle porch, shaking her head.

"This isn't your home," she said.

Maranatha awoke with the words pounding in her head.

This isn't your home.
This isn't your home.

She rolled over and stared at the wall until her vision blurred. For a moment, she panicked, remembering it was Friday and a school day—and she'd slept the morning through. Then she relaxed. Today was a teacher in-service, when the teachers worked but kids didn't.

Maranatha turned over and stared at the ceiling and realized she hadn't counted its cracks. When she first moved to the house so many years ago, it had been her ritual to count the cracks in the ceiling of her old room while recovering from a blow to the head. Though she had no concussion today, she felt something was broken in her heart, and the only way to calm herself was to count the cracks in the ceiling.

So she counted. Thirty-nine cracks.

She counted again.

And again.

Her mind drifted away from haunting dreams. She remembered the only thing worth remembering about yesterday: the legal papers.

Maranatha pulled herself up in bed, propping a pillow behind her. She started reading the documents but could make little sense of them other than her name and the address of the big white house. The rest were words she hadn't studied in honors English. Lawyer words.

She got up, pulled on a pair of shorts and a tank top, and walked to the window. Thankfully, Georgeanne's red Thunderbird was nowhere to be seen. She could phone in peace. She walked down the hallway past her old room and trotted downstairs. She picked up the one-inch-thick Burl phone book from the table under the hallway phone. Uncle Zane had said something about the courthouse. She flipped through the beginning section until she found the number.

"Johnson County courthouse, Ezell speaking, how may I direct your call?"

"I'm not sure," Maranatha said. Her heart thumped to her throat. She scolded herself for not thinking through what she wanted to say.

"Well, ma'am, I can't help you if you don't know what you want," Ezell said.

"Um, well, I need a lawyer."

"We have a district attorney here and a few ADAs. Which one would you like?"

"I heard there was a woman lawyer," she said, her words sounding three-year-old-ish.

"Miss Nichols? I'll put you right through."

A country song about a woman wanting custody of the dog after a nasty breakup wailed on the receiver.

"Jolie Nichols. How may I help you?" The woman's voice was not Burl. It wasn't even Texas. She sounded like a national newscaster. No drawl. Quick and to the point.

"I need a lawyer," Maranatha said. She ruffled through her papers, dropping most of them on the wood floor beneath her feet. She crouched on the floor, the phone cocked between shoulder and ear, and retrieved them.

"Would you like to report a crime? Because that's a police matter." The woman sounded so confident, so professional. For a moment, Maranatha envisioned herself in a power suit, sounding as assured. That passed quickly, subdued by intimidation.

"No, not really." Flashes of yesterday played about her mind. She shoved those memories down deep. She wondered if the police found the man in the red truck, wondered if this woman somehow knew the secret and would try to pull it out of her.

"Would you like to come in and talk about it?" The lady's

voice sounded inviting, empathetic even, but fear wrangled its way into Maranatha's mind. What if she knew? What if this woman forced her to be on the witness stand to face that horrible man?

"Are you there?" Again, more empathy seeped through the phone.

"Yes."

"I can't help you unless you tell me what you need."

Maranatha took a deep breath. "I'm having trouble understanding some documents. I need help reading them."

"Legal documents?"

"Yes."

Miss Nichols sighed. "Why don't you bring the papers to my office? I'll be happy to look at them for you."

Maranatha intended to say thanks, but the door opened, revealing a flustered Georgeanne.

"Just a sec," she said to Miss Nichols. She crooked the phone to her chin, still holding the legal papers.

Georgeanne set her large pink purse on the floor and fingered the mail at her feet. She found one apparently addressed to Maranatha and handed it to her. "Mail. For you."

Maranatha kept her neck crooked and took the scented-like-Georgio letter. Camilla. She transferred the letter to the top of the pile she held, letting her head sit straight again. She hoped Georgeanne would leave, but she stayed right where she was.

"Who's got your ear? That Charlie kid?"

She wanted to cup her hand over the receiver, but her hand held the papers. She stammered, "No one. It's the time lady."

"Well, why did you say, 'Just a sec'?"

The lawyer on the other end said, "I'm here all day. Come on by."

Maranatha pushed the receiver down, hoping this Miss

Nichols person would be an understanding Yankee. She nonchalantly dropped her left hand, which held the papers, to her side.

Then Georgeanne's hair registered with her. A Medusa-like halo of wild ringlets framed her face. Maranatha choked her laugh into a cough.

"You look suspicious," Georgeanne said.

And you look ridiculous, she almost said.

Georgeanne ran a hand through her hair, but once again, her hand got stuck. For a second, Maranatha saw a hint of vulnerability, could see Georgeanne was tormented by a bad hair day, like the rest of the Burl commoners who contended with the daily heat and humidity.

Georgeanne walked around her and then stopped. Right next to the papers. "The first day is the hardest, I always say."

Thank God she's changed the subject. "What do you mean?"

"Perms."

"You got a permanent?" Maranatha sat on the chair by the phone, slipping the papers under her left leg.

"Been getting them since I was seven." Georgeanne walked around her again, returning to her purse. She rummaged. "Stick-straight hair is my curse. Danielle is my savior."

"You go to Danielle for perms?" Danielle operated a salon on the Loop in the defunct "mall," catering to doctor's wives and women of old Burl money.

"Ever since she got here. She's the best in town, they say. But the first day's always the hardest. Your head smells like chemicals and you can't wash it for a while. That's why it's you and me all day today. I can't go out looking like this."

Maranatha touched the papers beneath her leg with a sly hand, smelling the wafting Georgio. "I have an errand to run. In town."

"What sort of errand? I imagine you can postpone it for another day."

Maranatha hesitated, unable to think of a creative lie. All she could see was Georgeanne's crazy hair coiling around itself like corkscrew pasta. "Hair appointment," she finally said.

"Really? That's not really an *errand*," she said, but in the next breath asked, "Who with?"

"Danielle." *What did I say?* Heat rose from Maranatha's neck to her eyebrows.

Georgeanne moved next to her. If she looked down a little, she'd see the papers sticking out kitty-corner from Maranatha's leg. "Funny, Danielle didn't say anything to me about it."

"Last-minute cancellation," Maranatha lied.

"I'm going with you." Georgeanne stood, a smile spreading across her curl-invaded face.

"But — "

Georgeanne put her hands on her hips, a sure sign of her seriousness. "No buts about it, girly. Truth is, Danielle's the most fun woman I've ever met. Tells the most hilarious stories. I miss her already. It'll do my soul some good to jaw a bit with her. Besides, we're the closest of friends."

"But, your *hair*." Heat crept above Maranatha's eyebrows, sweating her hairline. A trickle spilled from the corner of her forehead around the contour of her cheek. She should come clean. Right now. Just spit the words, *I lied about the hair appointment*. But something held her back.

Georgeanne patted her hair with her hands. "Ah, no matter. She's the one who did it anyway. What time did you say your appointment was?"

"I didn't." She looked over at the clock ticking on the wall. 1:00. She calculated how long it would take to call this Danielle person and explain her predicament and was about to blurt out

2:00, when Georgeanne interrupted her thoughts.

"No matter. I'll call her — see if she doesn't mind my company again today."

Maranatha wanted to throw up. The edges of the documents tickled her left leg. Georgeanne picked up the phone right next to Maranatha and dialed. Maranatha pulled the papers from underneath her and decided to whisk them by Georgeanne, up the stairs into the safety of her room.

"Danielle? It's me." She put a finger up to Maranatha to stop. Maranatha froze, papers at her side.

"Why, Georgeanne, silly. Hey, Maranatha says you fit her in today. That's awfully nice — "

Maranatha tried to motion with her eyes that she was going upstairs — anything to get away from being found out — but Georgeanne's pointed finger held a strange power over her, as if her bloodred nail polish wielded a secret spell. Georgeanne's eyes got bigger. "Oh really?" She narrowed her eyes. "*Interesting*," she drawled, enunciating each syllable, even adding an extra one on *ing*. Ay-ying.

"Must've dreamt it, I guess." Georgeanne relocated her finger from midair to her hip and smiled a sickly grin. "Well, how lovely you are. Yes, of course, Danielle. Same as me. Bye now." Georgeanne hung up, shaking her head. "Well, if we aren't the little teller of lies." She stepped toward Maranatha so close that perm solution stung her nose and tendrils of wild hair nearly brushed her cheek. "Mind telling me what you were going to do? Or were you avoiding me on your day off? Really, now, Maranatha, we're going to have to get along someday." She jutted her lower lip out in a toddler pout.

"I just — "

"You were going to go visit that boy, weren't you?"

Maranatha stepped back, fingered the papers in her hand,

and decided an exit plan would be a good idea about right now. Problem was, she couldn't think of one with Georgeanne blocking the staircase to her room. "No, ma'am. I . . . needed time alone."

"I told your uncle this the other day, you know. 'Zane, dear,' I said, 'that niece of yours is a recluse. Always stays in her room. If you ask me, she's got an antisocial disorder or something.' I studied those, you know, when I got my nursing training."

"I thought you were a home-health aid."

"Nurse. Home-health aid. What's the difference, really? Anyway, I did study about personality disorders." Georgeanne sat on the wooden chair near the phone, leaving a clear escape route, and sighed. "I told him I'd take you on. Teach you proper Southern manners. Teach you how to fit in."

"I can fit in just fine." She inched around Georgeanne.

"Well, I'm sure you would think that, what with the way you were raised and all."

A hint of fight made Maranatha turn away from escape and face Medusa. "What's that supposed to mean?"

"What I said. Your daddy's dead—a fine man he was. Your waif mama's dead. And you were raised by your uncle and an uneducated black woman. Of course you have problems in society. The Good Lord must've known. He brought me into your life at the right time. To help you." She crossed her legs and folded her hands on her lap. "And that's why I chose to overlook your transgression today—of lying to me. Because I'm genteel as all get out, I covered for you, Maranatha."

"Covered for me?"

"Yes, as you probably heard, I made you an appointment with Danielle. For a perm at 2:00."

"I don't want a perm," Maranatha said.

"I'll tell you what." Georgeanne stood, facing her. "I won't ask about those papers in your hand if you get your stringy hair some curl. Deal?"

Maranatha touched her hair. It'd been linguine-straight her entire life. But in one moment she made a snap decision. The papers could do more good to her and more harm to Georgeanne than a silly old perm. She'd play the game. Besides, a tiny curiosity wormed its way into her head. What if Charlie liked curly hair better?

"Deal," she said.

Maranatha stood in the center of her room, papers in hand. She had a smidgen of time before Georgeanne mounted the stairs to fetch her, so she sat at her desk and opened Camilla's envelope. For safe measure, she put Uncle Zane's papers in a drawer.

Georgio perfume, Camilla's favorite of late, taunted her, making Maranatha miss her friend more than ever. Inside the envelope were two folded wonders: pink paper pressed into a mouse, and white paper creased into a house. The mouse was labeled number one, the house number two.

She opened mouse number one.

Dear Nearly Homeless Maranatha,

I can't believe your terrible luck, what with mice invading and Georgeanne usurping (I like that word, usurp). If I were there, I'd welcome the mice back in like the Pied Piper, only I'd use a violin because everyone knows mice like orchestral music. And, you know what? I'd beat up that peachy wonder. Slice her through, right to the pit. I talked to Dad yesterday

*and he said you could live with him and Rose. Said in
his puppy-sad way that he missed having a daughter
around. You'd do them good, I know. So, I've solved
all your problems for you. What're best friends for,
anyway?*

The letter went on a little longer about cows and leather
and whether Camilla would wear suede. She wrote of feminism
rallies and how she thought bras were evil contraptions made
by oppressive men. Maranatha smiled. She opened the house-
shaped note. In it were the words of another one of Camilla's
truth-poems:

> Miss Winningham I am, I am,
> I will not bend to that Georgeanne
> I will not wrangle 'bout my house
> Unless I have a wee dead mouse
> To put before her smug-filled face
> Or underneath her panties' lace
> I will not let her take my home
> She's the one who's s'posed to roam
> This is my house, you see, you see
> She can live inside that tree
> While squirrels nest inside her hair
> And Burl society stands and stares
> At treed Georgeanne, no home to keep
> Sweet recompense, she's bound to reap
> Miss Winningham I am, I am
> I live to vex that pest Georgeanne.

"Thanks, Camilla," she said to the house-shaped poem.
The stairs squeaked familiar sounds as Maranatha finished

folding the poem back into a house.

She grabbed the papers from her drawer. Where could she hide them when Georgeanne snooped everywhere? Not between the mattresses. Not in the wardrobe. The room hadn't become familiar like worn slippers; she had yet to explore every nook and cranny with her eyes on lazy afternoons. She hadn't spent days breaking it in while she read or wrote in her journal. She spied the stack of *Seventeen* magazines under her bed and remembered Aunt Elma's *Good Housekeeping* piles. She smiled. For years, she believed that once she turned seventeen, she'd look like the cover girls. But nothing magic happened when sixteen turned to seventeen last April other than her having to shave her legs more often.

Georgeanne's footsteps sounded on the landing. Maranatha sat on the floor near her bed, pulled out an October 1986 issue, and slipped the papers between its covers. She stashed it toward the bottom of the pile.

"Ready?" Georgeanne's voice rattled her, a few steps beyond her door.

Maranatha left her room in a rush, slamming the door before Georgeanne could peer inside. "Let's go."

"I already love you," Danielle, a smallish woman with deep-set eyes, hugged Maranatha's neck as she gushed. "Georgeanne, she's told me all about you. You're lovely." Maranatha cast Georgeanne a puzzled look. Georgeanne averted her gaze.

Danielle's hair was blonde, very blonde. A long black line striped her part.

She directed Maranatha to a chair after scrubbing her hair with Pert shampoo in an uncomfortable sink. "Don't be looking at my hair. I'm trying to decide if I'll go back to brown. But my husband likes blondes, so I'll probably bleach again." She laughed like bleaching hair was a joke. Her laugh was so strong and unusual it reminded Maranatha of Camilla's laugh. She imagined Camilla sitting in this salon with her, egging her on, making fun of this strange woman, all the while trying to rhyme with *scissors*. As Danielle pulled at various sections of her hair and Georgeanne prattled on and on from a chair nearby about periwinkle being the new black, Maranatha decided she'd write Camilla another letter.

"You sure you want a perm?"

Maranatha looked over at a smiling Georgeanne.

"She's absolutely sure, aren't you?"

Maranatha nodded.

Danielle pulled one strand of hair toward the ceiling, Alfalfa-style. "You ever have a perm before?"

"No, ma'am."

"Don't 'ma'am' me, sweetie. I'm no ma'am. I'm just Danielle." She smoothed the cutting cape around Maranatha's shoulders and smacked her gum. Then she took a swig of coffee. "The reason I ask is that I need to know how easily your hair curls. Don't want to put the solution on too long, you know. I like poodles, but hey, let's face it, none of us wants to end up looking like one."

Maranatha nodded. A boiling fear churned her stomach like a witch's cauldron. What if she did end up looking like a poodle? Like Georgeanne?

Danielle pulled over a cart full of skinny rollers. "What color should I use? Hmm, let me see." She pulled out pink. It looked frighteningly slim. "No, too small. Here we go. We'll go with blue today."

Maranatha let out a breath. Blue was bigger.

Georgeanne sat reading a battered copy of *People* magazine. "Danielle, tell Maranatha some stories."

"Oh, she don't want to hear those."

"Yes, she does. Go on. Tell her the one about the kidney stone and Big Angus."

Danielle laughed again. Clients in other chairs didn't seem to pay any mind, as if her laugh had become elevator music. "It's a good one, I'll tell you that." She pulled a strand of hair from Maranatha's head and rolled it to her scalp, clipping the end to itself. "Big Angus was a scary man, I'm telling you what. That is, until the kidney stones got 'im. He was kind of like Paul Bunyan, could haul lead pipe around on his shoulder like he was carrying a cat. Not a soul messed with him, either. Legend has it that when he went to the emergency room at Mother Frances, he pointed his pistol at the doctor and yelped like a puppy. 'Doc,' he said, 'shoot me here and now. I can't take it.' Well, the doc, he shot 'im all right, with a needle full of morphine. In a few hours the stone passed. When the doctor handed the stone to Big Angus in a plastic cup, he was still on drugs. 'This is the thing that felt like I was being stabbed?' he asked. The doctor nodded. 'I'd like to put a hole through that blasted thang,' he slurred, 'but it's too darned small.'"

Georgeanne laughed. Everyone in the place looked at her. Maranatha glanced in the mirror at her reptilian head, a single long row of blue curlers from her forehead to the back.

Danielle spun more stories. John Crow, who tried to outrun a wild hog and lost. Elmer Grover, who, in his dementia, mistook a telephone pole for a pine tree and electrocuted himself after he tried to pick what he thought was a pinecone. Michael Martin, who liked to build crooked houses so that marbles would roll down the floors. Lester French, who tried to make his own dandelion wine and ended up sick in bed for weeks after drinking a gallon of the stuff. Danielle's mouth ran as fast as her fingers rolled hair.

She started squirting the stinky stuff on Maranatha's rollers.

"Danielle?"

"Yes."

"Do you have any funny stories about women?"

"Not a one, sweetie."

"Why is that?"

"One reason and one reason alone. Women aren't funny."

The chemicals burned Maranatha's eyes. She pressed a cloth to her forehead that was now on fire. She thought about Danielle's assertion. Maranatha didn't know many funny women — only Camilla when she was in a rhyming mood and Zady when she wasn't hell-bent on a task. "Why do you suppose that is?" She looked over at Georgeanne. Her eyes were closed; the magazine covered her ample bosom.

"Women are complicated," Danielle said, pulling a very ugly shower cap over Maranatha's head. "And mean as injured dogs. You ask me? I don't really like 'em."

"But your job — "

"Ironic, ain't it? I spend my days prettying up women, but I don't care much for them. Oh, I like myself all right — but that's only 'cause I can trust myself. Women are sneaky. They say one thing and mean another. They compliment you with words but kill you with their eyes. Men? They're simple. Feed them. Make sure they get enough sex. Plop 'em in front of the TV on Sunday afternoons during Cowboys season with Doritos and some queso dip and they're happy. You'll never hear a man say things like, 'Do I look fat in these Wranglers?' or 'Are you sure nothing's wrong?' If you ask me, men are simple."

Maranatha hadn't expected to receive life-altering advice

while getting her hair curled. But there it was. Men were simple. Women were mean. Tenets to live by.

Georgeanne snored so loudly Maranatha could hear the bellowing through Danielle's industrial-strength hair dryer.

"There!" Danielle said. "It took a long time to pull up, probably because you've got virgin hair." She pulled out a curler and let it dangle free.

Maranatha gasped. She hadn't meant to, but she couldn't help it. The big blue rollers wound curlicues of hair so tight, they bounced halfway up her normal hair length, like she'd gotten a butch haircut, only with curls.

"Well, hmmm, it's a bit kinky." Danielle looked nervous. "Best be pulling these out now before any more damage is done."

Damage?

She pulled them out so fast that with each tug, Maranatha winced.

Georgeanne snored.

As they hurried to the bank of sinks, Maranatha examined Georgeanne's hair afresh. What had she been thinking? Georgeanne *was* a poodle, and now she'd be her twin.

All the neutralizing and washing and conditioning done, Maranatha sat in front of Danielle's mirror with a towel around her head. She prayed God would do a miracle, that He would straighten her hair as easily as He'd sent boils on the Egyptians. *I'll take the boils*, she prayed.

But no boils erupted on her skin. Instead, when the towel was pulled away, poodle-tight curls erupted from her head in every direction. *Dear God! What have I done? I look like Shirley Temple's tighter-curled twin!*

"Don't worry, it'll relax. I promise." Danielle's words had pain attached, like she was working harder to convince herself than Maranatha.

"What can I do?"

"Wash the heck out of it."

"That's all?" Tears stung Maranatha's eyes. She looked over at an open-mouthed Georgeanne, magazine folded over herself, and hoped beyond hope that those legal papers would mess with Georgeanne's well-planned-out life.

"I'm afraid so. Looks like your hair takes kindly to curls."

"Will it grow out?"

"To your length? Might take years."

At the word *years*, Georgeanne's eyes opened. She yawned, folded the magazine, and looked at Maranatha the poodle. "I *love* it," she said. She stood next to Maranatha and ran her fingers through the wet curls. "Very chic. Danielle, you've done it again."

"I'm afraid I've done too much," she said.

"Not at all. This is miraculous. All that stringy hair now has life! Aren't you thrilled, Maranatha?"

Maranatha didn't know what to say. She worried if she spoke, the tears that threatened to burst from her eyes would view those words as permission to escape, so she stayed silent. The last thing she wanted was to let Georgeanne see her cry.

"Oh, she's speechless. Isn't that priceless?"

Mute Maranatha, or Poodle Girl Winningham, walked to the counter.

"How much will it be?" Georgeanne asked Danielle, who looked at her ledger without meeting Maranatha's eyes.

"Fifty dollars."

Maranatha gulped. She could've spent fifty dollars on hideous clothing at Value Villa and had the same effect, but at least she could shed a horrid wardrobe. Hair with a *perm* was *perm*anent. At least Georgeanne was paying.

Or was she?

"Didn't you bring your purse?" Georgeanne asked.

"No," Maranatha said.

"Well, I'll take care of it here, and you can pay me back when we get home."

Oh, I'll pay you back all right.

Nineteen

MARANATHA STAYED IN BED SATURDAY MORNING smelling chemicals and wishing she could will her hair straight. Curls twirled around her tired face, shrouding her vision while she lay on her stomach trying to write a newspaper-style letter to Camilla about the hair event. "Periled by the Perm," the headline read. Although she easily penned about the perilous perm, she couldn't bring herself to share about the red-truck man. Couldn't write one word about that.

Maranatha considered the benefits of becoming a nun. At least a nun could cover her hair. And she'd never be pestered with red-truck men. Too bad she wasn't Catholic.

But a part of her rejoiced in the disastrous head of hair. She hated being noticed, being leered at by men. Though sheets shrouded her body in a percale prison now, she felt naked. When the limping man in the red truck gawked at her, he seemed to possess Superman's roving X-ray eyes, could see right through her clothes to goose-bumped skin. At least with finger-in-the-light-socket hair, she'd be freed from any more Supermen. She finished her letter by signing, *Cheeks, Maranatha*.

The phone rang in the distance. Footsteps. Georgeanne's. Heeling their way toward the ringing. She could hear the murmured cackle of Georgeanne's laugh, the rising and falling of her drawled words, but not the words themselves. Georgeanne's heels slapped up the stairs like a fast metronome. Without knocking, she flung open Maranatha's door. "You got yourself a call. Downstairs. Best get up, lazybones."

Today Georgeanne's hair was tamed into submission, probably through the torture implements of hair dryer, hair spray, and curling iron. It gave Maranatha a slim bit of hope. "Who is it?"

"That Zady woman. Inviting us to a picnic."

"Us?"

"Yes, *us*, as in *our* family."

Family? Maranatha wanted to shake Georgeanne. Who appointed her to use that word? The nerve. "I'll be right there," she said, looking beyond Georgeanne's smirk. She pulled her robe around herself and walked downstairs.

"Hello?"

"Hi, baby, how's my Maranatha? Are you all right?"

Hearing Zady's voice choked her words.

"Are you there? Maranatha?"

"Yes, I'm here."

"Good. I wanted to remind you of the Founder's Day picnic at church. I can't believe I forgot to see if you were coming, but with that crazy man chasing you, I plum forgot. Tell Georgeanne we're celebrating fifty-seven years of being a church. There're games. Lots of food. And Charlie especially would like you to come." There was tenderness in her voice, as if all the angst from weeks past about Maranatha's pale skin had faded like a watercolor in the sun.

"You invited Georgeanne and Uncle Zane?"

"Well, that woman answered the phone and the words flew out. Must've been God's will. So you'll come then?"

"Yeah."

"That didn't sound too convincing."

"I'll be there. *With* my uncle and Georgeanne. That is, if they don't have other plans."

"Maranatha, do you mind if I give you a little advice?"

"No," she said. But she did mind. A little. Well, actually, a lot.

"She's your family now. It won't help if you keep her at arm's length. You don't have to like that woman, but you do have to be kind."

Maranatha watched the curls bounce in front of her eyes and remembered how Georgeanne had tricked her into poodle-izing her hair. Maranatha would be kind all right, but she wouldn't mean it way down deep. Soon she'd get even. But she wouldn't share that with the likes of Zady, who hollered Jesus phrases like *Turn the other cheek* and *Give an extra coat*. She'd keep her revenge behind her eyes, her own little secret.

"Are you there?" Zady asked.

"Yeah." She touched one curl and suddenly realized her predicament. She longed to be with her real family, the dear folks who populated Mt. Moriah Church, but her vanity held her back. What would they think of her awful hair? "I'm not sure I want to go."

"Why?"

Maranatha could hear the pain in Zady's voice.

"It's . . . well — "

"You and Charlie having problems? He has seemed a bit mopey lately. Don't let him stop you."

"It's not him that's stopping me."

"Then what?"

She took a breath. "My hair."

Zady laughed. "What? What do you mean your hair?"

"It's permed."

"And . . ."

"I look like Shirley Temple on steroids." The moment she said it, she laughed. She'd been so freaked out about her kinky hair that she'd forgotten how comical it all was. And how vain she'd become.

"What does it matter? I've had a perm my whole life. Welcome to my curly world," Zady said. "The picnic's at two o'clock. I'm bringing sweet potato pie. Best get there early if you want some."

Maranatha wrapped a ringlet of curl around her index finger. "I'll be there." *Hair and all.*

Twenty

"AH, COUNTRY LIFE. IT IS A bit quaint, isn't it, Zane?"
Georgeanne motioned out the Cadillac's window at the cow-
dotted pastures.

Uncle Zane nodded.

"You think so, Maranatha?"

Though she hated to admit that she agreed with the
perfumed lady sitting proper next to Uncle Zane, it *was* the
truth. She loved the country. "Yes," was all she said, though. No
use leaking out more words.

Uncle Zane crested a long hill. From that vista, Maranatha
could see the up and down hills of Burl's outskirts, painted with
straw-colored grass, pine forests, and man-dug lakes — a patch-
work of blues, greens, and yellows. She wanted to kick the door
open, roll out of the car, dust herself off, and go adventuring.
To meet new birds. To hold a pinecone. To be away from the
many eyes that would see her unruly, chemical hair. To meander without Georgeanne's cackling — a noise that had become
like antagonistic mosquitoes in her ears.

"There! I see them. Or their trailers at least." Georgeanne
pointed out her window, beyond a stand of trees where a
lazy ribbon of river mud cut through green banks. About ten

off-kilter trailers surrounded the muddy river.

"Pay no mind," Uncle Zane said, as if looking that direction was snooping.

"I'm fascinated by those people, Zane. Every year, they're in a different place."

"Maybe they like variety. Ever think of that?"

The anger in Uncle Zane's voice surprised Maranatha. Part of her wanted to pump her fist in the air, cheering his rare reprimand, but another part wondered why Georgeanne's comments riled her shy uncle. Maybe if she kept the conversation going, she could discover something new about him. "What do you mean, Georgeanne?"

"You know. The river-bottom people." She turned around, facing Maranatha, a wild look in her eyes. "Don't know where they live in the winter, but in the spring, summer, and fall, they camp in the river bottoms. Rumor has it that they're intermarried — ten families producing more than ten children a year, they say. They seldom come into town, except a few times a year, past midnight, stocking up on supplies and fuel and such. If you ask my opinion, they should be living somewhere else, not squatting on private land."

Maranatha remembered a snippet of Camilla's epic poem, *Burl, My Burl*, which Denim read proudly on KBBQ:

> Folks live on the river bottom.
> Yep, ol' Burl, they've sure got 'em.
> If you look hard, you can spot 'em,
> Gnawing on a leg of possum.

"What if they have nowhere else to go?" Maranatha looked behind her, eyeing the trailer compound, now growing smaller in the back window. Her stomach lurched. Car sickness. She looked forward between Uncle Zane's and Georgeanne's heads to the horizon.

Georgeanne kept her eyes forward, intent on the hot blacktop in front of the Cadillac's long hood. "Government should take care of them. Send them to Dallas. Get them out of here."

"So that's the solution for poor folks? Ship them off?" Maranatha could see red inching up Uncle Zane's neck. *Say something, mystery man.*

"There's more to a story," Uncle Zane said, "than what appears on the surface. Best leave it at that. You don't ship folks off just because they're poor."

His neck faded from red to pink to pale.

Silence settled into the car. Not the comfortable sort of silence living between two old married people who read each other's thoughts, but an icy silence, colder than air-conditioning vented high.

Maranatha squirmed. Only a few more minutes to go. While cows grazed and birds flew in formation even farther south than Texas, she wondered whether they'd ever really be like a normal family. She longed for it — a happy family with a mom and a dad, a sister or brother or two, a house in the country surrounded by hills and love — a *Little House on the Prairie* home, with Michael Landon as her pa. It ached her heart to long for it, but the longing was like an industrious disease, building the need for family into the very marrow of her life. If only she could save the house, then she could live there alone, perhaps marry someday, and fill the empty rooms with the chattering laughter of children. She may not have family now, but someday she'd make her own.

"I forgot to tell you." Georgeanne placed a slender hand on Uncle Zane's bony shoulder, not affectionately, but like it'd been written in *The Southern Belle's Guide to a Happy Marriage* and she was simply obeying its mandates.

"What?" He looked at the road, not at his wife.

"The house. Closing's happening next month. Our dream to live in the right neighborhood has come true!"

Next month? Maranatha felt like she'd been punched in the stomach.

"But the big house hasn't sold," Uncle Zane said.

"No problem at all. You're richer than rich — even *with* the medical bills. Surely you can handle it. Besides, the mortgage is paid on that rickety castle."

Rickety castle? Fight for it, Uncle Zane, like a prince defending his prized possession. Say something.

"Georgeanne?" Uncle Zane's voice had an edge to it then, almost like he was readying himself to tell her off.

"Remember, Zane, you told me to make the decisions." Georgeanne smoothed her words. "Told me you couldn't trust yourself to make good decisions. Leaving that excuse for a house is a wise decision."

Maranatha held her breath, waiting for Uncle Zane to speak up for himself. For their house.

"I suppose you're right." His shoulders slumped.

Georgeanne patted Uncle Zane and then brushed her polished nails through his thinning hair. He pulled away, only a hint of movement. "That's how you keep me happy," she said.

The right turn to Mt. Moriah showed up before Maranatha thought it would, rescuing her from the one-sided conversation. Uncle Zane pulled into the parking lot, careful not to spew gravel everywhere. He parked, predictably, under a large tree away from everything, the tires of the car exactly perpendicular to the fence in front of the Cadillac's grill.

He got out, secured hat to head, and walked around the car to let Georgeanne out. Before he could open her door,

Maranatha leapt from the car, slamming the door.

"Temper, temper," Georgeanne said, *tsking* her words.

Zady must've known she needed rescuing because the moment Georgeanne *tsked*, Zady appeared, carrying a covered dish. "Good to see you, Mr. Winningham, Mrs. Winningham. I'm so glad you could make it." She shifted the casserole to her left hip and extended her right hand.

Uncle Zane took it limply and let it go. Georgeanne ignored Zady's brown hand.

"Well, let's get you settled," Zady said, frayed dignity in her voice. "Maranatha, I could sure use your help, that is, if you're willing."

Maranatha nodded and moved next to her friend. Zady hugged Maranatha from the side and whispered so only she could hear, "I think your hair suits you fine. Don't you worry a stitch about it."

Maranatha leaned into Zady's side embrace, relishing her soothing words.

Zady directed Uncle Zane and Georgeanne to a picnic table decked in the familiar red and white oilcloth, a mason jar full of happy asters, and white plates stacked neatly at one end. "You two can rest here. Can I get you any tea?"

"Yes." Georgeanne smoothed out the tablecloth in front of her. "That would be nice. I'm sure Zane will have some too, although he doesn't like his too sweet. Best to mix one part sweet to two parts unsweet. Do you think you can do that?"

Maranatha shifted from foot to foot while her face flushed. She wished Zady'd take a swing at Miss Perfect, but Zady's face registered nothing, certainly not violence. All Maranatha wanted was to escape these people called family and join her *real* family laughing under the trees in groups. She spied Denim far away and wondered where Rose was.

"Two teas, coming up." Zady grabbed Maranatha's elbow and turned to leave.

Zady, you always know when I need to be rescued.

Georgeanne stood. "Uh, Zady, I hate to ask, but what will be on the menu today? I have a sensitive system to certain types of food."

Zady turned back around. "M'not sure, since it's a potluck and all."

"Specifically," Georgeanne twisted her wedding ring around and around like she was trying to twist off a stubborn lid, "meat. What kinds of meat are you cooking?"

"I'm not sure what you mean. The normal meat folks have at a barbecue."

"I know what *normal* folks have at barbecues, mind you. I don't know what types of meat *you* folks serve. Possum? Dove? Squirrel? I can't eat that stuff." She sat again, as if to say, *There, I said it. Now all is well.*

Maranatha wanted to twist off Georgeanne's curled head. Wanted to throw it out onto the field and play a friendly game of kickball with it. Bile singed her tonsils while venom breathed behind her almost-spoken words.

Zady cleared her throat and straightened her back. She stood taller than Maranatha had ever seen her stand — stately, like an old pine tickling heaven with its top branches. "I understand. I can't eat that stuff either, Miss Georgeanne. I'm glad we share the same food aversions. No need to worry. We folks like *normal* meat too."

Zady walked away then. Maranatha followed. When they were out of earshot, Maranatha said, "I'm sorry, Zady. I'm so sorry."

Zady faced her, the sun illuminating the whites of her eyes. "No matter, Natha. You're not responsible for her words."

"Why does it feel like it, then?" Maranatha grabbed a stick from the ground and dusted it off.

"Because she's your family. Folks feel responsible for their families."

Maranatha broke the stick in half. "She's *not* family. She's what I'd call an interloper."

"That's a mighty big word."

"It means she doesn't belong, Zady. She's not my family. Uncle Zane is."

"Let's pretty up the serving tables," Zady said.

They walked in silence to the open field, where Maranatha imagined God smiled down on the feast arrayed on two long tables.

Maranatha uncovered each dish, reveling in every distinct aroma that teased her nose. She wished Zady would talk. She felt like an uncovered casserole, her words exposed. *Georgeanne's not my family.*

Zady leaned in toward her. "Remember what it was like when you first met Zane?"

She nodded while black-eyed peas cooked in garlic assaulted her. Her stomach rumbled, aching for feast time.

"He didn't win any Father of the Year contests, did he?"

"No."

"Give it time, sweet Maranatha. You know what I've found?"

"What?"

"That the folks who are the prickliest on the outside are actually the most injured on the inside. Bishop Renny said once that hurt people *hurt* people. Like a gentle lapdog that bites his owner when he's injured, so do hurt folks. They bite when they're hurting—to keep others away from the injury. They don't realize that talking about the pain, sharing it with someone else, actually lessens it. That Georgeanne," Zady put a stout arm around Maranatha's shoulders, "is an injured lapdog, sure as pie."

"There are other dogs, Zady — dogs that are trained to kill. Maybe she's one of those."

"I'm willing to bet my sweet potato pie that you're wrong and I'm right, Natha. I can see through folks. Comes from walking years and years on this earth, experiencing all sorts of pain. I can spot me an injured lapdog a mile away."

Maranatha usually trusted every word Zady spoke, but this time she knew Zady was wrong. The older woman always tried to see the good in things, but Maranatha was sure that if you peeled away Georgeanne's surface, you'd find a Doberman.

They walked together, neither talking.

Something worried Maranatha, but she was afraid to bring it up. "Zady?" she finally asked.

"Yeah?"

"Are you doing okay?"

"Of course, Natha. Why do you ask?"

"With you not having a job and all, I've worried about you."

Zady laughed. "Oh, child. We's fine. God's been good. Pray for us, will you?"

"I will. I promise."

On her way back to the table, she scanned the groups for Charlie but couldn't find him. *I hope he doesn't call me a poodle.*

Denim approached Maranatha. "Hey there, Natha. How are you?"

She sighed. *Other than having a wicked stepmother?* "Fine," she said.

"You don't look fine."

"My hair," she said.

"No, it suits you, I think. Are you sure you're fine?"

"Yeah. I'm hungry." Maranatha wished she had what Camilla called a poker face. She knew her readable face gave away far more than she wished it would. Lord knew how many secrets folks detected through Maranatha's eyes and the curve of her mouth.

"You ever hear from Camilla?" Denim motioned to some nylon-strapped folding chairs under the wide embrace of a pecan tree, and they sat down. From this vantage point, Maranatha could see the church, the brown hill behind it, and the very top of a small water tower.

"Not much. Why?"

Denim rested his hands behind his head. "Oh, it's nothing. She's talking weird, that's all."

"We *are* talking about Camilla here, right? My rhyming friend? When has she *not* talked weird?"

Denim laughed, and Maranatha joined him, in spite of her earlier foul mood.

"She's talking about things like male dominance and oppression, about divine goddesses freeing women to be all they want to be. And she won't touch meat. Not a lick."

"She's going through a stage." Maranatha tried to say it with confidence, but the words tasted flat and dry on her tongue, like melba toast.

"I know it, but I don't have to like it. Makes Rose cry a river. Says she's lost her baby to communists — or liberals. Do you think you could talk some sense into her during Thanksgiving break?"

"I could try, but you know as well as I do that no one gives Camilla a talking-to. She's her own person." *And she's drifting away from us all.*

Denim stood. "Looks like it's time for food." He slumped away toward the feasting tables.

Maranatha watched him walk. Watched how his gait lacked kick and rhythm, one long foot plodding in front of the other. When she first met him, she thought him a brave knight, able to take on wily Burl politics with inexhaustible valor. Now he seemed wounded, more vulnerable. She'd needed Denim years ago, needed him to save her life. And he did, with a gallant clashing of knife and shield. She didn't realize until now that his shield had gaps and that Denim was walking around with a knife through his heart, the kind only wayward children can thrust.

All of Mt. Moriah gathered around the two feast tables and grabbed hands, while Bishop Renny thanked the good Lord for sunshine, food, and fellowship. Uncle Zane, Georgeanne, and Maranatha were the only white folks there, so Georgeanne made it a point to stand between Maranatha and her husband, her white shields. She seemed to have something against holding a brown hand.

Charlie sidled in next to Maranatha. "Like your hair," he whispered.

Maranatha shivered. And smiled. And then turned red. She couldn't tell if he was teasing or genuine. "Thanks."

He squeezed her hand as they prayed and let his touch linger after the "amen."

Georgeanne heaped piles of food on her plate. Zane spooned measured helpings of a few things, careful not to let any one food touch the other; it was his way.

"I didn't expect real meat, leastways not as good as this. I'm so glad y'all don't eat Spam," Georgeanne said to Zady, who smiled next to her, mischief dancing in her brown eyes. Zady's family and Maranatha's "family" sat crammed next to each other, devouring the amazing food.

Brisket cooked to blessed perfection.

Smoked ribs that would make Red Heifer green with envy.

Greens so green they'd make you sing.

Baked squash smothered in brown sugar and nuts.

Jell-O cottage cheese salad with bits of pineapple.

Molasses-baked beans with bacon and onions.

Iceberg salad with radishes and carrots.

Deviled eggs (that had been labeled "angeled eggs" in case Satan wanted the credit).

Turkey injected with Cajun spices.

Macaroni salad, creamy with mayonnaise.

Fried chicken with crispy skin.

Buttermilk biscuits lathered in honey butter.

Homemade pickles.

Cornbread with tiny kernels suspended throughout.

Georgeanne made *mm-mm-mm* noises as she put each bite of food in her mouth, like she was surprised that such good cooking could come from Mt. Moriah's congregation. She kept circling back to a pile of meat in the center of her plate. "This here meat, Zady. Amazing. What is it?"

Zady kicked Maranatha under the table and smiled. "Would you like the recipe?"

"Absolutely." She washed the last bit down with a gulp of tea. "Where would I find this in the store?"

"Well, it's a delicacy, really."

Maranatha could see Zady was ready to burst with laughter.

Georgeanne smiled. "I'm all for delicacy. That's why I like all that fancy French food. Is this French?"

"Could be. M'not sure." Zady swallowed what must've been a laugh.

Raymond opened his mouth to speak but was hushed by Zady's firm hand on his arm.

Charlie looked up at the sky, a smile playing at the corner of his lips. For a tiny moment, Maranatha wanted to kiss that corner.

Uncle Zane dissected his brisket, pulling strand upon strand away from the larger piece until it sat in a heap like curled noodles. For once, Georgeanne didn't cut his meat, humiliate him.

Georgeanne twirled her fork in the air in lazy circles while she chewed. Food in her mouth, she warbled, "The suspense is killing me, Zady. Spit it out."

"Calf fries." Zady's family ruptured laughter.

Georgeanne looked at the laughing family, a smile painted Mona Lisa–like on her bewildered face. "Well, then, it's veal, I suppose. I like veal."

Maranatha looked away, tears in her eyes from the laughter wanting to escape.

"Fried calf testicles," Uncle Zane said in scarcely more than a whisper.

Georgeanne's eyes rounded. A hand flew to her mouth. She tried to stand, but she was sitting in the center of the picnic table bench and couldn't escape. Charlie, Zady, and Raymond stood at once, pulling leg over bench, clearing a route.

"The bathroom! Where's the bathroom?"

"Oh, we don't have facilities like that. The outhouse is a few paces behind the church," Charlie said.

Maranatha almost corrected Charlie's words but decided it would be more interesting not to. The outhouse had been there a hundred years or so from when the land was a farm — forty-odd years before Mt. Moriah bought it. Folks only used it in emergencies, like when Zady weeded the grounds but the church was locked. It was most certainly a last resort. Smelled to high heaven, it did.

Maranatha thought Uncle Zane would follow his wife, but he didn't. He forked his pile of stringy brisket, then his biscuit, followed by macaroni salad. Zady laughed while Raymond scolded her. "You shouldn't have told her the truth," he said, but the way he said his words seemed more like, *That was the funniest thing I've seen all year.*

Charlie wiped his mouth and stood. "Natha, you want to take a walk with me?"

Maranatha's stomach hiccupped with joy. She glanced at Uncle Zane, but he didn't look up — too busy forking unruly greens into his mouth. "Sure."

"I didn't want to spend my day with you around them," he said.

"Me neither."

They walked a usual path, down the hill where the T intersection beckoned left toward town or right toward the lake. They turned right and curved around, following the paved road until it crunched gravel beneath their feet.

"The lake?" Charlie reached to take Maranatha's hand, but she shied away.

"Sure." *Why can't I seem to do anything right?* She fought the voices in her head. One said, "What're you waiting for? Hold his hand, you idiot." The other whispered, "He's like any other man, and you know too well what that means. He wants parts of you. He wants *all* of you, not merely your hand." Maranatha shook her head, hoping to quiet the argument raging there.

"Hey, Natha."

"Yeah?" She placed her hands to her sides, ready to take his hand if he offered it again.

"You going to homecoming this year?"

"What makes you think that? You know I'm not one for dancing."

"Just curious." Charlie fumbled with his hands, picked a hangnail, then placed them back in his pocket.

"Why? I thought you knew me better than that." The lake appeared in front of them, sparkling and wet, while the smell of fall swirled around them in a lazy breeze.

"I don't know," Charlie said, hands still in pockets.

From behind, Maranatha heard a vehicle sputter rocks under tires. She turned. A red truck rambled toward them.

Maranatha screamed. *He's found me. The man in the red truck. Just like General! Hunting me!*

Charlie hugged her shoulders with both arms while the red truck crawled by. A young boy stuck his head out the window and waved.

"Calm down, Natha, it's not even going fast, didn't come close to us at all. You okay?"

She shrugged off his arms, wishing she could shrug the memory of that leering man, the hot, wet feel of his hand on her thigh. "Yeah, I'm fine. It took me by surprise is all."

In silence, they walked to the end of the dock. Their place. Without words, they took off their shoes and socks and dangled their feet into the lukewarm water.

Maranatha tried to think of other things, tried to act normal. She made circles with her toes. In the distance a fish jumped.

"What is it, Charlie?" *If I ask him questions, my mind will wander from the memory.* Maranatha watched the lake ripple in front of her, wondering how deep it went and what Georgeanne would think if she jumped in.

"It would bother me if you went with someone, that's all." Charlie placed his hand next to hers — a millimeter away.

She enjoyed its proximity. She wanted to hold it. She

wanted to slap it. Caught in a tornado of swirling thoughts that connected Charlie to the likes of General and the red-truck man, she couldn't decide. *Should I take it? Or run away?* She forced herself to focus on what Charlie had just said. "Is that it?"

"Yep." He crossed his arms over his chest.

She traced the line of his jaw with her eyes and suddenly hated General and the red-truck man for tainting Charlie so. She hated that she lived in fear, spooked like an unloved cat when she was around any boy—all because of a few. Anger replaced fear, followed by determination. *Next time his hand's free, I'm grabbing it.* "Don't worry about it, okay? I have no desire to go to some high-falutin' dance with some corn-fed boy. It's *not* going to happen."

Charlie turned toward her, resting his hands beside him.

Maranatha covered his hand with hers. She swallowed. A stab of electricity warmed her back. She wanted to look into his eyes, but couldn't.

"I guess I need to know where we stand. Are we a couple, Natha?" He looked right into her eyes, but she looked away, removing her hand.

No. Don't ask me that. Wasn't it enough to touch your hand? Maranatha made more circles in the water with her feet, round and round for seconds upon seconds while her stomach fussed.

They sat there a long time, he now leaning back on strong arms, she wetting her feet. She didn't want to break the silence for fear that if it was broken, she'd have to speak words. And she didn't know which words would fly out. Would it be, "I love you, Charlie," or, "I hate the sight of you"? Best to keep it quiet. Words weren't trustworthy.

"Natha, you have to say something."

More circles.

"C'mon."

"Charlie?"

"Yeah, I'm listening."

What do I say? I have no idea what to say. "I'm afraid." There, she'd said it. Out there in the open. It was the God's honest truth.

"I know that, Natha. Have known it . . . for years."

What?

"I know *why* you're scared."

What? Panic seized her stomach. She placed a hand to her mouth just in case.

"But it happened so long ago, and it wasn't like you even knew him."

Maranatha stood, looking down on Charlie. Wondering if Zady had told him about General or if he'd found out on his own. Wondering how he saw her now—dirty, filthy, violated, used. Wondering how many folks knew. Did everyone at the picnic know her secret? Did Uncle Zane tell Georgeanne? She looked up, spying menacing leaves tinted slightly brown from the autumn cool. *Did Zady tell Charlie about the red-truck man too?*

Charlie grabbed her arm. "It's okay. Really."

Maranatha fought his grip loose. "It will never be okay, Charlie. Not now." She freed her forearm and lost her balance, falling backward toward the lake. Air greeted her backside, followed by the shocking welcome of warm lake water. She slipped deeper into the water as wet clothes clung to her body. From below she could see Charlie kneeling at the dock, peering in, a concerned look on his face. She descended further until Charlie looked like an indistinct lump.

In a moment, her lungs scolded her, screeching for air. As much as she wanted to escape the likes of Charlie who *knew* her terrible secret, the hysteria in her tightening chest forced her to swim upward, toward light, toward Charlie. Who *knew*.

She broke through the water's skin like a thrashing cat, groping for air.

Charlie reached a hand toward her.

She swam away.

"Natha, don't be doing that. We're best friends. Don't you remember our last talk here?"

"It was a mistake," she breathed. And she meant it. In that second between treading water and swimming, she remembered her mark — the mark General gave and the red-truck man saw as a green light to touch her. Now Charlie saw it. Who was to say he was any different from the red-truck man? That he wouldn't try something? She swam toward the shore until she could touch. Lily pads tangled around her while too-soft mud squished gooey between her toes.

"No, it wasn't a mistake." Charlie walked to where she fumbled ashore, her shoes in the hand she'd just held. "Here're your shoes. Come on out and let's talk. This is a big misunderstanding — "

Back on land, Maranatha grabbed her shoes and started walking, not bothering to look back. She tried to think of words that would keep Charlie away from her, to keep him from exploiting her mark, so she went for his jugular. "Misunderstanding? Is that what you call it? The only misunderstanding is that you *thought* we were friends." She stomped away toward church, not caring if he followed, not worrying about Georgeanne's inevitable *tsking*.

She found Uncle Zane and Georgeanne standing by the Cadillac, ready to leave, Zady extending a whole pie to Georgeanne. Shouts from a three-legged race filled the air.

"Land sakes, what in heaven's name happened to you, Maranatha?" Zady smiled, then covered her mouth. "Decided to take a swim, I see."

"I want to go home." Anger burned behind her eyes so hot, she could nearly see how scorched Zady'd become under her glare.

"Is something wrong, Natha?"

"Look in the mirror and ask yourself," she said, hating and relishing the sting.

By now Georgeanne and Uncle Zane sat stiff in the front seat, like crash dummies before a test. Maranatha walked around Zady, now pie-less, and *humphed* into the car, never meeting the bewildered woman's eyes.

Maybe her family really was the two statue people in the front seat.

Maybe it would never be anything else.

Twenty-One

COLUMBUS DAY WAS FIXING TO BE a peculiar day. Camilla's poem from last night played teasing games in Maranatha's head. A rose-shaped origami masterpiece held only these words:

A Perm by Any Other Name, it read. *A tragic but true couplet by Camilla Rose Salinger, girl of straight-hair persuasion.*

What's in a perm? That which we call a curl
By any other name would look as kinked.

In her room, Maranatha slipped the unfolded perm poem back into the recycled envelope. Camilla had taken to saving the rain forest one envelope at a time by carefully slitting its seams and refolding it outside in and regluing it. This envelope's first life had been sending solicitations about house siding.

A knock sounded downstairs.

At first Maranatha thought the brown-haired boy standing outside the front door, holding a pink rose, was part of some sick practical joke sent by Camilla in perfect comedic timing, but she soon realized he was serious.

She'd met him briefly during a debate tournament.

Maranatha had discovered he went to Burl High, across town. He liked drama and writing and especially playing the violin, an odd talent for Burl, where tackling and scrimmaging proved real manliness. Maybe that — and her belief she'd never see him again — is why a tinge of flirtation rose to her lips when she'd met him. She'd joked and averted her eyes, only to return them to his gaze for as long as she could think the word *ubiquitous*. It had been Camilla's number one flirting tip: "If you hold his gaze as long as it takes to think *ubiquitous*, kiss you, he must," she'd said. Maranatha was sure Camilla didn't even know what the word meant. She was always looking words up, writing them down, and promptly forgetting their meanings, which helped only during Scrabble, when she killed Maranatha every time.

It was strange to meet a white kid who attended school in her same town. She'd become so accustomed to the brown faces in her district that she plum forgot white kids went to school in Burl too.

The rose-carrying boy stood awkwardly on her front porch. His eyes scurried back and forth, almost as if he were watching a tennis match between Road Runner and Speedy Gonzales.

He swallowed.

She watched his Adam's apple bobble.

He cleared his throat, still watching the invisible match.

One more breath.

"Maranatha," he finally said, "I wanted to know if . . . you'd like to go to the homecoming dance with me next Saturday."

She knew it would be the perfect revenge if she could just say yes. But fear kept her mouth shut.

"I know it's last-minute," he said. "If you have other plans, I understand."

"Sure, Charlie, I'd love to," she heard herself say, though she questioned her sanity. Was life that simple? Exchange one Charlie who knew too many terrible secrets with another Charlie who knew nothing? Safe.

At least she hoped so.

Besides, she could tell Camilla about this Charlie. Violin Charlie, she'd call him. And the other Charlie would be sorry he ever mentioned knowing. Everything was tied up neatly with this one yes.

She knew Georgeanne was not coming home for a while yet, said she had shopping to do, and Lord knew that took forever and a year, or at least until late afternoon. The coast was clear. "You want some tea?" Behind Violin Charlie, she saw the pecan tree. Charlie's body blocked her view of its trunk so that the browning leaves looked like a lion's mane around his head. For a moment, she worried. Would he be like General? Or the red-truck man? She barely knew him, for goodness' sake. She swallowed, trying to force the fear back down.

"Well, yeah. I guess so," he said. He handed her the rose. "It's for you."

"Thanks." She swallowed again. What if his giving her a flower meant she owed him something?

Holding the flower reminded her of when her old friend Eliot initiated friendship in the form of a purple and yellow pansy so many years ago. It made her sad remembering. She wished Eliot was still planting violets on earth.

Violin Charlie sat on the porch swing. Maranatha ran inside and opened the cupboard, only to find Georgeanne's fancy schmancy glasses. She ran outside. "Charlie, do you mind waiting a little longer?"

He shook his head.

"I need to grab something. I'll be right back, okay?"

"Sure thing."

She took the stairs three at a time, ran down the hall, and

flung open the door to her room. She grabbed two plain, clear glasses from Uncle Zane's former collection and ran back downstairs, huffing.

These are better glasses. There was something humiliating about serving her guest on her porch with Georgeanne's glasses. This way she felt more genuine. She poured sweet tea into her glasses and took them outside, handing Charlie one. "To homecoming," she said.

"To homecoming," he replied. They clanked glasses and forced smiles.

She swallowed again, hoping the fear tickling her would pass away, but instead it lodged in her throat like a too-big vitamin. *I can't believe I said yes to homecoming. And why did I offer him tea?*

The red Thunderbird pulled up.

Georgeanne. Maranatha thanked Jesus for that pesky woman right then and there.

She got out of the car and spied them. "Well, I declare. This house is a welcome sight after all that shopping. My feet are plum wore out, that's for sure," she yelled. She opened the trunk and pulled out some shopping bags.

Go about your business. No need to chitchat. Just put away your parcels and be done with it.

Charlie stood as Georgeanne disobeyed Maranatha's silent directive and stopped on the porch, bags upon bags hanging like gypsy bracelets from her wrists.

"Well, now, who is this we have here? Aren't you handsome!" She shot a smile to Maranatha. "A vast improvement over the last boyfriend."

Maranatha could see Charlie's ears pinking. She tried to think of something to say to cut the awkwardness, but she knew this was one of those times in life when no amount of nouns and verbs could remedy the embarrassment.

Georgeanne plopped her parcels on the porch decking. "And what's your name, son?"

"Charlie." He extended his hand her way.

She sandwiched his hand between her two. "So polite too! I'm Georgeanne, by the way." She gave Maranatha a wide-eyed look. "Charlie. Hmmm. Seems to be a popular name with Maranatha, I'd say." Her grip on his hand remained steady. "And why are you here, Charlie?"

Charlie slinked his hand away from her lingering embrace. "Only a visit, ma'am. All in good propriety, I assure you."

Georgeanne pulled a wicker chair near the porch swing. "I'd like some tea, Maranatha." She looked directly at the two unmatched glasses sweating circles on the side table. "In my own glass, please."

"Don't you need to put those things away?"

"They can wait."

Maranatha ran inside and poured tea into one of Georgeanne's crystal glasses.

Georgeanne was talking to Charlie. "All this stuff is for the new house, you see. We're moving. To your side of town, I gather. In Brooke Estates."

"That's where I live, ma'am. It's a great neighborhood."

She reached over and grabbed his hand. "See, I knew I'd like you, Charlie. Maybe you can speak some sense into Maranatha here. She wants to stay in this horrid house with families of mice and peeling paint. It ain't proper, if you ask me."

I'd live anywhere, in a hovel, if it meant I could live far from you. Why'd I welcome the sight of you a moment ago?

Violin Charlie gave Maranatha a pleading look, something akin to, *Get me the heck out of here.*

Think. She looked at his silver Honda Civic parked in front of Georgeanne's red car. She picked at a fingernail. But no escape plan formed in her mind.

"I see you have a car. Very nice."

"My dad bought it for me, on account of my grades," Charlie said.

Maranatha stood, about to declare her need for homework, or its need for her, but Georgeanne blurted, "You should take Maranatha on a drive through your neighborhood. Maybe with you as the tour guide, she'd take a liking to it."

Charlie said nothing.

"Go ahead, Maranatha doesn't bite. You'd be doing me a favor."

"I have homework," Maranatha said.

"Oh, for heaven's sake. Just take a drive. You need to get used to the idea of living over there." Georgeanne picked up her parcels.

Charlie pulled out his keys, looked at them. "I guess it wouldn't hurt. What do you say?"

This wasn't exactly what she had in mind when she wanted to escape, but faced with the choice between a meddling Georgeanne and a violin-playing A-student, she chose the student. "All right, but just for a little bit."

Georgeanne opened the front door and turned back toward them. "A date. Maranatha, isn't this your first real date? Should I get the camera out? Didn't I tell you that once you got your hair permed, you'd finally land a man?"

I think I'll die right now.

"It was nice meeting you," Charlie said. He kept his hands in his pockets while backing down the stairs.

"You too, Charlie. Come back around again, you hear?"

It was fine to ride in the *other* Charlie's beat-up white truck. She had a few fears there, but at least they were knowable. She knew Charlie, knew his mama, Zady. Sitting in the Honda Civic next to a boy she'd met through debate tournaments worried her. Would Violin Charlie be like the red-truck man? *Why did I agree to this?*

Violin Charlie got in, buckled his seatbelt, and thwapped the tree-shaped air freshener dangling from the rearview mirror. "If I do that, it smells better," he said.

Maranatha smiled. "Thanks."

He started the car. "No problem at all. Mind if I turn on some music?"

"No."

He turned on the radio, dialing between stations until he landed on quiet music. "It's the only music that pleases Jesus," he said.

She laughed. *Pleases Jesus* would be a perfect Camilla word combo.

"What's so funny?" He maneuvered the car in a tight U-turn.

From her window, Maranatha saw Georgeanne waving from the porch. She didn't wave back. "Oh, nothing. The music reminded me of a funny friend."

"Well, this is serious music, Maranatha. About faith. And trust. And holiness." He turned left at the Loop and headed toward what Georgeanne called the "good" part of town. "I heard you were a Christian."

"Yeah, of course," she said, but her words sounded small. How did he know that? And what difference did it make? Was knowing Jesus some sort of get-to-ride-in-his-car permission question? She hoped his knowing Jesus meant he didn't try things with girls.

Violin Charlie let out a long breath. Maranatha could smell it. Tea breath.

The radio sang, "Jesus. Jesus. I'm calling for Jesus. He's on the line. Every time. Oh, Jesus."

"Good," he said. "Mind if I ask you a question?"

"No."

"Have you been baptized?"

Bishop Renny had chatted with her briefly about baptism, but she hadn't thought it important. Truth be told, the thought of being dunked in front of people frightened her. So she hadn't taken the plunge. Yet. She didn't want to admit that she hadn't. A bit of shame crept into her heart.

The radio blared, "It's time. It's time. To trust the Lord. To take that leap of faith."

Oh, great.

"Maranatha? Well, have you?"

"Not yet," she said. Hearing Violin Charlie say her name with the Mara connected to Natha made her miss the other Charlie. It occurred to her that she loved being called Natha, loved how Mara, which meant "bitter," had been conveniently eradicated from her name. Zady's Charlie had renamed her, a beautiful gesture of friendship he probably never even realized. One thing was sure, he never asked questions like Violin Charlie did. He wouldn't dare.

"It's a shame. You're missing out on fullness. On power. On true life. Getting baptized makes you a *real* Christian."

He slowed the Civic, his words dangling in midair as he took a left into a well-to-do neighborhood. "I can take you to my pastor. He's got all the important baptism verses on one sheet of paper. He knows 'em all too, by heart."

"Thanks," she said, but didn't know what else to say.

"You gotta obey, Maranatha. Gotta get yourself baptized."

She watched the porch-pillared homes go by like the slow pan of a movie camera. Trimmed yards, nary a weed in sight, sported too-green grass. It was as if the neighborhood had an unwritten gardening code to be certain every yard conformed to the others. Two trees each. Front flowerbeds surrounded by man-made pavers that made the flora look like it was captured behind a castle-walled moat. Four crepe myrtles planted an equal distance from each other across the span of each home. The sameness of it all made Maranatha shudder. "You like living here?"

"Yeah. It's a real safe community. We have barbecues, block parties, everything. You'll love living here." He turned into a half-circle driveway. "Here we are. Home."

Maranatha opened her door before Violin Charlie could get to her.

"I'm supposed to do that." He shut the car door and took her elbow, escorting her to the front door through tall white columns, reminding her of the burnt house whose pillars had been the only thing standing. It seemed like years ago now, the day she asked Jesus to show her He loved her, the day she and regular Charlie took shelter from an angry tornado, the day she found and lost a love ring from Jesus, the day Zady wore the coat of prejudice — a coat she shed for Jesus' sake. *What am I doing here?* But then she remembered the two-faced side of Zady, the Zady who probably told Charlie her secrets. For a moment, this new world of wealth and yard uniformity felt safe.

Two imposingly tall doors with a berry wreath on each shouted wealth to Maranatha.

"Hey, Charlie?"

"Yeah." He pushed through the doors, revealing a two-story entryway with an oversized cherub statue sitting coyly on a pillar, smack-dab in the center of the foyer. A skylight shot sun on the cherub's happy head that was wreathed in fake ivy and pink ribbons. The house echoed under their footsteps. Empty.

That they were alone rattled Maranatha.

"I need to be getting back," she said.

"But you just got here. Let me show you around first." He walked into the expansive living area. She followed. Floral wallpaper screamed country. Matching couches sat in quiet formation around a large pine coffee table, issues of *Southern Living* neatly fanned across its top. A two-story fireplace stood majestically on the left of the room, flanked by river rocks. "Isn't it beautiful? My mom's an interior designer."

"What's your dad do?" *Must be a doctor or something.*

"Don't you know? He's the judge. Been so since the other one died years ago."

Does he know that dead judge was my father? Did his father know mine? Are they the same sort of man? A tremor of terror shot through Maranatha. "I need to be getting back. Your house . . . it's real nice."

Violin Charlie smiled. "I understand. You're a right and proper Christian girl, aren't you? Don't want to have anyone suspicious of you being in my house alone. I respect that."

She expected him to morph into General right then, to grab her and force her down to the tiled floor while the cherub smiled above them. Instead, he stuck out his arm, pointing toward the doorway. "Let's go."

She let out a breath. *Thank You, Jesus.* "Thanks."

He shut the front doors and looked up at the house. "It's a beauty, isn't it? Do you know where your new home is? I can drive you by on our way out."

"No, that's okay. Just take me home. I have homework." She walked down the perfectly straight cement path toward the Civic. An errant buttercup, defying the lawn service, shot up on her left. She picked it, then twirled it between her fingers. "I'm not planning on moving, anyway."

"But your mom said—" He opened her door. He stood above her now, blue eyed and sincere.

"She's *not* my mom. If you want to know the truth, she's my stepaunt."

He put up his hands as if in surrender and shut the door.

Once in, he started the car. "It sounds like you need some inner healing."

"What?"

"Inner healing. Folks pray over you, and God heals you. Sounds like you're bitter."

Bitter? Why did you have to go and use that word? How much do you know about me? Who made you my spiritual guide? Has Zady been talking to you? Telling secrets to the likes of you? "I'm fine. Really. But I appreciate your concern." She looked at the buttercup lying on her jeans now and remembered his flower greeting—a pink rose. "When will you pick me up for the dance?"

"Next Saturday at five o'clock sharp. I'll be wearing a tux with a pink tie and cummerbund."

"Pink?" Maranatha looked over at him now. Dark brown hair. Long eyelashes. Strong jaw. White button-down shirt. Levis. He was handsome, that is for a guy who spouted strange religious talk and wore pastels.

"My mom's idea. She says it's all the rage right now. Anyway, you might want to wear a pink dress so we match."

"Oh."

"Is that a problem?" He looked at her now, his eyes holding hers longer than *ubiquitous*, too much longer.

She swallowed. Couldn't talk.

Maranatha looked out the window. "No, not at all. I'll have to go shopping, I guess."

"Don't you like to shop? My mom's near addicted to it."

"Not really."

"I thought all girls loved to shop."

She watched the golden arches of McDonalds rush by. It had been the first fast-food place to grace Burl's Loop, attracting quite a line of cars through its drive-through two years ago. Now it sat idle, down the road from Dairy Queen, Wendy's, and Pizza Hut that stood proudly in fellowship on the corner, a gas station completing the quartet.

Charlie cleared his throat. "Maranatha? Did you hear me?"

"What?"

"I said, I thought all girls liked to shop."

"Not me. Not so much."

"Interesting."

Why is it interesting? Because I don't fit your weird Christian girl mold? Or because I won't quite fit in with the pillared-house crowd? What exactly is interesting? "Yep, that's me. Interesting." She wondered how they'd find things to talk about at the dance. And then she realized she'd *have* to dance.

"Charlie?"

"Yeah."

"Do you *like* to dance?"

"I can't say."

"Why not?"

He kept his mouth shut and his eyes on the road. He swallowed hard.

"What do you mean?" She pushed a curl behind her ear.

"*Footloose*," he said, finally.

"The movie?"

He nodded.

"What about it?"

"I'm like Kevin Bacon's friend."

"A rebel?"

"No, not like his *girlfriend*. Rebelling's what Satan did. It's just, well, I want to dance. But I can't." He stopped at a stoplight and looked over at her.

A horrible thought took residence in her mind. *What if he's one of those boys who takes advantage of a girl at a dance?* Maranatha held her stomach. *Oh, Lord, I hope not.* She looked at him. "Why can't you?"

He blushed. "I'm embarrassed. My feet can't keep up with the beat in my mind. A terrible thing for a musician, don't you think?"

"No, not really."

"So that's why I don't think we'll dance at the dance. I hope you're not disappointed."

"Not at all."

"We can still listen to the music and eat stuff."

Relief swept through her. She smiled, almost laughing. "Okay."

"Thanks," he said, his lips pressed into a wide, horizontal line.

He turned right toward Maranatha's home.

She put a hand on his arm.

He jumped. "What?"

"Could you take me to the courthouse instead?"

"Why?"

"I'm meeting someone."

"But it's closed. It's Columbus Day, remember? My dad's out on a deer lease with his friends, shooting critters. Mom's out shopping the sales. No one's working today."

"Well, just the same, could you drop me off there? I have a feeling she'll be there." *I do hope you're there, Miss-Nichols-who-sounds-so-professional. I need to get working on this house thing.*

"Sure. No problem. You want me to stay and wait?"

"No, that's okay. You can drop me off."

He stopped directly in front of the beige courthouse. It was the kind of building that loomed, like it was meant to be built on a hill above a town. Its dome hollered Greek to Maranatha, making it look out of place in Burl, like a cowgirl toting a Gucci bag.

Maranatha kept staring at it, forgetting to get out of the car before Mr. Gentleman let her out. He opened her door.

"Here you are," he said. "In front of an empty building."

"Thanks, V—" She caught herself in time. He probably wouldn't want to be called Violin Charlie. "Charlie."

"No problem." He faced her, his eyes trying to catch her wayward gaze. "I'll see you next Saturday at five."

"Five it is," she said, looking above his eyes at his perfectly groomed eyebrows. No more *ubiquitous* glances. *Maybe I'll suddenly get sick.*

He drove away like Uncle Zane—slow and cautious. *That Violin Charlie's a paradox. Plays the violin, but can't dance. Parroting words his preacher probably taught him, things he likely doesn't even understand.*

She stood in front of the wide steps of the courthouse and shivered. Even though an eighty-degree mugginess seeped into her, she shook. Maranatha had made it a point to never come to this place. Sure, the town extended outward from the too-tall structure like spokes of a wheel. She'd pedaled past it many times like Miss Gulch hustling off with Toto — fast and purposeful. But she had never gone inside.

The father she'd never known used to pound a gavel here. Used to connive and banter. She'd never seen his face, not in person. Only saw him in faded photographs she found buried underneath peach crates in the attic. She and those photographs exchanged stares for a time, until she took the sharp end of her geometry compass and poked his eyes out. Evil man.

A large plaque stood like a rock to her right. It read, *Erected after the devastating 1913 fire that destroyed its predecessor. Built in the Renaissance Revival style by W. V. Butts. Unusual for its brick-over-stone façade and high-topped dome. Considered one of the prettiest courthouses in East Texas.*

Maranatha ran her finger over the word *prettiest* and wondered how a building could be described that way. Stately, yes. Solid. But not pretty.

The door at the top of the stairs opened, spitting out a young woman with long, straight, blonde hair. She clipped down the stairs and stopped right in front of Maranatha.

"You need something? Because it's Columbus Day. We're closed." She seemed cross, at least her words sounded that way, but her eyes smiled.

"Miss Nichols?"

The woman shifted folders from one hand to the other and whipped her head to one side to clear the blonde hair covering half her face. "Yes, that's me."

"I called you. A while ago. About some legal papers."

"Lots of people call. Can you give me a little more?"

Maranatha didn't know what to say. The woman in front of her did wear a power suit like she'd imagined when they first spoke — dark blue with a softening pink blouse. She had a pen poked behind her ear, car keys in one hand, files shifted in the other. She looked beyond Maranatha, then rested her eyes on her.

"Um, well, I did hang up on you."

Miss Nichols' eyes got larger. "Oh, yeah, I remember. You're here to see me? Today?"

Maranatha suddenly realized how stupid it all looked. She

looked like a reporter waiting around the courthouse for an exclusive. She held no papers in her hands, not even a pencil and notepad. Why did she come here without her papers? "Yes, ma'am. But I remembered that I forgot the papers. Is there any way we can schedule an appointment next week? After school?"

"What could you possibly need me for? How does a young girl like you fall into legal trouble?" She sat on the steps and patted the place next to her. "Sit. Tell me about it."

Maranatha sat, welcoming the cold brick. "It's my house," she said. "I don't want to lose it."

"That's something for your parents to worry about." She sighed a deep sigh, the kind that exhales a world of stress. "I'm so tired of this job. Parents making their kids deal with bankruptcies, using them as front people so I won't go after them. Makes me sick to my stomach."

"But, it's not like — "

She held up her hand. "You don't need to tell me. I know what this is about. Your parents wrote some hot checks. The bank's going to take your house. They send you to me for the feel-sorry-for factor."

"No, it's not that."

"Then what is it?"

"Do you really want to know?" Maranatha shifted to face Miss Nichols.

The lawyer set her papers aside and faced Maranatha. "Sure. Tell me."

Maranatha spilled her whole story, how the former judge was her father, how she never really knew him or remembered much of her mama. She told of Nanny Lynn and Aunt Elma, her life before Burl in the pastures of Little Pine. How when Nanny Lynn died, she and Aunt Elma moved to Burl, only to have cancer take Aunt Elma. She didn't say a word about General or Officer Gus. She described the big white house, silent Uncle Zane, and busybody Georgeanne.

"And now she's fixin' to sell our house — my house — and move me to the other side of town in the middle of my senior year!" Maranatha realized she was waving her hands. She sat on them.

"Well, that's quite an amazing story." Miss Nichols removed the pen from her ear and jotted a few words on a manila folder.

"You don't believe me."

"If you had told me this before I moved to Burl, I wouldn't have, but now that I've walked these streets a few months, I know you're probably telling the truth. This is a crooked town, you know."

"I know."

Miss Nichols gathered up her files and stood. "So, you want me to save your house. You say it's paid for, and part of the property, if not all, is deeded to you?"

"Yes, I think so."

"Good. Bring me the papers next week, say a week from today, after school next Monday."

"Thanks, Miss Nichols."

"And another thing. Don't talk about this with anyone, okay? Your father still has a lot of friends in this town, even from the grave. I wouldn't want to see you hurt."

"Hurt?"

Miss Nichols leaned in closer, whispering. "Be careful with those papers. Don't let a soul see them."

Twenty-Two

ALL THAT WEEK MARANATHA THOUGHT ABOUT the papers. She'd taken them from her magazine hiding place and hidden them four more times. In the quiet of her room she pored over them, wondering what all the legal words meant, worried that personal disaster lived encoded on the pages.

She wrote a lengthy letter to Camilla about the papers and how she'd met a strong woman in Miss Nichols — Camilla would be proud — even though Miss Nichols didn't seem the type to emancipate her chest from evil bras. She even spilled the beans about Violin Charlie, about how she was thinking of ways to get out of homecoming. She told Camilla it was her duty to return to Burl for homecoming, even though Maranatha knew well enough that she'd have to wait until Thanksgiving to see her.

When Georgeanne found out about homecoming, she went all aflutter. "I'll buy you the pinkest, prettiest dress known to prom queens," she said, while Maranatha rolled her eyes. "And you'll have to order a pink boutonniere."

"What's that?" Maranatha wished Camilla would come over this moment to distract this woman from saying indecipherable French words she didn't understand.

"A flower for his lapel, silly. I'll call Mateer's right now and order it."

Maranatha had learned the word *gallivant* this week in honors English. She thought she'd never use that word in the real world until she saw Georgeanne gallivant down the hall to the phone, humming and swaying her hips to the rhythm.

Before she could escape down the hall and up the stairs, Georgeanne stopped her, putting a hand on the receiver. "Your mum. Did Charlie say he'd order you one for the game? It's a tradition, you know."

"No, he didn't. I'm not going to the game, just the dance. No need for a mum."

"What?" She removed her hand from the receiver. "Can you believe that, Jenny? The girl's not going to the game! Yes, of course make her one, the biggest, ribboniest mum you can concoct. Tomorrow? Great. You're a peach." She hung up.

"You can thank me by polishing the floors this weekend."

"Call me Cinderella," Maranatha said.

"Very funny. I suppose that makes me the wicked step-mother? Really, Maranatha — after what I've done for you, you ought to try to be more original."

"Exactly what *did* you do?" Maranatha mounted the stairs.

"I saved your dignity, that's what. You can't go to a Burl High homecoming game without a mum. You'll die of embarrassment."

Didn't she hear me say I'm not going to the game? Maranatha walked up a few stairs and turned around. "You want my opinion? Mums are a stupid tradition."

Georgeanne gasped.

"I mean, it probably started out nice enough. Girls wore school-colored chrysanthemums to the big game. Have you seen them lately? You can't even see the flower. It's all ribbons and teddy bear pins and charms. I don't need one."

Georgeanne put her hands on her hips. "I know we don't exactly get along, Maranatha Winningham, but I do expect respect around here. Trust me, you'll thank me for doing this."

"I'm so glad you're looking out for my . . . popularity."

"Next semester you'll be going to that school, thank God, away from that excuse for a school you're in now. I'm preparing you for that place. You're a pretty girl, you know. You should fit in fine. Maybe they'll even crown you homecoming queen." Georgeanne smiled.

"I'll be in college by the time homecomimg rolls around next year. I'm a senior, remember?"

"Oh, yes, silly me. Though it breaks my heart that you haven't had a normal high school experience so far, with a *normal* student body."

Maranatha held the stair rail. "Georgeanne?"

"Yes."

"Why'd you never have kids?" The moment it left her mouth, Maranatha regretted it, which surprised her. Truth was, she knew the answer — that Georgeanne had wanted nothing more than to have a passel of kids but her former husband, Jimmy, had said, "No thanks." She thought she'd gain an upper hand for once and experience the ecstasy of putting Mrs. Nosy Winningham in her place. Instead, she felt plain empty.

Tears graced Georgeanne's eyes. She turned and left the room without so much as a word, leaving Maranatha holding on to empty glory.

"She's going to pinkify me," Maranatha said to Old Mack the next day.

"Can't say I've ever heard of that word." Old Mack poked his front fours with a soggy toothpick.

"It means to make someone all froufrou."

"I see. And that's a bad thing?"

"It is for me." She sat on the high stool on the other side of Old Mack's counter, placed there for his customers to have a sit and a chat.

"You say you're going to homecoming?"

"Yes. This Saturday."

"With who?" He winked at her like he already knew.

"Charlie."

"Charlie?" Old Mack slapped his hand on the counter. "Well, land sakes. That's the best news I've heard all October. What does Zady think about that?"

"I don't know."

"Why not? She must be tickled."

Maranatha realized then that Old Mack *didn't* know. The whole town practically buzzed with the news that Charlie Baker, Judge Baker's son, had asked her to Burl High's homecoming. Strangers in line at Kroger smiled at her with knowing looks. Girls at school said, "Natha, you hooked yourself a keeper," as if Violin Charlie were some sort of prized catch. He didn't even play football, for goodness' sake.

"Zady doesn't know, Old Mack. It's not the Charlie you're thinking of."

"What?" Old Mack leaned forward.

"It's Charlie Baker, the judge's son. *He's* taking me to Burl's homecoming."

He twisted his beard. "What does your Charlie think of that?"

"Why would I know?" And really, why would she? She hadn't talked to Charlie or Zady since the Founder's Day picnic fiasco, though she missed them desperately.

"Oh, dear. A love spat. Tell me, Maranatha Winningham. What went wrong?"

"It's not what you think."

"What do you mean?"

"It's not because he's black, you know."

"Maranatha Winningham. How well do you know me?" He didn't wait for her to respond. "I know that. I know skin color don't mean a thing to you. Now, what's really the trouble?"

"I don't want to talk about it." And she didn't. Even with Old Mack. She twisted a more-relaxed curl around her finger and didn't catch the old man's gaze.

"Enough said. These things of the heart have a way of working themselves out anyway. I won't pry. How about a Coke?"

"Sure."

He swiveled around and opened an avocado-colored refrigerator, circa 1972, and pulled out a bottled Coke.

"I thought bottles were done for." Maranatha watched him as he pried the cap off with the side of his mouth.

"Nah, I can get these from Frank's Fuel. Coke tastes better in a bottle, in my opinion."

She took a long, cold drink and couldn't agree more. "Thanks."

"No problem at all. Now, tell me about this other Charlie."

"I call him Violin Charlie because, well, he plays the violin."

"That's interesting. So he plays a fancy fiddle."

"Yeah, at least that's what he told me. He's picking me up on Saturday at five. Georgeanne ordered him a boot-in-ear, or something like that. And she ordered me this hideous mum thing. It looks like a grand prize horseshow ribbon."

"Mums are important," he said, stone-faced. He spat into an

empty Coke bottle with perfect aim.

"Don't know why," she muttered.

"Georgeanne, she's a funny one. I know she's hard to get used to, but you have to understand her a bit to love her."

"Love her?" Maranatha took another drink.

"Well, she does love folks. In her own way. It may not look like love, leastways not in the way you or I might understand it, but it's love, plain as day."

"What do you mean? Meddling and snooping and saying mean things is love?"

"No. But giving is. Ever notice how she loves to give things?"

Maranatha nodded.

"Well, it's how she gives love. My advice? Take the mum and say thank you."

"You sound like Zady. Everyone's trying to make me like her." Maranatha stood. Her angry heart beat hard, like it was trying to escape her ribs. She wondered if she'd holler. She looked at Old Mack then. Studied his kind face. "Even you," she whispered. "Nobody understands what it's like to live with her. Not a one."

"That's a true statement. I ain't never walked around in your Nikes, Maranatha Winningham. Don't really know what your life's like. But I can tell you that holding grudges long past their prime makes 'em spoiled. Makes you spoiled."

She set the Coke on the counter and turned to leave.

"And Maranatha?"

She turned to see him holding the most hideous homecoming mum known to high school game watchers — purple and green ribbons with a dried-up flower in its center. When he lifted it, dust wafted from it, like it'd lived its former life on the set of *The Munsters*. "My gal, she gave it back to me before the homecoming game. Never went with me to the dance. My first love. My only love. I wish to God she'd taken it. Taken me. This is all I have left of her." He set it on the counter. "Don't let that happen. If someone gives you something, take it. With gratitude. There're enough broken hearts in the world; even Georgeanne has one. Best take it."

"Best take it" reverberated through her as she pedaled home. She decided to take the mum, although she didn't know how to take it with gratitude. Bishop Renny once preached about everyone's GF — Gratitude Factor. He said that the closer folks were to Jesus, the more thankful they became. Said you could measure a person's relationship to God by their whining. "The closest folks to Jesus are ones who say thank you a thousand times a day," he had said.

She turned the corner and headed down the tree-lined street toward home. The trees responded to the evening's nippy air by releasing a scattering of brown leaves. Maranatha breathed in Burl air, filling her lungs with the town's dashed hopes. Truth be told, she'd let her mind wander to all things homecoming rather than concentrate on what would get her out of this pathetic town. She'd let her studies take a backseat to frivolity.

One block away, she saw the familiar truck. Rusted white. Charlie, *her* Charlie, leaned against its bed. She slowed her pedaling. Fear hiccupped inside.

She rolled to a stop about ten feet away from him, far enough away to avoid having to look closely at him, but close enough to sense the power of his fiery eyes.

He took off his Texas Rangers hat and stood away from the truck, its bed no longer supporting him. "I hear you're going to homecoming."

She looked at her feet.

"I thought you said nothing could make you go to a dance with some corn-fed boy."

Maranatha put her hands in her pockets.

"Come on, Natha, it's me here. Talk to me."

She looked up to see red-rimmed eyes. Not fiery eyes. Hurt eyes. She wanted to pedal away. To another town. Another state. Another world. Away from sad eyes.

"It was all a big misunderstanding at the lake. I don't know what you're all mad about. I said that I understood. Isn't that what boyfriends are supposed to do? Understand?"

Not this. How could he even look at her knowing what he knew? And what did he want from her now that he did? Maranatha found her voice. "You don't understand, Charlie. Just saying you understand shows you don't." Anger fueled her tongue, the kind of anger carrying bile. "So, yeah, I'm going to homecoming. With another Charlie. A Charlie who actu-ally *does* understand me." The lie hissed through her teeth. She wished she had something to throw at him, like a ring or a necklace or a stack of love letters, but their love — if she could dare call it that — was not of the gift-giving, word-sharing sort. It was a comfortable, warm blanket of friendship, one that she flung off with such ferocity that it startled her.

"Well, at least he's white. That should make things comfort-able for you."

"What are you talking about, Charlie?"

"I think this misunderstanding thing is just a cover-up for how uncomfortable my color makes you feel."

"Color has nothing to do with it, and you know it."

"Do I?"

"You're being ridiculous."

Charlie didn't even look at her. Didn't say a word.

She wanted to take back all her words, wanted to pull them back, away from Charlie's hurt eyes, but she couldn't. It occurred to her that she wasn't even really angry at him. It was General she hated, General she wanted to hurt, and Charlie just happened to be in the way.

He opened the door to his truck, got in, put it in reverse, and backed out of her life. Probably forever.

Safely inside her room, she couldn't shed her shivers. *I'm a heartless, terrible wretch.*

She attended her guilt party a good twenty minutes before she started convincing herself of her own righteousness.

Charlie shouldn't have said all those things on the dock.

He did it to get something from me. Maybe he thinks I'm easy.

That's it. He wants me for my body, plain and simple.

Who cares if he's hurt? He hurt me first. He deserves it.

From far in the back of her head, she heard the words *eye for an eye.* She remembered when Jesus said those words, somewhere in the book of Matthew, where He told folks to pray for those who hurt you. Somewhere around there He said that to hate someone was like murder. Zady had shown her those verses years ago when she wrestled with hot anger toward her father. There were days when she let the anger fall away, like water poured out. Other days she nursed the anger until her head pounded, her heart recoiled.

And now she'd added more people to the list she struggled to forgive.

Georgeanne.

Charlie.

Zady.

Maranatha balled up on her bed, holding knees to chest. The spent pink rose on her nightstand, with its erect head of baby's breath, reminded her of the dandelion wish she'd made last summer — that Jesus would show her He loved her. Instead of granting her wish, He'd added hard people to love to her life. It didn't make much sense. Why would He send her difficult folks when all she needed was His embrace? A tangible piece of hard evidence that He was there and that He loved her?

She picked up the picture of Mama. "Did you know Jesus loved you? Did you have a hard time forgiving? Did you have a bitter heart?"

Mama grinned back, a frozen smile that seemed to say, *Yes*.

Or was it, *No*?

Twenty-Three

SHE ALMOST CALLED VIOLIN CHARLIE THAT week. Almost made up a sickness and called the whole thing off. But the way Georgeanne preened and hollered about the dance forced her to forget about contracting a disease and actually go through with it. If she didn't, she'd never hear the end of it.

Maranatha stood in front of her mirror, examining her appearance.

"Your hair." Georgeanne barged into Maranatha's room, all the while shaking her empty head. "You're not going to the dance in *that* hair, are you?"

"Why not?" Maranatha looked again at her hair in the small mirror above her dresser. It looked like it had the last several days, a permanent wave that (thankfully!) had relaxed into loopier ringlets.

"Why not? Because you're my —"

I'm your what? Stepniece?

Georgeanne straightened. "I'm your friend."

Let's not say things we don't mean, now.

Maranatha pulled her hair back, securing it with a black ponytail holder. "How's that? Will that do?"

"Absolutely not. Would you please let me work with it?"

Georgeanne walked toward her, brush in hand, like a B-rated movie ghoul, ready to attack.

"No way. It's my hair. I'll deal with it."

"At least let me call Danielle. She'll do something gorgeous."

"I don't know."

"What do you mean, you don't know? Land sakes. First you made me take back the pink chiffon wonder dress I bought for you. You would've looked downright princessy in that beauty. And now you're refusing Danielle's help? What's wrong with you?"

Maranatha weighed Georgeanne's advice. If she called Danielle, then perhaps Georgeanne would stop prattling on about her hair, her dress, her anything. If she didn't let Georgeanne do her thing, she'd be pestered for the next three hours as she readied for the dance. "Sure, sounds like a great idea." For a moment, she congratulated herself, knowing Old Mack would be proud. Maranatha had allowed Georgeanne to give something. From the surface, it appeared as though Maranatha was letting bits of Georgeanne in, that she actually liked the perfectly groomed woman.

Georgeanne left the room. Where chattering had filled every empty space, silence now gobbled it up, making Maranatha smile.

Silence.

She looked at the three dresses laid neatly on the bed like headless cartoon women flattened by a pavement roller, none of them pink. Once she'd decided against pink, she started grabbing dresses from her mama's collection, but the white one soiled by punch, the one she really wanted, was gone. Still. *You'd think Georgeanne would admit she took it.* She'd settled on choosing from the three on the bed.

Maranatha picked up each lifeless dress and held it to herself, wondering. Mama's red dress seemed too grown-up, like something worn to a cocktail party. Before she put it down, she smelled it. Faint hints of roses dizzied her, made her long for Mama to be here, fussing over her. Made Mama's absence more real somehow. Maranatha glanced at her picture while a couple tears tumbled from her eyes. She wiped them away, then turned the picture over. No use letting Mama see her cry. Maranatha wiped another tear with the back of her hand and took a deep breath. She picked up the cream dress, put her head through the wiry hanger to see what it might look like on. But it screamed *prude*. High-necked and long-sleeved. Too Puritan. The sea-foam green dress, when she saw it against her face, washed her out, made her look sickly, sallow.

It was an odd thing indeed that she could change a dress and become a different Maranatha with each one. Cocktail party Maranatha would be alive, conversational, quick-witted. Prude Maranatha could be aloof, haughty, disinterested. Sea-foam Maranatha could utter tragic stories about contracting measles, mumps, and rubella. The white dress would've said the right things, would've shown who the real Maranatha was: intelligent, cautious, feminine, afraid, alive.

Maranatha smoothed each dress on her bed. None would do. If she had to pick, she'd choose the sickly one. But it wasn't her. She could make believe sea-foam Maranatha in the same way she pretended to let Georgeanne love her. It was all a show, anyway, this homecoming thing. Maybe life would be easier if she'd learn to be like a chameleon. She could lock the real Maranatha behind a secure door and become what everyone else wanted her to be.

Georgeanne's high heels rapped the hallway's wooden floor. She looked around the doorway. "My cousin's here," she said, a look of confusion painting her already painted face. "And he wants to see you."

"Old Mack?" Maranatha stood.

"One and the same. Not sure what he's up to, but he's a stubborn one, so you might as well go downstairs and oblige him."

Maranatha left the red, cream, and sea-foam disguises behind and trotted down the stairs.

Georgeanne ushered Old Mack into the parlor. "Why don't you have a visit in here," she said. "Do you want any tea?"

"No thanks." Old Mack was fumbling with his thumbs while he sat straight-backed on an old-fashioned chair.

"I'd like some." Maranatha sat across from Old Mack on their very uncomfortable settee.

"None for you, child. You'll stain your teeth. Best chat a little bit. Danielle will be here in a few minutes."

"Thanks, Georgeanne," she said, hoping the woman would leave. She did.

Old Mack twirled his beard with his left hand. "I, uh, have something for you."

"You do?"

"Yep. In my car out front. Want to come see?"

She nodded. Maranatha followed Old Mack outside. He opened his pickup, parked squarely under the shedding pecan tree, and pulled out a black garment bag. "I brought you a present."

"For me?"

"Yes, dear. You." He handed her the garment bag. "Now, don't be snooping in broad daylight. Take it upstairs and see what you think. I won't be hurt if you can't use it. But if you do, save me a picture, will you?"

"Of course," she heard herself say, but the curiosity of what the garment bag held made her antsy, like when she had to say a speech for the first time in Mrs. Kulhanek's class last year.

"Just git, you hear? There's not much time."

Maranatha looked at Old Mack. He seemed shorter under the pecan branches. Maybe it was because she'd mostly seen him on a high stool at his store or behind the mammoth organ at Georgeanne's wedding. Without the props of stool or bench, he seemed more, well, *human*. More vulnerable. She wanted to hug him, to throw her arms around his neck and say one thousand thank yous, but something held her back. She turned to see what prevented it: Georgeanne's stare from the front porch.

"Thank you, Old Mack. I'm sure whatever it is, I'll like it."

Old Mack kicked at the ground, then got in the truck and drove away.

Maranatha hurried past Georgeanne, but not fast enough to escape a pestering of words.

"Hurry up, now. Danielle will be here soon. The moment she pulls up, I want you downstairs, you hear?"

Maranatha nodded and mounted the steps two at a time. The garment bag *swish-swished* her legs.

She laid the bag over the three dresses and unzipped.

She gasped.

She pulled out a silky, satiny, sky blue dress, the same color as her eyes. There were no embellishments on it. No lace. Just a simple scoop neckline with capped sleeves. The waist dropped slightly with simple pleating around the skirt that looked to be tea-length. It was everything and anything she'd ever want in a dress. Elegant. Understated. Beautiful.

She slipped off her jeans and T-shirt and pulled the dress over herself. Crooking her arms behind herself, she zipped it halfway up, changing arm positions until she could zip it all the way. Maranatha stood in front of her small mirror and shivered. The perfect dress. It should make her smile, she knew, but having something like that wrapping itself around her skin made her vulnerable somehow. Like she was showing too much of her body, like it was on display to purchase and take. Would Violin Charlie let his eyes rest too long on her figure? Or would it enhance her eyes so much that he'd linger far too long there? Would he try to unzip what she zipped?

She held her stomach, willing it to stop gurgling and churning. Nausea nearly overwhelmed her. She swallowed.

The familiar clicking of heels made her straighten up.

"Good Lord!" Georgeanne said. "What in heaven's name?"

Maranatha turned to face Georgeanne. Danielle stood behind her. "Old Mack gave it to me."

Danielle walked right up to her, nearly toe to toe. "Yessirree, that's the prettiest dress I think I've ever seen. Look at this detailing." She pressed the piping on Maranatha's sleeve between two manicured fingers. "This looks custom made."

Maranatha remembered when she first unzipped the dress, she'd seen no label, no size tag. Every seam had been finished, not like store-bought clothes, where frayed ends were surged. *I wonder who made this.*

"That cousin of mine!" Georgeanne joined the compliment party around Maranatha. "He's an interesting one, buying dresses for near-strangers. I think the dress I bought was better."

Maranatha knew she should have said, "You're right, Georgeanne," but the words didn't form in her heart, certainly not on her lips.

"Well, we need to get to this hair," Danielle said, cutting through the thick silence.

At four thirty, Maranatha was Cinderella-ed. Mice, in the form of Old Mack, Danielle, and Georgeanne, had tucked, curled, hair sprayed, makeupped, and donned Maranatha until she wanted to fling everything off and take a bike ride. Truth be told, when she stared gape-mouthed in the full-length mirror in Georgeanne's room, she did feel the prettiest she'd ever felt.

The doorbell rang.

"He's an early one. I like that in a boy," said Georgeanne. "Best go down and invite him in for some tea and cookies."

Maranatha had forgotten about the dress, how it might welcome unwanted attention, but as she walked down the stairs, she remembered her fears. She breathed in and out through her nose, slow and long, to convince herself that everything would be fine. After all, Violin Charlie was a churchgoing boy.

She opened the door.

Regular Charlie stood there.

"Charlie?"

"Yep."

"But, what are you doing here?"

He looked into her eyes, held them for three *ubiquitous* moments, hands behind him. "I came to wish you a good time."

A rush of footsteps skittered behind Maranatha.

"I got my camera. Don't move a muscle." Georgeanne practically pranced downstairs until she landed on the last step with a thud and a loud, "Good Lord!"

Maranatha turned. "Charlie came to tell me to have a good time."

"Oh."

Danielle inched around Georgeanne. She offered her hand to Charlie. "Nice to meet you. I'm Danielle."

"Charlie," he said, shaking her hand while the other remained behind him.

"Oh, sorry, this is my friend Charlie," Maranatha said.

"Best be scatting along, Charlie. Maranatha's got a date to get ready for. Homecoming. On the *other* side of town." Georgeanne stood between them now.

"Please," Maranatha said. "A moment alone, okay?"

"Suit yourself." Georgeanne held on to the knob like an undecided gatekeeper. Her eyes willed Regular Charlie outside, but then the logic of it all seemed to change her mind. "Better sit in the parlor a moment. A real short moment."

Charlie, one hand still behind him, followed Maranatha into the parlor while Danielle and Georgeanne skirted around them to the kitchen, "To prepare tea for when your date arrives," Georgeanne said.

Alone, Maranatha looked at her feet, feeling the force of Charlie's eyes on her dress.

"You look beautiful."

The word singed through her like a lightning bolt looking for a home. *Beautiful.* It was the word General used to describe her so long ago. It'd taken years of Zady's prayers to convince Maranatha it wasn't a hideous word. Coming from the lips of Charlie who *knew* the whole terrible story revived the word for her, revived the meaning from "pretty" back to "hideous." She knew it was polite to say thank you, but she couldn't. Not today. Confusion about Zady settled in Maranatha's heart. *Zady, what did you tell him?*

"Well, I best be going. I brought you these — to say I'm sorry. About the black-and-white comment." From behind his back, Charlie brought out a tangle of wildflowers, tied haphazardly with baling string. "I know color doesn't matter. I was just mad at you, and the words came out." He handed the flowers to her. "I picked 'em from the pasture near where the tornado almost ate us. Maybe they'll help you remember me. Remember us."

Maranatha took the flowers, held them right out in front of her like she was the one presenting them. To pull them to herself and smell in the wild, woody scent of autumn on the bouquet's petals would mean Charlie's apology had touched something inside her. It took a herd of will to keep them at arm's length, far from her heart that ached and recoiled at the same time. "I'll put them in a vase. I'll be right back."

"All right."

In the kitchen she nabbed a florist's vase from under the sink while the eyes of Georgeanne and Danielle settled on her.

"Wildflowers. How ridiculous. Is he gone yet?" Georgeanne took a long drink of tea and threw her head to the side.

"I think it's sweet," Danielle said.

"It's as sweet as a molasses-colored boy trying to slither his way into our lives, I'm telling you what."

Our? Maranatha filled the vase and plopped the flowers in with a quiet thud. For one moment, she allowed herself the luxury of smelling the flowers, flowers that smelled like heaven in a bunch. She shook her head to rid herself of the crazy sentiment. "Don't worry." She turned to face Georgeanne and Danielle. "I'll rid the house of Charlie. Never you mind." She left the kitchen.

The doorbell rang.

Maranatha stopped, her low-heeled shoes stuck to the floor.

The doorbell rang again.

"Aren't you going to answer it?" came Georgeanne's screech from the kitchen.

She made her feet unstick themselves. In the parlor to her right stood Charlie, tall and lean, sorrow wetting his eyes. "I guess it's time you go," she said.

"I know." He walked past her, like she was a statue thwarting his path. Walked clear around her, not saying a word. He opened the door before she could.

There, a corsage of pink roses in hand, adorned in a black

tux with pink tie and cummerbund, stood Violin Charlie. His face, normally pale, now pinked, matching his outfit perfectly.

Violin Charlie, meet Regular Charlie. Maranatha stood there while the Charlies shared an awkward moment at the threshold.

"I'm here for Maranatha." Violin Charlie shifted his feet.

"I am too," Regular Charlie said. "But I was leaving." He inched around Violin Charlie and walked down the porch stairs in angry stride, each step reverberating the porch. "Catch you later, Natha."

"Bye," she said, but by the time her vocal chords said the word, he was clear out of the yard, sliding into his pickup. His revved engine roared its own good-bye.

"Who was *that*?"

"Only a friend," Maranatha said. "You want to come in for some tea?"

"Yes, come on in, Charlie," Georgeanne said from the hallway. "I've got a nice tea set up. Why don't you and Maranatha sit in the parlor?"

Violin Charlie handed the wrist corsage to Maranatha. She slipped it on. "Thanks," she said.

"You're welcome." He produced a bouquet of twelve pink roses from behind his back and handed them to her. "You look spectacular," he said.

Nausea bit at her throat. "Thanks. I'll put these in water."

A leaded crystal vase, one of Georgeanne's wedding presents, sat empty-mouthed on the kitchen counter.

"You can't put those beauties in a countrified vase, now can you?" Georgeanne took them from Maranatha and arranged them loosely in the vase. "Here. Take the flowers and set them in the middle of the coffee table. Danielle and I will follow with tea."

The four sat while silence decorated the room. Violin

Charlie played with his cuff links. Maranatha smoothed her skirt. Danielle pulled her gum from her mouth in a long string, examining it. Georgeanne finally filled the dead air with words about weather and pecan harvesting. Eventually, they spoke of Burl's glory decade, the seventies, when the Burl Stinging Scorpions nearly went to state — a safe enough topic.

The front door creaked open. In walked Uncle Zane. He stood in the parlor's wide archway, looked at Maranatha, and half smiled.

"Doesn't she look lovely for homecoming, Zane?" Georgeanne asked.

He winked at Maranatha. "Very pretty dress," he said. He walked away.

Violin Charlie stood. "Well, we best be going. Don't want to be late for our dinner reservation. It's an hour to Marshall, where we're eating."

Twenty-Four

ALONE IN THE CIVIC, MARANATHA REMEMBERED
she'd forgotten the boutonniere. She let it slide, hoping Violin
Charlie wouldn't notice. He'd started the car and put it in drive
when a harried-looking Georgeanne ran down the stairs, flail-
ing her arms.

She ran around the car's nose and knocked on Maranatha's
window. "You plum forgot his boutonniere, Maranatha. Silly girl!"

"Thanks," she said.

Georgeanne smiled. "Not a problem. What are friends for?"

Friends? She wondered if Georgeanne had read some self-
help column about getting in good with a stepchild. "Be a
friend," she imagined it saying. Hogwash.

Maranatha went to close her automatic window, but Violin
Charlie already controlled it.

"I could've done it," she said.

"I'm being a gentleman."

As the lazy hills of East Texas raised and lowered the car from dip
to horizon, Violin Charlie said little. He'd turned on Christian

radio right away. During every song, he gave a brief commentary on whether it was anointed or not and which artists were worldly.

Sitting next to him, hearing his explanations of what was acceptable or not, made her nervous. She knew it should reassure her; after all, he was speaking about spiritual things. But the more he rambled about music and rules, the more her stomach felt queasy.

A fast-paced Jewish-sounding song came on. "Worldly," he declared. "The Devil's beat, if you ask me." He turned it way down, so the hum of the engine filled in the blank air. "I need to ask you a question anyway."

"What?" she asked.

"Why are you wearing that dress?"

"What do you mean?"

"I specifically asked you to match to my tie and cummerbund. That doesn't exactly look pink."

What?

"I mean — it looks like rebellion to me."

"I'm not sure I'm following you," Maranatha said, heat rising in her voice.

"Rebellion. Like Eve. She took that apple plain as day. Rebelled against God. Sin is all a woman's fault, if you ask me. That's why it's up to us men to keep y'all in line. That's why God put us in authority over you, because you're of the weaker sex."

Maranatha searched through the filing cabinet in her mind entitled "Sermons by Bishop Renny." None of them had sentences like Violin Charlie uttered. Not a one. "The dress was a gift — at the last minute," she said.

Violin Charlie formed a press-lipped smile. "Really? From who?"

"You mean from *whom*, don't you?" Maranatha wanted to

go home. Right now. This date was not worth the anguish, even if it did make Regular Charlie jealous. Maybe if she kept being snippy, Violin Charlie would get the hint and take her back.

"Who, whom, whatever. You didn't get it from that colored boy, did you?"

Maranatha turned to look at Violin Charlie. She hoped he was joking, calling Regular Charlie *colored*. But he wasn't. Anger seemed to fill his half-slit eyes, pulse through his temples.

"No. From a friend. A *white* friend. Does that suit you?"

Violin Charlie wiped his mouth with the back of his right hand, like he'd been smacked a good one by a bully and was clearing the corner of his lip of blood. "Yes."

"You remind me of someone."

He looked at her briefly, then stared again at the road. "Really, who?"

"Georgeanne, my uncle's wife."

For several miles, neither of them spoke.

Maranatha found some lip-gloss, flipped down the car's mirror, and smoothed it over her lips. She looked over at Charlie. "You mind if I ask you a question?"

"Not at all," he said.

"Which Bible do you use?"

"The only one there is, the King James, of course."

"Well, I don't think we have the same Bible. I got mine from a lady in church. She loved me to death. Like Jesus does."

"That's great. I'm really glad you have someone to disciple you."

"She was black, Charlie."

Violin Charlie looked at her. Said nothing.

"In fact, if you need to know it, I'm the only white face in my church."

"You ever thought of going to a white church?"

He sounds like that Carla woman who spilled punch on my dress! "Last I heard, this country passed equal rights legislation. Far as I can see, black folks have as much right to live here as we do. Didn't Jesus die for them too?"

He didn't answer, not right away. He drummed the fingers of his right hand on the dash.

"Charlie?"

"Of course. Yes."

"What is it?"

"I worry for you." Maranatha looked out the window. "Black men, Maranatha. It's proven, you know, that they're more *sexual.* That they prey on women."

Maranatha laughed.

"What's so funny?"

If you only knew. General and the red-truck man briefly flashed through her mind like a picture taken — both with faces as white as lilies. "Nothing, really, I think it's funny you believe nonsense. It's ridiculous, if you think about it long enough."

"I'm trying to preserve your reputation, that's all."

Oh, how can I ever thank you? "So how can you go out with me and not be ashamed?"

Violin Charlie took both hands off the wheel and slammed them back down. The steering wheel vibrated.

Maranatha wondered if she should rename him. *Violent Charlie.* For a moment, she felt trapped in his car. Visions of the red-truck man, his sweaty hand on her leg, made Maranatha clench her fists.

Charlie took a breath. Then another. "I'm sorry. I let my temper get the best of me sometimes. I'm constantly going to God about it. I think it's my thorn in the flesh."

What in the world?

"This date isn't going the way I wanted it to."

Maranatha didn't respond.

Charlie stared straight ahead. He swallowed a lot.

"Maybe you should take me home," she said.

Charlie took in several long breaths. "Hey."

"Hey, what?" She kept her eyes on the horizon.

"I'm sorry. Really, I am. Forgive me?"

"I'll think about it," she said. "Can I ask you another question?"

"Yeah."

"Do you love folks, you know, like Jesus does?"

"Sure. I tithe. I give to benevolence. I memorize verses. I volunteer in Sunday school."

"That's not what I asked."

"Yes, Maranatha, I love people. But if you're trying to back me into a corner here and say I don't love black people, you're wrong. I like 'em just fine."

"I disagree. You know what I think?"

"I can hardly wait to find out."

"I think you're scared."

"How so?"

She watched the muscles of his jaw tighten. "You're scared to hold a different view from what you've been taught. Would I be right in assuming your daddy thinks the same way you do?"

"Yeah. So what?"

"Well, have you ever considered that there's another perspective?" Maranatha remembered Camilla lecturing her about this very thing. Called it having a liberal arts perspective rather than a Burl one. She used her logic to try to convince Maranatha that women have as much of a right to be preachers as men. She didn't buy all of Camilla's words, but Maranatha was thankful now for the opportunity to steal them. To prove a point.

"Not really." Charlie downshifted as they approached a light.

"I'm talking about your daddy's perspective, not God's." Maranatha flipped down her visor, looked at her face. Though well makeupped, she looked old. Felt old.

"You don't cross my daddy, don't disagree with him," he said. And said nothing more for ten minutes until he parked the car at Rosa's Mexican Family Style Restaurant.

Dinner was a festive affair, at least on the outside. Hundreds of sombreros, ponchos, and piñatas hung askew from the ceiling, cloth streamers dancing in between. Maranatha ordered the three-enchilada plate, one cheese, one bean, one chicken, while Violin Charlie selected the beef chalupas. Between them sat a ceramic bowl of runny salsa and a basket of hot chips. Maranatha contented herself on chips while Charlie remarked about the restaurant's decor.

"It's so *Mexican*, so authentic," he said.

"Yes," she said.

"Hey, listen," he finally said. "Can we keep our former conversation back in the car? I'd like to have a nice evening."

It wasn't as simple as imprisoning his words behind a locked car door. Like a dandelion blown to the wind, his words could not be returned. They floated through the wind of her mind, pirouetting, taunting. No, she couldn't keep them in the car. Couldn't even respond to his offer of conciliation. She kept picturing the folks at Mt. Moriah, imprisoned behind the bars of Charlie's making.

Violin Charlie hummed along to the restaurant's lively guitar music while keeping rhythm to its incessant beat with nimble fingers upon the table. "Do you like music?" he asked.

"Yes."

He bent toward her. "I love it. Makes me alive."

Maranatha always wondered about musical folks, how they seemed to savor music like a prisoner on death row relishes a final pizza, extra cheese. It seemed to worm into music lovers' souls, enlivening, awakening. "I can take it or leave it. Unless I'm in church. Then I can't help but smile when folks dance."

"Dance? In church?"

"Yeah, of course. You should come sometime. It's amazing."

"But . . . in church, really?"

"It's not like they're Texas two-stepping or anything. People start singing, the organ bounces a rhythm off the walls, and before I know it, I'm tapping my foot while others dance and whirl. I don't really know how it happens."

Violin Charlie ate a chip. He wore a face of confusion now, like her words didn't fit into his puzzle correctly. She liked that. Liked putting him off-kilter.

The meal went a little better. Although Maranatha was initially against the idea of fried ice cream, Violin Charlie persuaded her to try it. She loved it.

The dance, held in the Burl High School gym, began with loud music and few dancers. Corsaged and boutonniered kids clung to the outer walls as if a bomb were being dismantled in the gym's center. Furtive looks, awkward conversations, the lull of words not spoken added to the tension. A disc jockey, wearing a black trench coat, gelled asymmetrical hair, and heavy eyeliner, seemed to watch the dispersed crowd with amusement. Had that boy been walking Burl's streets at night, Maranatha was sure he'd run into shovel-wielding boys saying things like, "You're not from around here, are you now?"

The dazed people jumped to life when Prince's song "1999" bounced through the speaker system. Wall-clingers flat ran out to the floor, dancing, whirling, laughing. Violin Charlie tapped his foot a half step behind the rhythm of the happy song.

"I'm not one for dancing," Maranatha yelled above the bass notes pounding in her chest, "but I'd be willing, that is, if you are." A wildness, ignited by music, crept up on her. Seeing so many strangers laughing and dancing made her want to join in, like at Mt. Moriah. Only this time, she wanted to do more than tap her toes.

She was a stranger here, she knew. There was safety in that; probably no one here knew her secret. She could be anyone she wanted. Tonight, she wanted to be a dancer, despite her confusing conversations with Violin Charlie. Truth be told, she wanted to use him. For dancing, of all ironic things.

Violin Charlie looked around, surveying the straggling wall folks. "I don't know, Maranatha. I'm not sure I feel comfortable dancing—I mean out there where everyone can see me."

"What did you do in seventh grade?"

"What?"

"You know. When all Texas PE classes mandate you learn square dancing. What did you do then?"

"I had a note."

"Figures. You wouldn't want to make a mistake while doing the do-si-do around the corner gal. Might lose that image of perfection, right?"

Maranatha regretted her words when Charlie winced.

"No. I'm just shy about dancing in front of folks, that's all."

"So who cares what other people think? Honestly, what would happen? Is it really that bad?"

Violin Charlie shrugged, his eyes darting around the room, taking in the other dancers. "Besides, what would my church think?"

"Church?" She imagined the black Jesus smiling from the picture on Mt. Moriah's wall. That Jesus, with His kind, dark eyes, couldn't possibly scowl down on someone for dancing, even if he did skip a beat now and again. She often thought if He were there, He'd be kicking up His sandaled feet and hoofing it across the front of the altar, in perfect rhythm, no less. "I think you're going to the wrong church."

The music kicked back in, this time torturing Violin Charlie with "Footloose." "Oh, man! Why *that* song?" he said, tapping his feet, this time nearly on beat.

"You're practically dancing right now. You probably dance at home, don't you?"

Violin Charlie smiled as he nodded.

"Well, what are you waiting for? Why not just do it here?" Maranatha felt like a bad peer in one of those after-school specials, pressuring a friend to take one huff of a joint. *C'mon, everyone's doing it* danced in her mind like a mean joke.

In one instant, he grabbed her hand and pulled her toward the amoeba of dancers. For the next hour, they danced. Like happy children in *Romper Room*, they played to the rhythm of music. But when the music slowed, Maranatha made excuses. She watched the couples hug and move, hug and move, and wanted no part of slow dancing. She'd never been that close to a boy her age, pressed body to body like that. Watching it made her want to feign illness. "I'm thirsty," she'd say each time.

Violin Charlie didn't seem to mind. Tie loosened, cummerbund askew, hair sweaty, he emanated joy.

For the rest of the evening, they danced, Maranatha carefully avoiding slow songs, the majority of which were sung by Journey or Styx.

On the way home, Maranatha sensed Charlie's elation.

"Thank you," he said.

"For what?"

"For making me dance."

"I didn't make you."

"Yeah, you did."

Maranatha shook her head, smoothed her skirt. "I have a feeling I couldn't make you do anything you didn't really want to do."

"Yeah, but you let me be me. I haven't been me for a long time."

She wondered if his views about black folks would turn as quickly as he exchanged his wallflower status for dancing machine. Something inside her knew that would take a load of work. Prejudice was like a cancer, she knew. She wondered how much it had spread and whether it was incurable.

They rode in silence after that, his emancipated words about "being me" giving Maranatha a vague hope that he'd change. Something stirred inside her as he pulled under the pecan tree. A longing. A need. All she ever wanted was a father, someone who'd hold her tightly and say everything was going to be okay. Someone who cheered her, loved her no matter what. She wondered if Violin Charlie could be like that. If he could hold her while she cried and cried and cried, whispering comfort in her tired ears.

Violin Charlie got out. She watched him walk around the hood of the car. She let him open her door. He grasped for her hand and lifted her out. Instead of recoiling from his touch as she stood, she let him continue to hold her hand. They walked, hand in hand, to the door. The house's eyes were shut for the night. No lights on except for a solitary porch light.

"Want to sit?" Maranatha motioned to the green porch swing, the swing her mama used to push her in.

"Yeah."

They sat, hands clasped together. The night air was neutral, neither sweaty-hot nor nippy—a perfect fall evening.

"You know, Maranatha, I've been thinking."

"About?"

"Us."

"Us?" Her voice cracked a bit on the word.

"We make the perfect couple, you and me."

"How do you figure that?" Maranatha expected him to spout Georgeanne-esque words, like how they matched or how they resembled Barbie and Ken or other such nonsense.

"You and me, we need each other," he said. "Together, we're whole. Like two half notes joined together." He squeezed her hand.

Her stomach rumbled, protesting enchiladas and too much salsa.

"I'll be right back," he said. He ran to his car, opened the trunk, and pulled out a violin case. She watched as he removed the violin and bow, set the case at his feet, stood underneath the pecan tree, and crooked the wooden instrument under his chin. He pulled the bow across two strings, filling the autumn air with violin harmony.

Captivating. The piece had an American beat to it, like a cowboy was riding his trusty steed at full gallop to the rhythm of the music. She tapped her left foot. For a moment, she didn't even think about the neighbors as Charlie serenaded her in the night. She watched him play as if the violin were an appendage of his, a natural part of his body. She kept rhythm in her heart, thrilling at each rise in melody.

A car sped by.

He stopped.

"Lovely," she said.

"It's called 'Hoe-Down,'" he said. "By Copeland. My favorite. He also wrote this."

He slowed his pace now, melting himself into the music. The first part sounded like an orchestra warming up, low to high notes, followed by a simple melody. It held Maranatha in a movielike trance. She could almost picture a barn dance, ladies in full skirts twirling to the music's rhythm in the crook of dancing men's hay-bucking arms. Charlie finished. He carried the case and the violin, one in each hand, up the steps. He placed the violin back in its case, like he was putting it to bed, and set it on the swing.

He sat next to her, the violin between them. "That's called 'Saturday Night Waltz.' Appropriate, don't you think?"

"Yes," she said.

He stood, pulling her toward him.

His breath warmed her forehead. Violin Charlie wrapped his arms around her waist, pulling her closer, like they were slow dancing to remembered remnants of "Saturday Night Waltz." He looked in her eyes for five *ubiquitouses*. And she held hers there. On the porch, they danced, leisurely, to the meter of silent music, while their feet creaked the decking and the violin watched.

"Maranatha?"

"Yes." She scarcely said it.

"I want to kiss you."

A violence of emotion rumbled like war inside her.

Kiss?

She closed her eyes.

Me?

He held her chin.

Here?

He pulled her closer.

Now?

Before her crazy head could ask another question, his warm lips met hers in midair.

But all she could think of was her own Charlie, how she wished it were him standing there. She pulled away. "I had a nice evening. Thank you."

He flustered a few words and bent near.

She turned her head. "I'm sure Georgeanne is spying. Let's call it a night, okay?"

He held her near, breathing warm on her face. "But, I thought—"

What did you think? That I owed you more? Her longing for an innocent fatherly embrace faded like mist on a morning pond. Now all she wanted was escape. Scripture, pieces and tails of it, meandered into her head like a Savior. "A time to embrace, and a time to refrain from embracing." The words of Ecclesiastes poured out, while a bewildered Charlie pulled away.

He laughed. "You're a puzzle, sure enough."

She backed away toward the door. "What do you mean?"

"You make me dance, but you quote Ecclesiastes to me when I kiss you. Yep. One big puzzle. My daddy said you'd be trouble, but I didn't believe him."

Adrenaline shot through Maranatha's heart. She suddenly felt hot. "Your daddy said I was trouble?"

"Yeah, he told me to be careful with the likes of you." Charlie's words tumbled out lazily, not in spite, from smiling lips. His nonchalance and playful mood didn't match the words he rambled.

"What's *that* supposed to mean?" Maranatha was next to the door now, holding the handle tightly, hoping Charlie wouldn't notice the tremor of her other hand.

"Aw shucks, Maranatha. Nothing. He warned me. Nothing

more." He stepped to face her.

She pressed her back close to the door. *If he doesn't already know my secret, he will soon. Lord knows you can't trust a judge.* "I had a nice time. I need to go in."

Charlie cocked his head to one side like a curious bird. "One last kiss, and I promise I'll leave."

In one smooth motion, Maranatha kissed his cheek Camilla-style, then opened the front door. "Curfew. Good night."

Before he could say a word, she shut the door and stood in the safety of her home.

Twenty-Five

AFTER SCHOOL MONDAY, WEARY FROM FIELDING one thousand questions about homecoming, in which she used words like *good* and *fine* and *nice*, Maranatha gathered the legal papers from her hiding place, tucked them in her backpack, and rode her bike to the courthouse. It was one of those splotchy, shadowy days when the sun played peekaboo behind fluffy clouds. Her front tire wove in and out between shadow and light, playfully meeting the sun-shade checkerboard sidewalk. On her bike, Maranatha usually tasted freedom, but today, her mind entangled itself like morning glories in a chain-link fence.

While she rode past broken-down houses, she wondered if all this scheming was worth it. Did she really want the big white house that much? Was she ready to become a homeowner? How would Uncle Zane feel if she no longer lived with him? And what about Violin Charlie's neighborhood? Maybe this was all a silly mistake. Maybe she should concentrate on what really mattered anyway: getting good grades so she could leave this town. Wouldn't the big white house tether her here forever?

But those thoughts didn't needle her, not really. Not like the Charlie thoughts that somersaulted in her head while she rode her salmon bike nearer to the imposing courthouse. She remembered the kiss, her first, how the wrong Charlie bent low and sweet. She wondered why at that very moment she imagined the other Charlie pressing lips to hers. She so wanted to hate Regular Charlie for saying he knew her secret, but his presence in her heart would not be so easily dismissed. Maranatha shook her head to rid herself of both Charlies, but her heart stayed on one.

A striking blue bird wove a path in front of her. She wondered if he was a sign from God. Wasn't the Spirit like a dove? Should she follow the bird? *Don't be ridiculous. It's a stupid bird. God doesn't give signs to the likes of me. He doesn't even answer prayer.* The bird hovered for a moment, then dashed to Maranatha's right, landing on a porch. She stopped her bike, kickstanded it. Where the bike's front tire intersected sidewalk and lawn, an erect dandelion stood, head of fluff. She'd never seen one in the fall before. She bent low, pinching the stalk near its root, and stood. *One more wish.*

Maranatha examined the dandelion's fuzzy head, all the while stealing several wishes, though she knew only one counted.

Show me You love me, God.

Help me make it right with my Charlie.

I need to save my home.

Random prayers, she knew. Still, she breathed softly over the dandelion head. But it would not release its wishes, preferring to keep its happy wig intact. Maranatha let the stubborn flower fall from her hand. She crushed it under foot, mounted her bike, and rode for the courthouse.

"Let me see what you have," Miss Nichols said.

Maranatha handed the suited woman the folder. "Do you

think the house is mine?"

"If what you say is true, this should be a simple matter of paperwork and the house will be yours."

"Really? Even at my age?"

"You'd be under guardianship, but as long as your uncle agrees, you'll be fine."

Fear rumbled in Maranatha's stomach. Did she really want to live alone in that big house? And how would Georgeanne react? She looked around the small office, trying to rid her mind of pesky questions. Black-and-white 5 x 7 photos, framed with large white mats, hung in groups by silver thumbtacks on every wall except one. The pictureless wall held framed diplomas and awards. University of Washington. Southern Methodist University. Something about passing the bar exam with honors. "Where did you say you were from?" Maranatha asked.

"Seattle."

"I hear it rains a lot there." Maranatha peeled her pinky fingernail clear off. She stuck the moon-shaped thing in her pocket, hoping Miss Nichols wouldn't notice.

"Yes." Miss Nichols didn't look up, intent on scanning the document. She gasped, then pushed away from her desk. "What did you say your name was?"

Did I do something wrong? "I didn't. But it's Maranatha."

"Maranatha Winningham?"

"Yes, ma'am."

"I was going to call you today, and here you are sitting in front of me. What're the odds?"

Maranatha didn't know what to make of this, didn't know what was going on. Was her house really that important?

"Listen. I need you. To testify."

A kaleidoscope of memories jumbled through Maranatha's mind at the word *testify*. She remembered testifying before.

Ten years old, shaking with shivers, sitting in the witness stand. Answering questions about things ten-year-olds aren't supposed to know about. Seeing General's spite-pocked face. Holding back tears that disobeyed. Grabbing her stomach. Praying for it all to end.

"Are you all right?" Miss Nichols asked.

Maranatha nodded on the outside but shuddered on the inside.

"Are you familiar with Jake Gully?"

"No. Is that a place?"

"It's a man. Was arrested yesterday because of an incident that took place not too long ago, along the highway. Seems he picked up a girl."

No. Not the man in the red truck. She'd tried to send that memory away. She'd nearly done it until right now. Maranatha felt the color wash from her face.

"And raped her. Nearly killed her too."

Thank God. It's not about me, Maranatha thought, worried that she felt more relief for herself than pity for the poor woman.

"Turns out he'd tried that sort of thing before, but the first girl escaped. And knows what he looks like." Miss Nichols looked right into Maranatha.

Maranatha squirmed.

Miss Nichols walked around her desk and put a tentative hand on Maranatha. "I need your help. Your name's on that first police report. We can put Jake Gully away for good if you'll agree to testify next month." Miss Nichols bent low and faced her.

No. No. No. I can't go through that again. She bit her bottom lip — hard. She tried to think of a way of escape, like that temptation verse in the Bible. *Where is my way of escape?* It came in the form of a lucid question: "What about the other girl?

Wouldn't her words be better than mine?"

"Would be if she'd talk, but she can't. She's in a mental hospital. I need you to be her voice, Maranatha. Can you do that for me?"

Twenty-Six

MARANATHA SPENT TUESDAY IN HER ROOM. George-
anne poked her head in at least ten times asking her if she was
okay, if she needed anything, but Maranatha grunted replies. She
wasn't sick, but she didn't care. School could wait while she sorted
through things. She picked up the picture of Mama. "Sephie,"
she said to the silent girl, "you never did have to testify, now did
you?"

Georgeanne interrupted Maranatha's one-sided conversation. "I'm coming in. With soup. And a letter."

Before Maranatha could say no, Georgeanne was halfway to
the bed. She held a white wicker tray with rickety legs, a bowl of
something steamy on its top, a letter sitting like a napkin under
a spoon. "Now, there you go. Matzo ball soup cures any ills, my
mama always said." She set the sick tray over Maranatha's legs
and sat next to her. "Are you sure you're going to be all right?
You look pale."

"I'm fine. Really. Just a cold, I think. What's matzo ball
soup?"

"It's Jewish soup. Chicken usually, with dumplings made of
cracker meal."

"You're Jewish?"

"Not hardly," Georgeanne laughed. "But we had us a neighbor. Tatty, she called herself, though that wasn't her real name. She was a nonpracticing Jew, whatever that means. Whenever we had a snitch of a cold, old Tatty'd bring us a big ol' pot of matzo ball soup. It was downright mysterious how the stuff cured us all."

"It smells good," Maranatha admitted, though she hated to. "But I'm not hungry." Her stomach rumbled. Loud.

Georgeanne smiled. "But you didn't eat any dinner last night. You sure it's not the flu?"

Maranatha shook her head. She wanted to say, *Would you please leave?* but thought the better of it. She was too weary to be mean.

Georgeanne tucked a piece of hair behind Maranatha's ear. "If I were to guess, I'd say you were lovesick."

"Well," Maranatha said, sipping the chickeny soup, "you'd be wrong then." She slurped some more, then picked up the letter. From Camilla. It was fat.

Georgeanne rubbed her legs with both hands and then looked at Maranatha. "I saw you smooching on the porch. You two make a perfect couple, if you ask me."

Oh, bother. Another spoonful. She set the letter next to her. "I suppose that would fit right in with the plan you have for me."

Georgeanne seemed to ignore Maranatha's barb. "Saw how you pulled away all afraid and aflutter. I understand that, you know."

Maranatha thought of words she could say to rid the room of Georgeanne while she took another spoonful of heaven-on-earth soup. "Oh really? Because of all your smooching and pulling away from Uncle Zane?"

"No need to be snippy, Miss Maranatha." Georgeanne

looked away, studied the window for a long time. Probably twenty *ubiquitouses*. "It took me a long time to learn how to like kissing," she said, looking away.

Maranatha took another sip. As the broth made a home in her stomach, Georgeanne's words filtered through her mind, not making any sense. She tried to think of a clarifying question but couldn't, so she kept quiet, something that seemed to unnerve Georgeanne.

She stood. "No matter. I can see you're not interested. I'll leave you to your soup and that letter."

Maranatha heard hints of agony lingering in Georgeanne's voice, something she'd never detected before today. "I'm all done," Maranatha said.

Georgeanne took the tray. She frowned.

"But I'd like some more. It's delicious."

The frown smiled, albeit wearily. "I'll be right back then," Georgeanne said.

When the door shut, Maranatha wondered if Zady was right after all. That hurt people *hurt* people. Was Georgeanne carrying around a duffel bag of hurt? Really? The thought made Maranatha miss Zady all the more; she wished life could be like it was — Zady tending the house and her soul while Georgeanne stayed conveniently in the background. By now Zady probably knew all about the other Charlie and the dance, how Maranatha'd wrung her Charlie's heart out and hung it on a clothesline to flap in the Burl breeze. *Zady must hate me.*

She remembered the envelope and tore it open. Instead of an origami note, something was scrawled in permanent pen on the back of a large, folded Fritos bag. Maranatha laughed.

Dearest Homecoming Queen,

By the time you receive this, you'll have danced a
few good ones with Charlie Barley Buck and Rye. You
may've even hollered at my homecoming game without
me. I got to thinking about all that and got a little
teary. I miss football, if you can believe it. Up here
in Illinois, football's not a religion, it's merely a sport.
I miss the hype, the cheerleaders screaming their
hoarse voices, the nerdy band playing "Tequila," the
corn dogs sold by Burl Boosters, the insane crowd. But
you know what I miss the most? Frito pie. Yep. Folks
up here eat Fritos naked, if you can scarce believe
that. Just eat 'em like they're chips or something. Oh,
how I long for a Frito bag sliced down the middle,
cradling a steaming dollop of chili (vegetarian, if you
please), a plop of sour cream, and a swirl of molten
Velveeta on top. No, ma'am, there's nothing finer.
So, I wrote you a song, my first. Sing along with it to
the tune of "Elbow Room" from Schoolhouse Rock. You
remember that one, don't you? About America buying
the Louisiana Purchase from les Francaises! Anyway,
make of it what you will:

> One thing you will discover
> When you cheer next to one another
> Is everybody needs some Frito pie, Frito pie
>
> The game's nice meeting with your friends
>   and all, but
> Not when your stomach curls into a ball, and
> Hankers for some pie, a little Frito pie

O, Frito pie, Frito pie
Gotta gotta get me some Frito Pie
The bag we bust
In chips we trust
There's a new dish in there . . .

Camilla signed her letter, *Triple Cheeks, Camilla.*

Camilla's truth-poems are getting wackier by the day. Even so, reading the rhymed words made Maranatha ache for Camilla.

She put a tape in her small recorder, hoping to quell the ache in her heart. She missed Camilla something fierce. Songs with words like *sanctified, blood of the Lamb, holy fire,* and *streets of gold* eradicated the room's silence but couldn't salve her loneliness.

She'd lost Camilla because of geography and Zady because of mistrust. Maranatha tried to rile herself to believe the worst about Zady but couldn't do it, at least not with Jesus music singing happy songs in the background. *But Charlie knows. And how could he know unless Zady told him?*

Maranatha realized Zady couldn't be trusted, a sad fact.

And now Maranatha's secret was out there to Lord knows how many Burl citizens. Maranatha Winningham had her virginity stolen from her. She'd been *raped.* Just thinking how the word played on the gossip-prone lips of others lit her face red with shame. *Rape. Everyone will know. And it's all Zady's fault.*

But something inside Maranatha's heart wouldn't let her despise the woman who nursed her back to health years ago. Wouldn't let her disdain those beautiful, humble hands. Wouldn't let her begrudge the heart that shared Jesus with her. No matter how she tried, Maranatha couldn't, *wouldn't,* hate Zady.

It must be the music, she thought. She reached to turn it off right as a passionate-sounding woman sang, "Freedom, freedom, freedom."

Georgeanne stepped in, interrupting the last *freedom*. She held up her hand. "You have a guest," she said.

Miss Nichols stepped through the doorway.

Maranatha ran her hands over her head, wondering what in the world she looked like. She fingered a rat's nest at the nape of her neck. *Great.*

Georgeanne added, "She was asking for you, so I brought her on up."

Maranatha looked at herself, wearing pajamas — a marked contrast to Miss Nichols' navy suit.

"I can wait outside," Miss Nichols said. "Until you're ready."

It was Miss Nichols' suggestion to take a walk, that is, if Maranatha was up for it. She was. No use in risking an eavesdropping Georgeanne.

As they walked out the front door, Maranatha heard Georgeanne from the kitchen. "I thought you were sick," she called.

"I'll be fine." Maranatha closed the front door before Georgeanne could say another pestering word.

"You're persistent." Maranatha kept her hands pocketed while they walked under an awning of autumn leaves.

"I need you. I told you that yesterday."

Maranatha hated to disappoint this woman, hated to disappoint anyone for that matter, but the monster of testifying silenced her fear of Miss Nichols' disapproval. They walked a block without a word exchanged. "I can't," Maranatha said finally.

Miss Nichols sighed, shook her head. "That's not the answer I need, Maranatha."

"I know. I'm sorry."

"I want you to look at something." Miss Nichols stopped right there on the street while cars motored by. She ransacked her briefcase, pushing papers this way and that, finally pulling out a small rectangle of white. "Maddie Elmwood," she said simply. She turned the piece of paper over, right in Maranatha's face.

A haunted woman stared back at her from the photograph. Right eye purpled, nose bashed, a front middle tooth broken. Her left eye held an anguish Maranatha understood all too well.

Maranatha walked away.

"You can't turn your back on her." Miss Nichols followed Maranatha, matched her footstep for footstep.

Maranatha turned back around, headed toward home. As she passed Miss Nichols, she shot, "Last I heard we lived in a free country."

"That's the problem with freedom, Maranatha," Miss Nichols said. "It allows for folks like Maddie to get her face bashed in. She's pregnant, you know."

This stopped Maranatha's barn-sour bent toward home. "Pregnant?"

"Yes."

"And still in a mental hospital?"

"Yes."

Maranatha let this news pulse through her. *It could have been me. Should've been me.* Nearing home, she reconsidered Miss Nichols' request for the sake of Maddie.

She thought of seeing the red-truck man again while she sat high on the witness stand, enduring uncomfortable questions while Jake Gully sneered from his seat. She knew the man would have those same terror-eyes General possessed. Eyes that emanated an otherworldly hate. Maranatha turned to face Miss Nichols under the pecan tree. "I can't," she said.

"Listen, I know you're skittish. I know your story. Know about Robert E. The rape."

Does the whole town know?

Miss Nichols placed a thin hand on her arm.

Maranatha jumped. "I can't testify, Miss Nichols. Can't go through that again."

"I'd coach you." Miss Nichols' voice sounded smaller, but still held resolve.

"I've *been* coached. Prosecutors made it sound like coaching would make testifying easy as pie. Well, it wasn't." Tears nettled Maranatha's eyes, stung them something fierce. She leaned against the fence while the courtroom scene projected like a horror movie in her head.

Ridley Owen, a suited defense lawyer, was so near the witness stand a young Maranatha could smell his nacho-chip breath. "Maranatha." He said her name like she was a toddler being reprimanded. "Are you *sure* you didn't entice the defendant? Come on now. You *are* a pretty little girl. Tell the truth!"

Maranatha shook her head, trying to blur Ridley from her mind. She straightened. Looked Miss Nichols in her persistent eyes. "I told you, I can't. *I won't.*" She pushed around Miss Nichols, then wrecked through the front gate, tears barreling from her eyes.

Twenty-Seven

NO AMOUNT OF MATZO BALL SOUP would cure this ill. Maranatha stayed in her room all day, first muffling her sobs with a feather pillow that seemed to be designed for such a thing. But soon it smelled like damp gym socks.

Her diaphragm ached from one too many convulsive sobs. Her eyes felt aflame, mouth cottony. Partway through the crying spell, she'd given up her dream of keeping the house and then bawled some more. Logic told her if she didn't testify, that Nichols woman certainly wouldn't help her secure her big white home. After those cries quieted, she cry-babied about living near Violin Charlie in a perfectly trimmed yard while Georgeanne had teas and soirees and other such nonsense for pasty-white ladies. Then she boo-hooed for *her* Charlie—his hurt eyes, his knowing looks about all her terrible secrets. It didn't take long for her to weep a river for Zady, her dear friend, practically her mama, who probably boldface-lied to Maranatha, told her she'd *never* tell a soul, not on your life. She cried about Camilla's absence and prayed that she'd be brave enough to share every new secret with her come Thanksgiving. Camilla would keep her secrets zipped, at least she hoped so. And holding the secrets inside made every tear come easier.

But the deepest wails came from parts of her she didn't know existed. Angry, pillow-punching cries took aim at God. And fired.

What kind of God are You, anyway? she cried into her damp pillow. *Taking my house and giving me Georgeanne instead? Spreading my secrets? Reminding me of General, of the trial? Do You really love me, or is this a big, fat joke?*

She waited for God to answer, for a cherubic angel to swoop in low to earth to whisper the Almighty's secrets to her. But no seraphim flew in her opened window. Not even a breeze, like the kind God used to speak to Elijah. Just stillness that seemed heavy and awful, like a wet army blanket on her questioning heart.

The dandelion wish from months ago floated through her mind, taunting her like a schoolyard bully. Nothing made sense. It was Mama Frankie who'd told her to live expecting signs from heaven. It's probably why Maranatha wished on a dandelion head in the first place, hoping God was in the business of granting miracles and signs right there on the streets of Burl, Mama Frankie–style. Maybe God smiled down on some folks and not on others. Maybe He sent sunshine to warm Mama Frankie's head when she had breath to sing hymns to Him. Now that the earth had swallowed the old woman up, maybe it pained God to send more blessings down. Maybe He was plain tired. Or kept things to Himself.

She didn't want to believe God's disinterest or silence, so she reminded herself of the fragments of prophecies she'd heard this year, of Old Mack's dead-on admonition: *I have an inkling that this bike will save you. Will help you through this next year*, he'd said. And he was right. The bike carried her away from Jake Gully. It saved her from much less menacing things too, like the monotony of life in the big white house. The bike had helped her sort her mind, helped her clear her cobwebby head. It saved her from having to hear Georgeanne talk on and on about nothing and everything.

And then Mama Frankie's words sifted through her memory: *This'll be your green 'mater year. Someone's gonna attempt to pluck you before you're ripe, before you get a chance to sing.* Maranatha had promised she'd run away if someone threatened to pluck her, and she'd made good on that promise, soon after Mama Frankie died. But now the world seemed like it wanted to pluck her from the vine of security, to take her from her house, to make her testify to something she'd rather forget, to separate her from Charlie and Zady and everyone. She was being plucked, sure enough, but Maranatha didn't have the strength to run anymore. And certainly not to sing.

Before she consciously knew what she was doing, Maranatha pulled out a piece of college-ruled notebook paper and wrote, *Dear Camilla.* From her pen flew words she dared not say anywhere except in the relatively safe confines of long-suffering friendship. She told of two Charlies, one loved, the other tolerated. She wrote of Zady's treachery, her loose mouth. While tears blurred the neat, blue printing, she spilled the red-truck man story, every detail, down to throwing up on Bishop Renny's church floor. She painted Miss Nichols as a nosy Northerner, trying to force Maranatha into sitting in front of that horrible man, reminding her of courtrooms past. She apologized for not sharing it all right away. She hated holding secrets; it felt like bloodied hands pulling the reins of an eager horse. Once she let go and the horse of secrets was allowed to run unhindered, Maranatha was free. And a little scared.

I miss you, Camilla. That's the truth. I don't have anyone to talk to here except Old Mack, but he's not a

girl, can't understand some things. And Georgeanne?
Well, it's my fault she married my uncle. I shouldn't
have left Uncle Zane on fair day. It's all my fault,
Camilla. Nobody's but mine. When you come home for
Thanksgiving, will you promise to spend a few after-
noons with me? I'm a bit of a mess.

Too many cheeks to count, Maranatha

She folded the letter in sixths, hardly creative considering
Camilla's master folding, and shoved it into an awaiting (unre-
cycled) envelope. Day shrunk from the windows of her room,
leaving the light dusky. She flipped on her light, set the envelope
on a small, round table by her door, and went to the bathroom
to wash her splotchy face.

Maranatha couldn't concentrate the next day at school. All she
could do was think about that letter, conspicuous next to her
door. She counted the minutes until the final bell when she could
ride her bike home, grab the letter, and scissor it into confetti.
Two worries needled her mind. One was Georgeanne steaming the envelope and reading all her sordid secrets. Everything
was in there, including Maranatha's plan to get the house. How
could she be so dumb as to leave that letter out in the open for
the spying eyes of that woman? Stupid!

The other worry haunted her even more. Had she sent that
letter, someone would know everything, that someone being a
sometimes-loudmouthed Camilla whose father happened to
be *the* radio personality in Burl. Maranatha's mind played terrible tricks on her, of Camilla calling her dad right away with

a juicy scoop. Of Denim broadcasting Maranatha's every secret to the truck radios of every Burl citizen. Of her fleeing the town ashamed.

When two thirty came and the bell didn't sound, she wanted to scream. She watched the second hand tick to ten seconds, twenty. Mr. Ellington, the world's most boring American History teacher, didn't seem to notice as he corrected papers at his desk. Maranatha wanted to strangle him. *Look at the clock! Something's wrong with the bell!*

The bell rang stilted, eighty-three seconds late. Maranatha threw on her backpack, ran from class, and unlocked her bicycle. She stood on the pedals, pumping her bike faster than usual while the sidewalk roots bumped the poor bike nearly off-kilter. She threw down the bike under the pecan tree and ran inside.

"What's the rush, little Missy?" Georgeanne wore an apron of yellow ducks on parade.

"Nothing. I have homework," she breezed as she ran the stairs.

"I mailed that letter by your door."

Maranatha turned, now at the top of the stairs. "What?"

"The letter. To that Camilla girl. I figured you wanted me to send it. It wasn't stamped, so I put one of my stamps on it. You owe me one stamp."

No. No. No! Maranatha walked down the stairs with deliberate anger. "Did you *read* the letter, Georgeanne?"

Georgeanne averted her eyes, looked at the ceiling. "There sure are a lot of cobwebs in this house. I'll be glad to be in our new home by Thanksgiving."

"Answer my question."

"Of course not. I don't snoop."

Oh really? Maranatha turned. With each step, fear and anger wrestled for preeminence. *Did she read it? If she did, who will she tell? I could kill that woman. What will Camilla think? Why did I let my secrets out? Why?*

She slammed her bedroom door, let it reverberate its stout jamb.

"My life is over." The four words summed it all up. Over. Finished. Camilla would know everything. Georgeanne might know everything. Soon, everyone would know everything.

Zady appeared like a rare autumn mist that evening. Unexpected. And certainly not wanted. She cradled her hips in her hands under the porch light; that much Maranatha could see from the narrow window flanking the door.

Maranatha opened the door and slipped out, hoping Georgeanne wouldn't see. Zady stepped back.

"I come to talk," she said. "I miss you."

Miss telling my secrets to the world?

"I don't have much to say." Maranatha looked beyond Zady to her bicycle resting under the pecan tree.

Zady sat on the porch swing. "Come now. Sit a spell." She patted the slatted seat next to her. "We needs to talk, you and me."

Maranatha obeyed in action, but her heart stayed far away like she was East Burl and Zady was West.

"Charlie Boy, well he said there's been a misunderstanding." Zady folded her hands on her lap, interlacing brown fingers in a beautiful entanglement.

Maranatha couldn't keep her eyes off Zady's hands; watching them made her speechless. She wondered how much Zady had to work at odd jobs to put food on the table.

"He says you had a fight. At the picnic."

Maranatha looked away from Zady's hands. She fixed her gaze on the pecan tree, whose hair was browning and shedding one by one. Soon it would be bald, naked for the winter. "Yes. A fight."

"Care to tell me what about?"

"Why don't you ask Charlie? I'm sure he'll be happy to share his side of the story." She watched one leaf in particular, a lone leaf wearing shades of grass and earth on a near-to-the-porch branch. It trembled, but it wouldn't fall off.

"Won't talk," Zady said. "Clammed up."

"I see." Maranatha admired the tenacious leaf grasping the tree branch. "So you want me to tell you everything, is that it?"

"No. Only if you want to."

"Matchmakers are seldom happy, at least that's how it seems in *Fiddler on the Roof*."

Zady turned to her, but Maranatha kept looking at the tenacious leaf. "I don't care if you date him. I want my son back. What went on at the dock, Natha?"

"A spat. Charlie's probably overreacting. I'm seeing someone else anyway." Maranatha let the lie slide off her tongue like a Jell-O jiggler, easy and smooth-like. *What's a slippery little lie between friends? Besides, I can't trust you with the truth.*

"So Charlie says." Zady hummed "Amazing Grace" with such loveliness that Maranatha near cried.

Maranatha kept her eyes on the shaking leaf, marveling at its grip. "Is that why you came today? To pry?" Maranatha spat her words, reminding herself of Zady's treachery even as she longed to grab the woman's hands and cry a river.

"No, actually not. I'm here to encourage you."

Maranatha looked at Zady. *Encourage me?* "Why?"

"There's something needing doing, and I'm afraid the messy

task falls on you."

"What, Zady?"

"Testifying."

Maranatha returned to leaf staring while anger and fear battled like angry twins in her stomach. She wondered if Zady, like Denim, knew every last one of Burl's dirty little secrets. She sucked in a breath, letting it out through her nose. "What do you know about testifying?"

"Plenty. A Miss Nichols called me this morning."

"She gets around," Maranatha said. For a moment she thought the happy, clinging leaf would shimmer and fall, but it stayed put.

"Jake Gully's a terrible man, Maranatha. Your words could stick him behind bars."

"I can't." There, she'd said it. Again. Hopefully Zady wouldn't guilt her about it. She remembered Zady's hollow eyes the last time she testified. The poor woman seemed to pull all Maranatha's pain into her at the last trial. The same pain emanated from her now. Maranatha tried to convince herself that Zady couldn't handle another trial. *I'm doing this for you.*

The porch swing creaked underneath them while Maranatha's defiant words hung in the breezy air.

Zady hummed "Amazing Grace" again.

Maddening woman! Stop that humming!

A brown hand rested on Maranatha's knee, warm like an oven mitt after handling a hot cookie sheet. "It's about weakness, Natha."

"What do you mean?"

"God doesn't call us folks to be strong. He calls us to be dependent, weak even. That's when He shows up — in our weaknesses. I knows you can't testify. I knows it will stir all sorts of scorpion nests in your heart. Truth is, you can't do it — like you said."

"Yes, that's what I said."

"But God *can*."

Those three words made no sense to Maranatha. What *could* God do? He didn't protect her from General, at least not initially. He didn't protect Uncle Zane from a stroke. God watched as Maranatha sat in white-knuckled terror in Jake Gully's red truck. What could God do? Maranatha sucked in a breath. "Sometimes God seems far away, Zady. I'm not sure He'll show up to help the likes of me."

"I guess that's where faith comes in." Zady hummed "On Christ the Solid Rock I Stand." "Here's how I see it. God puts you on this earth to love folks. Show 'em His love. He takes you through terrible trouble so you'll understand all sorts of folks. And now He's asking you to obey Him. He shows up *after* the obedience, child."

Maranatha shifted in her seat, Zady's hand resting on her knee. "Why would God ask me to do such a thing?"

"For others. To save others from your hell."

"I can't." Maranatha swallowed a cry that threatened to shudder her. "I can't look at that man's eyes. Not on the witness stand. Not ever."

"I can't bear it either, Natha." Zady pulled away her hand. She cupped her face in her hands and wept.

And wept.

And wept.

While Maranatha watched her leaf flutter and hold.

Zady pulled out a hankie and blew her tears into its belly. "God as my witness," she said, "I don't want to tell you this, but I have to. When the Good Lord tells me to say something, if I keep it inside I'll burst. His hand is heavy right now, pressing on me to say something." Zady rubbed her eyes. She took in a sigh, exhaled. "Natha, I need you to look at me."

Maranatha looked into Zady's hot-chocolate eyes and nearly melted inside.

"Your life is like a story, you understand?"

Maranatha shook her head no.

"There're a lot of characters in a story. Bad folks. Good folks. Conflict. Resolution. In your story, you are running," Zady said, "running from villains. Sometimes you run from folks who aren't villains, but your mind can't be convinced otherwise. You'd be much better off if you'd stop running from villains and go searching for the one true hero." Zady stood and faced Maranatha, hands on hips. She examined the porch's bead-board ceiling. "I said it, Lord. Said Your words."

Zady plodded down the steps, leaving Maranatha to wonder at her words. Who was the hero? Charlie? And how could she ever stop running from villains?

By facing them, a quiet voice whispered in her head.

Maranatha watched Zady walk beneath the pecan tree. When she left through the gate, Maranatha's leaf released its grip and drifted back and forth like a feather in flight toward the tree's dusty roots.

Twenty-Eight

"DID YOU LOOK LOVELY?" OLD MACK parted his beard down the middle like a snake's tongue. He twirled the right piece until it looked like silver cotton candy. Then he did the same to the other side.

Maranatha smiled. "I don't know." She slid a glossy 5 x 7 toward the fork-bearded man. "You decide."

"Lovely. That dress fits you like I thought it would."

"Old Mack?"

"Yeah?"

"Who made that dress?"

"I did."

Mysteries and perplexities normally didn't define life in Burl. "You?"

"Yeah."

"Why? How?"

"Why? Because I knew you probably needed a nice dress. Georgeanne came in here all aflutter about you rejecting her poofy pink dress and how you were going to wear some dress of your mama's." He rustled some papers in the drawer in front of him. "How? That night I dug through the material in the back of the store and started sewing. In the morning I was finished."

Maranatha didn't know how to wrap words around her feelings. First, there was the astonishment that the hillbilly man before her reveled in domesticity by sewing. And second that someone would spend an entire night stitching love in the form of a dress — for her. "Old Mack," she said, but nothing more.

He raised his hand while a slight blush colored his cheeks. "No need for words, Maranatha Winningham. Truth is, you're the type of person I'd go on vacation with for five days, longing for a sixth and seventh."

Maranatha never thought of herself as good company for anyone, let alone a cotton candy–bearded man with a hankering for classical music and sewing.

Silence sat between them like a down comforter in winter. Eventually, Old Mack asked, "How's that bike holding out?"

"Great. I really can't thank you — "

"Enough said. I knows you're grateful. Have you had to use the bike to run away from folks like I said before?"

Maranatha had tried to quiet the debate in her head about testifying and not testifying but to no avail. A war raged in there, complete with cannons and artillery. Anytime anyone said a word relating to the epic battle, she panicked, as molten cannonballs flew inside her mind. Old Mack deserved the truth, but she couldn't bring herself to lob a bit of it toward him. "No, not really," she said.

He scratched his head. "Strange."

"What?"

"Usually my inklings from the Lord are right on the money. I felt for sure you'd already had to flee. Maybe it's for another time. Or maybe the whole thought was bad pizza from the night before. No matter. I'd rather it not be true. I'd rather it be that you rode your bike for the love of it, not for running from villains."

Running from villains? Maranatha said a quick good-bye and pedaled far away from Old Mack. Though he was no villain.

That Saturday, Violin Charlie waited for Maranatha on her porch. "Hey," he said when she mounted the steps.

"What're you doing here?"

"Enjoying November. Wondered if you'd want to enjoy it with me."

Maranatha had to remind herself that the Charlie in front of her, with eyes the same color as hers, had something against black folks, that he was just like Georgeanne, only handsome.

"A walk. That's all I'm asking for. Care to take a stroll?" He offered the crook of his arm to her and winked.

But the wink held pain, she could see it. Maranatha took his arm without speaking, matching her footsteps to his down the porch steps. She wondered how many times she'd walk these steps before she had to move to Violin Charlie's neighborhood. *No testifying, no house.*

The pecan tree was half-naked now after pelting cars, passersby, and small animals, first with bushels of pecans, then with a scatter of leaves. Like a balding man, its hair thinned mostly toward the top, leaving stragglers around its girth. Maranatha loved and hated the sound of crispy leaves beneath her feet. Loved it because it meant she'd be free from Burl's emberlike heat. Hated it because the tree looked vulnerable. Like she felt.

They turned left. Their feet crunched leaves to a steady rhythm. When Maranatha tried to off-step, Violin Charlie'd skip the beat with her, matching her pace again.

"Your friend Camilla wrote me," he said. Just like that. Like it would mean nothing to Maranatha.

Oh no. "She did?"

"Yeah. Wrote me what she called a truth-poem. Want to hear it?" His voice, normally low and steady, cracked a bit on *hear it.*

Maranatha said, "Sure, why not?" *Let's hope this isn't like her other truth-poems.*

He pulled a yellow piece of paper, creased kitty-corner here and there, from his jacket pocket. "Came to me shaped like a bird. She's a funny one, that Camilla."

"Yeah. A funny one."

"We're friends, you know."

"Really?"

"Yep." He exhaled. "So here it is," he said. "She said to sing it to the tune of *The Brady Bunch*, which, she was quick to add," Charlie looked at the paper, reading, "is a chauvinistic TV show portraying man's inhumanity to women, stereotyping women as subservient to society's ill-understood norms." Charlie laughed. "She seems mad."

"That's Camilla."

"Anyway, she apologized for using the song, but she couldn't write the poem any other way, said our story begged to be written to this song. Wanna hear it?" Charlie turned left into a park.

Maranatha shuddered inside. The park used to be a vacant lot, a place she vowed never again to step foot into. General had pushed her down there, her only escape being a swift left kick. She stopped at the park's entrance.

"Anything wrong?"

"I don't like this park."

"My dad's responsible for its restoration. He's mighty proud he turned an eyesore into a haven, at least those are his words. Come on, let's sit on that bench over there. I'll read the poem and we'll head back home."

Maranatha agreed, but her insides jumped.

"Okay," he said, smoothing the paper on his legs. "Here goes."

> Here's the story
> Of a right-smart girlie
> Who was spinning hard to mess up her love life
> Caught up in this whole love mess
> Was poor Charlie
> Inside her web of strife

Maranatha squirmed. She chastised herself afresh for being so stupid as to tell Camilla her whole sorry story. She should've known that nosy girl would turn it into a joke, a platform to write poetry.

Charlie shook his head. "There's more," he said.

> Here's the story
> Of a boy named Charlie
> Who was eyeing Maranatha one fall night
> She had pretty hair of gold
> In the moonlight
> But her eyes held fright

Blood warmed Maranatha's cheeks; heat reddened her face. *What are you up to, Camilla? Trying to ruin my life?*

Charlie continued reading.

> Till the one day when the two came to their
>   senses
> And realized that life was such a mess
> That their love

Was doomed from the beginning
Because she was in love with someone else
With someone else
With someone else
Because she was in love with someone else

Maranatha despised truth, particularly when delivered by stanza and rhyme from a former best friend. She sat stunned on the bench while Violin Charlie disobeyed Camilla's bird folds and crammed it square-like into his pocket.

"Care to fill me in, Maranatha?"

"I never said you were my boyfriend." Her voice sounded flat.

"Oh really? Then why'd you go to homecoming with me? To string me along? Why'd you kiss me?"

"Because," she searched for words but found none. Camilla's song of truth scrambled the words in her head, trembled her hands.

"I thought we were on to something here. Something special. According to Camilla here, there's someone else. Tell me the poem's not true and we'll start over from scratch." Charlie reached an arm around the back of the bench, touching only the hard back.

"I can't."

Charlie removed his arm. He looked away, so far away Maranatha wondered if he could see clear to Louisiana. "It figures."

"What do you mean?" Maranatha inched away, then sat on her hands.

"Girls like you, you can't trust 'em."

Maranatha looked at him. "What does that mean?"

"You're integrated," he spat.

"So?"

"It's not the way things are supposed to be. But I'm willing to overlook that."

"Oh really? How nice of you."

"The thing that bothers me most is your past."

Maranatha touched her forehead, wondering if General's mark lived there, declaring to the world that she was violated. The shame warming her face quickly became unvented anger. For a moment, she sat on her hands like she'd sat on her anger, tried to cram it back inside while Charlie stared at Louisiana. She pulled one hand out from its resting place, and then the other. Once her hands were free, her words followed. "Well, it's a good thing Camilla straightened us both out then, isn't it?" She stood, facing Charlie, who now looked small on the bench. "You wouldn't want to be seen with Maranatha-with-a-past. Folks would talk."

Charlie looked at his knees and mumbled something she couldn't make out.

Anger, once concealed and pressed, lashed out now. "What's that? More rumors about me to sully your reputation? Care to speak up?" The venom surprised Maranatha. She put a hand to her mouth, hoping to keep her words inside where they belonged.

Charlie stood. He looked beyond Maranatha to Louisiana again. "I'd written you a song. On the violin," he said.

"You did?" *That was unexpected.*

He walked away, words dropping behind him like bread-crumbs. "But I guess the only song you'll be hearing is *The Brady Bunch* song. Good-bye, Maranatha."

He left her there.

Alone.

In a park General haunted.

With the knowledge that she'd broken someone's heart. And she'd soon need to break off a friendship.

Twenty-Nine

MISS NICHOLS CALLED EVERY DAY THAT week. And every time, secretary Georgeanne would answer it and hand the phone to Maranatha, who was breezing in the door from school. Though she told her not to take this woman's call, Georgeanne did every time. Something had changed in Georgeanne, though, because the look in her eyes when she handed Maranatha the phone resembled compassion, not smug satisfaction. It unsettled Maranatha. Keeping Georgeanne in the nosy, ditsy, busybody box was easier than enduring bewildering snatches of compassion.

Like clockwork on Friday, Maranatha mounted the steps to the big white house as the phone jangled inside. Like a well-scripted life, she opened the door and put out her hand, where Georgeanne placed the receiver and looked at her like she was a lost puppy, a maddening choreography.

"Hello, Miss Nichols. The answer is no." With Georgeanne feigning dusting the parlor, Maranatha dared not be specific.

"Listen, it's one day of your life. Sometime after Monday, November 23. That's the first day of the trial."

Two weeks from now. "That soon?"

"An hour of your time."

"An hour's like a lifetime."

"If you don't testify, I have nothing." Miss Nichols' voice raised. "Jake Gully will likely go free. Is that what you want?"

Northerners! So good with guilt trips. "I can't, Miss Nichols, but I appreciate your situation."

"My situation could become yours soon. That man will be out on the street. And so will you."

Maranatha hung up the phone. Her hands shook.

Georgeanne flicked her wrist while a pink feather duster flitted about picture frames and displayed china. "I wonder what that Nichols woman wants, calling you every day." Again, crazy empathy laced through her words.

Was Maranatha's life a stage play, and she and Georgeanne its actresses? Didn't Georgeanne know everything anyway? *Or did she?* Weary from a long day of exams, with a Jake Gully–shaped worry sickening her mood, Maranatha left Georgeanne with her pink duster, an "it's none of your business" tacked on as she ascended the stairs.

A soft knock came to Maranatha's closed-on-purpose door.

"I'm busy," she said. Though she wondered why Georgeanne didn't just march in like she usually did, she half expected it to be Miss Nichols, coming to torture her with guilt words.

"It's me," came the voice.

Uncle Zane? Maranatha opened the door.

He stood there awkwardly, fumbling with his fingers. He, always the proper suited man, wore a T-shirt, of all things, with belted, pressed jeans, a crease running white down the front.

"Do you need something?" *Like your normal clothes?* The whole picture of him standing there in *jeans* rattled her.

"Mind if I come in?" His right hand pressed T-shirt between fidgety fingers, like they missed messing with buttons.

"Come on in." She pulled her desk chair to face her bed and offered it to him.

"Thanks," he said. "This came for you today." He handed her an envelope.

Every square inch of it blossomed a confetti of color, like someone had put glue over the whole thing and flung small bits of wrapping paper hither and yon until it was covered like pointillism.

Camilla. That colorful traitor.

Uncle Zane looked out the window, letting an uncomfortable quiet settle between them.

"Is there something you need?"

"Uh, yes, there is." He continued examining the windowpanes. "The house."

"The house?"

"This house. Truth is, it's yours."

"But the papers? Don't I need to do something with them?"

He pressed his hands against his knees like he was ready to push to standing. Instead, he sat, massaging skinny knees. "I had them checked for you. By my lawyer. If you want to stay here when we move, you're welcome to. It's all arranged."

"Really?" Maranatha jumped up. *I'm gonna hug that man's neck!*

"Really." Uncle Zane stood and backed away.

Maranatha hugged him before he reached the door. "Thank you, Uncle Zane."

Though his arms hung at his sides, his stiffening seemed to relax.

"You're welcome."

"I don't know what to say."

"The house'll be yours after Thanksgiving. Georgeanne's having painters come to the new house, so our moving out's delayed. Hope that suits you." Pain creased his eyes, something Maranatha didn't expect.

"Yes, sir," she said, but her voice came out quieter than she intended.

"I know if I were you, I'd be afraid to be alone in this big old house."

"I'm not you," she said. "I'll be fine."

Uncle Zane stood there, a stunned look on his face.

"I didn't mean —"

"I know I'm not the same as I used to be . . . not since the stroke." He spun his wedding ring around his thin finger.

Maranatha looked at her feet, ashamed. "I'm so sorry. I should've stayed home that day. Should've taken care of you."

"Shhh. That wouldn't have changed things at all. It just happened. Nothing you could have done would've stopped it."

She wanted to believe him. But as he shuffled across the floor, all she could feel was the weight of her guilt.

Maranatha sat on her bed, her back against the wall. She pulled her knees to herself, chastising herself again for riding her bike away from Uncle Zane on the day of his stroke. If only . . .

And yet, even in his state, he'd made it so that she no longer needed to testify to save the house. Miss Nichols had no more leverage other than guilt. Uncle Zane's words buzzed her mind like a pestering fly. Would she be afraid all alone in the house? What if Jake Gully escaped? And General, well, he knew exactly where she lived. She gave her prayers voice, while arms hugged her knees.

"Jesus, I guess You answered a prayer." Her voice sounded loud in the room—enough so a lurking Georgeanne could hear—so she spoke into her knees, letting denim muffle her voice. "Thank You. Really. But I'm not sure now. Living alone, well, it scares me a little. I don't even know how I'll shop for food with my bike. And cook. And clean. I've been so bent on keeping the house that I forgot what I'd be giving up. How do I pay bills? I don't even have a checking account. I don't know what to do. Don't know how to be. Not only that, I've made a mess of things. With Violin Charlie. With my Charlie. I hate to keep pestering You, but could You show me what to do? You know I can't testify, but is there something else You want?"

But Jesus was silent, probably off helping someone else right now.

Maranatha's eyes caught the chaotically colorful envelope. "Here goes nothing," she said. She slit the envelope open. She pulled out a flowery card. "Best Wishes to a Great-Aunt on Her Birthday," it read. *What?*

She opened it. Inside was a paper-folded scorpion the color of a manila envelope. Maranatha put it aside. Even though it was a papered bug, it gave her the willies. She read the card. Beneath "May the blessings of friendship and family be yours today and always," Camilla had written a note.

Dear Great-Aunt Maranatha,

I did a terrible thing. I wrote a truth-poem, sent it to Charlie (the white one, not the real one), and now I feel awful. Wrapped up in my own cleverness, I felt I must mail the thing, thought it would be a good laugh. But once I sent it, I knew I'd done something fiendish. I don't expect you to forgive me. Not yet anyway. I'm prepared to do penance, though. You can make me eat meat, even Red Heifer's ribs, next time I see you. You may torture me with dripping water on the forehead or stick my hand in warm water while I sleep. I'll run naked through Burl, if you require it, even through the rail yard. Whatever it takes . . .

I wanted to call, but I'm flat out of money (like Benedict Arnold, I spent my last twenty-two centimes mailing the poem to white Charlie).

I found this card and thought of you. Not sure why. But it was in this box of free stuff at the library. I scrounged a stamp from Fiona, my roommate. Now I have to cut her hair. So, see? I'm desperately sorry. I hope Fiona forgives me when she realizes I don't know how to cut hair. (I think I'll cut it like Georgeanne's. What do you think?)

Next time you see me, I'll be the one flagellating myself with sticks and pinecones and, well, anything I can get my hands on in that silly Burl town. Speaking of flagellating (great word, isn't it?), I'm going to take that stick you keep whacking yourself with over your uncle's stroke. It's not your fault. Sometimes things just happen. If it would help, you could blame me. The way things have been, I'd gladly accept it.

With one cheek offered for a slap,

Camilla-Arnold

PS Inside the scorpion's belly, you'll find my opinion about testifying. You probably won't like it, but, hey, I gotta rhyme the truth.

Maranatha held the card in her hand, considering. She'd loved Camilla since she first saw her spanking a red gym ball down her alleyway under a fading Burl sun. They'd weathered every storm imaginable, real and internal. Camilla knew her secrets. She knew Camilla's — about a nearly debilitating fear of turning into her agoraphobic mother, about her sometimes shame at Denim's rid-Burl-of-crooked-politicians crusades. They'd been through most everything together, even separation.

She unfolded the scorpion, remembering the time she'd stepped on one nasty critter that happened to be making a home in her shoe. Felt like a hot nail being driven into the ball of her foot. Pain with a capital *P*. Inside the scorpion, as promised, was Camilla's truth, scribbled in tiny penciled print.

> I know it must be terrifying,
> This business of your testifying.
> If you don't, it'd be denying,
> All the pain, the hurt, the crying.
> I think you'd rather be defying,
> Than sit inside, afraid and sighing.
> So, stand up now and start relying,
> On Jesus, whose great love is prying.
> He'll open up what's underlying,
> And set your spirit free to flying,
> All because of testifying.

Maranatha read the words over and over again, letting them rhyme their way into places of her heart that she'd kept untouched. Bishop Renny once said that life was like a journey up a mountain. Up and up the trail went, twisting and tortuous. At spots in the journey, God asked folks to trust Him as He wound them through a dark cave, what Bishop Renny called the cave of healing.

"It's mighty dark in there," he'd roared from Mt. Moriah's pulpit. "Plenty dark."

"Mm-hmm," the churchgoers responded, fans fanning.

"And in that cave's a load of hurt."

Maranatha remembered thinking, *Well, who in the world would go in that cave, then?*

"It's mighty dark in there," he'd said. "But Jesus, He's there. Holding your hand while the movie of your life flickers in the dark. The bravest souls are the ones who dare walk into the darkness."

The bishop's words set folks to weeping, but Maranatha remembered being unmoved. Her heart felt cold, dead.

Today, as Camilla's poetry entwined her heart, she was stricken, but alive. Camilla's poem took her into that cave. And it was dark. And scary.

Bishop Renny'd said that nothing could compare to the sight on the other side of the cave. "There's dancing," he'd said. "And the mountain, it seems closer, like you could reach right out and touch it. That's the way of things, friends," he said. "The way of grief and healing. It hurts. It agonizes. But if you hold Jesus' hand through the darkness, you'll taste His presence more sweetly."

The church had erupted in a holy, wild dance after that, the kind Violin Charlie would spurn yet long for. Maranatha remembered slipping out, preferring to sit under a tree while the healed folks danced.

Holding Camilla's letter, she wished she'd stayed inside.

Thirty

MARANATHA MISSED MT. MORIAH. SHE'D CAREFULLY avoided it since the Founder's Day picnic and the Great Charlie Fiasco. But this morning, when she rolled out of bed, the longing inside couldn't be squelched. It was time to go to church, whether Charlie shot hard looks through those brown eyes or not.

Zady'd chastise her for wearing pants, but Maranatha didn't care. Her only transportation today was her bike; riding side-saddle wouldn't work. So she pulled on her nicest black pants and an ironed white blouse, gathered her loosely curled hair into a ponytail, and set off.

Maranatha kept to the main road. If she timed it right, she'd have enough time for a quick detour before the service started. The cooler air revitalized her, made her believe life was actually worth hollering about. The Burl hills meandered before her. Funny how they sped past when she rode in a car. Though she pedaled like a madwoman, the hills stayed lazy, slow even. She passed the costume shop, now picked bare after its Halloween heyday. "Closed for the winter," a sign read. The farm imple-ment shop appeared naked. The only thing left in its yard was a skeleton crew of ancient plows. The bed and breakfast's For Sale sign was faded now. Too much Texas sun and no buyer. The off-kilter mobile home was gone. So was the goat. A large farm lay barren, its fields burnt.

Maranatha liked the putting-to-bed aspect of fall and winter. Time to curl inside, to hibernate. She wished for a roaring fire in *her* home, complete with a classic novel and a cup of hot chocolate. Under one of Mama Frankie's afghans, she'd read the day away, with no one to bother her.

A gust of chilly breeze attacked her, goose-bumping her arms. She pedaled faster. A car sped around her, then slowed. Her heart erupted in her chest, not from pedaling too hard, but from fear. The butterscotch-colored car stopped fifty yards ahead, its tailpipe puffing exhaust in the cold November air. No one got out.

She stopped pedaling and coasted slowly toward the idling car. She debated whether she should pass it on the shoulder or risk a pass on the road. She opted for the road. The car door opened as she flanked the car. She squeezed the handbrakes, coming to a stop in time. A bewildered Augustine, Bishop Renny's wife, stood wide-eyed, inches from Maranatha's front tire.

"Natha, what're you doing here?"

"Biking to church." She smiled. "Where's Bishop Renny?"

"He's already there," she answered. "He paces the stage, wrestles with the Lord a good hour before folks show up. Me and the kids want to sleep in a bit."

"Are you all right?"

"Yeah. We're fine. Someone blessed us with this car just a few weeks ago, but it only goes seven miles, supposedly a heavenly number, and then it gets tuckered out. So I stop it, let it get its feet back underneath, and I start it again." She put her hands on her hips. "Natha, we've missed you something fierce. I'm so glad you're coming to church today."

"Me too. I'd offer you a ride, but—"

Augustine's laugh cut off Maranatha's obvious explanation. "Child, you git yourself on to church, you hear? I have a feeling you'll be blessed. I know *we* will, just seeing you." Augustine kissed her own hand and pressed it to Maranatha's cheek. "Now git!"

Maranatha pedaled past the car. A mile later, she slowed, then turned right into the abandoned spot of land. The squirrel gate was still broken at its hinge, leaving a triangle of emptiness as a crawl-through entryway. She scurried underneath, stood, and brushed off dusty pants.

Heart pounding in her chest, she looked around. No dandelion fields greeted her. No pillared house. Only brown, bent-over grass, naked trees, and a black piece of scorched earth. *Like my life.*

The terror-feeling she'd had when Augustine's car slowed revisited her there. Every ounce of fear came flooding in. Maranatha shook, this time from fright, though the hard wind could've shaken her as well. Echoes of Old Mack wove through her, words about her running away from evil folks. Zady's voice slipped in and out, reminding her of being chased. She wondered if she'd spend her entire life running away from men, no matter whether they wore evil or goodwill on their hearts.

She sat on the dandelion graveyard and touched the hard ground. She sat there with her frightened, weary self and wondered for a moment what life would be without fear, without secrets. Was there such a thing?

She hoped God would speak to her then, floating like a breeze over her soul, but no voice came. No trees whistled a parable, a message. She stood, brushed dead grass from her pants, and walked back to her bike.

You have a funny way of answering prayer, she told a silent God.

Maranatha didn't ride with anticipation. Truth be told, she lollygagged. When the time came to turn left onto the county road leading to Mt. Moriah, she stopped, remembering the last frenzied time she'd pedaled there, away from the likes of Jake Gully. She swallowed the fear, but it kept coming up, stinging her throat.

She turned left.

Despite chewing on fear, no attackers chased her. The menacing road looked like an ordinary country road, dotted with grazing black cows that looked up with friendly faces. One mile later, she steered right into Mt. Moriah's parking lot, late. Warmth and light danced through the windows. Singing enticed her.

Inside, she slid into an empty back pew, hopefully unnoticed. The word *glory* bounced the rafters. Over and over again, the congregation sang "glory" in several-part harmony. Though everyone stood, Maranatha sat, letting glory sink into her heart, that is, if it could.

The songs lifted her, sorrowed her, chastised her, lavished her. Songs about heaven, earth, life, Jesus. She wanted her tears to stay behind the well-locked doors of her eyes, but they seemed to be winning, seeping in and around the crevices. She wiped away each one, sniffing.

Bishop Renny dismissed the singers, thanked them for their anointed worship. He stood behind the podium, silent. For a good minute, not bowing, not looking as if he were about to speak. Simply standing.

The once-electric air of worship quieted.

Bishop Renny walked away from the podium, Bible in hand.

He pursed his lips as if he would speak, only to pace the stage.

Quiet.

He turned, faced the congregation. "The Lord wants us to repent, folks."

An "amen" shot heavenward.

"But it's not what you'd expect."

Another "amen."

"Some of us haven't been listening to the Lord, haven't obeyed the last thing He said."

He opened his Bible and read. "This is from the second book of Kings, chapter six, verses one through seven." He cleared his throat. "And the sons of the prophets said unto Elisha, Behold now, the place where we dwell with thee is too strait for us. Let us go, we pray thee, unto Jordan, and take thence every man a beam, and let us make us a place there, where we may dwell. And he answered, Go ye. And one said, Be content, I pray thee, and go with thy servants. And he answered, I will go. So he went with them. And when they came to Jordan, they cut down wood. But as one was felling a beam, the axe head fell into the water: and he cried, and said, Alas, master! for it was borrowed. And the man of God said, Where fell it? And he shewed him the place. And he cut down a stick, and cast it in thither; and the iron did swim. Therefore said he, Take it up to thee. And he put out his hand, and took it."

Maranatha didn't know what in the world any of this meant, other than she never understood the difference between Elijah and Elisha.

"Some of us need to throw the stick," he said.

Mumbled "mm-hmms" answered back.

"The man lost his axe head, plain as day. It sunk to the bottom of the pond. If the pond was anything like our man-made lakes, it had lots of slimy mess all around. And if an axe head flew through the air, there's no telling where it landed in the water exactly."

Bishop Renny closed his Bible around his finger and paced. "That man didn't do the obvious. Sure, he cried. He lamented. He pouted. But he didn't return to the place where he lost his borrowed axe head. He didn't *return*."

A "preach it" echoed from the congregation.

"The man of God told him to return." He set his Bible on the podium. "He cast a stick into the water, and that axe head rose to the top. Yes, ma'am. Yes, sir, it rose." As he said it, Bishop Renny raised his hands ceilingward.

A few more "amens" rattled the church.

"God's been speaking to you," he said. "And you've run away, afraid. He's calling you back. Back to the word He spoke to you before. You gotta face your fears, go back, and obey."

"Halleluiah," Zady's voice echoed from the front of the church.

"And miracles will happen. Some of you lament the fact that God doesn't speak to you. Well, maybe He did, but you walked away. Too chicken to obey. He won't speak another word until you heed what He said first. Go back! Go back! Go back!" Bishop Renny jumped up and down now, the organ punctuating each leap.

The last thing God had said to Maranatha thudded in her heart, in her ears. She knew God had told her to face her fears, knew it after Zady had sat with her on the porch swing.

She chewed on her bottom lip, curling her fingers into the palms of her hands.

What did it mean, exactly, to face her fears? Could Bishop Renny read her thoughts?

The now-sweaty man took out a handkerchief, wiped

his face. He stood behind the podium and raised a funny-looking book. "This is a New Testament," he said, "paraphrased by a man named J. B. Phillips. I want to read you something astonishing."

He thumbed through its pages. "Here it is. It's from the book of James, chapter one, verse two." He looked at his family, then, tears shining his eyes. "This is our family's verse." He cleared his throat, gaining composure. "The Good Book says, 'When all kinds of trials and temptations crowd into your lives, my brothers, don't resent them as intruders, but welcome them as friends!'"

What? Maranatha thought the kindly bishop had lost his marbles. Why would anyone want to welcome trials as friends? And what did that have to do with a floating axe head? Was she supposed to welcome folks like General as friends? Maranatha stood to leave, but Bishop Renny's voice settled her back into the pew.

"Trials," he said. "We all have them. And they come like mischief-makers. But we are told to welcome them. Why? Because God has something up His mighty sleeve. He knows that if we welcome them, He'll use them in our lives to make us better folks. More compassionate. More brave. More holy. Trials are gifts. Not to be run from, like that foolish man and the axe, but embraced. Like the axe head, we think all is lost, but God asks us to go back to the place where the pain was. And what does He do? He redeems it all."

Bishop Renny spoke forty minutes more. About Israelites and wandering. About disciples who didn't understand. He rambled in and out of Bible passages. But Maranatha's mind stayed on his first words.

Go back.

Welcome trials as friends.

She thought of the upcoming trial, a genuine, real-life trial that she was avoiding like an enemy. Her heart recoiled when she went back to the last trial she'd testified at, how she felt naked while General sat leering at her.

I can't do it.

As the church ladies readied the outer hall for supper, Maranatha stayed in the back, hoping to slip out unnoticed. Before she could, someone tapped her on the shoulder. She turned.

"Hey, Natha," Charlie said.

"Hey." Charlie seemed taller. More like a man.

"Want to go take a walk with me? I promise I won't talk much."

Bishop Renny's words had so knotted her mind, she couldn't think of doing anything with anybody. Part of her wanted to walk with Charlie. Part of her was angry with him for knowing too much. Part of her wanted to kick him. Part of her wanted to kiss him. "No. I need to get back home. It's a long ride."

"I can drive you. I could put your bike in the bed."

Maranatha remembered Jake Gully doing that, hefting her bike into the red pickup's bed. "No thanks." She skirted around Charlie, leaving him standing behind the pew. "I have to go."

Her words sounded fearful on her lips, but she went anyway.

Thirty-One

HE FOUND HER.

General.

Maranatha knew it'd happen sooner or later, but she didn't expect to see him clean-cut under the pecan tree looking like he'd preached a sermon. "Hey, Beautiful," he said. The sun poked itself through the trees' near-barren branches, highlighting General's copper head. Funny thing, though. He hadn't aged a bit since she saw him last in the courtroom so many years ago. She expected him to look more like a man, but his boyishness, for a brief instant, made him look vulnerable.

Maranatha said nothing. She heard her heartbeat in her ears. The pavement beneath her warbled. She squeezed her eyes shut and opened them again. The world blurred, the trees' stark branches oddly blending into the sky like an artist had smeared them together. General stood under hazy sunshine, eyes scanning her body.

Nausea attacked her. Made her almost bend over, but she could not speak. She shivered her response.

"Why don't you and I go on a little date? It's been a long time. We have catching up to do, don't you think?"

No voice. Her hand trembled.

Maranatha looked around. The street was empty. *I'm alone.*

General walked toward her, but she didn't move. He touched her hair, tucking a strand behind her ear.

His warm breath polluted her face. She took one step back. A small victory.

"Don't you be shying away from me, Beautiful. You know I don't like that."

Say something! Do something! Anything!

General stepped closer, this time touching her jaw with a rough hand.

She knuckled her fist, backed away, and let rage fill her fist. Swing! *Crack.* She landed a swift punch to General's nose. He staggered back, wiping blood, cursing.

"What in the—"

"Get out of my yard," Maranatha measured.

"Now let's not get carried away, Beautiful."

"That's *not* my name." She kicked him under his buckle.

General crumpled to the sidewalk.

"I'm not afraid of you anymore."

A woodpecker's *knock knock knock* blurred General.

Knock. Knock. Knock.

She looked again. Where he'd fallen was nothing. Only pavement.

Knock. Knock. Knock.

"Maranatha? You all right?"

Uncle Zane's voice.

What's happening?

A hand touched her cheek. She balled another fist and swung, hitting air.

"Maranatha! Wake up!"

It's a dream. Wake up. Wake up! Now aware, Maranatha tried to force herself from the dream. It seemed to take hours.

Open your eyes. Now.

Her eyes obeyed. Sitting next to her was Uncle Zane, a look of bewildered compassion in his eyes. He wore striped blue and white pajamas, and his hair was askew. "You were hollering," he said. "Really loud."

"I was?"

"And fighting."

"I'm sorry," she said.

"No matter. It reminded me."

Maranatha sat up. "Of what?"

"Your mama."

"Really?"

"Yes. She had these dreams. Near every night. She'd scream and holler, fighting the air. Sounded like terror."

"And you woke her?"

Uncle Zane's eyes searched hers. "Every time. Like this. Your mama was a fighter. My brother, he tried to take her soul, but he couldn't do it. She fought him in her dreams. I'm inclined to think she walloped him every time." A shy smile upturned Uncle Zane's thin lips.

"Have I ever hollered in my dreams before?"

"A long time ago. Not lately."

"My father. Do you think he won? That he ruined my mama?"

Uncle Zane looked away. He pinched the top of his nose with his thumb and forefinger. "No!" He stood, punctuating a loud voice. "No," he said, softer. "Your mama . . ." He turned away. She could hear him breathe in and out several times. "Your mama was the most beautiful thing that ever happened in my life. Brought me joy. Sang me songs. Lit up the darkness. Nothing my brother did could take that away from me."

"She loved you?" Maranatha scooted to the edge of her bed,

covering her legs with her long nightshirt.

"Yes."

"You loved her?"

"Yes."

"Uncle Zane?"

He looked at her then, a trace of fatherliness in his eyes.

"I love you." Maranatha stood and grabbed Uncle Zane tight. Sobs, locked away for safekeeping, unlocked themselves, wrenching her body. He wrapped thin arms around her and pet her head.

"It's going to be all right," he said. "Shhhh."

Maranatha fell into him then, like a crying child falls into the arms of her awaiting father after skinning her knees. She never knew Jesus would answer her *Show me that You love me* prayer by masquerading as Uncle Zane.

But He did.

Thirty-Two

NO.

Maranatha told God no.

She didn't care that Bishop Renny seemed to know her secrets, that he preached a sermon right to her. So what?

Even if Old Mack asked her to testify, she wouldn't.

Zady either, though her words about fleeing villains unsettled her.

What if the hero Maranatha found herself running to was herself? Maybe she could only save herself by *not* testifying. Most of her life had been hers — hers to protect — and now she was determined to control it.

But at night a face haunted her.

Maddie's.

She'd be chased in and through Burl's streets, criminals out to get her. She'd run into the big white house, panting. She'd slam the door and run up to her room. But Maddie was there, lying on Maranatha's bed, weeping, hair knotted around her face, a sunken eye socket pleading, begging.

Maranatha awakened, feeling like she was being choked. She couldn't tell if it was by General. Or Jake Gully.

Or Maddie.

After school, Maranatha walked up the stairs to *her* home. Georgeanne greeted her, phone in hand, eyes sad. "It's Miss Nichols again," she said, her voice sounding pinched.

"I need you," Miss Nichols said. "Maddie needs you."

"Leave me alone." Maranatha slammed the receiver down.

"Maranatha! Your manners!" Georgeanne looked aghast.

She wanted to think of a snide comeback, but all sarcastic words had left her mind.

Georgeanne placed her hands on her hips and shook her head. "Hanging up? That's not you."

"Not me? How do you know who I am? How do you even dare to say—" Maranatha's voice choked. She sensed hot tears swelling her eyelids. She took a deep breath, looked away. "I'm scared," Maranatha blurted, surprised at her words. Surprised at the truth that exploded inside her. "I'm so scared."

"Scared? You? I just don't see—"

The phone rang.

"I'll get it," Georgeanne said, her voice smacking of kindness.

"No," Maranatha said. "I think I need to." She willed her heart to slow down. Told her mind to stop panicking. "Hello? Miss Nichols?"

"Yes."

"I'm sorry. That was rude."

Georgeanne nodded at Maranatha.

"I hate to push you," Miss Nichols said. "I just don't know what to do. I'm afraid he'll be back out on the street, hurting other women." She paused. "Is that what you want? Really?"

"No," Maranatha whispered. She twisted the phone cord

around and around her finger. She looked at Georgeanne, then turned away. With guts she didn't think she had, Maranatha said, "I'll testify."

Miss Nichols stayed quiet a moment. Maranatha could hear her let out a breath. "Good. Thank you."

"Tell me what I need to do before I change my mind." Maranatha took out a pencil and a small pad of paper from the drawer under the phone. She felt Georgeanne's curiosity. Maranatha put her hand over the phone. "Do you mind? This is private."

Georgeanne left.

For several minutes Miss Nichols told Maranatha facts about the case and what she'd like to accomplish when she questioned her. "Let me give you a brief legal lesson. I know you went through this before, but you were pretty young then."

"Yeah, I was." Maranatha's stomach gnarled.

"First the police arrest a suspect," Miss Nichols continued, "in this case one Harold Gully."

"But I thought his name was —"

"His friends may call him Jake, but his name is Harold. Anyway, when Harold gets the cuffs, hopefully the arresting officer says the Miranda rights —"

"You have the right to remain silent —"

Miss Nichols laughed. "Yes, that's right. You must've watched a few episodes of *Adam 12*."

"*CHiPs*," Maranatha said.

"Then he's interrogated, usually with a lawyer present. Evidence is gathered, including interviewing the victim. We as the prosecution see if there is probable cause. In this case, it was clear, and I was handed the case."

"What are you, exactly?"

"An ADA. Assistant District Attorney."

"Sounds important."

"Not really. I'm pretty low on the totem pole here."

"Well, *I'm* impressed." Maranatha jotted a few notes and then drew a picture of Miss Nichols.

"So, since this is a felony case, we had an advisement hearing, followed by a preliminary hearing. I basically had to prove I had a case, complete with witness testimony. Which I did."

"But I didn't testify."

"You're right. But I had enough evidence to go on, thankfully, and the case was bound over to district court for arraignment. You're lucky Burl's the county seat. This court is a district court, so you won't have to travel to testify."

"Yeah, lucky," Maranatha said, though she didn't think so.

"Now the trial starts." Miss Nichols gave her the same trial date as before, letting her know she'd most likely testify the second day, Tuesday, November 24, but it was always hard to tell with these things. Jury selection was underway, all according to schedule, thankfully. "I'll need you to come in. Can you make it after school this week? Every day?"

"Sure," Maranatha said. The word didn't roll off her tongue like she planned it to. She wanted it to sound, well, *assured*. Instead, her voice sounded shaken.

"It will be important for you to have a lot of support there," Miss Nichols said. "The prosecution will bring up the past. All of it."

Maranatha swallowed her jitters. She wondered if she'd be able to face everyone, sitting high in the witness stand, fielding uncomfortable questions. How would Uncle Zane handle it? Last time, he'd shielded his eyes with a hat brim pulled low. Maranatha resigned herself to the awful truth that Georgeanne wouldn't miss a trial, not if Zane were going. *Great.* And Zady? She knew everything anyway, as did Charlie and Raymond. Old

Mack didn't know, but she knew he'd be supportive. Camilla might smirk and try to make her laugh. She could see these folks lined up while she spoke of violation, rape, fear. *Can I really do this?*

"Maranatha? Are you following me?"

She shook her head, ridding her mind of the friends and family row. "Do I have to have people I know there?"

"Yes. I think it's wise."

Maranatha spent the week at school mulling over Miss Nichols' instructions. She couldn't concentrate. She met briefly with a financial aid person, followed by a short meeting with the guidance counselor, but college seemed further away this week. Instead, Jake Gully haunted her mind while the list of people she was supposed to contact to come to the trial stared at her from her notebook. None down, too many to go. She wished she could wave a wand and have all the people told, but her words kept to themselves. She couldn't seem to do it.

Maranatha imagined the conversation like this:

Hey, I'm going to be testifying in court, and my lawyer thought you should be there.

Be there? Why? the person would ask.

The man on trial, he tried to nab me. Oh, and by the way, the lawyers defending him are going to take all my secrets and spew them on the courtroom. I sure hope you can make it!

Over and over she'd try to rehearse the invitation, but it always ended with the same too-cheerful, *I sure hope you can make it!*

Maranatha welcomed Friday. She rode her bike home from school, this time avoiding the courthouse. Four days of coaching were enough. All she wanted was her quiet room. But Charlie stood at her gate, his white truck parked next to the pecan.

"Hey, Natha."

"Hey." She rolled her bike into the yard. Charlie followed.

"What's going on?"

"Nothing."

"You want to talk?"

"Yeah." She was careful not to climb the steps. She didn't want to sit on the porch swing and listen to Charlie ramble, so she stood under the tree while Charlie fumbled with his pockets, looking nervous.

"I suppose you already know all this. You know how news travels, especially from your mama's mouth." Maranatha could see pain in Charlie's eyes. And a hint of confusion.

"What, Natha?"

"I'm testifying next week. The attorney lady said I need friends there."

"You on trial?"

"No. I'm testifying in a trial for something else."

"Then why do you need folks there?"

"I just do. So, would you come? It's next Tuesday at the courthouse. Tell your mama and daddy, will you?" *Phew! Three asked in one conversation.* She turned to leave.

"But, Natha, I have something — "

"Save it 'til after the testifying," she cut in. "You'll have plenty of words, or none at all for that matter, after all this is said and done." She turned and mounted the stairs, not looking back. Before she shut the door, she heard the truck's engine roar to life.

"I'm testifying next Tuesday," she told Old Mack. Spilling the words to Old Mack was easier now that she'd invited Charlie and his family.

"What for?" He offered her a cold bottled Coke. She accepted.

"About the time I had to use the bike. To flee like you said. I *did* have to use it." She looked at the floor, ashamed of her previous lie. She hoped he wouldn't ask more. He didn't. She forced herself to look at him. "The lawyer lady said I should have some friends there. Will you come?"

"Of course," Old Mack said. "I wouldn't miss it."

"Old Mack?"

"Yeah."

"Do you have secrets?"

He braided his beard. He pulled a small rubber band from his cash register drawer and bound it around his beard's end. "Of course. All folks do."

"Are they terrible? The secrets, I mean." She took a swig of Coke.

"Aren't all secrets terrible? Otherwise, why'd they be secrets?"

"I suppose you're right." There was so much more she wanted to ask, but Maranatha lost the energy. The load of everyone she loved hearing terrible things about her felt like a truck tire hoisted between her shoulders.

"Maranatha Winningham?"

"Yeah."

"You're a brave girl. Remember that, okay? Tell the truth. I hear it'll set you free."

"I hope so," she said. But she wasn't so sure.

That night at dinner, she told Uncle Zane and Georgeanne the news that she'd be testifying in a trial. "Will you come? It's on Tuesday." *I hope you're happy, Miss Nichols. Inviting Georgeanne's like inviting Satan to my birthday party. No telling what evil might befall me.*

"A trial? How dramatic!" Georgeanne fanned her napkin in the air, her empathetic look gone. "You hear that, Zane dear? Our Maranatha's going to be on trial!"

Not our *Maranatha.*

"Not *on* trial. *In* a trial. The lawyer—"

"Is that that Northern woman with the straight teeth?" Georgeanne picked rib meat from hers.

"Yeah, that's her. Anyway—"

"She wears the most beautiful suits. I wonder if she buys them in Marshall."

Uncle Zane pushed peas around on his plate. "Georgeanne," he said, "let the girl finish."

What? A reprimand? From Uncle Zane? Maranatha expected an explosion of words from Georgeanne's ample mouth. And she wondered why Georgeanne said nothing about Maranatha's getting the house. She'd expected a stream of words about it.

"Sorry, Zane," Georgeanne said in a whisper, averting her eyes. "Yes, Maranatha?"

Maranatha swallowed. "It's just that, I'm testifying, and the lawyer thinks I should have friends and family there. For support."

"How nice." Georgeanne placed her silverware on her plate. She took a long drink of tea. "And she's calling me *family*. I'm touched, Maranatha."

"We'll be there, won't we?" Uncle Zane said with an edge to his voice that Maranatha'd never heard before.

"Well, of course! That way I could ask that Miss Nichols woman where she does her shopping!"

Maranatha couldn't bring herself to go to church Sunday. Couldn't get out of bed. A heaviness seeped into her, the kind that made her want to sleep the day away. She knew Zady'd be expecting her at church, knew she'd probably be advertising the trial to everyone in the congregation. She couldn't face it.

Soon the world would know what kind of girl she was. A stained one. A violated one. An easy target. Though Charlie already knew the General story, she wondered how he'd take it coming from her mouth. He'd probably walk out of the courtroom. Out of her life. She deserved it, she knew. She'd been horrid to Charlie the moment she found out he knew. Things between them had been easier when Charlie'd kept General's sad fact to himself. Why'd he have to go and spoil it? It'd been easier to vent her anger at Charlie than to wrestle through the feelings of longing inside her, easier to push him away because he knew than to pull him close and face her fears.

She counted the cracks on her ceiling seven times. The ceiling seemed too far away this morning, the house too large. Though the thought of living with Georgeanne and all her hair products galled her, being alone bothered her even more. In two weeks, Georgeanne and Uncle Zane would live in Violin Charlie's neighborhood. And Maranatha'd be left to count the cracks.

A knock at the front door startled her. With Uncle Zane and Georgeanne at First Baptist and Mt. Moriah's service well underway, she wondered who it could be. Maranatha looked out the window but saw no car. The street was quiet, still sleeping in.

The knock sounded again, this time insistent. Maranatha pulled on a pair of sweats and a Texas A&M sweatshirt and walked down the stairs. She opened the door.

Camilla!

Maranatha wanted to throw her arms around her truth-poetry friend, but Camilla shoved a Kroger bag into the space between them.

"I've come to do penance." She shook the bag, bothering Maranatha to take it. "Go for it. Cook it up."

"What is it?"

"Baby cow—veal. And a package of livers. And cow tongue."

"Nasty! Why would I—"

"C'mon, cook it up. It'll make me feel better."

"I doubt that. Besides, you know I don't cook."

Camilla brushed past her. She walked up the stairs, leaving Maranatha with a bag full of animal parts.

Maranatha laughed as she stashed the contents of the bag in the fridge. She ran upstairs, finding Camilla in her room.

Camilla stood in front of the window, the bright fall day emanating around her. "I'm sorry," she said.

"I know." Maranatha plopped on her bed. She noticed Camilla's clothing now. An old man's button-down, two sizes too big, over a "Choose Life" T-shirt, Wham!-style. Sticking out from the frumpy mess were pegged and dyed Levis. *Interesting.*

Camilla sat at the desk. "Don't you think you ought to get dressed?"

"Not if I'm going to look like a hobo. What's with the clothes?"

"I call it urban chic," Camilla said.

"It looks more like thrift store meets Waver." Maranatha had criticized Camilla's propensity for MTV clothing, a la Duran Duran, before, but this was plain weird.

"I've missed my daddy so much, I stole his shirt this morning. Now quit with me. You're not exactly Princess Di, you know. You need to put some clothes on."

"When I'm good and ready."

"You're missing church." Camilla stood. She opened Maranatha's wardrobe, touching each dress.

"So are you."

"Yeah, but I have an excuse. Jet lag."

Maranatha laughed. "You know Chicago and Dallas are in the same time zone, don't you?"

"Yeah, but flying makes me tired, so that counts for something. I got in at ten last night."

"Wow, that's late," Maranatha teased.

"Besides, my mama's sick and daddy's staying home to take care of her."

"She okay?"

"Yeah, a cold. But you know how my dad is. He's all about doting."

"You're lucky," Maranatha said.

Camilla pulled the desk chair to the bed and sat down. "How do you figure?"

"You have a father."

"*You* have one." Camilla rested her chin on her hands.

"He didn't exactly win Father of the Year. Besides, I never met him."

"Yes, you have. Lots of times."

"What?"

Camilla pointed to the cracked ceiling. "Jesus' Dad is your Father too."

"Well, yeah, but —"

"Don't 'yeah, but' me. Sometimes truth stares us in the face. And sometimes God comes dressed in surprising packages."

A long silence hugged the room.

"Uncle Zane hugged me," Maranatha said, finally.

"He did? Is he dying?"

"No. He hugged me, that's all. Like a father would."

Camilla leaned forward, put both hands on Maranatha's shoulders. "Hold a true friend with both of your hands," she said, releasing her grip.

"That's beautiful."

"It's not mine, unfortunately. It's a Nigerian proverb. Are you ever going to forgive me?"

"I already did."

"But you didn't say it out loud."

"I forgive you, Camilla. Does that suit you?" Maranatha leaned back on her bed.

"Suits me fine."

Maranatha filled Camilla in on the upcoming trial and testifying, how she was scared, particularly about saying all that stuff in front of folks she knew.

"So you heeded my poetry!" Camilla stood.

"Yes, happy? Though it really was a bad poem, from an artistic standpoint."

Camilla faced the window. The autumn sun angled through the near-barren trees, outlining her. "I'm about done with rhyming," she said. "It's part of the new me, I think."

"Will the 'new you' be at the trial?"

"No." Camilla didn't turn around, seemingly intent on the sun-streaked outdoors.

"Why?" Maranatha pulled on slippers and stood.

Camilla turned around, eyes watered. "I can't. That's all."

She ran past Maranatha. "Keep the meat," she said as she took the stairs.

The front door slammed, leaving Maranatha shivering alone in the big white house.

Thirty-Three

UNCLE ZANE CAME INTO MARANATHA'S ROOM that night. He sat on the edge of her bed. "What are you reading?"

"Your favorite book," she said. She showed him the cover. *To Kill a Mockingbird* by Harper Lee.

"How appropriate," he said.

"I suppose. It's a bit unnerving, though. Atticus, he did the best lawyering, yet they found poor Tom guilty."

Uncle Zane sat quiet for a moment. He looked at the wardrobe and shook his head. "Sometimes justice never comes in this life."

"So, what's the point?" Maranatha put the book down and crossed her arms over her pajama-clad chest.

"You do your best, that's all. And hope God sees."

Another bout of silence emptied the room of words.

"Uncle Zane?" she finally asked.

"Yes."

"Were you poor once?"

"Why do you ask?"

"It's just, when we saw those river-bottom folks a while back, you got real mad at Georgeanne, like you understood something about being poor."

"Things weren't always what they are now." He looked at his feet.

Silence shrouded the room, not an uncomfortable one where words like *awkward* or *impossibly long* described it, but a silence of hoping for a story that might never be told. Maranatha decided to let Uncle Zane keep his thrift of words for now. Perhaps someday he'd share.

Maranatha looked out the window. "Are you going to miss me?"

"Yes. I am."

"Me too. I'll miss you too, I mean."

"I know," he said. "You're always welcome to stay with us, you know."

"I am?"

"Of course. Georgeanne may not show it, but she's been boo-hooing the last couple days about the move."

"Why?"

"Because she doesn't want to leave you here."

"I thought she'd be throwing me a good-riddance party. I'm surprised she hasn't danced a jig in my presence. She hasn't even mentioned my staying."

"She's sad you're staying. She loves you. In her own way, of course."

"She sure has a funny way of showing it. She snoops, you know. And takes my things."

"Give her time." Uncle Zane stood. "There's more to her than meets the eye. You'll see."

He left her alone, but for the first time she didn't feel lonely.

Thirty-Four

MARANATHA'S CLOCK RADIO CAME ON AT six to the words to The Romantics' song about someone hollering secrets in her sleep. "How appropriate," she muttered.

She sat on the edge of her bed. There was something off-kilter about her room. She couldn't figure it out. She waited while her eyes adjusted to the shadows. Then she saw it. A white something hanging from the handle of her wardrobe.

She padded across the room, warm feet meeting cold hardwood. "My dress!" Her mama's white dress, perfectly pressed and perfectly white, hung like a mystery from the wardrobe's handle. She turned the hanger around. Perfectly white. How did Uncle Zane do it?

She ran downstairs to the kitchen, where he ate his egg and toast. "Thanks," she said.

"For what?" he mumbled through chewed toast.

"The dress. How did you get it clean?"

He swallowed. "What?"

"The dress hanging in my room. Mama's dress."

Georgeanne scooted around Maranatha from behind. "What's all the commotion?"

"You know anything about a dress?" Uncle Zane asked.

"Of course. I meant it to be a surprise for Christmas, but I couldn't wait." Georgeanne poured herself a cup of coffee from the percolator under the cabinets.

"You had my dress cleaned?" Maranatha sat. Her joy over the beautiful dress waltzed with sadness. She sat down while regret sifted through her. *All those mean thoughts I nursed. And then this.*

"Thought you'd need something lovely to wear while you testified today, beings as how that Miss Nichols lady would be all pristine. It took a lot of mileage, though. Had to travel up to Dallas to have it professionally cleaned. That spot was mighty pink."

Maranatha reached a hand across the table where Georgeanne now sat. "Thank you." She touched Georgeanne's hand for the first time, then left the room.

In her bedroom, Maranatha wept. From confusion. Life had become manageable with Georgeanne as an enemy, but this act of kind treason jumbled everything up in Maranatha's head. If Georgeanne was capable of kindness, love even, Maranatha would have to grapple with forgiveness, something she wanted to hold on to and not give away easily.

She picked up the dress, the white, white dress, and held it to herself. She could no longer smell her mother there, but she could feel her. She wondered if the dress would be like Zady's tale of stained baby clothes.

"It's the oddest thing," Zady told her last summer. "A gal from our church had a baby, so I got out all our baby clothes, fixin' to give them to her. I put them in the box pristine clean, and they came out stained, like I'd never used any bleach."

Maranatha could see herself on the witness stand, wearing the white dress like armor. Each question about Jake or General would cause the punch stain to return little by little until the whole dress bled pink. Everyone would know.

She sat on the bed, hugged her knees. "Jesus, I can't do this. I can't." She said the prayer over and over, hoping to convince God to please intervene, say something kindly like, *Don't worry, Maranatha. I'm actually coming back today, right before the trial,* or, *I asked you to be willing, and you were; now, you're free. No need to testify,* or, *Jake confessed it all last night in his cell.* But God was silent. Deafeningly so.

She said one last "I can't do this" when the door opened.

Uncle Zane stood there, his eyes red. "You want a ride? I'm leaving in fifteen minutes."

"Sure," she heard herself say while her stomach entangled itself.

I'm going to throw up. Maranatha trudged up the courthouse stairs as though it would be the last time she'd ever see daylight. Dread filled her. She'd walk into this courthouse a person with secrets; she'd leave exposed. She looked down at her dress rippling in the slight breeze. *Soon you'll be pink. Red, maybe.* Inside, she excused herself from Georgeanne and Uncle Zane to find a bathroom.

She stood in the stall long after she needed to, her hot forehead pressed against the door. She whispered, "Jesus, I need You. Help." She longed for peace, the kind Bishop Renny preached about, but her stomach only churned war.

Maranatha washed her hands over and over again, scrubbing absentmindedly.

Miss Nichols entered the tiled bathroom, her heels clicking a hello. She put a thin hand on Maranatha's shoulder. "I need to tell you something," she said.

"What?" The way Miss Nichols spoke twirled Maranatha's insides.

"I hope you can forgive me."

Maranatha stepped back. She pulled a paper towel from the dispenser and dried her hands. "For what?"

"For willfully withholding information."

Without thinking, she grabbed another towel and rubbed her hands raw. "Such as?"

"The defense attorney. It's Ridley Owen."

"No." *Oh God. Not that man!*

"Yes, I'm afraid so."

Maranatha held her stomach. "We spent every afternoon last week together, and you didn't tell me this?"

"I'm sorry." Miss Nichols didn't sound like she meant it.

"I can't do it. Can't face *him*." Tears bullied her eyes, taunting her to release them. She took in six breaths. Slow and steady.

Miss Nichols faced her now, put two hands on Maranatha's shoulders, and looked into her nearly bursting eyes. "You can do this. I know you can."

"That's easy for you to say. Why didn't you tell me until now?"

The ADA in the perfect brick red suit let go of Maranatha's shoulders. "I need you to testify. I knew if I told you that you'd face the same lawyer, you'd balk."

"Maybe you should test your skills as a lawyer without me. It'd be a good challenge, don't you think?" Maranatha looked away.

"Listen, I understand your reticence." Miss Nichols' voice grew quiet. "But the jury needs to hear the truth."

"If the jury hears the truth about Jake, they'll also hear the truth about me."

"Granted, a terrible catch-22."

"Granted," Maranatha spat.

Miss Nichols opened the door. "It's time."

For my funeral.

The court's center aisle had grown to yellow-brick-road proportions. Maranatha took each step in slow motion. Her leaden feet followed Miss Nichols. She felt the stares of everyone there. The subject of the murmuring, she knew, was her.

Maranatha sat. She wanted to turn around, to catch a friendly gaze, but fear held her head forward.

Jake Gully looked small, but his effect on her was big. Nausea. Sweaty palms. A sudden headache behind her eyes. She watched the jury as they eyed the man and wondered if they'd feel sorry for him. She sure didn't.

Someone hollered, "All rise for the Honorable Judge Horatio Baker."

Horatio? She remembered the interim judge who presided over the last trial — a very tall, gaunt man with an angular face. This was no gaunt judge. Maranatha could see how Violin Charlie resembled old Horatio. Same eyes. Same mouth. But Horatio was a good 150 pounds heavier, like two Charlies stuffed into one black-robed body.

When Ridley Owen sat his bald self down, Maranatha held her stomach. He was already starting to sweat. She could almost smell his breath.

The Honorable Horatio settled into his seat while his "congregation" rose and sat. Maranatha wished Camilla could be here. She imagined the poetry Horatio alone could generate.

"The People call Maranatha Winningham," she heard Miss Nichols say, but her voice seemed far away, echoing in a cave.

I can't do this.

Defying her weak will, Maranatha stood. She walked over to the stand, placed her hand on the Bible, and swore to tell the whole truth. *I wonder what folks will think of my whole truth.*

She looked down, afraid to scan the crowd for faces.

Miss Nichols approached.

"Miss Winningham," she said. "Please describe for the jury what you were doing the afternoon of Thursday, August 27."

Maranatha swallowed but did not look up. She directed her eyes only at Miss Nichols. "I was riding my bike."

"Where?"

"To an abandoned piece of property. I go there to think." *Steady your voice. This is the easy part.*

"Were you aware that the property belonged to someone else?"

"I never really thought about it that way," she said. "No one was ever there, and I never meant any harm."

Miss Nichols gave her that *look*, the one signaling her to please not answer more than the question. "Stick to the facts," she had said. "So," Miss Nichols said, "you rode your bike to the property. Then what?"

"I parked the bike outside the gate, then I went inside the gate."

"Did you see anyone?"

"Not at first." Maranatha looked down at her dress. No spots. "But as I was leaving, a red truck pulled up."

"Had you seen the truck before?"

"No, ma'am."

"So it was a truck you'd never seen before."

"Correct."

"What happened next?"

"A man got out. He said I was trespassing, that it was his property."

"What did the man look like?"

Like that man over there who I can't look at. Maranatha

inhaled, then exhaled. "He walked with a limp. He had dark hair that covered his eyes." *And he looked right through me.*

"Is the man who got out of the truck in this courtroom?"

"Yes, ma'am."

"Would you care to point him out?"

Not really. Maranatha looked beyond Miss Nichols and saw the defendant's face for the first time, hair combed neatly back, shaven, a smile pasted on his lips. She swallowed. "Yes, ma'am. He's right there." She pointed, her finger a perfect trajectory to Jake Gully's nose. If her finger were a gun, she'd have a good shot.

Maranatha fought to return her gaze to Miss Nichols.

"And what happened after you saw him get out of the truck?"

"He said I was trespassing and to get off his property. So I said I'd get my bike and head back to town." Maranatha saw the whole scene replay in her mind, like she was an angel looking down from above. "Before I knew it, he said he was heading back to town and that he'd like my company. He put my bike in the back of his truck, and I got in, not thinking."

"Why did you get in?"

"I don't know," she said. A murmur rustled through the court. Maranatha allowed herself to scan the crowd now. Her hands shook. There, in one long row, sat her friends and family. Bishop Renny to the far left, followed by Zady, Raymond, and Charlie. Old Mack sat next to Georgeanne and Uncle Zane. At the row's end sat Denim and Camilla, notebook in hand. *Dear Camilla. You came!* Seeing them there should've scared her, but their faces, particularly Camilla's, gave peace. She allowed herself one more look. Sitting behind Charlie was Violin Charlie, no expression on his face. *Oh, Lord, why him?*

"You said you don't know why you got into the truck."

Maranatha looked back at Miss Nichols, whose eyes registered a hint of alarm. "Um, no. I mean yes. I . . . it all happened so fast."

"So, you got in the truck."

"Yes."

"Did you feel uncomfortable?"

"Objection." Ridley stood. "What do emotions have to do with this?"

The Honorable Horatio allowed the line of questioning.

"Go ahead and answer the question," Miss Nichols said.

"Yes. Terribly."

"Then why didn't you leave?"

"He had started the truck and drove away before I knew it. Drove the wrong way."

"The wrong way?"

"Yes, away from town. He drove very fast. I kept my hand on the door handle and scooted all the way to the right of the cab."

"Did he do anything that made you uncomfortable?"

"Yes." Maranatha closed her eyes. "He touched my leg. Then he said, 'Just relax,' or something like that. He said that we'd be there in a minute."

"Where?"

"I don't know."

"By now you must've been panicked."

"Objection," Ridley said. "Leading."

Miss Nichols redirected. "Please tell the members of the jury what happened next."

"He said something about wanting to get to know me better. That I knew what he was talking about."

"What do you think he meant by that?"

"I don't know."

Miss Nichols pursed her lips, then frowned. She paced, then

returned. "How did you escape?"

"Longhorns were crossing the road. As soon as Mr. Gully slammed on his brakes, I opened the door. I grabbed my bike from the back of his truck and started riding."

"Did he follow you?"

"Not at first. I saw him following me as I neared Mt. Moriah Church. I threw my bike down and ran inside."

"And who was there?"

"Zady Wilson. She called the police. And after Mr. Gully left the parking lot, Renny Jefferson, the pastor, drove in. Then the police came." *There, I told the story. Please let this be enough.*

"What do you think Mr. Gully was going to do if you didn't escape?"

Tears nipped at Maranatha's eyelids. She looked up at Zady, held her eyes for a moment, drinking in her peace. "I'm sure he was bent on raping me," she said.

"Rape is a pretty strong word. Are you sure?"

"I have no doubt," Maranatha said.

Miss Nichols' mouth hinted at a smile. "No more questions, Your Honor."

Ridley Owen rose. He unbuttoned his suit coat, put his hands on his hips. Beyond him, Maranatha met Jake Gully's terrible eyes. They seared fear into her, burned her will clear away. She looked away.

"That's a nice story you tell, Miss Winningham."

"Objection," Miss Nichols said. "He's editorializing."

"Get to the point, Mr. Owen," Honorable Horatio said.

"My point is that you've told a lot of stories in your life, haven't you?"

"I'm not sure what you mean."

Ridley stepped toward her. Close. The overhead fluorescent lights cast a ghostly hue on his shiny head.

"You've been raped before, is that right?"

Maranatha's heart hiccupped. The room seemed smaller now, whirling and spinning, leaving only Ridley Owen, Jake Gully, and General there, taunting her. She closed her eyes. Grabbed her stomach.

"I asked you a question," Ridley said, this time softer, like he cared about her. "You can tell the court."

Maranatha looked down. "Yes."

"You were in this very courtroom before, weren't you?"

She fidgeted with her fingers. "Yes."

"You accused a young man of rape, is that right?"

Maranatha smelled his fried-egg breath. "Yes."

Ridley Owen stepped back, giving Maranatha another clear view of Jake Gully, but she didn't look up. "Seems to me you like to make up stories."

"Objection!" Miss Nichols nearly screamed.

The Honorable Horatio scolded Ridley Owen.

"The records show, members of the jury, that Miss Winningham accused a young man of repeated rape seven years ago. Interestingly, he pursued her in an out-of-the-way place. Is that right, Miss Winningham?"

"Yes," she said. "In a remote area of Central Park." *Where is he going with this?* Maranatha wanted to look at Zady again, for strength, but she couldn't risk catching Charlie's gaze.

"In a remote area. So there were no witnesses to the so-called rapes?"

"Your Honor." Miss Nichols rose. "I'd like to remind the jury that the man accused of repeatedly raping Miss Winningham was convicted and is serving time."

Repeatedly raping. Repeatedly raping. The words bounced through Maranatha's heart like a skilled girl skipping rope. *Why'd she have to go and say that?* While the judge gathered the two lawyers to the stand and said a flurry of words, Maranatha could only think of what her row of friends and family were thinking. She glanced at her dress. White. Her soul bloodied while her face flushed.

Ridley Owen sauntered back her way. "I'll ask again. Were there any witnesses to any of the rapes?"

"No."

"Did anyone see Mr. Gully offer you a ride?"

"No, sir."

"Are you in the habit of accusing men of rape, Miss Winningham?"

"Objection!" Fury filled Miss Nichols' single word.

"That's all I have, Your Honor," the bald man said. He buttoned his suit coat and sat down.

When she left the stand, she noticed two things. Georgeanne was weeping. And one Charlie had left the courtroom.

Thirty-Five

THE SUN STARTLED MARANATHA. SHE THOUGHT
she'd walk out of that courtroom and a storm would be churning the sky. Instead, it rained brightness on Burl. She breathed
in the sun and was surprised how the warm air lifted her from
the bleakness of the courtroom. Her feet danced lighter down
the stone steps as she skipped to the cadence of *I-testified*,
I-testified.

I did it!

Thank You, Jesus.

Though speaking the horrid words had reddened her face
with shame, she now felt free. Maybe Old Mack was right. The
truth did have a way of setting folks free.

Though she didn't relish facing her friends and family,
something in her heart sang a short line of liberation. Maybe
it was bits and pieces of her shame flying on the breeze. She
looked down at her dress. Still white.

Zady ran toward her, engulfing her in an ample hug. "I knew
you could do it," she said.

"Where's Charlie?" Maranatha asked.

"I don't know," Zady said.

"He left."

"I know. But don't you be minding him. Your news on the stand probably startled him, made him sad. Let's sit a spell." Zady sat at a picnic table under an enormous sycamore tree.

Maranatha sat across from her, puzzled. "Why?"

"Well, when you're in love," Zady smiled, "the last thing you want to hear is that the person you love has been hurt so bad."

"But Zady —"

"Give him time. He's grieving, if you ask me."

"But, he knew already!" She picked up a brown leaf and twirled it in her hand.

Zady leaned back, eyes filled with alarm. "You told him?"

"No," Maranatha measured. "You did."

"Natha! I would never do such a thing. My Charlie knew nothing about what went on back then. I told you your secret was kept with me, and I meant it."

"But Charlie said at the dock that he understood why I was so afraid."

"Lord knows what he meant," Zady said, "but it wasn't about General. I guarantee it."

"Then what was it?"

"I have no idea."

Maranatha pressed her temples with the heels of her hands. *I'm a miserable wretch.* "Zady, can you forgive me?"

Zady stood, walked around the picnic table, and put her hands on Maranatha's shoulders. "I forgive you because I already had."

"Really?" Maranatha looked over her shoulder. Zady's brown eyes exuded warmth.

"Really." She sat next to Maranatha, holding her in a side embrace.

"But I was so horrid to you. So distant."

"It's no matter. I grieved, sure. But then I realized something about the Lord. He holds my reputation in His big, able hands, child. And Jesus, well, He understood how I felt being misunderstood and all. Think of all the times folks misunderstood His intentions. He was God with skin on and some religious people accused Him of using Satan's power. Can you imagine that?"

"No."

"So, He understood. Knew how I felt. It's His kindness that's letting us clear the air, don't you think?"

"Yeah." Maranatha traced her finger over a carved *Donny loves JoAnne* on the picnic table's top. "I've been awful, Zady."

Zady didn't say anything, let Maranatha be alone with her accusing thoughts, thoughts that fought inside her.

"I assumed Charlie knew because I believed you told him." She looked at her hands as if they were a stranger's. "And I held it against you both." Hearing her words out there just made her feel worse. That it was true: She was a self-absorbed mess.

Zady removed her arm from Maranatha's shoulder, then rubbed her temple with her hands. She said nothing.

"I'm so sorry." Maranatha rubbed her eyes now. She felt the weight of her betrayal, her snippy words in her ribcage.

"I know," Zady finally said.

They sat together, hip to hip, in silence, while tears ran down Maranatha's cheeks.

Maranatha wiped her eyes, turned to Zady. "But what about Charlie?"

"I don't know, Natha. Best let him be. These things take time." Zady stood, placing her hand on Maranatha's shoulder.

"I haven't even asked about your life." *I'm so selfish!*

"You carry too many folks' worries around. Best let them rest. We'll be fine, Raymond and me. We's got food, clothes, and a roof. That's enough."

"I should've prayed more for you."

"We all should pray more for everyone, that's true. But remember, Natha, Jesus is all about grace. Him giving us food and shelter. That's grace. Totally undeserved. And He gives grace to you for not being prayerful. He loves you whether you're lovable or not."

"Good thing. I don't feel lovable right now."

"*I* love you. You know that, right?"

"Yes." A wail erupted from her this time. All the stress and worry about testifying, all the misunderstanding, all the fear bottled up came gushing out. Maranatha didn't look around, worried about what people thought of her weeping. She cried while Zady's hand soothed her shoulder, her heart.

Bishop Renny and Raymond stood behind her now, praying under their breath. Denim joined the circle of people under the shedding sycamore. Camilla sat next to Maranatha. Old Mack sat in front of her, twirling his beard. Like a baby fresh out of the nursery, Maranatha was bundled by the love and prayers of these friends. Whispered prayers wafted past the tree above, heavenward. They were allowed unhindered access, few leaves to prohibit their flight.

Through tear-stained eyes, Maranatha looked up, watching the sycamore's arms caress the sky, reach for the heavens.

One by one, folks left the sacred circle. Bishop Renny and Raymond each took a hand and squeezed. Zady kissed her head. Denim said, "Thanks," tears in his eyes. Old Mack knelt down, wetting his knees on the damp ground. "I'm proud," he said. "So proud. I've always known Maranatha Winningham was the bravest girl around, and I was right." He touched her cheek.

"Thanks," Maranatha choked.

Camilla stayed behind.

She handed Maranatha a piece of paper, creased simply in fourths. "I didn't have time to fold it proper," she said.

"A poem?"

"Yep. But it's not like the other ones."

"How so?" She unfolded the paper, flattened it over *Donny loves JoAnne.*

"Read it."

Quietly, she scanned the page.

> Anyway
>
> Swaddled with aching truth,
> You speak.
> Tangled in listless hope,
> You mourn.
> Smothered from slavery,
> You breathe.
> Crumpled by circumstance,
> You live.
>
> And I smile to see it.

The words turned the soil of Maranatha's soul, preparing it for seeds of life to sprout. "Thanks," she managed to say.

"You're welcome."

"You finally took my advice."

"What do you mean?" Camilla asked.

"About rhyming."

A quiet moment passed between them as they sat side by side, an unrhymed poem between them, the title "Anyway" floating through the lazy breeze like a detached leaf.

Camilla stood. "You understand it?"

"Yeah." Maranatha remained on the bench.

"Really? Because the poem slipped out of me before I had

time to think it."

"It says that life is hard, but we live it anyway."

"Maybe I should've rhymed it."

Maranatha shook her head. "No. It's better this way. My life's never rhymed. Neither has yours. The poem is perfect."

Camilla smiled, squeezed Maranatha's shoulder. "I'll see you soon."

"Sure."

Maranatha watched Camilla walk away while the sun dappled her brown head. "Thanks," she said to the breeze.

"Maranatha?"

She jumped. Violin Charlie stood on the other side of the picnic table. "You startled me."

"I see that."

"I saw you. At the trial." Maranatha outlined the carved *Donny loves JoAnne* with her left finger.

"Yeah. I figured I'd see what it was all about."

"Your dad told you I'd be testifying?"

Violin Charlie nodded. "Said it would help me stop chasing after you. He didn't tell me anything, but now I know what he meant, you being damaged goods and all."

Maranatha looked at her hands, suddenly embarrassed.

He sat, facing her. He reached across the table, his hand obscuring the *loves* of *Donny loves JoAnne*. He held her hand.

She looked into his eyes, but they didn't butterfly her stomach.

"I can't see you anymore." He squeezed her hand, let go, turned, and walked away. A single leaf floated to the table, covering the *loves*.

Thirty-Six

LEFT ALONE.

Maranatha was used to that.

She looked beyond the picnic table to the parking lot, but Uncle Zane's white Cadillac was not there. Georgeanne probably saw her with the mixed-color crowd and scooted him away.

Maranatha walked home.

When she turned the corner toward the big white house, she half expected a white truck to be parked there, a handsome boy leaning against its bed. The white Cadillac sat parked under the pecan tree instead of in its usual place by the back door.

On the porch swing sat Georgeanne and Uncle Zane, like they were waiting for her.

She climbed the stairs, heart heavy from Violin Charlie's shaming departure.

Georgeanne's eyes were rimmed red, her makeup running black races down her cheeks. Her hair was flat on one side, her lipstick smeared. Uncle Zane's arm draped around her, not wooden, but alive.

"Thanks for coming," Maranatha said.

"Maranatha? I have something to say." Georgeanne shifted in the swing. It creaked. "I want you to consider living with us."

What?

"The truth is, I'd miss you. And the thought of you living in this house all alone makes my stomach curdle."

"Uncle Zane?" Maranatha leaned against the porch pillar. "I'm not sure what to say."

"This house is yours," he said. "Always will be." With those words, he stood. He placed his hand on Maranatha's shoulder. "But I'd miss you."

Georgeanne cried softly, streaking her face with the back of her hand. "Tell her my idea," she choked out.

"Georgeanne's decided the house needs fixin' up. She's hired Zady and Raymond to keep it up, to look after it. That way it won't fall apart when you go to college. In the meantime, you can stay here or you can stay with us." He squeezed her upper arm and let go. "Think on it."

All Maranatha could say was, "Thank you." But it didn't seem enough.

Thirty-Seven

THE NEXT DAY GEORGEANNE AND ZADY had themselves a spat on the front porch about the proper way to make sweet tea. Zady'd come to finalize the arrangements for the house and invite everyone to the Thanksgiving feast at Mt. Moriah, but Georgeanne said they'd be in Louisiana visiting relatives.

"Would you like some tea?" Georgeanne asked her then.

And that's when it started.

"Yours is too bitter," Zady said.

"And yours too dark." Georgeanne put her hands on her hips. So did Zady. Like sisters pulling hair, they kept to their stance, neither backing down. While Maranatha listened to the barbed words fly, she smiled. Earlier Georgeanne would've dismissed Zady's opinion flat out; at least now they were talking. Or yelling.

Zady left in a huff, but not without Georgeanne asking her to come over to learn how to make proper tea in her new house. "On the good side of town," she added.

"We'll see about that," is all Zady said.

True to her word, Georgeanne took Uncle Zane away to Louisiana for Thanksgiving. When they returned, Maranatha would help pack the house, her room included.

Maranatha waited for Raymond and Zady to pick her up for the church's annual Thanksgiving feast. She waited under the pecan and shivered, not from fear, but from a cold sting in the air. Zady pulled up in the Dodge Aspen. She motioned for Maranatha to get in.

"I hear they found Jake Gully guilty." Zady shut the door.

"Yes, just yesterday. The jury deliberated only five hours." Maranatha buckled herself in.

"You relieved?" Zady asked.

"More than I can say."

Zady started the car and pulled away from the curb.

"Where's the rest of your family?"

"Already at church. You know how much work it is to make a feast. I've been slaving them since the wee hours of the morning."

"Is Charlie there?"

"He was, but I'm not sure if he'll stay."

"Oh."

"Say a few prayers. You just never know what the Lord Almighty will do in a person, Natha."

They drove in silence past businesses and farms on the same road Maranatha had bicycled more times than she could count. Soon, the squirrel-gated parcel of charred land came into view. Zady slowed. She pulled over to the gate, idling the car. "Say your piece," Zady said. "I'll wait here."

Maranatha got out. The gate swung open now, so she walked through to the awaiting field. The sun angled its autumn light, casting a long Maranatha shadow. She walked to the slab where a pillared home once lived. Standing on what could have been the kitchen or den, Maranatha spread her arms wide, as if to take flight. "I love You, Jesus," she said. "I don't understand Your ways, but I love You. I hope that's enough."

Dandelions dead under her shoes, she walked back to Zady's car. The last time it idled there, she and Charlie had been caught in a tornado path. Maranatha had found and lost a Jesus ring. Her bike had flown away. And Zady's heart had burned mother-anger.

The next time a vehicle idled there, a limping man with a red truck had leered at her. Maranatha shut the gate as best she could, closing a door to memories she'd rather forget.

She got in the car.

"Thanks," she told Zady.

Mt. Moriah's insides were decked to the rafters with leaves, pumpkins, squashes — anything resembling a harvest. Two long tables lined the church's center aisle, food steam wafting toward the ceiling like prayer. Several round tables with eight chairs circling each one decorated the lobby. Though folks at Mt. Moriah liked feasting under the open sky, the chill in the air had brought festivities inside.

Maranatha stood in line, paper plate in hand. She looked for Charlie's face but didn't find it. She ached for him. Mt. Moriah meant Charlie to Maranatha. Without him, the church lost a little of its luster.

She said her thanks with Bishop Renny's long-winded prayer and ate with Zady and Raymond. Though the food looked like joy on a plate, she didn't really taste it, preferring to chew and swallow, say a few things, and then chew and swallow again.

As Zady and Maranatha cleared the tables, she worked up the nerve to say something. "Zady?"

"Yes."

"I think you were right."

"Really? That's news! About what?"

"Georgeanne."

"How so?"

"I think she's hurt, so she hurts others. Just like you said."

"It's the Lord's truth, I know it." Zady stacked a pile of soiled paper plates from Bishop Renny's table and handed them to Maranatha. Maranatha threw the plates away.

"Do you think Georgeanne and I will get along?"

"Hard to say. It's a bit like knots."

They grabbed some pie and sat next to Raymond.

"What do you mean, knots?"

"Folks are all tied up with each other. And sometimes to tie 'em rightly to each other, you got to untangle them. And that's hard work."

"Sure is," Maranatha said. She patted Zady's hand, then excused herself.

Maranatha found the same tree she'd sat under after Bishop Renny's healing cave sermon and sat underneath its gaze. The sun tickled her face, stung her eyes.

A shadow obscured the sun.

"Hey, Natha," it said.

Charlie!

She stood up.

"Want to take a walk with me?"

She nodded.

They didn't walk hand in hand toward the lake. Pavement gave way to gravel. Naked trees bowed branches to the silent pair. Charlie and Maranatha walked to the end of the dock. Both removed shoes while the cold air teased their toes.

Charlie put his feet in first. "Natha," he said.

Maranatha put her feet in the cold water. Shivers leapt up her spine. "Yeah."

"I have something for you."

"I have something for you too." She looked at Charlie with his browner-than-brown eyes. "I owe you an apology."

"What for?"

"What for? For running away from you. For thinking the wrong thing."

"You were scared," he said.

"I thought you knew my secret."

"I didn't. Not until you said it in court."

"Charlie?"

"Yeah."

"Why'd you leave?"

"I was angry."

"At me?"

"No. At the men. At whoever that person was who stole from you. At that Jake Gully man who tried to nab you. Rage grabbed me. I thought I'd explode, so I left to control myself."

"So you weren't mad at me?"

"No. How could I be? You're my best friend, Natha." He touched a strand of blonde hair that dangled in front of her eyes. He tucked it behind her ear.

She shivered.

"Cold?"

"No. Yes. I don't know."

Charlie laughed. He took off his coat and wrapped it around her.

"What did you mean," Maranatha asked, "when you said you understood why I was scared?"

"I thought you were scared because you didn't have a daddy to protect you. To give you stability. To take care of you. Bishop

Renny talks all the time about how important a father is. I figured you were scared because you didn't have one."

Maranatha let the words surround her while the cold water shivered her feet. "Can you forgive me, Charlie? For jumping to conclusions?"

"Of course."

They sat on the end of the dock while Maranatha's feet numbed. The sun settled itself lower, behind the pine trees, leaving the two of them shaded.

"You said you had something for me?"

Charlie laughed. "It's in my pocket." He put an arm around Maranatha and reached into his coat pocket. He grabbed something and quickly put it behind his back, along with his other hand. "Which hand?"

Maranatha faced him. "That one," pointing to the right.

"Nope. Try again."

"That one."

Charlie pulled out a gold ring. "I found this on Tornado Day. It caught the sun as the paramedics came down the cellar, hollering. Is it yours?"

Maranatha took the ring from Charlie. She turned it around in her hand. *Forever my love*, it said. She nodded.

"I meant to give it to you last week, but you wouldn't let me."

Maranatha flung her arms around Charlie's neck. Charlie answered by wrapping strong arms around her. "Everything's going to be all right, Natha," he said.

Maranatha pulled away, examined his face. Fear erupted inside—not the same old fear of being near Charlie, but the fear of him not being near.

He looked into her eyes. Three good *ubiquitouses*. "Are you afraid?"

"Yes," she said. *Terrified.*

"Me too." Charlie bent near. He dusted her lips with his — a sweet, agonizing brush — and pulled away. "I love you, Natha. Since way before when."

Maranatha thought she'd want to grab her shoes and run miles away. Instead, she whispered, "I love you too," while her feet made circles in the dark water and the barren trees clapped branches like God's applause.

bonus content includes:

- ▶ Maranatha's Birthday Journal Entries:
  1983–1987

- ▶ Reader's Guide

- ▶ Author Interview

- ▶ About the Author

Maranatha's Birthday Journal Entries: 1983-1987

April 12, 1983

Today's my thirteenth birthday. To celebrate, Zady gave me this empty notebook. I know it must've cost her more than she can afford, even though it's just a little spiral thing from Value Villa. I love how she pretty-fied it, though, with magazine pictures pasted on willy-nilly and a thick coating of something she called decopahhge (I don't know how to spell that word!). Well, I love it. Zady said, "I keep thinking there are snatches of a writer in you, child. Maybe this will help." When she handed it to me, I nearly boo-hooed. I've only told her once, but I wish she were my mama.

 I can't believe I'm thirteen. Camilla told me today, "You're a woman now." She said it so serious-like, I couldn't tell if she was joking with me or not. That's the weird thing about Camilla. When you first meet her you think she's more somber than a funeral director, but it's not long until you know she's a bit wacky and there's always a smirk under her frown.

When I woke up today, Uncle Zane was acting strange. He kept looking out the kitchen window and then looking at me. When I stood up from the breakfast table, he told me to go upstairs immediately. So I did. I've learned it's not helpful to argue with him. When he raises his voice, it's best to listen.

I could hear the back door opening and shutting, his steps down the back porch, and then a rustling as he must've tried to walk up the stairs again. When he opened the door, all sorts of racket broke out. "Maranatha," he yelled up the stairs, "get yourself down here."

So I did.

There, in the parlor, stood a brand-spanking-new bike. Uncle Zane had tied a ribbon around it best he could. He half smiled. I smiled all the way.

"It's for you. Happy birthday."

I hugged him real tight. He mumbled words like, "Be careful," and, "Don't get yourself killed now."

April 12, 1984

It's my birthday again. I'm fourteen. Almost an adult, Zady said.

Since Uncle Zane's stroke, I haven't spent much time hanging out with friends. Mostly I go to school, come home, and read to Uncle Zane. He's still in there, I know, but he's changed. It's like his brain that used to be like a block of cheddar is now Swiss cheese. He remembers some things, like lighting matches when he was seven or what he wore the day his daddy had a heart attack, but he forgets others. Today he asked me who that black boy was.

"It's Charlie, Zady's son," I told him.

He nodded but didn't say a word after that. I wonder if he knows his memory is Swiss cheese.

Everyone at school is talking about boys and who likes who. I think it's stupid, to be honest. I have decided I'll never marry. I'll be like one of those girls I've read about in the missionary biographies Zady gives me. Single for Jesus. On the mission field. Bishop Renny, he says he's proud of me. Last week he said my name in his sermon about the call of Jesus. "Take Maranatha, here," he said. "She's going to be a missionary someday." The congregation said all sorts of "amens" after that. Mama Frankie patted me on the back.

Camilla surprised me today with a poem:

> Roses are pink
> Violets are azure
> I hope to be
> Like you so pure

I'm sure she meant it in a nice way. But I didn't like that last word. Pure. I'm not sure what that means. Last night I had another dream about General. I woke up feeling dirty. I try to tell myself he's far away now, locked up in some camp, but I can still hear his voice when I walk alone.

April 12, 1985

Fifteen. A year from now I can get my license, if Uncle Zane ever lets me. I'm fed up with Georgeanne, more than I can say on this notebook page. (Georgeanne, if you're reading this, shame on you. God is watching.) She's taking over the house. She's got us all on a silly schedule, while Uncle Zane just putters along. He obeys her like she's his drill sergeant. I can't stand her hair. Her voice makes me want to run away.

Charlie came over today to wish me a happy birthday after school. We sat on the porch swing and talked a good hour. Sometimes I think he's my best friend, but I don't dare tell Camilla that. She'd disown me.

Zady gave me a new curling iron today. It reminded me of Aunt Elma, how she used to curl my hair once in a while when she was experimenting for new styles. I still can't believe she was a beautician. It's weird, I know, but I miss her.

Today I wanted my mama. I wanted her to run her hand through my hair and tell me she thought I was pretty. I wanted to hear her voice sing. I wanted to sit with her in the kitchen, sipping a glass of sweet tea. She'd tell me about becoming a woman, and I'd ask lots of questions — the questions I can't ask Uncle Zane, won't ask Georgeanne, and am too embarrassed to ask Zady. She'd put me at ease with the sticky questions. I see us laughing. When I look in her eyes, I see mine.

April 12, 1986

Sweet sixteen and never been kissed. At least that's what Vonda Rae said to me today. I laughed and told her I'd be a spinster and not to worry about my love life. She told me I needed to worry more.

Uncle Zane is coming out of his fog. He's doing crossword puzzles for hours at a time. When he watches the news, he argues back.

I don't know why, but I had another General dream last night. I got a call from the school office saying I needed to go there immediately. When I got there, General stood in a police uniform. "I'm here to take you in," he said. Though I tried to scream and tell the office ladies not to make me go with him, I couldn't find my voice. The ladies smiled, and General handcuffed me. I wonder how long he will haunt me.

All I want is to be normal. I wonder how many people in Burl know my secret. I worry sometimes that Camilla has spilled the beans. I doubt Zady would ever tell, and Raymond certainly wouldn't, but still I worry.

April 12, 1987

I wonder what this next year has in store. Mama Frankie says I need to be on the alert now that I'm seventeen, whatever that means. "Blessings are coming your way, Maranatha," she told me. "And whens they do, you gotta dance, child." She tried to dance with her walker. It made me laugh. "Blessings are a serious matter," she said. "Serious indeed." And then she laughed full-out. I hope she's right. I could use a few blessings.

Reader's Guide

1. Besides Maranatha's changing her name from Mara to Maranatha, what kinds of changes do you see in her between *Watching the Tree Limbs* and *Wishing on Dandelions*?

2. DeMuth once again uses the device of having Maranatha reflect back on life at age seventeen while an adult. She still tells the story, though, in third person. What does this say about her level of pain as an adult?

3. How does Uncle Zane's stroke affect the dynamic of life in the big white house?

4. In what way is a wish on a dandelion the same as a prayer? Are wishing and praying different? Why or why not?

5. Discuss the changing state of the vacant piece of land as a parallel to Maranatha's spiritual state throughout the book.

6. How does the bike symbolize freedom for Maranatha?

7. Maranatha experiences a tug-of-war in her heart when it comes to loving Charlie. Part of her recoils. The other part wants to embrace him. Discuss this dichotomy.

8. How does Zady's relationship with Maranatha change throughout the story? Why does a misunderstanding throw such a wrench in their relationship? Reflect on your life. Has a similar thing affected you? If so, how was it resolved — or not?

9. What role does Old Mack play in the story? What specific acts define that role?

10. How does the idea of prophecy or premonition play into the overall story? What do you think of Mama Frankie's and Old Mack's warnings? Have you experienced prophecy in your life?

11. What objects does Maranatha lose in the story? How are they restored?

12. How has Camilla changed by the book's end? What portrays this inner change?

13. How did you feel about Uncle Zane's marrying Georgeanne?

14. Discuss how Maranatha's dreams portray her inner anguish and her need for healing.

15. How is Old Mack a good example of the adage, "You can't judge a book by its cover"? How did he break out of his eccentric stereotype?

16. What evidence shows that Georgeanne is a hurt person who hurts people? When does the reader see the chink in her armor?

17. Discuss the metaphor of Maranatha's home. Why does she want to cling to it, to save it? What does it represent to her?

18. Describe Jake Gully. Though a minor character, discuss why he is central to the story.

19. Maranatha believes she is marked because of General's earlier abuse. Why?

20. What does Maranatha's giving in to Georgeanne's demand

that she get a perm show about her desire to save the house?

21. The lake is Charlie and Maranatha's special place. Trace the evolution of their relationship through the scenes at the lake.

22. Does Violin Charlie change by the book's end? Explain.

23. Later in the book, we see Maranatha's thoughts about Georgeanne: "Keeping Georgeanne in the nosy, ditsy, busybody box was easier than enduring bewildering snatches of compassion." Why is it hard for Maranatha to deal with a compassionate Georgeanne?

24. Can Georgeanne be trusted?

25. Why does Maranatha eventually decide to testify?

26. Does Maranatha ever get over her guilt for leaving Uncle Zane on the day of his stroke? Do you think she is guilty? Why or why not?

27. Discuss Bishop Renny's cave of healing, how Jesus heals folks in the dark places.

28. How does Charlie demonstrate Jesus to Maranatha?

29. Secret keeping is Maranatha's modus operandi throughout the book. How does letting her secrets out change her?

$\mathcal{A}uthor\ Interview$

This book deals with difficult subject matter: childhood sexual abuse and its residual effects. How did this book emerge?

My passion is to write about redemption through the avenue of story. I started the first book, Watching the Tree Limbs, *in a flurry. In my mind I saw the streets of Burl and a girl who didn't know where she came from. Because my personal story involves different instances of sexual abuse, I wanted to write a story that shows the reader how God can intersect an abuse victim's life and make a difference.*

So are you Maranatha?

In some ways yes, some no. Like Maranatha, I feel like God has transformed my life in such a radical way (like her name change from Mara — "bitter" — to Maranatha — "Come, Lord Jesus"). Like Maranatha, I endured sexual abuse, but I was much younger when it happened. Like Maranatha, I wondered if I had been marked, if every sexual predator could tell I was a ready victim. I wrestled through relationships in my teens with Maranatha's twin feelings of revulsion and attraction. But she is not me in many other ways. She is more independent. She has no parents. She lives in an entirely different culture. She is less ambitious. She has the privilege of many wiser people to mentor her through life.

What made you decide to write a love story?

The book didn't start out in my mind as a love story, but it evolved into it as I continued writing. Characters have that uncanny way of taking your prose and running in all sorts of directions with it. Charlie just kept being faithful. In a sense, I fell in love with him!

What made you choose East Texas as the setting for both novels?

The South fascinates me. I grew up in the Northwest. When my last child was born, my husband was transferred to East Texas to start a department in a hospital. Because I was a stay-at-home mom and was homeschooling my children, I didn't have much else to do there except observe small-town Southern culture. Because I didn't grow up in that culture, my senses were heightened, and I eventually began to really appreciate the differences.

Childhood sexual abuse is not talked about very often and is seldom covered in novels. What made you decide to write about it?

For that very reason. The quieter victims are, the less healing they will receive. The more we talk about it, bringing heinous acts to the light, the better able we are to know we are not alone. I wrote this book so other abuse victims would feel validated and heard. And to offer hope.

Why do you end your books with hope?

> *Because hope is essential to Jesus' gospel. Even when things are bleak, there is always hope — if not in this life, then in the next. I'm not interested, however, in presenting hope in a superfluous way. I don't want to tie up every story thread neatly. The truth is, life is tragic and difficult and bewildering, but God intersects that life and brings hope.*

Have you always wanted to write?

> *Yes. Since my second grade teacher told my mother that she thought I was a creative writer, I've wanted to write. I've kept a diary since the sixth grade. Though I was an English major, I didn't start writing seriously until my first daughter was born. I wrote for ten years in obscurity before my writing career took a turn for the better.*

Who are your literary heroes?

> *I love Harper Lee. I only wish she'd written more. Leif Enger, who wrote* Peace Like a River, *greatly inspired me to write visually and artistically. I love Sue Monk Kid's* Secret Life of Bees *— how you can almost taste her characters. I'm fascinated and intimidated by J. R. R. Tolkein — how he managed to create an entire world with several languages is way beyond my literary prowess.*

What do you want your reader to take away from *Wishing on Dandelions*?

> *That redemption of a broken life takes time. We're all on a journey of healing. Sometimes it's slow going, but if we can endure through the dark times, God will bring us to new places of growth. I want the images and characters to stay with the reader for a long time.*

About the Author

MARY E. DEMUTH has spent the last thirteen years as a writer. Her weekly column appeared for two years in the *Star Community Newspapers* in Dallas. She now splits her time between writing women's fiction and nonfiction books about parenting and risky faith. Her titles include *Ordinary Mom, Extraordinary God* (Harvest House, 2005) and *Building the Christian Family You Never Had* (WaterBrook, 2006). Mary lives in Le Rouret, France, with Patrick, her husband of fifteen years, and their three children, Sophie, Aidan, and Julia. Together, they are planting a church.

EXCITING NEW FICTION FROM NAVPRESS.

At age nine, Mara knows many things (how to do laundry, for instance), but there are lots of things she doesn't know — like her mother, her father, or even God.

Watching the Tree Limbs

Mary E. DeMuth

1-57683-926-5

Nine-year-old Mara loves playing Nancy Drew with her best friend, Camilla. With an attic chock-full of treasures and a whole summer ahead of them, they're set to find the home of the mysterious and controversial radio disc jockey, Denim. But then there are the mysteries that Mara's afraid to share: Who is her mother? Her father? And how can she stop the biggest criminal of all, General?

Visit your local Christian bookstore,
call NavPress at 1-800-366-7788,
or log on to www.navpress.com.
To locate a Christian bookstore near you,
call 1-800-991-7747.